Cop

MW00463273

This book is a work of fiction. Any resemblance to actual events or locales or persons, living or dead, is entirely coincidental.

THE ROLEX BANDITS

ISBN 1482528878

Cover illustration by Carrie Santa Lucia

Printed in the United States of America

# The Rolex Bandits

Alan Mowbray

# 1

From the corner of his eye Elliot Anderson, lying on his hotel bed, watched two naked women approach him as if in a mist. The room swam before him, moving, spinning. Tears stung his eyes. He was numb. A doughy, boneless feeling. A cold, creeping terror went through him once he realized he couldn't move any part of his body. He heard the women snickering at his helplessness.

A wine bottle and his half-filled glass were on a table next to the bed, inches away from his hand. He was naked, except for a sock on one foot and a droopy condom on his limp penis; a few minutes ago his erection had pulsed while he watched the women undress.

His heart suddenly started beating violently, punching through his chest. He struggled to breathe. His gasps seemed to suck all the air from the room. Sweat covered his face. He went from cold to feverish to dizzy. His lips turned blue. Gurgly noises belched from his throat, and he felt that he was going to swallow his tongue. For a brief moment his thoughts turned to Karen, his wife, and to her reaction once she learned that her overweight, fifty-one-year-old, philandering but condom-conscious husband had died of a heart attack while being mugged by two call girls.

Breathless, he gulped air until the shock subsided. The room stopped moving, became stationary. At the periphery of his vision he drowsily watched the women and their menacing movements, watched them slowly close in on him, one by the headboard, the other near the foot of the bed.

Raven-haired, the woman by the headboard strutted back and forth alongside the bed. She was petite and thin-waisted with strong-calved legs. Stiletto heeled. The slow sweep of his eyes caught the other woman sneaking around the foot of the bed; she was tall with bouncy, thick-nippled breasts and electric blue-streaked hair. He stared at their tanned, shapely bodies, suddenly ashamed of his pale and flabby flesh.

Then he noticed that the woman with the colorful hair was aiming something at him. He blinked back his tears to get a better look. Through his watery vision he recognized that she was holding a cell phone camera and was filming him and the prancing woman. Back and forth the other woman continued that sassy-ass walk of hers, tossing her long hair over her shoulders. Her painted face made her look ghoulish. She took his discarded necktie and dragged it between his thighs. Her voice was full of mockery as she teased and taunted him and his flaccid penis. She flicked his ear with her pierced, viper tongue, then kissed and bit him hard on the side of the neck. He cried out. She grinned, baring fangs. His painful reaction aroused her, her nipples becoming hard and erect. In a frenzy of impotent rage, he wanted to hit her, to smash her leering glossily red lips, but he couldn't even make a fist.

What had they slipped into his drink? He knew he must be hallucinating because the one who was tormenting him kept morphing from a woman into a she-devil. To further torment him, she made lewd gestures by gyrating her hips, thrusting and pumping her groin at him. On hands and knees, she slithered up and straddled his face, simulating various sex acts while moaning with exaggerated pleasure. Meanwhile the other woman continued to film the entire performance.

Immobilized like a tranquilized bear, Elliot lay pinned between the woman's knees, her bush flattened stickily against his face, smothering him. He smelled her perfume, her sweat. All he could do was stare at that impenetrable mound. He became morbidly fascinated at her overabundance of pubic hair, which spread from her inner thighs to an inch or so below her pierced navel. Those tiny hairs seemed to come alive, to move, to twitch and tickle his face and nostrils. Was this another of his hallucinations, or was she really this hirsute? He wondered if this untamed growth was meant to hide something unsightly, perhaps a scar or some disease. From his business trips to South Florida, he knew that many women kept their pubic hair trimmed in neat triangles because they wore bikinis throughout the year, but this painted savage creature had no such grooming habits, though the rest of her legs and underarms were cleanly shaven. Her bush aroused a mixed feeling of revulsion and attraction; he found its mystery perversely appealing.

She sat back from his face but remained on his chest, straddling him as she tried to unsnap his diamond-studded Rolex. The woman with the camera stopped filming and was going through his fat wallet.

The mugging had begun.

Through half-open eyelids, he watched as the women swarmed over him. It was hard to follow their movements because he kept drifting, drifting. The soft, soft bed was swallowing him. His thoughts wandered back to his wife and to Jeremy, his seven-year-old son. He was with them in Needham, Massachusetts, in the security of their living room, sitting before the fireplace . . .

Her red taloned-length nails on his wrist forced him to open his eyes; she had momentarily lost her seductive playfulness when the Rolex wouldn't unsnap. Her dark, flashing eyes gleamed wild. She hissed and cursed him because she had expected an easy theft. Her frustration soon turned into an obsession, and she scratched and clawed at his wrist. Then she broke the wine bottle against the table, glass flying everywhere. She pointed the broken bottle at him, threatening to slit his wrist.

Dazed and slack-jawed, he tried to speak. He had forgotten her name. Earlier, a friend of his had introduced her as a dancer at a topless lounge, but his mind was in such a fog that he had a hard time remembering any details, even his friend's name. He moved his lips, trying to form some coherent sound. He slobbered. Enraged, she pressed the broken bottle against his throat and snapped her teeth. For a second or two, her eyes rolled all-white.

Fear had given him an adrenal surge, and suddenly he could clench his fists. He took aim for her nose. One solid hit might knock her out, even drive her cribriform plate into her brain, but he couldn't raise either arm to swing. He soon lost what little strength he had, and his fists slackened.

The other woman grabbed her friend's hand and attempted to take the bottle. They gestured angrily and argued, their dream-babble of words rushing by him in a gust of sound. Then the woman on top of him, red in the face, flung the bottle across the room. Turning back to him, she raked his wrist with her nails, finally unsnapping the Rolex. Her face broke into a wide smile. A kind of mad laughter came into her eyes. Her companion looked rushed and was trying to tell her something, but the woman on top of him waved her off; she was having too much fun to leave. She pressed the Rolex into the moist blur of her bush and then rubbed it against his lips.

He despised her arrogance! He tried to say, *You goddamn thieving whore*, but the words just drooled. She laughed at his effort to speak, then leaned over and tongue-kissed him. Her unruly mass of hair fell across his face.

She grabbed his hand and tried to squeeze off his wedding band, but his finger was too stubby. As she sat straight up on his chest, shaking her head and laughing, he noticed a four-inch tattoo of a flaming arrow or spear above her pierced navel. Crawling out of her jungly bush were more tattoos of swamp-looking animals – a coiled snake, a spider web, a panther, at least two hawks (or were they bats?) – all poised to attack. Yet another tattoo, this one a gargoyle, inked next to her pelvis bone, leered at him. He closed his eyes, hoping that the grotesque assortment of tattoos were just in his imagination.

A flurry of blood-colored dots flashed before his eyes when he opened them. The overhead light went into spasms, and the room started spinning again. He was so groggy he could barely focus, and he fought the temptation to blink. Closing his eyes again, even for an instant, might be the end. He blinked anyway.

Something warm and damp touched Elliot's face. The woman with the bluish hair was sitting next to him with a washcloth in her hand, her breasts brushing against his arm. A double strand of imitation pearls hung on her neck. Was it her turn to torment him? Were the women trying to see who could humiliate him the most? He figured the washcloth was dipped in chloroform and would soon cover his nose. Instead, she pressed it against his forehead, trying to comfort him. She whispered something soothingly in his ear. Was this her way of teasing him? He expected her to turn on him. When would she reveal her fangs?

Her chocolate brown eyes, however, looked sincere, full of warmth. Her breasts were now only inches from his mouth, and he felt as though he were being cradled like an infant. He expected her to rock him, to embrace and gently kiss him. She was attractive but flawed, her slightly crooked front teeth separated by a noticeable gap. A tattoo of a flower rooted in her cleavage and grew to the base of her throat. Smaller flower tattoos, with butterflies and bees surrounding them, decorated her wrists and forearms. He tried to talk to her, to plead for help, but he was still too thick-tongued to make any sense.

Who was this woman, anyway? He had briefly met the other woman at the topless lounge, but this one had just shown up with her companion at his hotel room. He tried to reach for her, to touch her, but she left him and joined the other woman by the dresser.

He started to giggle at his helpless condition, finding it ridiculous that while fighting for his life, he had been become fascinated, even obsessed, with each woman's hair, the one's thick bush, the other's coiffure lit up with streaks of dazzling blue. He tried to stifle his chuckles. *Shut up*, he mumbled to himself. *I'm going to get killed if they hear me.* For now, both women seemed preoccupied with his wallet and other belongings.

He found himself sinking into the bed, sinking into an unknown gloom. Wave upon wave of delicious fatigue rushed through his body. A cloud seemed to grow in the room into which both women floated away, disappearing.

He strained to stare at the ceiling. He struggled to stay awake because he feared his tormentor would return, cut him up with the broken bottle, and leave him to die in the blood-soaked bed. With great effort, he focused on that one task: to keep his eyes open.

His eyes watered. Tears streamed down his cheeks. *Keep your eyes open, damn it. Don't you dare close them.*

A moment later, his heavy eyelids descended, but his eyeballs were still twitching, still straining to see as he fell into a dark sleep, whirling into oblivion.

# 2

Polita Flores emerged from her red convertible Mustang and headed for a four-story apartment building. Before she had walked thirty feet, a man appeared under a distant streetlight in the parking lot. As she quickened her pace, high heels clicking on the pavement, the man turned silently away. When she reached the stairwell door, she turned in time to see him fade into the darkness.

Inside, the building's walls were spray-painted with graffiti. Styrofoam food containers and beer cans littered the hallway. When she had reached the second flight of stairs, the stairwell door opened on the ground floor. She listened but heard no one on the stairs. Then she heard voices above her. Two teenage girls, smoking dope, descended past her.

On the third floor she opened the stairwell door and walked down the deserted corridor. The carpet was stained and smelled of urine. She stopped at an apartment, knocked, and then immediately rang the doorbell. Across the corridor, a poster on the wall showed a teenaged girl holding a baby. She scanned the long corridor. At one end, an EXIT sign glowed above the stairwell door, and a man suddenly appeared in the doorway beneath it. He looked like the same man under the streetlight. She knocked harder.

"Kim, open up. It's me. Polita."

The door cracked open. A young woman appeared behind it, wearing a sleeveless T-shirt and shorts. Polita looked down the corridor and noticed that the man had disappeared. Then she slipped into the apartment and went into the living room. The woman chain-locked the door and followed her.

The apartment consisted of linoleum floors and no carpeting. It was minimally furnished. A torn-and-taped lumpy sofa, one wooden chair, a plain coffee table, and a flat screen TV completed the living room's décor.

"Were you in bed?" Polita said.

"I was watching TV," Kim said. She turned off the TV and lit a cigarette.

Polita went to the living room window and stared down into the parking lot.

"Did you work tonight?" Polita said.

"For maybe an hour. I wasn't feelin' good, so I left early."

"You hear from Carmen?"

"Not since this afternoon. Why?"

"You knew she was supposed to meet a man tonight at the Luxuria?"

"Yeah. Some rich businessman from New York or Boston. She said she wanted me to help her, but I never heard back from her."

Polita sat on the lone wooden chair. She watched Kim as she glanced at her cell phone. Kim Ellis worked with her as a topless dancer at Café Sinsations. She was twenty-four, a year younger than Polita. She had a lean, severe face, lightless eyes, bleached eyebrows, and a spiky, peroxide-blond mohawk. Tattooed on the shaved part of her head, just above her left ear, were the words *No Exit*. Her nose-, lip-, tongue-, ear-, and eyebrow-rings could set off a metal detector. Tattoos of barbed wire wrapped around her ankles and wrists. Skull-and-crossbones tattoos covered both her forearms. She looked gladiatorial with piercings, tattoos, and blade-sharp hair spikes.

"I was with Carmen at the hotel," Polita said. "She asked me to meet her there."

"So?"

"Just thought you'd want to know, that's all."

"Then I guess she needed you more'n me." Kim blew smoke in Polita's direction.

"Carmen told me you weren't feeling good. You just said so yourself."

"Yeah. Whatever."

"Carmen wanted me to come along for the ride. I think she was worried about this CEO. He was old, but huge. I bet he weighed over three hundred pounds. He was bigger'n me and Carmen put together."

Polita thought of Elliot lying on the hotel bed; the mental image repulsed her. She could still see his blubbery nudity, the curly gray tufts of his chest hairs, his pinkish, stubby, sausage-link prick. She thought his heaving milk-white chest and stomach would explode. She remembered his slobbering wine-stained lips, his large, fat-knuckled hands balling into meager fists, his bulging, blood-veined eyeballs looking up at her pleadingly. His eyes were what haunted her.

"After we drugged him," Polita continued, "I went with Carmen to a party down by the hotel's marina. It was a stupid thing to do, and I told her so. I mean, we'd just robbed a man. Anyway, I stayed with her at the marina for maybe fifteen minutes. Then I got the hell away from there. She was being just careless. One minute she was afraid of him, then she wanted to party at his hotel. Made no fucking sense to me. But try telling her anything. She knows everything."

"You said you drugged him. What was there to worry about?"

"You never know how long those knockout drops last. Carmen put enough in his drink to turn him into Rip Van Winkle."

"Who?"

"It doesn't matter. Anyway, I only saw him take a couple of sips. We couldn't get him to drink much. He just wanted to fuck. He was so horny he didn't finish taking his socks off. You'd think we mixed viagra in his drink. And I think he was suspicious, or maybe he thought we poured him some rotgut wine. It wasn't good enough for his rich ass. He was probably pissed that we didn't have the most expensive champagne for him."

"I know what you mean. One night me and Carmen waited almost an hour for a dude to take a sip. It got to be real nerve-rackin'."

"This whole thing is nerve-racking. The three of us are in on it together, and Carmen's bullshit is going to get us all in trouble."

"Maybe it's time for us to quit while we can."

"Tonight might be it for me. I can walk away from it, but Dante won't like it if you go with me. He counts on you and Carmen for the gold."

For a minute or two neither woman spoke.

"I don't have a good feeling about tonight," Polita said, pacing. She returned to the window and looked out. "Speaking of Dante, where is he?"

"He left here a while ago. I guess he's back at his place waitin' to hear from Carmen. You think she went to the Bahamas? She told me she wanted to get away for a few days."

"That's what she told me. Dante won't be happy if she leaves. He wants the gold as soon as we can get it to him. Any delays, and he comes after us."

"What'd you get off this guy?"

"Some cash. No credit cards because I got rushed. And the fanciest Rolex you've ever seen."

"You got it on you?"

"Carmen has it," Polita lied.

Kim was curiously tense and fidgety. She rearranged cigarette butts in an ashtray, then checked her messages on her cell phone. Most of the time she wouldn't meet Polita's gaze.

"Next time we see Carmen," Polita said, "I think the three of us need to sit down for a long talk. We know she's into drugs big time. She's getting out of control. I used to catch her doing lines in the bathroom at work. Now she's a meth head. Tonight she was so jacked up on meth that she was even freaking me out. You should've seen what she was doing to that fat-ass CEO. I thought she was going to kill him. I was going through his wallet when I saw her trying to cut his fucking hand off to get to his Rolex. That's why I was so rushed."

"Me and Dante think Carmen's leaving Miami for good. Her days here are numbered. She's burned too many bridges." Kim tugged deeply on her cigarette.

"Yeah, I figured that much. That's why she doesn't give a shit about us. While she'll escape to Atlanta or wherever, she'll have the cops breathing down our necks here in Miami."

Kim was thinking. Her eyes showed her confusion.

"It's been a long night," Polita said. She was ready to leave and opened the door.

"You can stay here if you want."

"Not tonight. We still going to the Marlins game tomorrow?"

"Yeah. Carmen wants to come too, unless she went to the islands."

"I'll pick you up around noon."

Polita closed the door and walked down the corridor. She avoided the stairwell and took the elevator to the first floor. A gust of wind blew her hair as she stepped outside. Lightning flashed and revealed a man standing near the entrance to the building. She walked to her car with little, frightened steps, not looking back. The palm trees swayed in the wind. A frond fell behind her, a rattling sound as it blew across the sidewalk. She got into her car cursing, closed her convertible top, and pulled out of the parking lot. After a mile or so she stopped at a red light at a busy intersection. While waiting, she took out her cell phone and e-mailed the video clip of Carmen and Elliot to her computer. She drove on, weaving in and out of traffic. The car's panel lights glowed green. Slants of light rain hit the windshield. Approaching headlights - like sparks - shone in her eyes. The city lights of Miami misted-over behind the rain.

She turned into her apartment complex and parked. Despite the rain, a construction crew was working under massive Klieg lights on the adjacent highway. Jackhammers breaking concrete made her car rattle. Handbag strapped over her shoulder, she headed for her apartment, hurried inside, and double-locked the door. She said hi to Jazz, her brown cat, and checked her answering machine. There was one call, from her mother, in Tampa: "Just checking on you. Call me if you get in before ten. Love you."

She changed into a bathrobe and then brushed her teeth. Her reflection in the mirror disturbed her. She stopped brushing and looked closer. A strange light, a glint of fear, shone in her eyes.

She tightened the sash on her bathrobe and went in the bedroom. From her handbag she produced her cell phone, over $600 in cash, and the Rolex. At the bottom of the handbag she found Elliot's business card:

> Elliot Anderson III
> Owner and President
> Anderson Healthcare
> Medical Equipment and Supplies
> Boston, Massachusetts

She opened her laptop and checked her e-mail, eyeing the video clip of Carmen and Elliot for just a minute. Once she burned the video clip onto a DVD, she deleted it from her cell phone and laptop. She taped Elliot's business card to the DVD and placed it in a Ziploc bag. Then she counted the money, attached a paper clip to it, and slipped it into an envelope. A sharp reflection, like a flash of light, off the Rolex attracted her attention. She picked it up.

She held the watch for a lengthy time. In the glow of the lamp it gave off gleaming reflections. Her eyes sparkled with fascination as she admired it. For a minute or two she tinkered with its wristband, unsnapping it on the third try. She remembered how Carmen had clawed frantically to remove it from Elliot's wrist.

She placed the Rolex in a jewelry box and slid it, along with the rest of the stolen goods, under the bed. Tomorrow morning she planned to transfer everything to her safe deposit box. She turned the lamp off and went to bed. Her cat crawled up next to her feet.

She thought it was unusual that there were no sounds from the tenants above or on either side of her. The parking lot was empty. The construction crew had gone silent. The rain and the wind had ended. The bushes no longer scraped against her window. The night was a vacuum.

# 3

Elliot was sitting slumped in a chair. His head lolled from side to side as if he were drunk. An aberrant, organic odor hung in the room. Sweat thick as oil covered his face. His eyelids burned. He had an acid taste in his mouth. The Caribbean colors of the hotel room - bright florals, cobalt blue, tropical turquoise, peaches and terra cottas - nauseated him.

Gravity shifted under him when he stood. Groggily he moved from chair to table to minibar with a heavy numbness. He tried to make it to the bathroom, but he had a hard time keeping his balance. He didn't know if he had to vomit or shit. Knees shaking, he collapsed in another chair. The bathroom was a few feet away, but he had to rest. If he got sick, he just would have to let it happen from where he was sitting. He was breathing with deep, wheezing sounds. His chest ached.

That odor still troubled him. Where did it come from? The smell made him congested; he must have been having an allergic reaction to it. His eyes watered, and he sneezed repeatedly. *Take a deep breath*, he told himself. *Just relax and breathe*. He wanted to open the sliding glass door, to let some fresh air in, but he felt too queasy to stand, and the sliding glass door was in the opposite direction of the bathroom.

After a few minutes, it occurred to him that the odor was the stale, perfumy scent left behind by the two vaporous beings who had robbed him.

He realized that he was dressed in a pair of slacks, a pullover shirt, and shoes. Vaguely he remembered having awakened sometime after the call girls had left. He had no clear idea of any time sequence, but he knew he had tried to call his friend who was staying in a room six floors above his. When his friend hadn't answered his cell phone, Elliot had gone looking for him at the hotel's lounge and marina. After that he didn't remember much. The next thing he knew, he was back in his room passed out in the chair. His drug-haze and reality had fused into a hallucinatory world of fatigue and delirium.

He stared at his wallet on the floor. What was it doing there? Then he remembered that one of the women had gone through it. He leaned over and picked it up. Hands shaking, he went through it. Pictures of his wife and son. The cash was gone, but it surprised him that all his credit cards were still there. He wanted to report his stolen Rolex and the money, but he wasn't sure how he should go about it; after all, hadn't he paid for two call girls?

None of these details – his wallet on the floor, how he had dressed and had made it out of his room – had made any sense to him earlier, and he thought he was once again drifting in and out of a dream. Not long ago he had managed to go downstairs; now he couldn't make it five more feet to the bathroom. Why was he worse off? He should be more coherent, not more delirious. Maybe the drug the women had slipped into his drink was having a delayed reaction.

The thought of it all exhausted him. He needed more time to clear his head. He would have to wait for his friend's advice.

At least the feeling of having to vomit or to shit was subsiding. For the moment, at least, he felt safe staying seated. He started to doze off, but the sudden ring of a phone shocked him awake. He moved in sluggish spurts and looked on the dresser for his cell phone. He couldn't find it. Then he noticed it was the hotel's phone on the nightstand that was ringing. He picked up and heard his wakeup call; he had a breakfast meeting in a half hour. He dialed his friend's room and let it ring a full minute. No answer. He again tried his friend's cell number but could only get his voice mail.

He craved fresh air. He stepped out onto the balcony, which from the fifth floor overlooked Key Biscayne, and inhaled deeply, filling his lungs with the salty breeze. The fragrance from tropical trees in the hotel's courtyard floated up to his balcony. He could breathe again.

A crack of predawn light revealed pleasure boats on the bay. Yachts and sailboats were docked in the hotel's thirty-slip marina. Two women jogged along a nature trail that wound around the hotel and through a small forest of moss-covered oaks and cypresses.

He aired out his room by leaving the balcony door open. In the bathroom he unwrapped a plastic cup in cellophane and turned on the tap, but instead of water, a dark slimy liquid bled into the cup. The plumbing made a vomiting sound. He found it odd that there would be a problem with the plumbing at a five-star resort. The vomiting sound made him want to puke again, and another wave of nausea came over him. For the next five minutes he sat on the toilet, sweating and braced to empty his insides, but once again, nothing happened.

He struggled to untangle himself from his pants. He got them past his knees, but he had to get on the bathroom floor to kick them free from his feet. Given the condition he was in, it continued to amaze him that he had ever managed to get dressed in the first place. His goal was to make it to the shower where it would be easier to clean up the mess that was sure to come flowing out of him. Finally, he made into the shower stall and stood under the warm flow of water. The small bar of soap kept slipping from his grip, and it made his head throb every time he had to lean over to pick it up. The soap stung the scratches on his wrists. He didn't remember the woman's nails tearing up the wrist without the Rolex. Dried blood crusted on the deeper cuts.

He stepped out of the shower and toweled off. For the first time he felt steady on his feet; the powerful sensation of having to shit or vomit was gone, but he remained in the bathroom just in case. Hands no longer trembling, he opened his zipper bag, produced a razor, and started shaving in the bathroom mirror. He recoiled when he saw two purplish teeth marks – more like fang wounds - on his throat pulse in his reflection. He touched the flesh around the swollen bite, remembering the inflection in the she-devil's teasing voice, her derisive laughter as he drooled and stuttered, her hirsute cunt in his face. He flinched as he recalled her cat claws, the broken wine bottle, her nipples stiffening while she abused him.

He cut himself because he was so upset, watching as blood mixed with shaving cream ran down his chin. He dabbed his chin with a washcloth and applied a piece of tissue paper over the cut. He then slipped into a cotton knit striped pullover and a pair of slacks belted below his potbelly. A glance in the mirror revealed the hickey-sized bite mark above his collar. He adjusted the shirt to cover it, but it remained visible, as if spreading its purplish poison.

He changed into a starched white longsleeved shirt. He noticed that his face had a rosy hue, almost a burn, from yesterday's game of golf in the Florida sun. He knotted his tie and tucked in his wattled throat behind the stiff collar, concealing the bite mark. The starchy shirt irritated the wounds on his wrists.

On his way into the room, he stepped on a small piece of glass from the broken wine bottle. He cried out and hopped from the dresser to the bathroom. How had he missed stepping on the glass before? He shouted, "Goddamn her! Fucking slut!" He sat on the tub and ran warm water over his foot. It took him several minutes to pick out the piece of glass and dress the wound.

Back in the room, he got on his hands and knees and very carefully picked up and trashed the remaining pieces of glass. He put on his socks, shoes, and blazer, found his cell phone and stuck it in his pants pocket, and with his foot still throbbing, he limped out of the room.

# 4

The feeling that something cold was crawling up inside her made Polita bolt upright in bed. The cat at her feet jumped off the bed and ran down the hallway. In the dark, she remained still, hands held tightly between her legs to protect herself. She took a deep, trembling breath. Her entire body shivered. She drew the comforter up to her shoulders.

Fragments of the dream slowly came back to her; a slimy penis had slowly penetrated her, and had begun to eat away at her insides. The room in the dream had been the blackest dark, and the man on top of her had been unrecognizable. The sour smell of his stale breath on her face almost suffocated her. He had whispered something in her ear, but that too had been unclear.

Gradually she relaxed by taking a couple of deep breaths. The pain in her stomach went away, and her thoughts returned to the hotel room where she was diverting Elliot's attention while Carmen was pouring the wine. She remembered the lust in Elliot's eyes, his gluey tongue groping in her mouth, his big hands touching and grabbing her. Over his shoulder she watched as Carmen slipped the knockout drops in his drink, then lured him away and started to seduce him while the knockout drops took effect. She could still see him clearly, and the image of his helplessness wouldn't leave her. His jowly chin had shook with each gulp of air, with each gurgling, choking, raspy sounds. She feared she would have to grab his tongue in case he started to swallow it.

She got out of bed and turned on almost every light in the apartment. Her cat was restless, meowing and pacing back and forth in front of the sliding glass door. She peered through the curtains at some of the tenants who were leaving to go to work. Then she took three Advil. Her eyes were swollen and her hair was knotted and disheveled. She walked through the apartment, turning off the lights while brushing her hair with long strokes. The cat remained by the sliding glass door, crouched low to the floor, ears alert. She turned off her bedroom light and got back in bed. With wide eyes she stared up at the pale gleam of light that stretched across the ceiling.

Sounds of a jackhammer meant the construction crew was at work. A dumpster was close enough to her bedroom window that she thought she could smell it. She was tired but couldn't go back to sleep.

# 5

Alone on the glass-walled elevator, Elliot pushed the "lobby" button and the doors closed. He sat on the built-in sofa to take the weight off his sore foot. He watched the palm trees and tropical bushes and flowers of the twenty-one story atrium-lobby as the elevator descended through the flora and stopped on the third floor. A dark-haired bellhop, impeccably dressed in khaki pants and a safari shirt with epaulets, wheeled an empty luggage rack into the elevator. He was tall and lanky. The palest blue eyes, almost gray. His nameplate above his shirt pocket identified him as Phil.

"Good morning, sir," the bellhop said.

Elliot nodded and tried to smile. The doors closed and the elevator continued its descent.

"Sir, do you have the time?"

Out of habit Elliot turned the cuff of his sleeve back to look at his watch but saw only his scratched wrist. "I, ah, forgot my watch," he said. Then he pulled the cuff over his wrist. "It should be about six-thirty or so." He felt naked without his watch.

"Thank you. I forgot my watch, too, which almost never happens. My shift should almost be over."

When the elevator reached the bottom floor, the bellhop held the door open, and the two men exchanged niceties. As Elliot limped through the atrium lobby, he could hear the bellhop whistle at a macaw preening itself on a stand.

In the pink dawn, the tuxedo-shirted servers on the pool deck were waiting on the gathering guests, the males of whom were mostly dressed casually in slacks and shirts unbuttoned at the neck. One server poured Elliot a cup of coffee, and he sipped at the steaming beverage as he stood almost hidden between two giant vats of hibiscus. He avoided mingling with the guests; the only person he wanted to see was his friend. He tried calling him on his cell phone again but still couldn't get an answer.

The indistinct clouds, touched by the morning light, slowly began to break up. Pelicans perched on pilings of the marina. The bay was flat, waveless.

More guests were arriving, but Elliot still saw no sign of his friend. He limped around looking. The pool area, with its three interconnected pools and a massive rock grotto, complete with waterfalls and suspended bridges, was too spread out to cover on a sore foot, so he sat on a marble bench and passed the time by watching the kitchen staff setting up the tables and chairs on the pool deck. The air carried the scent of jasmine.

He listened to a nearby fountain bubbling and splashing with the music of water. The dome of the sun finally rose, firing up the horizon in reds and yellows. A tall-masted sailboat pulled out of the marina. Gulls swooped in and scavenged the area for any scraps of food.

Elliot was taking a sip of coffee when he spotted his friend, Stan Ferrell, coming forward with extended hand. His friends called him "Wink" because he was always winking, smiling, shaking hands, and patting backs. He gave Elliot such a vigorous handshake that he practically pulled him off the bench. Elliot stood and eased his hand free.

"Ah do declare, Mistuh Anderson, where'n the hail have you been?" Wink drawled, imitating a twangy, country-boy accent. He was freshly shaved and smelled of cologne.

"Where the *hell* have you been? I've been trying to call your cell since last night."

"Ah've been lookin' for you all mornin', pardner."

Wink smiled, very whitely, and mock-punched Elliot in the midsection. He was forty-six, of medium height, and going slack in the stomach. The breeze off the bay barely tousled his spray-stiffened pompadour hairstyle. Permanent smile-wrinkles creased the corner of his eyes. Elliot had known him for fourteen years, ever since he had worked for him as a sales representative in Boston. For the past six years he had lived north of Miami in Ft. Lauderdale.

"Don't you look handsome," Wink said, dropping his accent. He touched Elliot's gold stickpin beneath the knot of his tie. "You're color-coordinated. Except that little piece of white tissue paper on your chin doesn't quite match your tie."

"Damn." Elliot removed the bloodied tissue from his chin. "You'd think someone would have reminded me. I feel stupid."

"Why are you so dressed up? This is just a little shindig that we're attending. Remember, you're in Florida. Even though it's only April, you're going to burn up with all those clothes."

Wink was dressed casually, white-shirted and suspendered but tieless. A cell phone was Velcroed in a holster clipped to the waistband of his white slacks. He wore tasseled loafers without socks.

"I've got to tell you what happened to me last night," Elliot said in a hushed voice. He led Wink toward the marina away from the crowd.

"Why are you limping?"

"I stepped on a piece of glass."

"Bummer."

"It happened in my…room." He glanced up at the fifth floor of the hotel.

"How'd glass get on the floor in your room?"

"I can't wait to tell you."

"You'd better be careful. You're cutting yourself all up." Wink snickered, "Well, are you going to tell me about last night or not?"

Elliot was about to speak, but Wink interrupted him by calling out to a server, who quickly came over and handed him a glass of orange juice.

"You should be drinking fresh-squeezed Florida orange juice," Wink said, smiling and sounding like a commercial. He held his glass up and touched it against Elliot's cup.

"I should be drinking something a lot stronger than coffee after what I went through last night."

"Classy place, isn't it?" Wink gazed at the Mediterranean-style hotel that resembled a pink stucco palace. "First time I've been here. I live only forty-five miles from the hotel, but when my company said they'd pay the bill, I wasn't going to argue. Why not lead the good life on company time? It's one of Miami's two or three best resorts. Of course, someone like you is used to staying in such fancy places."

"You gave me a tour of the place yesterday; I don't need another one. I've got to tell you what happened in my room last night."

"I've been waiting to hear it."

"You haven't listened to a word I've said. And I can't believe you never answered your cell."

"Maybe we had a bad connection or something."

"Bad connection my ass. You're always on your cell. It's practically attached to your ear - even when you sleep, except for the one time I needed you the most."

A friend of Wink's, Dave Kornick, suddenly stepped between them and gave Elliot a slippery handshake with no vitality. The limpest of handshakes. Elliot had met him yesterday when he and Wink had picked him up at the airport. In his late thirties, Dave was tall and trim with a gentle manner. He combed his blondish, thinning hair crosswise from ear to ear. A bald spot was beginning to form at the crown. He wore white slacks, a flower-print shirt, and sockless loafers.

"You look tired," Dave said to Elliot, with a tight smile. He gave Wink a side-long glance. "Wink and I were hoping that you had a good time last night."

Wink and Dave broke into wide smiles. Dave had been with Elliot and Wink at Café Sinsations, and the two of them were the only people who had known about Carmen's visit to Elliot's room.

"Elliot keeps stalling about telling me what happened with him and Carmen," Wink said.

"That's something to keep between you and a very sexy woman, isn't it, Elliot?" Dave said.

"Maybe," Elliot said. He noticed that Dave had an eye tic which he didn't remember from yesterday.

"I'm all ears," Wink said.

Elliot wanted to separate Wink from Dave and talk to him privately, but several more of Wink's friends came over and joined him. Standing in the middle of everyone, Elliot found it confusing to keep up with all the conversations. Then Wink became dominatingly loud by telling stories and obscene jokes. It was the salesman in him, charming and effusive.

As the conversations swirled around him, Elliot gradually edged away from the crowd. He was so tensed up that he dropped his cup. A server appeared, cleaned up the mess, and offered Elliot another. He held the new cup with both hands.

A sharp pain shot through his chest. He was still tense. He tried to calm down by taking deep breaths and by walking around, but the bright colors of the surrounding landscape only further distressed him. Upon his arrival yesterday from winter-worn Boston, the sub-tropical scenery around the hotel seemed tranquil, but today everything overwhelmed him, as though the greenery was closing in on him, strangling him. It was the same feeling he'd had in his hotel room. Was he going to have a heart attack? Should he call rescue? The botanical plant life dazzled him with its exotic reds, purples, yellows, and different shades of greens. Flowering vines covered the statuary and fountains. The freshly mown lawn, with its pruned shrubs and hedges, appeared smooth and velvety. Bougainvillea draped the hotel's iron balconies. Flowerbeds of dusty millers, marigolds and daylilies framed selective trees. Groundskeepers in khaki shorts, green sports shirts with hotel logo, and pith helmets were weeding and mulching nearby gardens.

Impatient with Wink entertaining his friends, Elliot, desperate, interrupted him and led him to the marina, where he backed him up against a railing on the seawall. A narrow strip of beach lay between them and the tideline.

"For once will you give me your undivided attention?" Elliot said. "I've got to talk to you about last night."

"I've been listening."

"No, you haven't. You've been too busy performing for everyone." Elliot stared into Wink's eyes. "Those two women you sent to my room last night robbed me."

Calmly incredulous, Wink looked at Elliot for a few seconds. "I'm not sure I heard you."

"I said I was *robbed*. They stole my Rolex and over $600 in cash."

"Now dagnabit, slow down. You're goin' way too fast for this here country boy." Wink's only expression was a raised brow. "What do you mean *they* robbed you?"

"Those two women...I'm having a hard time remembering the name of that exotic dancer."

"I only introduced you to Carmen. She must've brought along one of her friends. I warned you that she was a hellion."

"She's a thief. And a fucking psycho."

"What'd you do, not pay them what they wanted so they took some of your things? I told you she was pretty expensive."

"They ripped me off right before my eyes. I watched them do it."

"You mean they pulled a gun on you?" Wink's near-permanent smile slowly faded.

"Uh...not exactly." The words were slow to form off Elliot's lips.

"Did they or didn't they?"

"Ah...there was no gun."

"No gun? Then Christalmighty, how in the hail did two women rob a man your size?" Wink's smile returned, toothy and bright. "What happened, you let Carmen handcuff you to the bed? She probably took a few of your things as some kinky joke."

"It wasn't a joke. I don't find any of this amusing."

"OK. I can tell you're not too happy."

"Believe me, I'm very angry."

"I just can't believe that a woman I set you up with would have the nerve to rob you."

"She drugged me."

"She what?"

"She slipped something in my drink. The next thing I knew, I was paralyzed."

"Sounds like you got drunk and passed out."

"I wasn't drunk. I had maybe four or five sips of her cheap-ass wine."

"Come on, El."

"I'm serious. I was awake but couldn't move a finger while they robbed me. They had it all planned. Things were going smoothly for them until she couldn't unsnap my watch. Lately, I've had some trouble unsnapping it myself. So much for owning a Rolex. I've been meaning to take it to a jeweler, but I just never got around to it. My procrastinating almost got me seriously injured. Maybe even killed."

"Killed? What are you talking about? You said they weren't even armed."

"Your cute little exotic dancer threatened me with a broken wine bottle. She could've cut me up and left me in my room to bleed to death. How do you think I ended up stepping on a piece of glass?"

Elliot unbuttoned one sleeve and showed Wink the scratches on his wrist. For a moment Wink was speechless.

"Her damn nails were as sharp as knives," Elliot said, buttoning his sleeve. "Nothing like this has ever happened to me before. It was my personal introduction to a few minutes of terror."

"I don't know what to say."

Elliot glanced up to the fifth floor. "I know it doesn't sound like much, but it scared me that I thought I was going to have a heart attack. And I still have the feeling that I could croak at any time. Whatever they put in my drink has totally fucked me up. I don't know where I am half the time. One minute I start feeling a little better, then I have a relapse." He pressed his hand against his chest. "I swear, I may have to call a doctor. I get acid reflux all the time, but this feels twenty times worse."

Distracted, Wink didn't respond to any of Elliot's comments. He gazed out at the bay, drifting into his own thoughts. A silver-haired security guard drove by in a golf cart. The sun's rays spread out over the bay. Already it was humid, enough that sweat beads glistened on Elliot's forehead. He took off his blazer. His starchy shirt tormented his wrists and neck, and he scratched and scratched as if a cloud of no-see-ums were attacking him. The wounds on his wrists had turned into festering sores.

"This really burns me up," Wink finally said, though he didn't look upset. His attention returned to Elliot. "What makes Carmen think she can rob a good friend of mine and get away with it? I know her. I know where she works. I can't believe she's that stupid. Doesn't she know that I can have her arrested?" He stared directly into Elliot's eyes, gripped him by both shoulders, and said in a reassuring voice, "El, don't you worry about a gah-damn thing. If she skedaddled with your Rolex and money, I'll find her. You can count on me, pardner."

Wink's fake country-accent had worn on Elliot's nerves. He escaped from Wink's grip and stepped away from him. He was sweating, his shirt clinging transparently on his skin. Wink, meanwhile, looked cool and calm. He returned to Elliot's side.

"Yep, that was one dumb bitch to mess with us," Wink said, clinging to Elliot like the humidity.

"She's not dumb." Elliot stepped another couple of feet away from Wink. "She sounds pretty damn street smart to me. I'm the one who looks stupid. We can't go to the police and she knows it. She's got me by the balls."

"Why can't we go to the police?"

"For a number of reasons. Because having call girls in my hotel room was illegal. Because that fact means my insurance wouldn't cover my stolen Rolex. Because Karen gave me the Rolex for a wedding anniversary and would divorce me for adultery. Need any more?"

Wink thought for a moment.

"I have an idea," he said. "Tell the police you were robbed by two thugs. Just don't tell them they wore dresses."

"Your aw-shucks Southern bonhomie shows me that you're still not taking this seriously. I've never been so scared - and humiliated - in my life."

"I'm not treating this lightly. I'm serious about my idea. I've already got everything figured out." Wink's cell phone rang and he answered it, tersely saying, "I'll call you back. Can't talk right now. Maybe later. Bye." Then he continued where he left off. "We stick to our plan for this morning. We play a round of golf, then Dave takes us downtown to show us his new warehouse and offices, which are smack-dab in the middle of Miami. The whole shebang. While the three of us are returning to his car, we get robbed at gunpoint. Happens all the time in Miami. It's the crime capital of the U.S! We tell the police that a couple of punks pulled a gun on us and took our money and watches. At least Karen won't find out about the two women. And you can collect your insurance on the Rolex."

Elliot brooded over Wink's plan for a while. The sun's reflection off the bay mesmerized him.

"I don't know," Elliot said. "That's filing a false report."

"Just tell the police that some punks robbed you. That part is true. Then you don't have to worry about catching hell from Karen. And your insurance will cover your Rolex."

"I'm afraid it's more complicated than that."

"It isn't as long as we leave Carmen and her friend alone. Let them go. Anyway, I'm sure they've already spent your money and cashed in on the Rolex."

"I'm sure they have. My problem is that I'm being set up to be blackmailed. It's a classic case of extortion."

"I'm not following you."

"That other woman used her cell phone camera and filmed Carmen and me in bed. With our clothes off."

"You were filmed fucking her?"

"I barely touched her. I was so drugged I couldn't raise my little finger. But that doesn't matter. The video clip will show me in bed with a naked woman. I was serious when I told you they had me by the balls."

"That does it. I'm going to the café tonight ending this little crime spree of Carmen's."

"We won't be able to go to the police with your story until you can get that video clip from her."

"Yeah. You're right there. That makes it a little more complicated. But I'll have it all figured out by tonight."

"What makes you think you can get the video clip from her?"

"I'll tell her our plan. We won't press any charges if she will hand over the video clip. She can keep the money and the Rolex. If she doesn't agree to go along with that, we'll just have to tell the police the truth. Then at least she couldn't blackmail you because Karen will then know everything anyway. The video clip would be worthless."

"They're probably watching it right now and laughing their asses off." Elliot smacked the railing with the palm of his hand.

"I'll take care of everything. Trust me." Wink gripped Elliot's shoulder and squeezed it. His intense, prying eyes stared at him. "I'm really sorry I put you through all this. I knew she was wild, but I never dreamed she'd do this. This other woman must've put Carmen up to it."

"It was Carmen, not the other woman, who tore me up." Elliot unbuttoned his shirt collar and pulled it down to show Wink his neck wound. "She acted like a damn vampire and took a chunk out of me. In the condition I was in, I could've sworn that she had venom dripping from her fangs."

"Holy shit."

Another security guard, holding a cell phone to his ear, strolled by. He was dressed in blue slacks, a white, short-sleeved shirt with epaulets, and a blue clip-on tie. He said hello to Elliot and Wink.

"What was the other woman's name?" Wink said.

"I don't know." Elliot's face was dark with concentration. "I'm not sure if she ever told me her name. When I answered the knock on the door, I was expecting only Carmen. The other woman just happened to show up with her."

"What'd she look like?"

"Dark eyes and sexy, like Carmen. Wild-colored hair. An athletic figure. Probably an exotic dancer."

"There are at least thirty dancers at the café. Carmen's good friends with a dancer by the name of Kim, but she has blond hair." Wink thought for a moment. "You said her partner in crime had colorful hair. Hmm. Those exotic dancers have all kinds of funky hairstyles. I've seen fluorescent hair, spiked mohawks, Afros. One dancer has a shaved head. And some of them wear wigs."

"Maybe the hair color was just one of the many hallucinations I was having last night. Neon, straight black, curly blond – how the hell can I be sure? Fuck, maybe she was an hallucination. I can't be sure of anything right now."

"I'll find out who she is through Carmen."

"I don't care who she is, just get the video clip back and all will be forgotten."

"I'll get it and the Rolex."

"That'd be nice too, but at least the Rolex is insured."

"If you don't mind my asking, what's it worth?"

"Around seventy thousand."

"Gah-damn, son. I didn't know a Rolex cost as much as a Mercedes."

"Karen had it customized."

"My ex was always jealous of Karen's expensive tastes."

Elliot's eyes watered from the bright sunlight. "I'm so tired I can barely hold my head up. I think I'll go back to my room."

"They're serving breakfast now."

"I've got to put my head down. I feel as though she spiked my drink with strychnine."

"I hate to be the one to tell you this, but you fell for an old trick."

"Thanks for the warning."

"I read about the same thing that happened to a pro football player a few years ago. A call girl drugged him and ripped him off, including his Super Bowl ring."

"Then why did you have such a hard time believing me when I told you that the same thing had happened to me?"

"I had no idea Carmen would've done something like this, especially to a friend of mine. I'm certain this other woman must be behind it."

"I've already told you, this Carmen was the one who ran the show. She got into it. The more she humiliated me, the more it turned her on. The other woman stayed in the background and let Carmen do the dirty work. Or so it seemed to me. But again, what do I know? I was drugged most the time."

Elliot and Wink returned to the pool deck. Nearby the guests dined in a flowering arbor where the tables were covered with pastel linen and fresh-cut flowers in crystal vases. Two white-aproned omelet chefs stood behind a table on which the hot plates were arranged. Servers in their bow-tied tuxedo shirts pampered the guests with exaggerated politeness. The aromas of coffee, of flowers, and of the salt breeze filled the air.

"I need about a two-hour nap," Elliot said.

Wink walked with Elliot to the entrance of the lobby.

"We tee off at 9:30," Wink said. "We should keep to our schedule and act like everything's normal."

"I'll see how I feel." Elliot noticed that Dave was staring at him from across the pool. "Are you sure we should tell Dave any of this? He might not want to get involved."

"He's already involved because he knows about you and Carmen."

"How well does he know her?"

"He's been with me to the café a few times."

"Then keep this between the three of us. I don't want anyone else to know."

"It's top secret. Don't worry." He gave Elliot a fist bump. "Go take a nap, big guy. I'll check on you in an hour or so."

From the entrance of the lobby Elliot watched Wink return to his friends with a little trot. Wink made a call on his cell phone, then stood near a table in the arbor and immediately joined in on his friends' conversations. His hands were a blur as he gestured, shook hands, squeezed elbows and shoulders, handed out his business cards, and gave openhanded slaps on backs, grabbing and pulling on everyone who came into contact with him. Outside of Wink's circle of friends, Dave stood alone by the pool, holding a glass of orange juice and gazing out at the bay.

Elliot limped to the elevators, passing two bright, multicolored macaws that were perched on their stands in the atrium-lobby. He rode an elevator to the fifth floor, and on his way down the corridor he loosened his tie and rolled up his sleeves. The first thing he did when he entered his room was peel off his sweatsoaked shirt. Then he showered again, careful not to get soap on any of his wounds.

Overcome with fatigue, he collapsed on the bed and fell asleep.

# 6

Lying on her stomach on a lounge chair by the pool, Polita reached both hands behind her and unsnapped her bikini top to expose her bare back to the sun. The heat penetrated to her bones. She relaxed as the rays soothed her neck and shoulders, still sore from last night's restless sleep. Nearby, two women in lounge chairs were sitting next to each other, their faces raised to the sun as they talked on their cell phones. Across the pool, a man was leaning back in his chair, listening to his iPod and staring in Polita's direction. A combination of a concrete wall and a chain-linked fence surrounded the pool.

Polita, drowsing, felt a cool shadow come over her. She thought it was a cloud blocking the sun. For a long moment the coolness remained, sending a chill over her. When she opened her eyes, she noticed a person's stationary shadow on the concrete. Holding her loose bikini top against her breasts, she turned over and squinted at a vague shape that stood at the foot of the lounge chair. After her eyes adjusted, she recognized Seth Watson, one of the bouncers who worked at Café Sinsations.

"I was wondering how long it was going to take for you to turn over," Seth said. "Were you asleep?"

"I think I dozed off some."

Seth wore sandals, shorts and a T-shirt. His dark-tinted, wraparound sunglasses reflected the sun's glare off the concrete, and it hurt Polita's eyes to look at him against the sun. She shaded her face with her hand. When he didn't move, she repositioned herself in her chair and started watching his shadow.

"I thought you were going out of town for a few days," Polita said.

"I was planning to go to my brother's place, but I've got some big tests coming up that I have to study for. Nothing comes easy for me. You've met my rich brother Paul, the whiz kid. He's the one with the brains and the luck in my family."

Polita felt Seth's eyes on her. It was odd for her to feel uncomfortable around him since she had known him for the full ten months she had danced at Café Sinsations. A twenty-six-year-old senior at Florida Institute of Technology, he was short and bowlegged but solidly built. His arms bulged in their sleeves. His brother's place was in Everglades City, an hour's drive from Miami. Polita had been there once before, when he had invited her and Carmen and Kim to a party.

"Must be crazy at times going to college and working the late hours you put in at the café," Polita said.

"It's not so bad." Taking off his sunglasses, he pulled up a lawn chair and sat next to her. "I hope you don't mind my dropping by like this without first calling you."

"You don't have to call. We're friends."

She thought that his unannounced visit was unusual. He had been to her apartment only twice before: once to help her move in, and another time for a birthday party with some employees from Café Sinsations.

The man across the pool with the iPod gathered up his things, glanced at Polita, and walked out of the gate as she and Seth sat quietly. She turned her neck stiffly as Seth watched her. His hair, somewhere between blond and light brown, was combed back against his forehead. He was fair-skinned with light blue eyes. For some reason, she preferred that he kept his sunglasses on.

"You keep rubbing and twisting your neck," he said, moving his chair closer to Polita's. "Do you have a headache?"

"I tossed and turned last night."

"Turn over and I'll rub your neck and shoulders." He picked up her container of suntan oil.

"That's OK."

"I won't take no for an answer."

"Really, I'll be fine."

"I'm ready," he said, rubbing the oil on his hands.

"You don't have to."

"I insist."

She straightened her towel on the chair and turned over. Lying flat on her stomach, her palms resting on the warm concrete, she braced herself for his touch as his shadow loomed again over the concrete like a cloud. He applied the oil on her back, massaging it in. His hands moved upward to her shoulders and to her smooth, bare neck. He avoided getting any oil in her hair. His massage generated great warmth, and she could feel the tension leave her body. His hands controlled her, rubbing, rubbing. She closed her eyes. His touch was tender but resolute. His thick, strong, uncalloused hands massaged her shoulders, her lower back. Her legs.

"You're very good," she said.

Seth was quiet.

"I might fall asleep on you," she said.

"I guess that's a compliment." His massage went deeper, deeper. His hands returned to her neck. "You're tense."

"I sometimes get bad headaches when I can't sleep."

"Why can't you sleep?"

"All those late nights at the café are starting to get to me."

"But you're in great condition. You're an athlete."

"Tell that to my feet. One time last week they were so sore they kept me up all night. Dancing in heels for six to eight hours almost every night is making them look deformed. Sometimes they feel like stubs. In a few more years I'll probably have to get them operated on."

He turned his attention to her feet and massaged them.

"I didn't mean that as a hint to rub my feet," she said, turning slightly to smile at him.

"I was working my way down."

She turned back around and closed her eyes.

"If your feet are bothering you that much, you should take some time off," he said. "Take a vacation."

"I can't afford one. I just like to complain. Don't pay any attention to me."

"Why don't you take a few days off and come out with me to my brother's?"

"I might."

"You said you had fun last time you were there."

"I had a blast."

"It's only an hour away, but it feels more like a thousand miles from here."

"You and your brother planning on having another party?"

"I'm tired of parties and loud music. We hear it every night at work. I need some peace and quiet."

"I know what you mean."

"I'd like to take my brother's boat out into the Gulf and do some fishing or diving. Maybe go hunting. I'd just like to get away from the café and from my studies and take it easy for a few days."

"Sounds like fun."

They were quiet for a few minutes. He went from her feet to the small of her back.

"You must be getting tired by now," she said.

"Just warming up. If you feel like it, after work tonight, I'll give you another massage."

She didn't respond. She listened to his breathing. His hands tightened their grip. The massage was beginning to hurt, and the pressure on her back almost took her breath away. She stiffened. Didn't he realize he was being too rough? She opened her eyes and stared at his shadow on the concrete, at that dark cloud looming over her. She wanted to turn over but was pinned down, unable to move.

He momentarily stopped to squeeze more suntan oil on his hands. She used that time to turn over.

"Thanks," Polita said. She adjusted her bikini top, and in doing so thought it odd that she was trying to cover herself up when he was used to seeing her topless at work.

Surprised at her sudden move, Seth showed Polita his oily hands.

"I'm good for at least another twenty minutes," he said.

"I've got to be somewhere in a little while."

"I guess I don't get the job as your personal masseuse."

"That's the best massage I've ever had. Look at my towel, you had me drooling on it."

Polita, grimacing, felt a sharp pain in her side when she stood up.

"You OK?" he said.

"Yeah. You took my breath away with that massage." She held her side.

"I hope I wasn't too rough with you."

"You weren't, really."

Polita slipped on a pink cotton mesh tunic and gathered up her things. While gazing at her, Seth used the towel to wipe off his hands one finger at a time. He had a strong-boned face and a sharp jaw that came to a point.

"You going anywhere special?" he said, slipping on his sunglasses.

"Not really. A Marlins game."

"I didn't know you were a baseball fan."

"Baseball bores me. I watch the people instead of the game. I'm only going because Kim and Carmen invited me. Carmen's the real baseball fan."

Instead of leaving for his Jeep, Seth followed Polita to her apartment. She unlocked her door and opened it but didn't enter. His eyes hidden behind his sunglasses, Seth lingered in the doorway without saying anything.

"I guess I'll take a shower and get ready," she said. She debated whether she should invite him inside.

"I keep looking for distractions - anything - to keep from studying for my tests. I can't study tonight because I've got to work."

"Am I a distraction?" She smiled.

"You're a good reason for me to keep from having to study." He was being more friendly than affectionate.

"Thanks for coming by. And thanks for the massage."

"You and your potted plants and flowers." He was gazing over her shoulder into her apartment. "I've never known anyone who loves flowers as much as you."

"One day I hope to have my own florist shop."

"When I helped you move that time, you wanted me to be more careful with your plants than with your furniture."

"After dealing with some of the customers at the café, it's nice to come home to something sweet-smelling and pretty to look at. It's like going from a sewer to a garden."

"Hope you enjoy the game. I'll see you at work tonight."

Seth headed for the parking lot, turning once to wave at Polita. She went inside and watched from her living room window as he climbed into his Jeep and drove away. In her bedroom, she gathered up the stolen goods and put them in her handbag. She planned to go to her safe deposit box and then pick up Kim.

Sleek with suntan oil, she slipped out of her bikini and took a shower. She could still feel Seth's hands on her, touching, probing, rubbing. And she felt a slight pain in her ribs.

# 7

After they had played golf and had dropped by Dave's warehouse and offices, Elliot and his two friends returned to the hotel's pool deck where lunch was being served. Wink had told Dave about the robbery, and Dave had advised Wink and Elliot to contact Carmen before they went to the police. Nothing more had been said on the subject, and for the rest of the time they had talked mostly about golf and a business deal between Elliot and Dave, but Elliot had noticed that both men occasionally stared at his scratched wrists. Luckily, his neck wound was partially covered up by his shirt collar, so it hadn't attracted much attention.

All three men wore visored golf caps as they stood in line at the buffet table. Servers bearing trays of hors d' oeuvres approached the guests. Elliot had an appetite after having played nine holes. He admired the assortment of food. Chicken and pasta dishes. An assortment of sliced luncheon meats and cheeses. Fruits so colorful they looked plastic. Oysters on the half shell, broiled jumbo shrimp, scallops, crab cakes. Every dessert imaginable. He served himself a smoked turkey croissant and chocolate mousse, and then he joined Dave at a table in the arbor. Wink had slipped away unnoticed.

For the next couple of minutes Dave talked to Elliot about their business deal; both men owned a medical supplies business and were planning a joint venture in the Miami area. While Elliot was explaining his business model, though, he saw that Dave's attention began to wander and became remote, disinterested. Elliot had noticed since they had met yesterday that at one minute Dave could be friendly, and at the next he would be withdrawn and coldly detached.

Without saying anything, Dave got up and walked over to a mosaic fountain adorned with flowers and potted palms. He picked off a thick-petaled jasmine flower and smelled its fragrance then wandered over to the seawall where a crowd was gathering.

Elliot finished his dessert and leaned back in the chair. His recovery from last night was going well, and he felt stronger and more clear-headed. He had eaten slowly, so as to avoid acid reflux. He raised his face to the sun; everything he touched was sun-warmed. The sky was clear, cloudless. Palm trees swayed in the breeze. A brooklike gurgle of a fountain relaxed him. Peacocks crossed back and forth across the lawn. A gull tilted toward the marina and away. The far-off drone of recreational boats sounded in the bay.

He returned to the buffet line for a soft drink. When he got back to his table, he noticed that more and more people were wandering over to the seawall. Curious, he stood up and passed through the crowd, only stopping once when a server presented him with chocolate-dipped strawberries on a tray. With a Coke in one hand and several chocolate strawberries in the other, Elliot stepped up to Dave who was standing at the railing of the six-foot concrete seawall and sipping a beer. Everyone's attention was directed at the narrow strip of beach in front of the marina. It was lowtide. Policemen and paramedics were standing between the seawall and the tideline, looking at something.

"What's going on?" Elliot said.

"Probably a dolphin beached itself or got tangled up in a fisherman's net." Dave pushed his visor back on his head.

"I don't think paramedics would be down there to help a dolphin."

"I wouldn't be surprised. They beach themselves. No one knows why. Maybe they get disoriented. Or maybe it's suicide. Last summer, a dolphin beached itself and someone tried to give it mouth-to-mouth. I should say mouth-to-blowhole." Dave giggled. "Imagine an animal-lover crazy enough to try to resuscitate a damn fish. Although, when you think about it, with AIDS and everything else, I guess you're safer to revive a dolphin than some stranger who croaks next to you. It happened to me one time. I was at an airport and this man sitting next to me slumped over and started choking. I let someone else try to revive him. No way would I do it."

Dave's eyes seemed to have sunlight in them, making them sparkle. He had finished his beer and was teetering on his heels. From his rambling conversation, Elliot assumed that Dave had had a few.

"That's no dolphin down there," Elliot said. "With that many policemen and paramedics, someone must've drowned."

"Maybe so." Dave shrugged and viewed the activity below with dispassionate curiosity.

Now that people began to separate, Elliot could see more clearly. Paramedics placed a corpse into a blue vinyl body bag and carried it away on a gurney. Police cruisers and rescue and fire trucks were gathered at the far end of the hotel. An evidence technician knelt on one knee and videotaped under the marina and the surrounding area. Yellow-crime scene tape restricted access to the marina.

The crowd, many of them dressed in citrus colors and talking on their cell phones, slowly returned to the buffet tables. A few curious bystanders, among them Elliot, looked on as several detectives gave instructions to two police divers who were standing knee-deep in the water. Dave gazed past the police, past the marina. His unblinking staring eyes were wide and vacant.

Several minutes had passed when Elliot felt someone grip his arm.

"Have you seen Dave?" The voice belonged to Wink, who appeared next to Elliot.

"He was just here a second ago," Elliot said. "I didn't see him leave. Where have you been? Lately you've made it a habit of disappearing on me. I thought you were going to join us for lunch."

Wink was quiet. For a long moment he stared at the marina while chewing on the rubber end of his sunglasses. A breeze came up and created a light chop on the water.

"Your visitor from last night was found floating under the marina," Wink said in an uninflected voice. He turned his gaze from the marina to the rescue truck into which the corpse was being wheeled. "That's Carmen they're taking to the morgue."

Wink's comment hung in the warm air for a while. Elliot was stunned. He glanced from the rescue truck to Wink, whose eyes seemed colorless.

"I watched the police put paper bags over her hands while they were photographing her," Wink said. His voice was as soft and calm as the breeze through the palms.

Elliot took a deep breath. "Are you sure that was her?"

"I'm positive. I was talking to some friends when we noticed the police walking around the marina. We went over to the seawall before the crowd showed up. I got a good look. I couldn't believe it at first. I even walked down to the beach. It was Carmen, all right. I was standing no more than five feet from her."

Elliot, whitefaced, broke into a chilly sweat. He stared at the policemen who were observing the divers in the water, their shadows passing back and forth under the marina like slow-moving sharks.

Wink drummed his hands on the railing. "Unbelievable, huh? From what I've heard, a man was getting his sailboat ready and noticed this red thing floating a few feet under the boat next to his. He thought it was a swimsuit or a piece of sail that was snagged on one of the pilings. When he got a better look, he noticed it was a woman in a red dress. All this was going on while we were coming back from Dave's warehouse. Someone said it was hard to see her because she was hung up between the pilings. Otherwise, the tide would've taken her out to sea."

Elliot tossed his Coke and one half-eaten chocolate strawberry into a trashcan. He remembered the swish of Carmen's red dress when she had entered his hotel room.

"Are you absolutely positive it was her?" Elliot said. "When someone drowns, aren't they all bloated up? How could you have recognized her?"

"I told you, I was standing just a few feet away from her." Sweat darkened the underarms of Wink's shirt. "How she ended up in the bay is beyond me. I guess she was here at the party."

"Did you see her last night?"

"No."

"What do you think happened?"

Wink avoided Elliot's eyes.

"I'm not sure," Wink said, watching the divers.

Gulls skimmed the water.

"What did the police say?" Elliot said.

"Very little. What I overheard was said among the employees."

"Was she identified?"

"The police are quiet on things like that."

"Why didn't you identify her?"

"I couldn't believe it was Carmen. Then I thought about you and the Rolex, and I kind of froze. By the time I could think clearly, they were already taking her away. For all I know, they probably found some identification on her, so I doubt they needed me anyway."

"Damn, damn, damn." Elliot placed his hands on the railing, gripping it. "If they found her purse, that means they have my Rolex, which has an identification number on it. That'll look real good. My Rolex is found on a dead woman. Not to mention they'll have a video clip of me in bed with her."

The rescue truck, emergency lights flashing, left the premises.

A detective near the tideline looked up to where Elliot and Wink were standing.

"We can't talk here," Wink said. "Let's go inside."

Elliot followed Wink past two policemen who were talking to a hotel official. Across the pool, Dave was sitting by himself and talking on his cell phone.

"There's Dave over there," Elliot said. He pointed him out to Wink. "Since he's in on it, we need to tell him what happened."

"I'll tell him later."

They passed sun-bathers lounging by the pool. The air was thick with the smell of chlorine and suntan oil. The animal gluttony of the guests was still evident, as they were piling their plates with food, smacking their lips and sucking fruity drinks through straws. Elliot and Wink went inside and ascended to Elliot's room where they sat on stools in front of the minibar. Elliot took a bottle of water from the small refrigerator and drank half of it in several gulps. He mopped the sweat on his face with a towel. The back of his shirt was soaked. In the long silence that followed, Wink sipped a diet drink and stared out the sliding glass door. Deep-drawn sighs sounded between them until Elliot, flooded with doubts, got up from his bar stool and paced the room. His limp was getting worse.

"I can't believe this is happening to me," Elliot said. He stopped pacing because his foot was hurting. He took off his shoes. "It wasn't that long ago that she was in this room. In that bed. Now she's dead."

"When was the last time you saw her?"

"When she was mugging me. It was probably around ten o'clock by the time she and that other woman left my room."

"You sure it was ten o'clock?"

"I was goddamned drugged, Wink, so I can't be sure of the exact time. From the time I was drugged until this morning when I first saw you I can't be sure of a goddamned thing."

"OK. You don't have to raise your voice." He flashed a smile and momentarily slipped into his country imitation. "And quit sassin' me, dadgummit. When you're mad, you can be a real sumbitch."

"That fucking hick routine is wearing me down."

Wink remained calm. "OK. I get your hint."

"It's not a hint. I don't find any humor in any of it, especially at a time when I think my head is going to explode."

"Let's go over this again. You told me that after you woke up you went looking for them?"

"I went looking for *you*. Why would I try looking for *them*? I figured they were long gone. I must've called your cell a dozen times. For someone who's always jabbering away on it, I found it strange that I could never reach you. But we've already been over that."

"You didn't see Carmen at the marina when you were trying to find me?"

"Hell, no. I didn't know I was supposed to be looking for her. You were at the party. Did you see her?"

"No. I was only at the party for maybe fifteen minutes."

"Then how was I supposed to see her when you didn't? I wasn't at the marina for more than five minutes. And I was drugged – totally fucked up – during that time. I didn't know what was going on. Sometimes I doubt I was ever at the marina. I think I just dreamed it."

"She either drowned or was murdered." Wink's expression said nothing.

"Drowned?"

"Who knows? She could've been drunk and fell off the dock." Wink took several sips from his drink. "Looks like we'll have to revise our story about getting robbed."

"Revise it?" Elliot got up from his chair. "We've got to drop the entire story now. There's a dead woman out there who had my watch and a video clip of me."

"Maybe she didn't have them."

"Maybe the police or her murderer has them now."

"We don't know if she was murdered."

"Jesus Christ, Wink, I seriously doubt she just fell into the bay. The music wasn't that loud; someone would've heard her screaming and splashing around. At least I think that's what people do when they're drowning."

"As I said, I bet she was drinking. Then she slips, hits her head, and ker-plunk, she sinks to the bottom."

"Frankly, I don't give a damn. She didn't show me any compassion when she was torturing me, so why should I show her any now? I'm more concerned about my wife's reaction. Now I'll have to tell her the truth about the Rolex."

"Don't give up on our story yet. Let's keep to our schedule as if nothing had happened."

"Tell me again, I forgot. What's our schedule?"

"At two o'clock we're supposed to meet with Dave and a real estate agent about a new office building." Wink consulted his watch. "At three we have a seminar to attend here at the hotel. But we can cancel that and go to the driving range."

"I don't know if I can concentrate on golf after what happened."

"You outplayed us this morning. That was an impressive performance, especially considering what happened to you last night. You also haven't played in almost six months. Dave was certainly impressed, and he plays at least twice a week while you're snowbound in Boston for half the year."

Wink stood up and practiced swinging an imaginary golf club. He was unnervingly composed.

"You knew this woman," Elliot said. His voice was low, urgent. "You don't seem too upset that she was murdered."

"What happened to her was terrible." Wink shrugged. "Yeah, I knew her. But we weren't friends. Women like her don't let you get close to them. Besides, my concern is with you, not her."

"Ever since I set foot in this hotel I've..." Elliot didn't finish his sentence. He continued shaking his head in disbelief.

"Let me handle everything." Wink patted Elliot's shoulder. "I know this has taken a toll on you. As I told you, my main concern is to look after you. We've got to protect your marriage.

I've known Karen for a long time, and I know how hot-tempered she can be."

"She'll just have to deal with it. But the thought of how messy our divorce could get isn't looking too attractive."

"You don't sound very convincing. A divorce would almost devastate you."

"I wouldn't go that far."

"Do one thing for me."

"What's that?"

"Stop pulling on your wedding band. You've been doing it since breakfast."

"I'm lucky I have it. She tried to steal it, too."

"Her ripping you off is still the damnedest thing I've ever heard. She knew me. What was she thinking?"

Shaking his head in disbelief, Wink finished his diet drink and started to leave. Elliot stopped him at the door.

"Where are you going?" Elliot said. "What did we decide? I feel lost."

"I've got to find Dave. And you, Mistuh Anderson, have got to take it easy. Relax. We'll come get you in a half hour or so." Wink cocked his finger and pointed it against Elliot's stomach. "Put your shoes on. I don't want you stepping on any more glass."

"What are you going to tell Dave?"

"I'll tell him what happened to Carmen and ask him if he has any suggestions."

"Let him know it was no beached dolphin."

"Huh?"

"Dave made a sarcastic comment when he saw the corpse on the beach."

"He had a few drinks when we stopped at the clubhouse. I know Dave; two beers and he's talking in riddles."

"He'll sober up once you tell him who the corpse was."

After Wink left, Elliot went back to the minibar and sat down. The whirl of events had been too much for him to comprehend. His thoughts scattered. What was he supposed to do? Should he let Wink handle things? Should he call the police? What would he say to the police if he decided to talk to them? How would he handle Karen? Whatever happened to his Rolex and to the video clip?

He found himself panting and short of breath, and he continued to have those same chest pains. He stepped out onto the balcony. The divers were out of the water, conferring with the detectives. The yellow crime-scene tape at the entrance to the marina fluttered in the breeze. He spotted Wink at the pool deck, weaving through the crowd until he found Dave. The two talked for a while. A few minutes later they joined a group of businessmen who were standing under some multicolored umbrellas. Elliot observed the two for a while. Slap-happy Wink was back to handshaking and storytelling. Dave, meanwhile, returned to his cell phone while staring at the marina.

# 8

For over an hour Polita and Kim had sat through four innings of a Miami Marlins-New York Mets baseball game. Polita's hair was done up in a bandanna, and she wore shorts and a tank top. She enjoyed sitting in the sun, though she soon lost interest in both the game and the crowd. Kim, listening to her iPod, had said little since Polita had picked her up. Kim looked tired, her eyes withdrawn.

Fifteen minutes later Polita told Kim she was ready to leave.

"OK," Kim said. "I guess Carmen's got other plans."

"It's not the first time she stood us up."

A loud crack sounded as they were walking down the aisle, followed by a cheer from the crowd. Polita turned and watched the soaring homerun ball disappear over the centerfield fence, but Kim continued to walk straight ahead without turning, indifferent to the excitement around her. Polita wondered why Kim was disinterested in the game. When she and Carmen had come with Kim to the ballpark before, Kim had sought the players' autographs, cheered them on, and socialized with the fans. But something was troubling her today; she seemed strangely guarded and uneasy.

When they reached the concession area, Kim took out her cell phone and called someone. She ignored Polita and carried on a conversation that lasted several minutes. After some cursing and arguing, she snapped the cell phone shut and tossed it into her purse. Then she pushed ahead of Polita as they walked out of the stadium.

In the car on their way home, Kim put in a heavy-metal CD, turned up the volume, and gazed out the passenger window without saying anything. Several times Polita had to turn the music down because it distracted her.

"Take me to Dante's," Kim said, ending her silence. She lit a cigarette. "He's got some things of mine I want."

"You know I don't like being around him."

"I also promised him I'd drop by to check on my cats. He's been keeping 'em for me while my apartment building's being sprayed for insects."

Ten minutes later, they were pulling into a trailer park just off I-95. At its entrance a pastel-colored neon sign shone dully in the sun: WALDEN BY THE POND – THE AMERICAN DREAM FOR EVERYONE. The surrounding industrial area looked blighted. Vacant lots with stripped hulks of cars, robbed for parts, gave way to boarded-up warehouses with rusting chain-linked fences topped with coils of razor wire. A deserted freight yard and a scattering of pawn and porn shops, neon lights blinking, completed the bleak scene.

Polita drove past an abandoned security booth with broken windows. Excessively high yellow speed bumps were spaced every fifty yards or so on the narrow pot-holed road. Trailers with neglected yards and barred windows were pressed tightly together, many with single-unit air conditioners affixed to the windows. Retention ponds throughout the trailer park fed into a swampy-looking lake.

Polita turned into a weedy yard with one wilted scrub oak and plaster lawnbirds and parked next to a wheelless car on cinder-blocks. A tire swing hung from one of the oak's lowest limbs. Next door, two small children played unsupervised in a plastic swimming pool. Polita and Kim got out of the car and approached a double-wide trailer. The air conditioners nearby made loud, rattling, chirping sounds like giant swamp bugs. Kim rapped on the screened door, and they entered the sun-baked trailer. Two men in their late twenties, Dante Rivas and Ramón Martinez, were in the living room working on a disassembled window air conditioner. Legs crossed on the floor, Dante glanced up and eyed each woman while unwinding some electrical wire.

"I'll be done in a little bit," Dante said.

Polita caught Dante's hostile glance. The shaven-headed Ramón watched the two women with an open-mouthed, indifferent expression as they sat down on a red naugahyde couch. Kim remained silent while she glanced through a magazine, moving her lips as she read. Two cats played at her feet.

The living room consisted of a chair and coffee table, stained carpet, vinyl drapes. A wide-screen plasma TV took up an entire side of the room. Mildew crawled on the walls. An oscillating fan circulated warm, dusty air. The trailer smelled of mildew and catshit.

Restless, Polita stood, parted the drapes, and looked at a fetid, steaming retention pond. Ramón, naked to the waist, went into the kitchen to throw something away, each of his steps shaking the floor and the thin walls. He was a hulking figure with a big, sloppy belly that drooped over grease-stained shorts. He had a glass eye and a stiff-legged walk, ramifications from a shotgun blast. He walked back through the living room and resumed working on the air conditioner.

Dante stood up and stretched, then lit a cigarette and inhaled deeply. Its smoke merged with that of Kim's, creating a cloud in the living room. Dante was a rodent of a man with quick-darting eyes, protrudent teeth and ears, a wispy goatee, and acne-scarred cheeks. He was always smirking. Freakishly thin, almost skeletal, his tank top revealed tattoos that seemed to drip off his scrawny arms like messy Dali paintings. Gold jewelry clinked around his neck. A ponytail reached past mid-shoulder.

"Fuck," Dante said, wiping his face with a paper napkin. "It's only April, but it already feels like the middle of fuckin' summer, don't it?"

Neither woman said anything.

"I'm getting tired of babysitting your fuckin' cats," Dante told Kim. He kicked at one of the cats as it walked past him.

"Ramón must think I'm queer 'cause I've got cats runnin' all over the place. Ain't that right, Ramón?"

Ramón, squinting, grunted an inarticulate response.

Kim made no reply. She chainsmoked while flipping through her magazine. Her sulky silence seemed to bother Dante. He placed some tools on the Formica counter, paced the living room, and constantly grabbed at his crotch. He was hyper. Tightly wound. Polita tolerated him only because he was Kim's boyfriend. She had seen him argue and fight with Kim over inconsequential things; he could terrorize her with just a glance.

"Where's Carmen at?" Dante said.

"I think she went to the Bahamas for a couple of days," Polita replied after Kim didn't answer.

"I thought she was going to the Marlins game with you two."

"We tried calling her several times, but she didn't answer. And we went to her apartment, but she wasn't there."

"Shit, she ain't got no business going to the Bahamas." Dante took the cigarette from his lips, held up the lighted end to his eyes, contemplated it, and stared at Kim. "Is that where she's at?"

"Huh?" Kim said. She stopped flipping through the magazine and raised an eyebrow.

"*Huh*? Pay fuckin' attention to me when I'm talking to you. I asked if Carmen went to the Bahamas."

"I dunno where she's at."

"Duh. I dunno. Fuck, man. If you only had a brain." Dante looked at Kim with disgust. He undid his ponytail and let his hair fall over his shoulders, then shook his head several times and tied it back again. "She didn't tell me shit about going to no islands."

"She did, too," Kim said. "I was there when she said she might go away for a while."

"I didn't hear her. Carmen was always running her mouth about taking trips. Where was she getting all the money? She was always telling me she was broke. Shit, man. Like, she was always living in LaLa land."

"I heard her tell you."

"Are you gonna sit there and argue with me? Huh? Goddamn. Don't cha think I know her? What the fuck do you know anyway? You're also in LaLa land half the time. A goddamn airhead."

Kim sat through Dante's abuse with a confused look.

Dante ignored her and stared at Polita.

"Carmen told me she had an appointment last night to see some CEO at the Luxuria," Dante said. Through his cigarette smoke he studied Polita. "She told me she wanted you or Kim in on it."

"I was there," Polita said.

"I waited up all night 'cause she told me she'd have something for me."

"What was it?"

The cigarette smoke coiled slowly from Dante's nostrils. He smiled.

"You talking about a Rolex?" Polita said.

"You said the magic word." Dante's smile broadened. "Of course that's what I'm talking about. After Carmen met this CEO at the café, she called to tell me that he had the most expensive Rolex she'd ever laid her eyes on. She said that the dial and the bracelet were both diamond-studded. A fuckin' Presidential Rolex. Custom made. We're prob'ly talkin' in the neighborhood of a hunnerd grand. Worth maybe half that on the street. Shit, man. That Carmen, she had an eye for the gold. She once told me she could size up a man's worth in a split second by glancing at his watch and the kind of shoes he wore. This dude must've been an Arab sheik or something. You was there. You saw the Rolex. You think it was worth that much?"

"Beats me."

"You mean to tell me you ain't got no idea?"

"I'm no jeweler. You and Carmen do all the wheeling and dealing when it comes to the gold. All this is still new to me. You're trying to make it sound like I'm keeping something from you."

"Are you?"

"No."

Now and then Kim paused from reading her magazine and looked at Dante. She fabricated a yawn.

"Tell me something," Dante said to Polita. "Why were you with Carmen last night? Kim said she wanted to go with her, but you talked her out of it. Ain't that right, Kim?"

Kim nodded.

"I told Carmen I got off early last night and that I'd meet her at the hotel if she wanted me to," Polita said. "Kim told me she had to work till midnight."

"Did this Mr. Rolex ask for two women?"

"I don't know. Like I told Kim, I think Carmen got bad vibes from him."

"What was wrong with him? You girls always pick the safe, CEO types who can fork out the dough for a little entertainment."

"I guess she sensed some trouble from him. Or maybe she was worried about someone else. I don't have a clue. All I remember is Carmen telling me this man was looking at her kind of funny when he met her at the café. But we're always dealing with weirdoes. Men are men. Makes no difference if they're rich or poor. We dance in front of them every night."

"None of this answers my question. Where's the Rolex?"

"I told you I don't know. I haven't seen Carmen since last night."

Out of the corner of her eye Polita saw Dante and Kim exchange a quick, collusive glance. Had Dante and Kim argued just to put on an act for her?

It began to rain, a light drumming sound on the thin roof.

"Besides the Rolex," Dante said, "what else didja get off this dude?"

"That was it."

"I don't believe you."

"Whatever money or credit cards we take belongs to us."

"I know that. How much you stuff your pockets with is your business. I ain't your pimp, am I?"

"We don't need one."

"You're right there. But you do need me to turn the gold into cash. I've got all the connections. Ain't I right?"

"We've kept to our agreement. The two Rolexes I stole I gave to you."

"And I gave you good money for them. Right?"

"I guess."

"You guess. Well, Carmen promised me another Rolex."

"You'll have to ask her about that."

"You sure you don't have it?"

"How many times do I have to tell you?"

A rainy dampness settled in the trailer.

"Know what I think?" he said, cutting both women a glance. "You girls ain't being up front with Dante."

"There you go again," Polita said. "You can have all the Rolexes you want. I don't care if I see another one."

"That how you feel?" Dante said to Kim. He pushed her magazine down with his forefinger. "Huh?"

In a whiny voice Kim said, "Seems you and Carmen are the only ones who have this thing for Rolexes. I think they're more trouble'n they're worth."

"They pay the bills."

"They pay your bills," Polita said.

Dante gave Polita a hard-eyed squint through his cigarette smoke. Ramón glanced up from the air conditioner to look at her.

"Let's add it up," Dante said. "Between Carmen and you two, we've taken in - what? - about a dozen or so Rolexes? Not to mention rings and money and credit cards and whatnot. We prob'ly average at least a couple grand between us for each Rolex. That ain't too bad, if I say so myself."

Dante waited for either woman to agree with him. Polita stared out the window at the rain. Kim returned to her magazine and read with dull interest.

"You know," Dante said, "no one's forcin' you to steal these Rolexes."

"You never threatened Kim?" Polita said.

Dante followed Polita's eyes to Kim and stared at her, unblinking. She moistened her lips with her tongue and lit another cigarette.

"I ever threaten you?" Dante said.

Kim wilted under Dante's glare.

"No, not really," she said after a long pause. She took out her compact-mirror and checked her makeup. Her hands shook.

"See," Dante told Polita. He stabbed out his cigarette in an ashtray. "Man, ain't no one being jerked around here. You girls are my boss, I work for you."

The slow-moving, slow-talking Ramón finally got the air conditioner to run. He got up and started closing the windows in the living room and kitchen, telling Dante what he thought had been wrong with the unit as he trudged around. Ramón was asthmatic and breathed heavily through his mouth. His "Uh-huh" replies to Dante sounded like gasps for air.

As soon as he turned it on, though, the air conditioner made popping sounds as if it might explode. Aggravated with the increasing noise, Dante smacked his hand against the appliance and cursed it. His sudden display of anger almost made Kim drop her compact-mirror.

"Thought I had it workin' right," Ramón said. "Sorry motherfuckin' piece of shit." He stared at the air conditioner, his mouth slackly open. Gang tattoos covered his arms.

"I've got to get some rest before I work tonight," Polita told Kim. She stood up. "I don't know about you, but I'm ready to leave."

"Me too," Kim said.

Another look passed between Kim and Dante. Her eyes were troubled, sometimes furtive. Polita went to open the door but Dante blocked her exit. He raised his arm and grabbed the top of the door so that his damp armpit hair was next to Polita's face. She stepped back.

"I'm really disappointed in you," Dante said.

"Leave her alone," Kim told Dante. "We've got a long night ahead of us."

"Was I talking to you?" Dante barked. He lowered his arm from the door. "Was I?"

"All I was tryin' to say was – "

"Shut the fuck up."

Kim pouted by taking out her cell phone and checking her messages.

"I just wanted to say one more thing," Dante said to Polita. Despite holding his head high in order to add another inch or two to his height, he was still level-eyed with Polita. "I know you're holdin' out on me."

"No one's cheating you, Dante," Polita said.

"Then why didn't you mention anything about the video clip?"

"I, um, thought maybe you already knew."

"Don't *I um* me. Shit, now I know you're cheatin' on me. You never would've said anything about it had I not brought it up. Huh?"

"What's so important about a video clip?"

Polita took her bandanna off and tossed her hair. She noticed Ramón staring at her; his glass eye had the look of a taxidermied fish's gaze. Strangely, his good eye looked away from Polita, while the fake one seemed to be following her every move.

"Oh, but the video clip is a big deal," Dante said. "Carmen and me decided that we wanted to try something different. Like film a CEO trying to fuck to see how much it might get us. If this one went off OK, we'd try a few more. These men run corporations. They have families and reputations to protect." Dante flicked his cigarette out the door. "By the way, all this was Carmen's idea, not mine."

"Then what's so important about a Rolex if what you're really after is a video clip?"

"You can always count on gold. At least that's what the conquistadores believed." He beamed. "I should know 'cause I'm a descendant of one. Gold's in my blood, know what I mean?" His smile turned to a frown as he looked around his trailer. "I figure what I have comin' to me from Carmen'll be my ticket out of here. I don't like living in these tin cans no more, 'specially with all these fuckin' hurricanes slamming into Florida. I want a big brick house that ain't no big bad wolf gonna blow over." He looked at Ramón. "The next hurricane should be named Dante or Ramón, huh? And it'll be one of those cat-five hurricanes that'll huff and puff and blow this whole fuckin' trailer park down."

A sly, fleeting smile crossed Dante's lips. His face was slick with sweat.

"Carmen put the Rolex and the video clip in her purse," Polita said. "That's the last I saw of them."

"You know, Polita, you're awright. Know what I like about you? You're a lot like Carmen. You're a con artist, man. You're fuckin'-A-OK. I think you're cut out for this business."

Polita walked past Dante and headed for her car. Kim followed her. As Kim was opening the car door, Dante came up behind her, gently turned her around, and kissed her.

"Love you, baby," Dante said.

Kim got into the car, and Polita pulled out of Dante's yard. Though it had rained for only ten minutes, the narrow road was flooded. The yellow tops of the speed bumps were barely visible over the water.

"I wish you'd dump him," Polita said. "He's nothing but trouble."

"Don't worry about him." Kim was relaxed now that Dante wasn't around her. "Behind that tough act he puts on, he's really pretty good to me. He has to show off when he's got an audience. When we're alone, he treats me like a queen."

"A queen? Right. You tense up when you're around him."

"You're too hard on him. He's all bark'n no bite."

"You're always defending him."

"'Cause you're always criticizin' him."

"He thinks I'm stealing from him. He doesn't even trust you."

"He's just lettin' off some steam. He gets that way when he's broke."

"He's nothing but a lowlife. A dirtbag."

"What the fuck are we?" Kim laughed while taking a long drag on her cigarette.

Without further comment, Polita drove over the last speed bump, and they sped out of the trailer park. The smell of Dante's mildewed trailer followed her all the back to Kim's apartment.

# 9

Elliot was sitting between Wink and Dave, listening to a speaker deliver a PowerPoint presentation on the technology of medical supplies to a packed conference room. Elliot was too distracted to pay attention. Since Carmen's death, his mind had been in a kind of numbing suspension.

Halfway through the presentation, Elliot stood up without saying anything to Wink or Dave and walked out. In the atrium-lobby, he passed one bellhop and hotel attendant after another. They almost all looked the same: young, well-groomed, tanned, resplendent in their crisp uniforms. They fussily went about their work, always cleaning, always sweeping, always serving.

He went outside to the pool deck where another buffet was being set up. One table gleamed with fruit. No breeze came off the bay, and it was humid. A security guard was standing by the yellow crime-scene tape that roped off the marina. Elliot followed the tiled walkway that led to the mulched and bark-covered paths that wound around the resort. He walked through a topiary garden where butterflies of almost electric hue flitted about the azalea and camellia bushes. Weeping willow trees leaned over the banks of a pond. One walkway he strolled along was shaded by a coppice of five-story oak trees covered with Spanish moss. The lush density of bright flowers and leafy plants gave the area the appearance of a bird-filled mini-rain forest. A perfumed tropical scent was in the air. He breathed it all in, trying to clear his head.

After sitting on a bench and resting his sore foot for a while, he circled back around the resort and wandered over to a 9-hole pitch and putt course. He entered the pro shop and looked on as a golf pro was instructing several guests on the science of sport biomechanics with video and computer graphics. The golf pro, a tall, blond man, whose nameplate identified him as "Jeff," asked Elliot to step up to a small platform. Elliot took one swing with a golf club, after which an audible beep sounded to verify that a speed reading was taken. Jeff explained that the device measured clubhead speed at impact and calculated the approximate in-air distance the shot traveled. He then handed Elliot a read-out of his swing, congratulated him with a handshake, and led him to a golf cart that was parked inside the shop.

"Tonight the Luxuria is giving away this brand new golf cart," Jeff said. The golf cart, decorated with red, white and blue balloons, was a four-seater with leather interior, sunroof, radial tires, gold-plated castings, walnut console, dash clock, radio and CD player, refrigerator, and in-dash fan. "Just sign your name and put your room number on this portion of the read-out and I'll drop it in the box next to the golf cart."

Elliot did as he was instructed.

"This might be your lucky night," Jeff said. He tore off the portion of the read-out that Elliot had signed and dropped it into the box. "Enjoy your stay at the Luxuria."

Elliot checked out a putter and practiced on the greens. His thoughts, however, were hijacked by memories of Carmen's face. He found it strange that he could remember her appearance but not much of what her companion looked like; he could only vaguely picture her blue-streaked hair and dark eyes.

Off in the distance, with the marina in the background, a security guard was sitting in a golf cart under an oak tree. Elliot wondered if the man was watching him, but soon he started up his golf cart and drove away. Another person who kept glancing his way was the golf pro. He was standing on a green behind Elliot and was helping an elderly woman with her putting. Why was everyone staring at me, thought Elliot? Perhaps he was becoming paranoid?

After he practiced on the greens, he returned to his room, changed into a white terrycloth bathrobe, and drank a bottle of water. He tried to relax, but that same bitter perfume smell returned to his room. The odor so distracted him that he called room service and complained.

Within minutes, a chambermaid appeared and scented the room with a herbal fragrance. She was a thick-shouldered woman of sixty or more. Elliot noticed that the Luxuria employed a wide range of mostly young to elderly employees, at least half of whom were foreigners.

"The person who was here before me must've been a smoker," Elliot said. He watched the woman spray.

"Smells like perfume," she said with a Spanish accent.

"Whatever it is, I must be allergic to it."

"We apologize, sir. We scent every room after a guest leaves. Would you like another room?"

"It's too much trouble. I'll probably be checking out tomorrow, anyway."

After the chambermaid left, Elliot felt dehydrated, so he drank another bottle of water. He had debated all day whether he should call his wife. He had a compelling need to speak to her, to hear her voice. The thought of sleeping in this room one more night troubled him. He wanted to leave the hotel immediately and return home; after all, there was no reason for him to remain in Miami, and he could leave the four-day convention at any time. The business deal he had with Dave could wait.

He called his wife's office number at her marketing firm. His hand was trembling a bit, and he hung up before the third ring. He decided he needed more time to compose himself.

A knock sounded on the door. He opened it, and Wink, smiling, entered.

"I dropped by to check on you," Wink said. "You feeling all right?"

"I've got a headache."

"I was concerned when you left during the presentation."

"I couldn't concentrate. And I got tired of hearing the speaker talk about how profitable portable commodes are."

"Yeah, pretty boring stuff." Wink sniffed the air. "Smells like a pine forest in here."

"I had a maid spray my room. I couldn't get rid of the thieves' cheap perfume. It was beginning to smell like death."

Wink gazed at him with an arch expression. Elliot sat in a chair, propped his sore foot on the bed, and applied a clean Band-Aid to his cut.

"I'm thinking of going back to Boston tonight or tomorrow morning," Elliot said. "Whenever I can get the first available flight."

"You think that's a good idea?"

"Considering that I've been mugged, that I almost had my throat slit, that one of the thieves showed up dead, and that the other thief is somewhere out there, I think it's a damn good idea to get the hell out of Miami."

"But you and Dave are about to close on an important business deal."

"That can wait. I need to get away from here before something else happens."

"I was hoping you'd at least stay another couple of days. Enjoy the weather. Play some golf. You just left three inches of snow."

"I went from a snow storm to a shit storm."

"Stay at least another day?"

"Give me one good reason."

"Because somewhere in Miami someone has your Rolex and a video clip of you in bed with a call girl. And if the police find any of your things on Carmen...Well, it wouldn't look good if you left town in a hurry. Cops check little details like that."

"Why are you so concerned that I stay?"

"We're both in on it, El. That's why. So is Dave. Several dancers and a bouncer saw us talking to Carmen at the café. And that other woman who robbed you knows all about you.

Sooner or later we'll probably have to answer some questions. I think it'd be best if the three of us kept to our schedules, at least for now."

"I'd like to put all this behind me."

"So would I."

"Dave's been awfully quiet. He didn't say two words to me when we were in the conference room."

"I don't know what he could've said. Carmen's death surprised him as much as it did us."

"He's so casual about it all. In fact, both of you are acting like it's nothing much to worry about."

"Looking cool is part of the business. Listen, it's my fault that I got you involved with her in the first place. I still plan to go to the café tonight to see what I can find out."

"In the meantime, what am I supposed to do if the police find my Rolex on a dead woman? They would've had time by now to trace the ID number on it."

"If it comes to that, we'll have to tell them what happened."

For a couple of minutes they sat in silence. A deep frown creased Elliot's forehead.

"Your neck looks a little better," Wink said, eyeing Elliot's bite wound.

"I've been going around like a teenybopper trying to hide a huge hickey from his parents."

"You don't want Karen to see that thing. That's another reason why you should stay for the rest of the convention. Give it a chance to heal."

"Hell, it would take a week or more for the swelling to go down."

"I've got a sales rep to meet in Coral Cables. I'll leave from there and drop by the café, and then I'll check back with you around nine or so."

"What time do I meet back up with Dave?"

"At eight." Wink gave Elliot another one of his fist bumps. "I'm glad you decided to stay for at least another day."

"I'll see you around nine."

"Okey-doke."

After Wink closed the door, Elliot decided to call his wife's cell phone. She answered on the third ring.

"Hey, hon," Elliot said.

"Hello, sweetie."

"Are you busy?"

"Not really."

"Still at the office?"

"Since early this morning."

"I wanted to tell you how much I love you and that I miss you."

"Oh, how sweet. What brought on that outburst of affection?"

"You make it sound like I never tell you that I love you."

"Your voice sounds so…different."

"It's the connection."

"I love you, too. I was hoping to hear from you last night."

"You were?"

"You said you would call."

"I did? Oh. I was with Dave Kornick, Wink's friend. He's the one I'm doing business with. It was late by the time we finished. I didn't want to call and wake you."

"I went to bed early anyway. I would've called this morning, but I've been putting out fires since I showed up. It seems everyone in the office is having issues."

"Hmm."

"So how's Florida?"

"Hot and humid."

"In April?"

"Must be a heat wave for this time of year. But, hey, it's the subtropics."

"I think that April in New England is the cruelest month. We get two or three warm days, and then we get blasted with another cold front."

"You had your chance. I asked if you and Jeremy wanted to come with me."

"I don't remember you inviting us."

"I thought I did."

"You must have mumbled it. Anyway, what have you been up to?"

"The boring stuff, like going to conferences and workshops. And I've been doing some research on this new business that I'm opening up with Dave."

"Are you sure you want to invest in another expansion?"

"Dave has a very successful business down here, in both Miami and Naples. Retirees are everywhere, and they're the ones who buy our supplies."

"Well, is the Luxuria Resort and Spa as good as advertised?"

"It's" - Elliot stared at the bed where he had been rendered helpless – "…um…nice."

"Just nice?"

"It's a very pleasant resort. Definitely ranks up there with some of the best I've visited. Great view from my balcony." He could still smell the bitter odor of the call girls' perfume. "You would enjoy it. It has the feel of a private estate. And Jeremy would have fun in the pool with its slides and waterfalls. There's enough here to keep both of you entertained."

"I'll come down with you next time and we can stay there."

"Sure. Sounds great. I'd like that. This place is very family-oriented."

Two quick raps sounded on Elliot's door.

"I think I hear Wink," he said. "He was just here and must've forgotten something. Hold on a sec."

With the cell phone pressed to his ear, he opened the door but saw no one at the entrance. He was about to say something to Karen when he glanced down the corridor and saw a woman in a tank top and snakeskin jeans walking away with an exaggerated shake of her ass. Her stilettos could impale a rodent. Abruptly, the woman turned and gave Elliot a sharp side glance over her shoulder before disappearing into the elevator. She resembled Carmen with her curvy figure and dark eyes, and she even had the hair of the drowned – wet and stringy, like rotten kelp, it hung past her shoulders without any bounce or movement. From the railing on his floor he looked down through the trees and waited for her to appear. He heard her stilettos snap on the marble floor like caps going off. A few seconds later, through a clearing in the trees, he watched as she walked through the atrium-lobby and out the main doors. Her perfume, which lingered outside his room, had the same scent as Carmen's. Shaken, he returned to his room. He had forgotten that he was holding his cell phone.

"Elliot, are you still there?" Karen said.

"Oh. Yeah. Sorry I kept you waiting."

"What did Wink want?"

"He, ah, nothing really..." Elliot's thoughts were on that woman. Who was she? Why had she knocked on his door?

"Hello? Honey Bunny, I think we've got a bad connection. Do you hear me?"

"I hear you now."

"What's Wink up to? I haven't seen him in at least a year."

"He's the same."

"Charming and full of shit?"

"That's Wink."

"I think he always dreamed of being a standup comedian, but he had to settle for a sales job instead."

"There's never a dull moment around him, that's for sure."

"Remember how he would always try to impersonate famous people?"

"Yeah. He still does that, except now, for some reason, he's into imitating country hicks. Been driving me crazy with it. Well, I'll be seeing you in a few days, maybe as early as tomorrow evening. I'll call if I can wrap things up down here. Tell Jeremy I love him. I love you, honey."

Elliot's conversation with Karen had ended but he found himself still holding the cell phone to his ear long after she had hung up. He was thinking about the woman who had knocked on his door. He told himself it was nothing to worry about; perhaps she had mistaken his room for someone else's.

He stepped outside again. At the railing, he peered down through the trees in the atrium-lobby. The woman was nowhere to be seen.

# 10

Through a parted backstage curtain Polita watched a topless dancer perform on a runway around which mostly well-dressed patrons, polite and subdued, were seated. Lean and graceful, the dancer did a straddled handstand to the applause of the audience while a second dancer swung on a trapeze in a cage and a contortionist performed on a smaller stage. No shouting, whistling, or rude behavior came from the audience. The music was loud but inoffensive. Strobes and lasers flashed. Several topless waitresses carried drinks on trays from table to table. Standing at the entrance were two bouncers, Seth Watson and Allen Seagraves; they wore neatly pressed blue trousers and white pullover shirts that fit tightly across their chests and biceps. "Café Sinsations" was inscribed in cursive above their shirt pockets, a buxom devil with her pointed tail poised provocatively around the letters 'Sin.'

Polita closed the curtain. She sat at the vanity in the powder room and rubbed lotion on her legs while she waited for her turn to go on stage. A dancer named Michelle Labelle entered the room and started talking. She was a big-boned woman, at least six foot one, in her mid-thirties, waistless, with curly dark hair and a husky voice.

"I'm finished for the night," Michelle said, sitting in a chair next to Polita. She slipped off her high heels and rubbed her large feet. Her toenails were painted black. "I'd better start thinking of retiring. After seven years of this I'm already burned out. My knees and feet are killin' me. I'll have deformed feet if I dance another year or two."

"I told Seth the same thing today," Polita said. "Some nights I can't even go to sleep because my feet hurt so bad."

Polita got a good look at Michelle under the fluorescent light. Dark little shadowy hairs above her lip formed a vague mustache. Her sunburned, peeling face appeared to be rotting around her sunken cheeks and fat, silicone-injected lips. Her hands were hairy-knuckled and large enough to palm a basketball.

"What do you call a foot doctor?" Michelle said. She noticed Polita was staring at her.

"Starts with a 'p.'"

"I can think of pediatrician and proctologist."

"Oh, it's a podiatrist."

"That's it. Anyway, I went to this podiatrist and she told me I already have bunions forming on both feet. I knew a dancer who had to quit because her bunions were so bad that one of her big toes needed surgery and the other one had to be completely redone."

Polita smiled. "Don't we have a health plan at the café that covers operations on bunions?"

"Honey, we ain't got diddly. You'd better be making some big tips to cover any medical expenses."

Both women laughed. A knock sounded on the door. The manager, Mark Cerone, stepped into the room.

"Polita, Miss Wanda and I need to see you in her office," Mark said, meaning Wanda Cassala, the owner of Café Sinsations.

"I'm up next," Polita said.

"I've got another dancer to take your turn," he said in a high, thin voice.

Polita glanced from Michelle to Mark. She was confused. Why would the owner want to see her so urgently? She slipped on a robe and followed Mark down the hallway. Murals of sand dunes and palm trees decorated the walls.

"Is something wrong?" Polita said.

But Mark said nothing else. He was in his mid-forties, trimly handsome, haughty, almost elegant. Perfumed. He kept his sleek, graying hair combed close to his head. He wore an expensive gray suit, gold neck chain, and bracelet. They entered Miss Wanda's office and sat at the opposite ends of a leather sofa. Hands folded on her desk, Miss Wanda looked at Polita with sad eyes. She lit up a cigarette, but abruptly snubbed it out in a fish-shaped ashtray.

"A detective was in my office a while ago," Miss Wanda said, coughing. Her voice was raspy, as if permanently hoarse from smoking too much. "He told me that Carmen was murdered. Her body was found in Biscayne Bay this afternoon. That's all I was told."

Polita received the news without expression as Miss Wanda loomed in her vision. She was maybe sixty-five and was so heavily made up that she looked like an embalmed corpse propped up in her wingback chair. Her dye-damaged hair was coarse and straw-like. Nicotine stained her teeth. Reading glasses hung from her necklace. Polita squeezed her eyes shut to hold back any tears. A half minute passed before she opened them. Her eyes were dry, though Miss Wanda's were moist.

As Miss Wanda and Mark whispered briefly to each other, everything seemed to collapse around Polita. Their voices were lost in the thumping background. The walls of the office closed in on her and her eyes became unfocused.

"Polita, are you all right?" Miss Wanda said.

"Uh-uh." Polita's lower lip trembled. "Um, I'm OK…"

"The detective asked me a lot of questions about Carmen. He wanted to know the names of all my employees. We need to help him in any way we can. I told him that Kim was probably the closest to Carmen. He went to her place to see her, so she won't be coming in tonight. I'm telling each employee one at a time." Miss Wanda went into a brief coughing spell. "You're one of the first I wanted to tell because I knew that you two were pretty good friends. Didn't you share lockers with her?"

"Ah, yeah. No. I mean, our lockers were next to each other. I just can't think right now." Polita's words were a whisper.

"I'm sorry I had to be the one to tell you."

At her last words Miss Wanda lowered her eyes, and Polita lifted hers to the ceiling fan above Miss Wanda's desk. The vagueness around her deepened. A film seemed to develop over her eyes.

"Miss Wanda has owned, and I have managed, Café Sinsations for six years," Mark said. His voice had a boyish pitch. He touched his thin mustache. "We've always treated our dancers like we're one big family. We've had some problems with Carmen, some disagreements. But we've stayed with her. We cared for her. She will be missed."

"You should go home now and rest," Miss Wanda said. She got up from her desk and sat next to Polita. "Take as much time off as you need."

"I don't understand," Polita said. Her lower lip still trembled.

"Shh. You don't have to say anything." Miss Wanda wrapped her hands around Polita's. Cold, veiny hands with a lot of rings.

"I mean…"

"Shh."

Polita glanced up at the wall on which hung photographs of all the café's dancers. Carmen's eyes burned through her print.

"I'll go with you to the dressing room so you can change," Miss Wanda said.

"OK," Polita said.

Miss Wanda escorted her out of the office and down the hallway. Inside the powder room, two dancers stopped their conversation when Polita and Miss Wanda passed them. At the far corner of the room, Michelle, the wide-shouldered dancer, watched Polita open her locker.

Polita changed, took her handbag, and walked with Miss Wanda out of the powder room. Mark, examining his immaculate fingernails, was waiting for them in the hallway.

"I'll walk with her to her car," Mark said.

"There's no hurry," Miss Wanda said. "If she wants to, she can stay in my office till she feels better."

"You're busy," Mark said. "Let me help."

"I'm not busy when it comes to something like this," Miss Wanda said, interrupting Mark.

"I'm OK," Polita assured her. She detected some tension between Miss Wanda and Mark.

The door to a storage room opened, and Allen Seagraves, one of the bouncers, rolled out a dolly with cases of liquor on it. He was smiling and whistling until he noticed the sullen expressions of the three standing in front of him.

"Is something wrong?" Allen said. Rangy, thick-chested and muscular, but going slack in the stomach, Allen's hulking presence filled the hallway. He was in his late thirties and had receding light brown hair, a boxer's blunted nose, and a dimpled smile that softened his rough-featured face. The creature from the movie *Alien* was tattooed on his right hand.

"I'd like to see you in my office," Miss Wanda said to Allen. "You also need to hear the news."

"You want me to drop this liquor off first?" Allen said, but he was looking at Polita.

"Leave it all here," Miss Wanda said. "Mark will take care of the liquor after he escorts Polita to her car."

"I'm not sure if I'll have time to unload all of that," Mark said. "Let Allen handle it."

"It won't take more than two minutes to wheel those cases to the bar," Miss Wanda said.

Mark gave Miss Wanda a sharp look but averted his eyes when she continued to stare at him. The older woman hugged Polita and told her goodbye, then led Allen into her office and closed the door behind her. Mark, leaving the cases of liquor in the hallway, straightened his tie, smoothed his mustache, and walked with Polita to the back door.

Once outside, Mark started complaining. "She treats me like I'm her flunky instead of the manager of this place. I run one of the classiest lounges in Miami. Without me, Café Sinsations would be just another topless bar."

Polita gazed straight ahead, into the greasy drizzle of neon lights that advertised Café Sinsations. The bluish-purple colors of the lights matched the colorful streaks in her hair. The traffic was bumper-to-bumper. A police siren wailed past them.

Mark seemed to calm down a bit and got a wistful look in his eyes. "Miss Wanda is taking Carmen's death pretty hard. I think Carmen reminded her a lot of herself when she was a young dancer."

Without saying anything, Polita walked to her car. The glow of neon lights grew thicker, descending - pulsating - in a sickening motion. She stopped, afraid she might lose her balance. Mark, sinisterly lit by the neon, caught up to her and held her by the arm. Up close, his breath smelled of garlic.

"Do you need to sit down?" he said. "You don't look well."

"I can make it." She resumed walking with his arm around hers.

"You know how it's our policy that dancers have to leave in pairs or be escorted by a male employee. That Carmen, though; I always had to get on to her about leaving alone. I remember she once said, 'When your time's up there ain't much you can do about it.' She said that three, maybe four months ago. It's almost like she had a premonition."

While trying to find her car keys, Polita's handbag slipped from her grip and fell on the pavement. Polita and Mark scrambled to pick it up simultaneously, and when they pulled at it from both ends, its contents spilled onto the asphalt. Makeup, a pair of shorts, two blouses, a hairdryer, and the empty jewelry box in which she had kept the Rolex scattered at their feet. Both of them were squatting.

"I'm sorry," he said. "I'll pick it all up."

She quickly took the jewelry box from Mark and stuffed it back into the handbag. She then gathered up the rest of her things.

"See what happens when you're trying to help?" he said. "I've always been a klutz."

"It was my fault."

She unlocked her car door, got behind the wheel, and put her handbag on the passenger seat. Before she could close the door, he leaned in and touched her gently on the hand.

"I don't mind following you to your apartment if it'll make you feel safe," he said.

"Why shouldn't I feel safe?"

Polita's question surprised Mark. In the blinking neon glow his face changed colors. From green to red to purple.

"You shouldn't be out alone," he insisted.

"I don't have far to drive. Thanks anyway."

Mark closed Polita's door - almost slammed it - and stepped back from the car. She drove to the end of the parking lot. In her rearview mirror she noticed that Mark's small, lean frame was standing in the same spot. She waited for a break in the traffic, glanced again in the mirror - he was still in the parking lot - and then pulled out.

Polita drove to Kim's apartment. She went up the stairwell and knocked on Kim's door. Two teenage boys down the corridor were kicking a soccer ball back and forth. She knocked again, louder. The hallway smelled of insect spray.

"Kim, it's me. Polita. Open up."

Kim cracked open the door, saw who it was, and let her inside. In one hand she held a wad of tissue paper; a brush was in the other. Her eyes were red and swollen from crying.

"Where's Dante?" Polita said.

In a soft-dazed voice Kim said, "I don't know. I haven't seen him since we were at his place. Why?"

"Because I don't want him anywhere around me." Polita gripped Kim by both hands. "Kim, tell me what happened to Carmen."

Kim's fear-filled eyes gazed helplessly at Polita. "I don't...I can't..."

"Talk to me."

"I can't believe Carmen's dead. It wasn't that long ago that..." Her voice faltered. She was shaking.

"I know how you feel. I've been in shock ever since Miss Wanda told me."

Kim staggered to the couch and lay down, her head resting on two pillows. She stared at nothing in particular. Across from her, Polita sat in the lone chair and rubbed her aching feet.

"I tried calling you when the cops told me about Carmen," Kim said. "All I got was your voice mail. I hung up each time I called. I don't feel like tellin' no machine about Carmen being dead. That don't seem right. I had to hear your voice, not just a recording."

"You called both my home number and cell?"

"Yeah."

"I left early to go to work. I guess I had my cell turned off for some reason."

Kim sat up. Her face was blank and dull. Mascara smeared her cheeks. Absently, she brushed her hair.

After a moment of silence, Kim said, "A couple of detectives were here. They were rude to me. They made me feel like shit."

"What'd you say to them?"

"Nothing much. I couldn't think straight. They kept asking me one question after another, like, how long did I know Carmen? Did she have any jealous ex-boyfriends? Were there any regular customers who showed up to see her dance? Did she ever brag about any big tippers? On and on. They wouldn't stop. So I started cryin'. They said they want to see me tomorrow."

"Miss Wanda said a detective was at the café."

"I'm sure the cops'll talk to all the dancers."

Kim stopped brushing her hair. She wrapped her arms around her chest and rocked back and forth.

"You mention my name to the cops?" Polita said, with anticipation.

Kim shook her head.

"Nothing?" Polita pried.

"I didn't say nothing to 'em about you."

Polita was visibly relieved.

Her voice clear but shaky, Kim said, "Someone murdered Carmen. It's not like she died in a car wreck or something. It was no accident. Polita, what are we supposed to do? What if someone is after us?"

Polita got up out of the chair and stood in front of a half-curtained window from which the moonlight entered.

"Dante said the cops are gonna for sure find out about us and the Rolexes," Kim said.

"I thought you said you haven't seen him since we were at his place."

"I...um...I called him to tell him about Carmen."

"Is he coming over here tonight?"

"He said there ain't no way he'd be seen here with all the cops roamin' around."

Polita looked at her image in the window. Kim was staring at the guest bedroom for a long time.

"Me and Carmen worked together for a year and a half," Kim said. "We were even roommates for a while. That's where she stayed, in that bedroom. I can still see her in there, always combing her hair and singing. She had loads of talent. She didn't let no one get close to her, but I prob'ly knew her better'n most anyone. Now she's dead. She's...dead."

"How many times are you going to keep saying that? I know she's *dead.* You don't have to keep reminding me."

Polita was ready to leave. She headed for the door, but Kim stopped her.

"Stay with me tonight," Kim said. "I don't want to be alone. Not tonight."

"I don't like being here with Dante hanging around."

"Please. You can have my bed. I'll sleep on the couch."

"I'll stay tonight. But if you let Dante or Ramón in, I'll leave."

"I promise I won't. You don't have to worry about them. It'll be just you and me."

"I've got to take a long bath. I feel dirty."

"I'll show you where everything's at. If you want you can..." Kim tried to say more, but she choked up. She threw herself face-downward on the couch, covered her head with a pillow, and wept.

Polita went into the bathroom and filled the tub with hot water. The sound of the faucet running kept her from having to listen to Kim's sobs. She locked the bathroom door, took off her clothes, and got into the tub. She lay submerged with her head resting against a bath pillow, her face tilted upwards. Her hair floated around her shoulders. The water was almost scoldingly hot, and steam rose from her body. The hotter the better, she thought.

As the water washed over her, cleansing her, Polita stared at the ceiling. Her gaze was wide-eyed and vacant, her blinks slow. She was unable to concentrate on anything. Her eyes followed the lazy pace of a cockroach directly above her as it made its way from the ceiling to the wall and finally to the window.

# 11

After attending a trade show in the conference room, Elliot and Dave went into the lounge and sat at the bar. It was past nine o'clock, the time Wink had told Elliot that he would be back from Café Sinsations. The bartender, his thick black mustache too big for his thin face, served them drinks and a basket of popcorn. They passed the time by watching a baseball game on a wide-screen TV. They were silent for some time, each waiting for the other to speak. Dave kept glancing at his Rolex as if bored. He ate his popcorn compulsively. Elliot saw him as a cold, silent, aloof man. Whenever Dave smiled, it was a condescending smirk, and his laugh was humorless and forced.

After two drinks, Dave began to loosen up by making small talk about business, baseball, and golf. He even made an obscene remark about an attractive woman who was sitting by herself at a nearby table. Elliot was beginning to think that Dave might have a drinking problem; the man had had at least three beers during lunch, and he was practically gulping his drinks tonight.

A few more minutes of desultory conversation followed until Dave surprised Elliot by saying, "Sure was unfortunate about what happened to that exotic dancer." It was the first time tonight he had mentioned anything about Carmen. "An incredibly sexy woman who probably got involved with the wrong crowd. I guess this puts you in a bit of a predicament."

Elliot stopped itching around his shirt collar, and his jaw tightened.

"What happened to her after she left my hotel room has nothing to do with me," Elliot said. "If I'm in a bit of a predicament, as you say, then all three of us are."

"I didn't even know her. All I did was watch her dance a couple of times."

"I didn't spend more than thirty minutes with her while I was in my room. And half that time I was semi-unconscious."

"The little I know of her is only because of Wink. According to him she had several select customers. And she more than danced for them." Now and then Dave flicked the lime slice on the rim of his glass. "I once told her that I fantasized about her. But that was all she was - an erotic fantasy."

"That's what she turned out to be for me. A very short-lived fantasy."

Dave was silent.

"How many times have you been to the café?" Elliot said.

"Yesterday was probably the third or fourth time, all of them with Wink. The café is his home away from home. He's into the topless scene."

"When he lived in Boston, I remember he had a thing for exotic dancers. Maybe it's an obsession with him."

"He says that some men prefer sports bars so they can watch ballplayers spit and scratch themselves, while others, like himself, go to places like the café because they enjoy being around half-naked women. A matter of preference."

"I can understand an occasional visit, but Wink was making it a habit."

"The café is a place where he can do some strutting. It's a place where he can feel important. As you probably know, he isn't doing very well financially. He always seems to be struggling, especially in this recession. He had to sell his condo, and now he's renting an apartment. He has tried a couple of times to go into business for himself and either went bankrupt or had to sell out at a loss. He's great at networking, and he knows his products, but when it comes to selling, well, the contacts he has don't always translate into money."

"He was always a good salesman when he worked for me."

"The café is one of his escapes. The golf course is the other. I've watched him at the café. He pisses away his commission on sexy women and booze. He likes to make everyone think he's something he's not. You know him as well as I do. He's a good friend, but we know that we can't take him too seriously. The women at the café really play up to him, especially the one who was murdered. I can't even think of her name."

"It was Carmen."

Dave's scalp moved. He was staring at the TV, but watching nothing. Elliot noticed that Dave had lost that nervous eye-flutter of his.

"That's weird," Dave said, after a lengthy silence. "Until you told me, I couldn't think of her real name, but I remembered the name she used at the café. It was Chechoter. The customers called her Che or Checho for short. You'd think I could remember a simple name like Carmen rather than Chechoter."

"I didn't hear anyone call her by that name."

"That's because Wink knows her pretty well and introduced her with her real name. She likes to go by the other one when she's with customers at the café."

"It was Checho-what?"

"Chechoter."

"Sounds demonic. Is it a cult name or something?"

"Wink told me it means Morning Dew."

"Morning Dew? That's a soft drink, isn't it?"

"You're thinking of Mountain Dew." Dave chuckled, his smile almost a grimace. "Wink told me that Chechoter was the name of one of Chief Osceola's wives. The Seminoles are big in Florida." He rattled the ice in his glass. "That was her gimmick at the café, to dress up like an Indian."

"I remember her Indian outfit when she was dancing - what little there was of it. But I saw her from a distance. She was wearing something over her costume when Wink escorted her to our table. I guess that explains her flaming bush. I thought she was trying to be a nature child or some new-age hippie."

"Wink said that her father's Cuban and her mother's Seminole or Miccosukee, or maybe it's the father who's Indian. Anyway, she's half Indian. I don't know why she picked that name. Maybe she has a thing for Indian chiefs. She did look damn good in that outfit of hers. Give her some credit; Chechoter is more original than Dusty Busty or whatever these dancers usually come up with."

"Wink seems to know quite a bit about her. Was he ever involved with her?"

"He claims he wasn't. Oh, he was attracted to her." Dave thought for a moment. "She had a certain charming savagery about her that would attract any normal man. You saw it in her."

"I don't know about the charming part, but she was a savage when she attacked me."

"Think about it. These women live off tips. Some of them try to make you think they're accessible. They're performers. Cock teasers. Any level-headed man knows that. Wink knew it was all an act, or at least I think he did. As I already told you, he just likes being around sexy women. Nothing wrong with that. He likes to impress them by bringing in his business friends, like you and me."

"She sounded more like a shrewd businesswoman than an exotic dancer."

"She was too shrewd for her own good. You've got to admit, her type would make one hell of a saleswoman. I need someone like her selling for me. I should've offered her a job when I had the chance." Dave glanced at his Rolex. "Wink should've been back from the café a half hour ago. I'm curious to know if he found anything out about that other woman. Her involvement in this sounds creepy."

"Wink needs to stay away from that place and quit trying to play detective."

"He feels bad about what those two women did to you. So do I. What in the hell were we thinking? The shenanigans of three middle-aged men playing around with exotic dancers. Shame on us. You would've thought we were horny college kids on spring break."

Elliot listened as Dave had gone from rattling his ice to chomping on it.

"After what I did, I'm more stupid now than when I was in college," Elliot said.

"Those two women took advantage of you because they knew you were from out of town. It's always open season on tourists and executives at business conventions."

Dave ordered for himself and Elliot, and the bartender soon returned with the drinks and another fresh basket of popcorn. Elliot was amazed that Dave could drink and eat so much and still be so thin. Dave, burping, stirred his drink with his forefinger. On another wide-screen TV the local news came on. Elliot had missed the evening news because of other commitments and was curious if there had been any story on Carmen's murder, but with both TVs on and with the music playing, he could barely hear the anchorman.

"To be honest with you," Dave said, "that dancer had it coming to her." He was becoming more talkative with each drink. "Chalk up another homicide for Miami. It doesn't really bother me when criminals knock each other off, and that's all she was - a criminal. So is that other woman who was with her. Before it's all over, the cops will probably be fishing her body out of the bay."

Elliot remembered the soft look in Polita's eyes when she had touched his forehead with the warm washcloth.

Dave said, "These young women - some of them right out of high school - they dance topless for the quick money and to stroke their egos. Some of them just eat up the attention, like the ones who robbed you."

"Tell me something, did you or Wink ever see her at the hotel last night?"

"I didn't." Dave stuffed his mouth with more popcorn. "I hardly saw Wink last night."

"He told me that you two spent a lot of time together." Elliot smelled the liquor on Dave's breath.

"For maybe a half hour. Then he disappeared. You know how Wink is. He's here one minute, gone the next." Once again Dave checked his Rolex. "It's getting past my bedtime. Tell Wink to be quiet when he comes in the room." Yawning, he placed two fifty-dollar bills on the counter. "The drinks were on me. Don't lose any sleep over this dancer."

Elliot watched Dave walk out of the lounge, then gazed up at the TV and sipped his drink. A short time later Wink entered the lounge and sat next to Elliot.

"Where's Dave?" Wink said. He waved at the bartender.

"He just walked through those doors. I'm surprised you didn't pass him in the lobby."

"She alone?" Wink nodded in the direction of the woman who had been sitting at the table.

"She's been there since I sat down."

"She might be a cop."

"What makes you think that?"

"The police already know that Carmen was a dancer at the café. Maybe they've figured out that she worked business conventions at posh hotels like this one, which means they could have a stakeout here. That woman over there could be a decoy. She could be all wired up and have contact with another undercover cop. I've learned to be alert to these things. There's one person we both know who could tell us about female undercover cops."

"Who?"

"Promise to keep it between you and me?"

"Who else would I want to tell?"

"You've got to promise me, big guy."

"All right, I promise."

"OK, now I'll let you in on a secret. Dave was arrested - oh, I guess it's been about three years now - in an undercover police sting for soliciting a prostitute."

Elliot stared at the empty chair where Dave had been sitting.

"Dave told me the whole story about his arrest," Wink said. He spoke to the bartender for a moment, then turned back to Elliot. "He pulled into a 7-Eleven and saw a hooker talking on her cell, at least he thought she was a hooker. He propositioned her, and they went to a motel room. His conversation with her was recorded with an undercover microphone transmitter that alerted other cops. They busted him with his pants down. Literally. His arrest made the newspaper. Fortunately, his two daughters were too young to understand, but Ashley, his wife, threatened to divorce him. He ended up resigning his position from the Naples Chamber of Commerce. The publicity ruined his political aspirations. At one time he had considered running for the Florida Legislature, maybe even for Congress. He showed up for court with his wife and pastor and told the judge how sorry he was for having hurt his family. I think he got sixty hours community service and was ordered to attend an AIDS awareness program."

"The Marlins can't hold a lead," the bartender said, referring to the game on TV as he served Wink a drink. Then he spent a few minutes talking to Wink about the strengths and weaknesses of almost every pitcher on the Miami Marlins baseball roster. Once the bartender left to serve other customers, Wink returned to his conversation with Elliot. "Dave jokes about his arrest now. He admits that the decoy was one good-looking cop."

"Soliciting a prostitute…" Elliot was silent for a moment. "I could get charged with that."

"You're not going to get charged with anything. I'm not sure I'd call Carmen a hooker. She was just an expensive date."

"Too expensive."

"Besides, you'd have to proposition an undercover cop to get arrested. What happened to Dave was completely different."

"Yeah. He still owns a Rolex and the woman he tried to fuck didn't show up dead. And his wife never divorced him."

Elliot stared out the window at the moss-draped oaks that were lit up by the hotel's floodlights.

"Sometimes I can't figure Dave out," Wink said. He sipped his drink thoughtfully. "When I first met him, I thought he was one of those dull but decent types. He's got everything - money, looks, beautiful kids, a loyal wife - but he has a wild streak in him that can get out of control. He admitted to having picked up some whores since his arrest. Not expensive call girls at some escort service, but street whores. And this is a man who could have just about any woman he wants."

"He's kind of strange. But I'm sure he thinks the same of me. Anyway, let's change the subject. What did you find out at the café tonight?"

"Very little."

"What have you done for the past four hours?"

"My client didn't help by showing up late. But I did get a chance to talk to some of the dancers. They're not saying much. I was hoping to see Carmen's ex-roommate, Kim, but she wasn't there. Kim's white-trash from some podunk town near the Florida-Alabama border. Room temperature IQ. Great bod, though. Just another redneck who's trying to make it in the big city."

"What about the other woman who was with Carmen? Did you find out anything on her?"

"A little. Turns out there are at least three dancers with fluorescent hair. One's black and the other one is blond, so your description narrowed it down to a dancer named Polita Flores."

"Did you see her?"

"No. One of the girls said that some of the dancers left early after they found out about Carmen's murder, and this Polita was one of them. I've seen her dance a few times. Like Carmen, she's quite the performer. Probably one of the top four or five dancers at the café."

Elliot noticed the bartender kept glancing in his direction.

"So, her name is Paula?" Elliot said.

"Polita. Polita Flores."

"Polita...Well, I'm ready to call it a night." Elliot stood up. "I hope this completes the worst twenty-four hours of my life."

"I'm going to stay here for a while."

"Before I forget, I need you or Dave to take me to the airport tomorrow. I booked a flight for three-forty five."

"I thought you were going to stay for a few more days."

"None of this sits well with me. I need to go home where I hope I can sort through everything. I just don't feel comfortable here."

"I wish you wouldn't, but it's your decision."

"I don't need to be here. I've seen Dave's operation. Everything looks good from the business end." Elliot took a step toward the door and turned around. He noticed the woman who had been sitting by herself was ready to leave. "I'd like to know something."

"Sure."

"Was Dave involved with Carmen in any way?"

"He was just another customer at the café."

"He tried to act like he couldn't remember her name."

"He only knew her through me."

"He told me that Carmen went by some Indian name. Checho-something. Is there supposed to be some deep hidden meaning behind it?"

"You mean Chechoter?"

"Yeah, something like that."

"I don't think it has any secret meaning. It was just some fancy alias she went by. Chechoter was one of Chief Osceola's…"

"Don't waste your breath. Dave already told me the story. I'll remember her Sioux war cry for the rest of my life."

"The Sioux are Plains Indians. Carmen was part Seminole or Miccosukee."

"Whatever."

"Now, I could be wrong. She could be Miccosukee. I think Miccosukee actually means swamp Indian. Sucaw is hog, and Nikasuki means hog eaters. The Everglades are full of wild hogs and…"

"Like I give a flying fuck about a bunch of swamp Indians. Damn. I'm going to bed. In case I have another panic attack in my room, I want you to keep your cell on you at all times. Keep it plugged to your ear if you have to. Don't go disappearing on me again. Goodnight."

Elliot left the lounge and took the elevator to the fifth floor. When the doors opened, he found himself facing a woman in a black leather dress slit up at the side and a low neckline exposing her cleavage. She entered as he was leaving, and a sliver of tanned flesh showed from the slit in the dress. He turned for a second look and recognized her as the same woman who had knocked on his door earlier that day; her hairstyle and dress gave her a different appearance, but her perfume was unmistakable. She stared directly at him as the doors closed, and the elevator descended to the atrium-lobby.

Elliot peered over the railing and watched her disappear through the main entrance. That same snap of her stilettos could be heard all the way up from his floor, and their clap-clap-clapping infused him with a dizzying, out-of-focus strangeness. He pushed back from the railing and went into his room, where he collapsed across the bed, fully clothed, and felt himself falling into a black hole.

# 12

A deep gloom had settled in Kim's apartment. Kim, chain-smoking, paced the living room mutely. Immersed in the heavy-cushioned couch, Polita held a plastic wineglass in her lap. They had stayed up into early morning, smoking dope and drinking themselves into a near-stupor while they reminisced about Carmen. Two empty wine bottles were on the coffee table. A single lamp burned in the corner.

Kim, with dark smudges under her eyes, stopped pacing and sat on the other end of the couch. She stared at the lipstick-stained cigarette butts and half-smoked joint in an ashtray on the coffee table before her. Polita, dry-eyed, sloshed wine in her mouth before swallowing it.

"I'll never forget when Carmen was arrested by a vice officer," Kim said. Her voice was drained. Their stories about Carmen had become a mix of drunken silliness and sadness. "Before we worked at the café, me and Carmen danced at a low-rent place that had private booths. One night a vice officer went into Carmen's booth pretendin' he was a customer and paid to watch her dance. After she finished, he showed his badge and arrested her. I have all them legal words memorized. The charge against her was called 'panderin' obscenity.' I guess panderin' means trying to sell sex, but Carmen just danced for him; she never intended to fuck him. He cuffed her right there in front of me and took her away. She was released later when a friend posted her bail.

"Then Carmen got herself a big-shot lawyer and went to court. One of the questions her lawyer asked the detective was if Carmen turned him on when she'd danced in front of him. The detective answered that Carmen didn't do a thing for him. That was the wrong answer. When the judge heard, he dropped the charge against her. He used a lot of big legal words, like the 'arousal factor' had to be important in provin' that Carmen's dancin' in the booth appealed to the detective's 'prurient interest.' Don't ask me to spell that word." Kim was beginning to slur her sentences. "I think prurient means perverted. So Carmen got the charges dropped, and the dancers gave her a big party afterwards. She became a kind of celebrity among all the exotic dancers in Miami. Of course, the cops were pissed off that they couldn't keep her in jail. They couldn't believe that the reason she went scot-free was because she didn't get one of their men excited. Like, what was he supposed to do, jerk off and then cuff her?" Kim giggled. "The cops promised they'd find a detective who would get turned on to her dancin'. Then they'd charge her with that prurient thing. Only something like that could've happened to Carmen."

Kim tried to stifle some more giggles. "Wanna hear another funny story?"

Polita shifted in her chair. She was deep in thought and didn't respond.

Kim seemed to talk more to herself than to Polita. "Carmen's very first john at the Luxuria was this egghead-lookin' president of some college in Florida. After she drugged him, she tried to open his briefcase but couldn't, so she took it to Dante and had him do it. I was there while she went through his wallet, important lookin' papers, and whatnot; Dante already on his cell about the dude's Rolex. Then she pulled out this paperback that was titled *No Exit*, which we tried readin' while we was getting totally wasted. Since we couldn't concentrate, we left to see a friend who owns a tattoo parlor. We didn't plan to get a tattoo but just to visit. Well, shit, while I was there I decided – with Carmen talking me into it – to get the title of the book tattooed here." She pointed to the side of her head. "I guess I did it 'cause Carmen said that her john talked down to her the whole time he was with her. Made her feel stupid." She laughed. "I know one thing, this tattoo sure is a good conversation piece at the café. Like, some of the men there even start tellin' me they've read the book. I guess they think I'm one of those dancers workin' my way through college. Dumbass Dante thought I got it as a street sign meanin'" – she again pointed to her head – "that what goes in one ear ain't comin' out the other."

Kim's laughter made her snort, which in turn made her laugh even harder. She looked at Polita for a response, but she was expressionless. Kim stopped laughing and started to say something else, but her voice soon trailed off. Despairing, she buried her face in a pillow. Polita listened to Kim's muffled sobs.

"I've always wondered why Dante and Carmen started this Rolex scam of theirs," Polita said. "Of all the women Dante knows or claims to know, why did he recruit Carmen? She was too much of a free spirit to've let some chickenshit like him control her. She had to've gone to him out of desperation."

"Do we have to talk about this now?" Kim stared glassily at Polita while she blew her nose. Her cell phone rang in her lap, but she ignored it.

"I knew Carmen was into drugs, but I didn't know how deep she was involved."

"I don't want to talk about any of the bad stuff."

"So we just sit around, get shitfaced, and tell funny stories about Carmen?"

"I'm not in the mood to talk about any drug problem she might've had."

"Might've had? Both you and Dante knew she had a drug problem."

"Are you saying we took advantage of her?"

"I don't know about you, but I'm sure Dante did. Of course, when it came to taking advantage of other people, Carmen was the expert."

"Like we're innocent?"

"I didn't say we were. Carmen just seemed to be in a league of her own."

They relapsed into silence again. Polita had observed Kim's reactions to her comments, having thought all along that there had been something false in her voice and that her sobs and deep, weary sighs had seemed exaggerated. Moreover, her eyes, no longer soft and teary, looked intent, suspicious.

"Why didn't Dante depend on you, instead of Carmen, to run his Rolex operation?" Polita said.

"He never liked the idea of other men touching me."

Polita's eyebrows jumped. "You've gotta be kidding me, right? You've already done at least a half dozen johns." She laughed. "As far as Dante's concerned, once you've fucked that many, what's a dozen? Two dozen?"

"He wants me to quit soon."

"He doesn't want you to quit. He's feeding you full of shit. And you know I don't believe any of it. So stop playing the dumb blond."

"Why do you care? I don't know why you're so worried about me and Carmen."

"Because I don't want you or me to end up *like* Carmen."

"You never liked Carmen anyway."

"You keep making it sound like you two were best friends."

"We were roommates."

"For two whole weeks. So? Big fucking deal. Then you kicked her out because you knew that she was fucking around with Dante. Carmen told me all about it. She even told me you threatened to shoot her. So, yeah, try to convince me how close you two were."

"We fought like sisters, but we were still friends. That's more'n I can say for you."

"None of us are friends. I don't trust you. You don't trust me. Dante doesn't trust his own mother. We're thieves and prostitutes. Even among thieves there's supposed to be some code of conduct, but that's bullshit with us. We put up with each other only because we have to."

"I don't care what you say. I was close to Carmen."

"You're putting on a good act with all that crying and stuff. And don't think I didn't see those sneaky glances between you and Dante at his place yesterday. What're you two really up to?"

"I haven't seen you shed one tear for Carmen. You've always said mean things about her. You..." Kim spoke breathlessly, then choked on her words. More tears rolled down her cheeks.

Polita and Kim turned their backs to each other. Eventually, Kim stopped crying. Each woman listened to the other's breathing. Polita checked her nails. Kim stifled a yawn.

"Kim?" Polita said, a few minutes later.

Kim silently stared at the cell phone in her lap.

"Kim?"

"What?"

"I'm sorry I got you mad."

Kim shrugged. They continued to sit with their backs to each other, and for a long time, no one spoke. Kim yawned again.

"You were right," Polita said. "I said some mean things. Instead of being sad, I'm angry."

"We're both pissed off." Kim, brushing her hair, turned to face Polita. "You gonna stay over tonight?"

"Yeah. I'm not going anywhere this late."

Polita finished her glass of wine.

"Wanna toke?" Kim said.

"I'm already stoned. And drunk."

Kim smoked the joint by herself.

Both women grew silent and withdrew into themselves. Kim looked nervous, eyes glancing around the room. Mindlessly, she tapped her long nails on her cell phone.

# 13

A cackle of giggles outside Elliot's room woke him. Then he heard a security card enter his door slot, but it was rejected each of the three or four times that it was tried. The person on the other side of the door soon gave up and the giggles now came from across the hall. Elliot slipped out of bed and cracked open his door. Across the hall stood a man and a woman, arms around each other's waist and obviously drunk. The well-dressed man aimed his security card into the door slot but kept missing. The blond woman, statuesque with long, suntanned legs, swayed back and forth, laughing at his futile attempts to enter the room. She wore a skintight mini-skirt and severely pointed spike-heeled shoes with ankle straps. While she waited for her companion to open the door, she turned and, as if expecting Elliot to have been watching all along, gave him a lewd wink. She was the same woman whom Elliot had seen twice before on his floor, except this time she was wearing a wig. A bemused half-smile played around her lips. Her companion finally got the door open, and they entered his room.

Elliot closed his door. Who was this woman? Why did she keep appearing on his floor? What was she up to? Was she taunting him? Everything about her reminded him of Carmen. Too restless to go back to sleep, he got dressed and left his room. He took the elevator to the atrium-lobby. At the bottom floor, he sat in a cushioned chair under a jacaranda tree. Despite the late hour, there were numerous bellhops and hotel attendants working.

He passed the time by reading through brochures of different home healthcare companies that were sponsoring the convention at the hotel. Dave's business, MedTec Health, was one of the main sponsors. Slow-moving paddle fans tousled his hair. While he was reading Dave's glossy brochure, he heard the ding of the elevator open in front of him, but no one exited. The doors closed and the elevator rose again to the top floor.

For the next couple of minutes the elevator repeated the same pattern of passengerless rides from the top floor to the atrium-lobby. The two other elevators, meanwhile, were inactive and sat with doors open.

He ignored the active elevator, figuring some teens must be playing around, and glanced through another brochure. A while later, the elevator returned to the atrium-lobby and, when its doors opened, a lone bellhop appeared. He passed by Elliot, smiled, and stopped at a vacant macaw's stand. Elliot recognized him as the same tall, lean, dark-haired bellhop who had asked him for the time the previous morning.

Weirdly, the bellhop started to whistle and talk to one of the vacant stands as though he were trying to get a macaw to imitate his voice, but there were no macaws in any of the three stands; they'd been put up for the night. After a minute of this, the bellhop, with his hands behind his back, strolled through the atrium-lobby. Every few seconds he would sound a sweet, warbling whistle. Unlike the other employees who were performing their tasks with almost stiff, soldierly discipline, the bellhop was either loafing or was on break. He lingered. He sat in a chair. He paced. Then he disappeared down one of the corridors.

Elliot finished reading the rest of the brochures and found a magazine to flip through. All three elevators were quiet. A few minutes later the same bellhop appeared again. He walked back and forth from one macaw stand to the next. Elliot kept an eye on him until the bellhop, his khaki uniform helping to camouflage him, wandered behind some thick foliage and out of view.

Irritated by the all the activity around him, Elliot went outside and took a stroll around the pool deck. A security official rode by on a Segway in the direction of the pitch-n-putt course. The hotel became unnaturally quiet, full of secrets. Only a few lights shone in its many rooms.

He walked to the seawall and stood at the same place where he had viewed Carmen's corpse. The moonlight lay on the water like a white sheet. He listened to the night's different sounds. Wavelets lapped against the seawall. Yachts creaked in the marina. A far-off cry of a seabird sounded.

Elliot remained at the seawall for a long time, staring at the city lights across the bay. A mist off the water grew thick and turned to fog, and a strong taste of salt filled the air. The moon became a yellow smear and then slowly disappeared. The city lights were extinguished. The cries of the seabird ceased. The fog, dense as the dry-ice smoke from a low-budget movie, slowly wrapped itself around the marina, starting at its entrance and covering each yacht until it blanketed the seawall, the pool deck, the surrounding landscape, and, within minutes, the entire hotel, dulling all its lights. He could only see about two feet in front of him. Droplets of moisture touched his skin.

Distant sounds, as if from a party, came from somewhere. Giddy with voices, laughter, and music mixed with the clink of silverware and the clatter of plates, the sounds came not from the hotel but from beyond the marina, carrying across the water like ghostly echoes. An unseen sailboat must be passing by, he thought, for he heard no motor sounds.

As he turned to leave, he noticed a figure move silently away from the seawall; someone had been standing but a few feet from him the entire time. The figure was vague and featureless, blending with the fog. "Who's there?" Elliot called out. "Who are you? What do you want?" No response. Elliot headed across the pool deck, then stopped and turned. "Why are you following me? I know you're there! I'm going to call security!" He peered through the fog, trying to see if someone would materialize, but he saw nothing but a shifting grayness.

He quickened his pace and entered the hotel. His hair was damp from the fog. As he walked to the elevator, he heard that same whistling again. Then it stopped. This time he saw the bellhop talking to a security guard. Nonchalantly the bellhop put his hands in his pockets and strolled through the atrium-lobby, never once looking in Elliot's direction but walking parallel to him.

Elliot took the elevator past his floor, past the tallest trees. He stopped on the eleventh floor and went to the room where Wink and Dave were staying. He pressed his ear against their door and listened, but he heard nothing. He moved away from the door when he heard footsteps coming around the corner. A security guard approached him, smiled, and continued walking down the hallway.

He returned to the elevator. On his way down to the fifth floor, he looked through the glass for the bellhop in the atrium-lobby, but he couldn't see him. Before he unlocked his door, he listened for any sounds coming from the room across the hall where the woman of many disguises was entertaining her date. He heard nothing. He entered his room and stepped out onto the balcony. The fog was dissolving, fading from around the hotel, and within a few minutes, he could see clearly past the lighted marina.

# 14

Dawn came, and Polita had not slept. For the past couple of hours Kim, curled on the couch, had slept soundlessly. Polita washed her face and brushed her teeth. A slight hangover gave her a headache, so she took two Advil. She quietly gathered up her things and, without disturbing Kim, closed the door behind her, descended the stairwell, and walked to her car. The sun shone dimly behind the pink glow of clouds.

To avoid the rush-hour traffic, she drove down a number of secondary roads back to her apartment. She thought of how good it would feel to sleep in her own bed. She parked her car and walked briskly through the courtyard.

When she opened her apartment door, she stepped back in disbelief. The sofa and chairs were overturned. Cushions were ripped open. Desk drawers hung empty and exposed. Plants and flowers were strewn across the floor. Framed pictures with fist-sized holes punched through them dangled precariously on the walls. She gasped, and a shiver ran through her. Her face lost color.

Leaving the door open, she walked very carefully through the stale-aired apartment and looked for any signs of forced entry, but she saw no broken windows or suspicious marks of any kind on the two doors. Suddenly, something moved behind the closet door in the hallway.

"Jazz?" she called out.

A scratching sound came from behind the door, followed by a meow. She opened the closet and her cat darted between her legs and ran out of the apartment. She stopped before she entered her bedroom. At her feet lay the smashed framed pictures of her mother and of her grandparents. Dresser drawers and clothes and slashed stuffed animals were scattered across the floor, joined by slashed pillows and a ripped open and overturned mattress. A foul smell made her gag. On the mattress was a soggy clump of seaweed and some dead fish.

"*Fucking* Dante," she fumed.

She started to call the police, hesitated, then hung up. The police would ask too many questions. She would deal with Dante later, on her own terms. She began straightening up the overturned furniture, working until the fish and seaweed stink made her ill. Even with the bedroom door closed, the odor was too strong. Her stomach churned, and vomit rose in her throat. Light-headed, she grabbed her handbag and keys and closed the door.

With no destination in mind, she found herself driving in dense traffic. She was swept along with everyone else, traveling farther and farther from her apartment. "Get out of town," she said aloud. "Just get out of town." She gripped the steering wheel so tightly her knuckles turned white. She cranked up the volume of her CD player so loud she couldn't think. The music numbed her. She rolled down her windows and drove faster. The in-rush of wind and the blaring stereo whirled in her ears. She wanted to scream. To cry. But she did neither.

Polita stopped at a traffic light at a busy street corner where a middle-aged man with scraggily hair was holding up a hand-lettered piece of cardboard – LOST JOB – and made eye contact with her. Across the street, on a sidewalk next to a strip mall, a young man with headphones entertained passing motorists by dancing with a sign that read BREAKFAST AT GINO'S – HALF PRICE. She gave the panhandler a dollar bill, and he thanked her by saying, "God bless." As the light changed and she started to pull away the panhandler said, with a near-toothless smile, "Please be careful." In her rearview mirror she noticed that he was still smiling as he was holding his sign chest-high.

Polita traveled on I-95 North, heading out of Miami, and an hour later she ended up in Ft. Lauderdale at the Riverwalk where she had taken her mother on a water taxi ride several months ago. Her mother had driven from Tampa to visit her, to try to convince her to return home. It was the last time she had spoken to her in person.

*I get sick worrying about you,* her mother had told her. *I know deep down you're a good person. You've always been my most sensitive child. But I can't stand the thought of you working at strip joints. There are too many shady characters who'll try to take advantage of you.*

*I'm a big girl, Mama. I don't put up with no one's shit.*

*Why can't you get a job at a travel agency, like the one you had in Tampa? You had a decent job. Another year there and you could've made office manager.*

*You call what I did there a decent job? The owner was an asshole who paid me next to nothing. He cut back my hours, telling me how bad the economy was, but he was really doing it to punish me because I wouldn't go to bed with him.*

*I'm sure that kind of stuff happens all the time. But you've got to start somewhere.*

*For two years all I did was book tourists on fabulous vacations. Me - I couldn't afford a bus ride out of Florida.*

*You young people want it all right away. I'm pushing fifty and I've never been out of Florida since the day I got here from Cuba in nineteen –*

*Eighty. Mama, don't you think I've heard this same story since I was a little girl?*

*And you'll keep hearing it till the day I die.*

*I guess I will. OK. I'm just saying I saw no future at Sandcastle Travel Agency. I had to say it - Sandcastle Travel Agency - every time I answered the phone. I was repeating it in my sleep.*

*You have a future dancing at strip joints?*

*Maybe.*

*Oh, and you plan on doing that till you're my age?*

*Of course not. But dancing can help me get started into something else.*

*Like what?*

*Like maybe owning my own little business.*

*What in God's name kind of business are you talking about?*

*I just want to own a flower and gift shop, or something like that.*

*Trying to open up a business now is very hard. It's tough out there. A lot of people are being laid off left and right. People are losing their homes in record numbers.*

*I know that. I'll wait for the right time to open a business. I've been trying to save my money. Mama, I made over fifty grand in less than a year where I dance. I bought a nice used car, some clothes, some decent furniture. And I'm saving to get my teeth fixed. A dancer at the café introduced me to a dentist who told me about this treatment called Invisalign. It's like wearing invisible braces, and I'm planning on making a down payment in a couple of weeks.*

*I couldn't afford to get you braces when you were a girl.*

*I know you tried, Mama. I'm not blaming you. In high school, someone I had a crush on told me that I was pretty if I didn't smile.*

*You've always been beautiful.*

*Have you ever seen a TV anchor with ugly teeth? I want mine to look like theirs.*

*Come back home with me. I can help you now. My job's pretty secure. I'm pleading with you, I'll pay for everything till you can get on your feet. Just leave that strip joint.*

*It's not a strip joint. And I'm not a stripper. I'm an exotic dancer. A performer.*

*You're only fooling yourself with talk like that. You expose yourself to strangers for damn tips. How can you make a living on tips? Huh? Please tell me. I'd like to know.*

*I just told you that I made over fifty –*

*Don't raise your voice at me. I'm still your mother.*

*I'm sorry. Mama, I make a whole lot more dancing than I ever did at Sandcastle Travel Agency. While people are losing their jobs in this economy, I'm making good money.*

*But the jobs they're losing is honest work. What you do…*

*What I do? Look, the way I see it, dancing topless is a business opportunity, especially during these times. Mama, did you know there are at least a dozen women at the café who are putting themselves through college by dancing? And one of the dancers managed to make enough to –*

*I don't care how much she made.*

*Look, Mama, I go around without a bra on. And I wear a thong. OK? Big deal. In Europe women don't think twice about going topless in some places.*

*You ever been to Europe?*

*No, but that's what I've heard.*

*You don't know what you're talking about. Your head's filled with nothing but fantasies.*

*I wear a little less than what some women wear on Miami Beach. OK? In fact, some women there make me look like I'm wearing too much.*

*Polita.*

*Mama, what I do is a job, nothing more. I'm not proud of it, but I'm not ashamed of it, either. I damn sure wasn't proud of the job I had at Sandcastle. Mama, I never lied to you about how I was making a living. I've always been up front with you.*

*If your father ever finds out…*

*If he finds out? When did he ever care? Since he remarried and started on his second family, he doesn't give a damn about us. He calls me twice a year - Christmas and my birthday. And that's twice too many.*

*I know he loves you.*

*Yeah, right.*

*I just want you to stop what you're doing. I don't want to get a call one day telling me something bad happened to my daughter.*

*Mama, after two or three years of this I'll be ready to quit. Just give me a little more time.*

Polita could still see her mother, crying, getting out of the car and walking away from her, her heaped-up, slightly crooked hairdo making her appear off-balance. Their only contact since then had been several brief phone calls.

She parked her car, boarded a bright yellow water taxi, and stood next to a group of colorfully dressed elderly tourists. She felt comfortable and secure among them as they talked to each other and took pictures. She noticed that one of the old codgers was looking her over. He winked at her. On his wrist gleamed a Patek Philippe. His wife, who wore an Omega and carried a Louis Vuitton purse, stared with disgust at Polita's tattoos and blue-streaked hair. The tourists looked so trusting, so vulnerable. If she decided to, she could rob them blind.

The water taxi traveled down the Intercoastal Waterway, passing high-rise condominiums and canalside homes with private docks. Off in the distance, Polita caught glimpses of the Atlantic Ocean. A shower of sunlight poured through the clouds. She leaned against the railing and breathed in the fresh air as the wind whipped through her hair. The scenery had a calming effect on her. The smooth water, the sailboats, the gulls whirling, gliding, dipping, all put her to ease.

The water taxi docked at the Riverwalk, and Polita departed with the group of tourists. She walked down a tree-shaded sidewalk of upscale boutiques, open-air stalls, and canopied kiosks. After window-shopping for a while, mindlessly wandering from one shop to the next, she grew tired. Another surge of nausea came over her, like the one she had experienced at her apartment; though she had tried not to think about it, the fish stink had stayed with her.

She entered a public bathroom and stood at the sink, staring into dark-circled eyes she barely recognized in the mirror's reflection. Her face was pale and her hair was tangled from the boat ride. Half-fainting, her legs going limp, she entered one of the Lysol-smelling bathroom stalls and began vomiting so violently into a toilet that she collapsed to her knees. Each time she heaved it was as if someone were punching her in the stomach. The pain doubled her over, and she moaned. Her vomit reminded her of the stench on her overturned mattress; and she puked again until her stomach was empty. Hunched and dry-heaving, she remained kneeling over the toilet, too weak to stand. Her entire body was cramped. It took her a few minutes to regain her composure. She wiped her lips and chin with toilet paper, then wiped around the stall where she had missed and flushed the toilet.

After a while the nausea receded, and she went to the sink and washed up. The unventilated bathroom and the smell made her shaky. Outside she sat on a bench in the shade, remaining near the bathroom in case she got ill again.

A half hour passed before she felt confident enough to leave the bench. She walked down the block to a CVS Pharmacy and bought a toothbrush, toothpaste, mouthwash, and a pack of chewing gum. In the store's bathroom, she brushed her teeth until her gums bled and gargled half the bottle of mouthwash.

She then boarded the water taxi. The weather had changed to an overcast sky. The water was no longer smooth but choppy and had a dark, brackish look. She fought the motion of the boat. The diesel stench made her nauseous, and she felt wobbly and green-faced. The vomit taste came back to her. She dry-heaved once when she saw a clump of slimy seaweed and dead fish float by, so she avoided looking at the water and instead focused on the passing high-rise condominiums. For the remainder of the ride, she imagined herself standing on firm ground.

Fifteen minutes later the water taxi docked. Once in her car, Polita transferred a small pistol from her glove compartment to her handbag. It was time to pay Dante a visit.

# 15

Elliot finally got out of bed sometime after ten o'clock. He had slept little and felt sluggish and headachy. After he showered and shaved, he called room service for coffee and a blueberry muffin. He was packing his clothes in his suitcase when a chambermaid, this time a young woman, entered and set a tray of food and *The Miami Herald* on the table. He tipped her and closed the door after she left.

He went out onto the balcony with his food tray and newspaper and sat in a lounge chair. A breeze rustled the palms, and the scent of bougainvillea wafted across the balcony. A gull swooped by, flashing in the sun. He opened the newspaper and looked for the story on Carmen's murder. The shooting of two fast-food workers dominated the front-page headlines; Carmen's murder was in the metro section, second page, without photos.

### Woman Slain

A Miami woman who was found Monday in Biscayne Bay died from being beaten on the head, an autopsy revealed.

Carmen Rafael, 25, of Seventh Street and King in Miami, was discovered floating in the marina at the Luxuria Resort and Spa.

"The official cause of death was blunt-force trauma to the head, inflicted by a weapon," police spokesman Sid Ortiz said.

Police refused to comment on

the weapon used in the murder. No arrests have been made, and police would not say if any suspects have been identified.

Rafael's empty wallet was found in her handbag, and police have said that robbery may may have been a motive.

"The autopsy was not able to determine immediately whether Rafael had been raped," homicide Sgt. Maurice Hawkins said. Further tests are being conducted.

Rafael, a topless dancer at Café Sinsations, was last seen at a party Sunday night at the Luxuria Resort and Spa. The Luxuria was sponsoring a party for a business convention, a resort spokesperson said.

While Elliot glanced through the rest of the paper, his cell phone rang.

"I'm meeting Wink on the first floor at the health club," Dave said. "Care to join us?"

"I've got a flight this afternoon."

"We won't be long."

"All right."

"I'll be down to get you in a few minutes."

Elliot changed into a pair of shorts and a T-shirt. He waited for Dave by practicing his golf swing. The feel of the wand-like weightlessness of the graphite club in his hand tempted him to cancel his flight for two more days of golf.

Dave showed up in gym shorts, tank top and running shoes. They took the elevator to the atrium-lobby.

"I was hoping we could've worked something out before you returned to Boston," Dave said as he led Elliot outside.

"After what happened to that dancer, I haven't been able to stay focused."

"I understand."

Elliot tried to keep pace with the quick walking Dave. They passed through a pergola and a banyan tree under which some elderly guests were playing a game of bridge. The lower limbs of a nearby ancient oak tree were so thick and heavy and dripping with moss that some of them drooped to the ground.

"Give me a week or so and I'll be back down to finish business," Elliot said.

"Good. You can stay at my place. No more hotels. Too much mischief in a place like this."

"You're walking too fast. My foot still hurts from the glass I stepped on."

"Sorry." Dave slowed down. "I didn't mean to be in such a hurry."

"Did you see today's newspaper?" Elliot noticed that Dave was staring at his neck wound.

"No, but Wink told me there was a story on the murder. The health club's this way. Watch your step."

Dave led Elliot down a tunnel-like passageway inside the massive rock grotto. The roar of a thirty-foot waterfall tumbled into the pool, winding sections of which cut through the grotto like underground streams in a deep cave. A lone swimmer, with goggles and fins, explored the bottom of one of the streams. A steaming hot tub seemed to bubble up through the rocks around each turn in the bend.

Elliot followed Dave up a steady incline of steps and entered the health club. Wink, on a treadmill, waved them over. Elliot and Dave climbed onto stationary bicycles and began peddling; before them a picture window revealed the other half of the pool, the marina, and the bay. Hotel attendants were attending to the guests at poolside.

While Wink and Dave discussed their plans for the day, Elliot peddled his bicycle and looked out the window. A sailboat leaving the marina was radiant with sunlight. The lowtide revealed the marina's barnacled pilings.

Elliot waited for Wink and Dave to finish their conversation and then said, "What did you think about the story on that dancer's murder?"

"Weird, huh?" Wink said, walking at a fast pace.

"What was weird about it?"

"At least now we know she was murdered."

"There was never any doubt in my mind."

"How was she killed?" Dave said.

"The paper said she was struck over the head," Elliot said.

"With what?"

"The police didn't say."

They fell silent for a minute. There were only three other people in the health club. A hotel attendant folded towels behind a counter, and a muscular man and a lone woman worked out at opposite ends of the carpeted weight room. When the man wasn't lifting weights, he was flexing in the mirror.

"I've got some inside scoop that you two might be interested to know," Wink said without slowing his pace, though his breathing was heavy. "Looks like someone tomahawked our Indian dancer with a golf club. A six iron. She was dead before she hit the water. By the way, no one's supposed to know this."

"How'd you find out?" Elliot said.

"Last night I overheard some of the employees talking in the bar. People just can't keep secrets. Half the staff here already knows most the details. Rumor has it that one of the groundskeepers found a golf club with a bent shaft next to the seawall."

"So a golf club was the murder weapon?" Dave said.

"It's a good possibility," Wink said. "The police think the murderer might've tossed it in the water."

Dave looked incredulous. "Can they fingerprint something after it's been in the water?"

"I'm not sure. I'll have to start watching NCIS to be able to tell you." Wink laughed.

"I wouldn't be surprised if the police are purposely circulating false information," Elliot said.

"They could," Wink said. "You never know what they're up to in murder cases."

Dave peddled at a rapid pace. "If a golf club is the murder weapon, I wonder if the killer used his own club."

"Who'd be playing golf that late at night?" Elliot said.

"The pitch-n-putt course is open until midnight," Dave said.

"What are the police going to do, search every golf bag at the hotel to see who's missing a club?" Elliot said.

"They'll need a search warrant for mine," Dave said. He winced a smile; all of his smiles evinced a certain tension.

"Same here," Elliot said.

"The killer would've been stupid to use his own club," Dave said.

"Unless he was in a rage," Elliot said.

"Maybe it was a *she*," Wink said. "You can't rule out that other woman who was in your room."

"That's a thought," Dave said.

"The police already know who owns the golf club," Wink revealed, ever the showman.

"Who?" Elliot and Dave said simultaneously.

"It belongs to the Luxuria Resort and Spa," Wink said. "The hotel's logo and ID number are on it. Someone - a guest or an employee - left it lying around."

"The pitch-n-putt course must have dozens of clubs that could get misplaced," Elliot said. "A place this ritzy isn't going to keep tabs on every one of its clubs."

Dave said, "It sounds too coincidental that there just happened to be a golf club conveniently lying there near the marina."

"I agree," Elliot said. "Who knows, maybe a guest got upset after making a poor shot and threw the club in the water. Or a disgruntled employee got chewed out by his boss and tossed one of the clubs. I'm sure the divers who were out there yesterday could find dozens of discarded clubs."

Wink broke in again. "If you two would let me finish, I'll tell why the golf club might be the murder weapon." He touched and patted his perfect hair as he continued on the treadmill. "Now, this could be just more scuttlebutt, but one of the employees said that a piece of brain tissue and hairs were stuck to the club."

"Gross," Dave said. "That's probably some illegal-immigrant-groundskeeper running his mouth."

"Maybe," Wink said. "I also learned that she may've put up a fight with her killer. There was someone else's skin under her broken nails, so she obviously saw her killer up close. That's all the info I have for now."

"That also could be a rumor," Dave said. "I'd bet there are a couple of minimum-wage employees just trying to impress their friends."

"At least the info I'm getting is something," Wink said. "The cops aren't releasing many details."

"For obvious reasons," Dave said.

While Elliot and Wink were panting, Dave was peddling effortlessly. The only other sounds were the male weightlifter's straining grunts and the slamming of his weights.

Between breaths, Elliot said, "The newspaper said that robbery could've been a motive. That means the killer would have my Rolex and the video of me."

Wink nodded in agreement. "Sounds a little strange that our Indian dancer, Ms. Chechoter, gets scalped but what's-her-name – Polita? – manages to escape. The more I hear about this

Polita, the more she's beginning to give me the heebie-jeebies. Nosiree. I don't trust her one bit."

Elliot, already lathered with sweat, stopped peddling and leaned over the handlebars. He was exhausted, and his sore foot had started to hurt.

"Did you notice there wasn't much written on her murder?" Wink said, slowing his pace. "A couple of short paragraphs on page two of the local section. But those two fast-food workers who were shot got front page."

"I didn't hear about that," Dave said. He showed no sign of slowing down on the stationary bicycle.

"A night manager and a part-time worker at McDonalds were shot while they were closing up. The worker, an honors student at a local high school, died. The manager is expected to survive, but he'll be spending a long time in a wheelchair. He had recently married and his wife is six months pregnant. Now that's a tragedy."

"Not a good night for fast-food workers or topless dancers," Dave said.

Elliot used a towel to wipe off the sweat on his forehead and around his neck. He listened to Wink's and Dave's conversation.

Wink said, "In another couple of days, Carmen's death will be just another statistic."

"So will that honor student who was killed," Dave said.

"The public doesn't care what happens to a topless dancer. But that honor student, he'll at least get some sympathy."

"I read not long ago that there had been more than twenty-four thousand people murdered in Florida over the past twenty years. That's just the statistics of one state."

"Unbelievable. Our murder rate is comparable to a war zone. Last year, in Miami alone, it got so bad because of the drug wars that the county morgue was filled to capacity. The excess corpses had to be stored in refrigerator trucks."

"Violent crime among teens has been rising. With the number of teens due to increase, it'll only get worse. This country is turning into a dystopia."

"Remember when those teens attacked that woman in downtown Miami? The term they used to describe the attack was 'wilding.' They went after her like a pack of wild animals."

"Those two women who attacked me were like a pair of wild animals," Elliot said.

"Sure sounded like it," Dave said. "Something else about our crime problem; there's been a steep increase in women using violence, especially female teenagers."

"There are some very hostile people out there," Wink said. "You know, it used to be where the wealthier neighborhoods barricaded themselves against violence by building tall fences and walls and hiring their own security people. Now even middle class neighborhoods are getting into the act."

"I just got back from Acapulco a few weeks ago," Dave said. "During two days of turf warfare between drug cartels, more than forty bodies, half of them headless, were found. I won't be going back there anytime soon. They have to send in the military when crime gets out of hand because the police are almost helpless. Or corrupt. Instead of sending our troops to Iraq and Afghanistan, we should have them stationed in some of our own cities. Like Detroit, Atlanta, New York, Miami, D.C. - they're just as bad as some of the Latin American cities I've been to."

"Worse, I bet, because here the criminals do get away with murder. I blame those big gummint liberals. Back in the day, crime wouldn't't've gotten out of hand like this."

"A friend who lives in my neighborhood bought a $150,000 guard dog to protect his home. Can you believe that?"

Elliot watched the woman in the health club wander over to the weightlifter, and the two began talking. The weightlifter's loud grunts and groans, Elliot decided, had been mating calls.

Wink said he was finished and stepped off the treadmill. Elliot and Dave followed him into the locker room, where they undressed and climbed into a Jacuzzi. Their conversation changed from homicides to medical supplies. Elliot remained mostly quiet.

In a shower stall a silver-haired man with a snoutish nose was shampooing his hair. After he finished, a young hotel attendant, dressed in all white and standing almost unnoticed against a white wall, wheeled his cart a few feet to the shower stall, opened the glass door etched with seabirds, and handed the man a fluffy towel with hotel logo. On the cart were stacks of towels, towelettes, body lotions, bottled water in an ice container, a box of Kleenex and other toiletries. After the man dried off, making sure that he cleaned himself thoroughly between the legs, he handed the damp towel to the attendant, who placed it into a small hamper attached to the cart. Still naked except for a pair flip-flops, he stepped over to use the urinal. He requested a Q-tip, and, while urinating, he used his left hand to clean out his left ear and his right hand to hold his penis, alternating hands as he switched to each ear. He scratched his rear end twice and farted once. The attendant looked on impassively while the man struggled to empty his blander, even moaning a few times, but once he finished, he shook his penis four or five times with one hand and used the other to return the used Q-tip to the attendant, who disposed of it in a wastebasket attached to the cart. The attendant helped the man into a terryrobe, retreated with his cart back to his station in the corner of the locker room, and stood at almost parade rest until Wink requested three bottles of water, whereupon he wheeled his cart to the Jacuzzi.

Fifteen minutes later they got out of the Jacuzzi. The attendant handed each man a towel and disposed of their empty water bottles. He told them that their sweaty clothes would be delivered to their rooms, washed and folded. While Dave went to the bathroom, Wink wrapped a towel around his waist and went up to Elliot, who was drying off. Wink and Elliot stood belly-to-belly.

"I can tell you've got a lot on your mind," Wink said. His voice was soothing, almost demure. He started to whistle some country-western tune.

"Seems like you and Dave are deserting me."

"Why do you say that?"

"Listening to you two talk, I don't detect any concern for me at all."

He pulled up a chair and straddled it backwards. "Ah-shucks, El. That's horseshit and you know it. We're behind you all the way."

"See, there you go again with that damn country hick accent. Neither one of you sound serious about any of this."

"Knowing the strain you're under, I guess I'm trying too hard to humor you, to put you at ease."

"Do me a favor, don't humor me. It only makes my mood worse."

"I wish you'd reconsider and stay for a few more days. You need some more time to prepare for Karen. I also heard on CNN that another cold front is moving toward New England."

"I don't care about the weather. I just want to get as far away from here as I can until all this blows over."

As Dave approached them, Wink got up from his chair, squeezed Elliot's fleshy sides, and said, "Come on, big guy, lighten up. Things are looking good. Let's get a massage. There's a Croatian woman here that Dave and I went to yesterday – she's the best masseuse in the business. You should see the ass on her. And good looking."

"I've got to get ready for my flight," Elliot said.

The three men left the health club in terryrobes, returned to the atrium-lobby, and took the elevator to Elliot's floor.

"We'll be down to get you in a little while," Wink said.

Elliot entered his room. While he was gone, his bed had been made and his room had been cleaned. Crisp white linens and embossed towels were in the bathroom, and a vase filled with tropical exotic flowers was on a glass end table. He found it odd that some of his personal items had been rearranged; his briefcase, which had been on the dresser, was on a chair, and instead of his suitcase being on the floor next to the bed, it was next to the minibar. Also, his golf bag stood in the corner by the sliding glass door and not inside the closet where he had kept it. He rearranged everything the way he had had it. After he finished packing, he dressed in a blue suit. A few minutes later Wink showed up.

"Where's Dave?" Elliot said.

"A valet went to get his car. He'll wait for us at the front entrance."

"Look, Wink, while we're alone I want to tell you something. In the health club, you made a comment about that dancer having someone's skin under her nails."

"I knew from the look you gave me that I hit a nerve."

"Well, we both know that some of my skin is under her nails. I don't want Dave to know about how she slashed up my wrists."

"No one else will know. That's our secret. You know you can trust me."

"Also, I need to tell you about something else that's been bothering me."

"I hope it's nothing else I said. I know that my attempt at some comedy has fallen flat."

"There's been this woman hanging out on my floor."

"Yeah?"

"She looks at me as if she knows something."

"She an employee?"

"She acts like she belongs to an escort service."

"You think? How many times have you seen her?"

"At least three or four times. She looks like Carmen."

With a quick smile Wink said, "Looks like Carmen?"

"Could at least be her sister. Dark-haired, slim, Latino. Very sexy."

"That's strange."

"Everything about this whole damn thing is strange. Let me rephrase what I just said. When I first saw her, she looked like Carmen, but she keeps changing her appearance. One time I see her she's dark-haired, the next she's blond. But everything about her still reminds me of Carmen. The way she looks at me. The way she walks. Even the perfume this woman wears smells like Carmen's."

"Are you sure she's the same woman?"

"I can't be sure about anything at this hotel. The first time I saw her, when she looked like Carmen, I was ready to make a run for it. I didn't want another encounter with that little demon."

"The stress has made you paranoid."

"Maybe so. You'll really think I'm paranoid when I tell you about the bellhop."

"What about him?"

"The morning after I was robbed, he was with me in the elevator and just so happened to ask me for the time."

"What's unusual about that?"

"It was the way he stared at me that struck me as peculiar. Then, very early this morning, I couldn't sleep so I went downstairs. Guess who was following me around? The same bellhop."

"If he makes you feel uneasy, let's report him to management and they'll fire his ass."

"I'm not making any complaints. I want to be as invisible here as I can make myself."

"Speaking of bellhops, I need to call for one to load up all your things."

"I don't trust anyone from this hotel. If you'll take my golf bag, I'll carry the suitcase and briefcase."

"You've got that collar so tight you're going to choke yourself to death." Wink touched Elliot's necktie.

"I have to hide my neck wound from Karen."

"Gah-damn, son, she's sixteen hundred miles away. Put your tie on when you land. You can take it easy for now. Ah ain't never seen you act like this before."

"I fear Karen more than I do the police asking me about that dead dancer."

"Heck, I reckon you do." Wink undid Elliot's top collar button and loosened his tie. He dropped his country accent. "Karen's quite a woman. I know she never liked me, so I made sure I always kept my distance from her."

"I wouldn't say she never liked you."

"I know better. Well, you've got a flight to catch."

Wink wheeled Elliot's golf bag to the door and opened it for him. With suitcase in one hand, and briefcase in the other, Elliot took one last look at the hotel room, relieved that he would never see it again. Wink closed the door and they rode the elevator to the atrium-lobby. On their way to the main entrance, three different bellhops offered to carry Elliot's things, but he told each one, "No, thank you." One of the valets opened the main doors for Elliot and Wink, and the two went outside.

"Were any of those bellhops the one you were complaining about?" Wink said.

"No."

"Did you see any Carmen look-a-likes in the lobby?"

"No."

"I plan to go back to the café again tonight. I'll try to track down this Polita."

"It almost doesn't matter anymore. I've resigned myself to expect the worst."

"Everything's going to be all right."

"Every time you tell me that, something bad seems to happen."

"Have you decided what you're going to tell Karen?"

"I'll probably have to tell her the truth."

"Until you hear from me, don't tell her anything."

"I don't know how I'm going to hide not having my watch from her."

They approached Dave's black Mercedes. Without getting out of his car, Dave popped open the trunk from the inside. Elliot and Wink loaded up the suitcase and golf bag and then got into the car. Dave, talking on his cell phone, drove down a flower-boarded road that circled the hotel. Easy Listening music played on a CD. Sitting alone in the back seat, Elliot gazed out the open window. Gulls glided over the marina. Flower-hung statuary stood strategically placed in the median. The sunlight shone greenish through the trees. Pith-helmeted groundskeepers, armed with rakes, machetes and gas-powered lawn equipment, attacked a dense area of underbrush and palmetto near the road.

As they drove past the wrought-iron security gate, the pink hotel and the blue expanse of the bay disappeared from Elliot's view.

Dave clicked his cell phone closed. "Have we decided what we're going to tell the cops if they ever ask about the dancer?"

"You go first, big guy," Wink said. He turned around and squeezed Elliot's knee. "Let's all three get our stories straight so there won't be any inconsistencies."

"Then we can forget about this mess," Dave said. He glanced back at Elliot and gave him one of his chilly smiles. "When Elliot comes down next week, I just want us to talk about business and golf. Nothing else. Right?"

"I hope so," Elliot said.

Wink squeezed Elliot's knee harder, and then tickled the inside of his thigh. "I hope so isn't good enough for me. I want you to sound more positive than that. I'm going to go over my story one more time. Don't deviate from it, OK?"

Wink was smiling, scheming, as he began to coach Elliot on what to say.

# 16

Polita turned into the trailer park where Dante lived and drove to his place. In the front yard Dante and Ramón were working under the hood of a car. They looked up when they heard Polita park along the side of the road. She got out of her car, adjusted her handbag over her shoulder, and approached them. Dante resumed working on the engine, while Ramón went to the rear of the car and opened the trunk. Both men ignored Polita, who stopped ten feet in front of Dante.

Polita was about to say something when, across the road, seven or eight young men came out of one trailer. They were smoking, drinking, and talking on their cell phones. Some of them waved or yelled out to Dante and Ramón. Dante waved back. One man was eyeing Polita. He was shirtless, and the mass of lurid tattoos on his chest and back made him look like a mural. Two of the men got into separate cars and started them up. Gangsta rap blared from the vehicles. The group seemed evenly divided between whites and Latinos. Then two black men – one wearing a do-rag, the other in dreadlocks to the middle of his back – came out of another trailer and joined their friends, all of them wearing familiar gang attire, complete with baggy clothes and heavy gold jewelry. Several of them wore baseball caps turned sideways. Those standing outside the cars, including Dante, were hocking and spitting while pulling and scratching at their crotches; either they shared some disease or they were communicating in a crude and wordless language.

Dante called out to the man wearing the do-rag, "What's happenin', Tyrone?"

The man raised his fist to Dante and glared at him. After the men spat and scratched for a few minutes, they climbed into the two cars and sped out of the trailer park. Their high-decibel music could be heard all the way to the main highway.

"Kim ain't here," Dante said without looking up.

"I didn't come here to see Kim," Polita said. She glanced at Ramón, who was changing one of the rear tires. Despite the humidity, he wore a black skull cap.

"Oh?" Dante looked at Polita. "If you're not here to shoot the shit, then I take it you're here to talk business. Didja bring me my Rolex?"

Polita said nothing. Both of her hands gripped the strap of her handbag. Her silence prompted Dante and Ramón to stop working. Over Dante's shoulder she saw Ramón clutching a lugwrench in one hand and a jack in the other. Polita shifted her weight from one foot to the other.

"Did you and Ramón find what you were looking for?" Polita said.

"What was we s'pose to be lookin' for?" Dante squeezed his crotch once.

"You know what I'm talking about."

"I ain't got a clue where you're coming from, but I'm happy you're here, 'cause we've got some unfinished business between me and you."

"I won't have any more business deals with you. Ever."

"Man, I think you're forgettin' that you've got a few thingamajigs – I think one's a Rolex and the other a DVD - that belong to me."

"I told you last time I was here: I don't have the Rolex or the DVD." Polita spoke in a cold, hard tone.

"And I think you're bullshittin' me."

"Was Ramón with you?"

"With me where?"

"When you broke into my apartment."

"You ain't making no sense." Dante slanted an eye to Ramón. "She making any sense to you?"

Ramón, mute, leered at Polita with that one small, shrewd eye. He took off his skull cap. His shaved, blunt head shone like a miniature sun.

"I'll make sure you pay if you ever fuck with me again," Polita said. Her voice never faltered. Without flinching, she took several steps toward Dante. He measured each step she took with narrowed eyes. "I really appreciate what you did to my apartment. Tearing it up is one thing, but leaving the dead fish and seaweed was real fucking sick. I'll get you back for that."

"You threatenin' me?" For an instant Dante's face darkened.

"You heard me. For you to do that after Carmen was found in the bay shows..." Polita was so angry she left the sentence unfinished.

"Oh, man, now I know now why you're so upset." A smile returned to Dante's face. He looked strangely innocent. "I heard what happened to Carmen. That was terrible. You mark my word, I'll find out who did it. Kim's all tore up about it too. When's the funeral?"

"*Fuck* you." Polita's eyes sparked fire.

"Aw c'mon. All of us are shook up over her death. But it don't give you no reason to come out here and abuse poor Dante."

Polita and Dante stood a few feet apart. They studied each other's eyes.

"Like you, Kim was acting awful weird this morning," Dante said. "One minute she was sad, then she was kind of crazy. I know you're both scared shitless, but don't be. Me and Ramón will look after you. Won't we, Ramón?"

Ramón stared at Polita with his perpetual mean squint. His mouth opened, but he didn't speak.

"I came here for one reason," Polita said. "That's to warn you to leave me alone."

"I didn't know I was bothering you." Dante gave her that same innocent look.

Polita reached into her handbag and pulled out her pistol, not aiming it but holding it down at her side.

"Fuckin' A..." Dante eyed the pistol. He and Polita showed opposite expressions: he looked amused, she was nervous. "Hey, Ramón, you see what she's packin'? I heard these little weapons are called purse pistols. They're so cute. So girly lookin'. I like the pretty colors – hot pink and black. Matches your pink blouse. You look like a model, all color coordinated. Looks a little like a derringer. You know, it's hard talkin' business while you're holding that pistol on me. That's not good company policy, bro. Better be careful you don't blow off one of my fingers with that thing."

"Don't fuck with me!" Blood rushed into Polita's face, shading it.

"Have I ever?"

Polita aimed the revolver at Dante, never taking her eyes off him. For the first time he showed a slight uneasiness. Only his dark eyes moved with nervous intensity from Polita to Ramón, from Ramón back to Polita. Open-mouthed and holding a lugwrench, the glaring Ramón approached Polita.

"Everyone take it easy," Dante said. He again pulled on his crotch. He eyed Polita sideways. "Ramón, I need you to fix my car. I can handle her."

"Tell her to put that peashooter away," Ramón said, a tiny flicker of light in his glass eye.

"You shouldn't be pointin' no little pistol around here," Dante said. "We've got kids in this neighborhood."

Dante looked across the road. In a vacant lot two children were playing. Polita returned the pistol to her handbag but continued to hold it by the handle. Ramón walked back to the car and tossed the lugwrench in the trunk.

"That's better," Dante said. His mouth twitched. The armpits of his T-shirt were stained. "Now that we all are calmed down, we can talk business."

"Let's talk about how much you owe me," Polita said.

"I owe you? It's the other way around."

"You owe me five-thousand dollars. That'll cover my bed, sofa, recliner, and some of my clothes."

"There you go again. You're not making a bit of sense."

"I know you and Ramón broke into my apartment."

"I don't know nothing about your apartment."

"You're a goddamned liar."

Dante took several steps toward Polita, but stopped when she started to pull out her pistol. He glared at her for a moment, and then laughed nervously. Ramón, eyeing Polita, was tinkering with something in the trunk. Everything about Ramón was menacing: that fishy one-eyed stare, his silence, and his slow deliberate movements.

"Run that by me again," Dante said. "You claim I owe you five grand."

"You really think I'm stupid, don't you? You treat me just like you do Kim."

"Now I do admit, Kim ain't the sharpest knife in the drawer. But you, you're smart. And scary. Maybe a little on the crazy side. I don't know if I want to mess with you. 'Specially knowing that you carry a pink pistol."

"Too bad you didn't find the Rolex and the DVD."

"I ain't done nothing." Dante held his arms up over his head as if surrendering. "You don't believe me, then call the cops to fingerprint your place. On second thought, I guess you don't want no cops snoopin' round your apartment, 'cause they might find some stolen goods. Ain't that so?"

Polita was trembling. That same vomit taste rose in her throat.

"I'm worried about you," Dante said. "I think you're in real grave danger. Now don't get me wrong, I'm pissed off that you and Carmen cluster-fucked me like you did that CEO. Carmen owed me a lot of money. And like I said, I was s'posed to get my fair share from the Rolex and the DVD. That's 'cause

Carmen was runnin' up a debt. She had a $150-a-day coke habit. Now, a rock star might be able to afford a habit like that, but it was getting outta Carmen's price range. Know what I mean? Shit, when you do the math, we're talking a grand a week."

"What are you trying to say?"

"You know what I'm getting at. There's someone who's more pissed off at you than me. Someone else out there has a score to settle with you, maybe some john or customer at the café. That worries me when it might involve Kim too. I don't want no-one else to get murdered. I care about both of you. I think you'll do me right in the end. You just made a mistake. Got a little greedy, man. But we can still work things out."

"You don't give a shit about anyone. All you care about is Dante. You'd stab Ramón in the back if it meant saving your own scrawny ass."

"I can't believe you'd talk to one of your business associates like that. I think it's time you start showing me some respect. Ramón, show her what I mean by respect."

From the trunk Ramón pulled out a pistol-grip shotgun and mimicked a gunslinger by drawing on Polita. With the huge barrel aimed at her, Polita stood motionless. Perspiration beaded delicately on her forehead.

"Bang, bang," Ramón said. "You dead."

"Whatsamatter?" Dante said. He stepped up to her. "You don't like Ramón's weapon? Lemme tell you something, next time you point that BB gun at me, there won't be no friendly negotiations. I'll just tell Ramón to open fire."

Polita's face was only inches from Dante's. Through his eyes she saw herself clearly. As a scared little girl. She squared her shoulders, chin upraised as if daring him to hit her. For a few seconds no one moved. His breath smelled of alcohol and cigarettes. Then a crooked smile appeared on his lips.

"Babe, you in the big leagues now. Take a hint from me: that there pistol you're holding won't impress no one. And it damn sure won't protect you against someone who's after you. Like Carmen found out, you don't fuck around in this city. You saw those men who just left them two trailers. Would you fuck with them? Any one of 'em would just as soon slice you up into tiny pieces of meat and feed you to the sharks."

"I wouldn't hesitate to shoot you or Ramón." Polita took three small steps backward. "You two are nothing but scumbags. Two dumbass, overgrown punks."

"Who the fuck you think you are? Huh?" Dante went into an eye-bulging, finger-pointing tirade. "You're nothing! Talkin' to me and Ramón like you was someone important. You think you're some sophisticated call girl? You're nothing but a snaggletooth whore."

"I don't have to listen to this."

"Then fuck off. We didn't invite you. I ain't got nothing to do with you, unless you're ready to talk business."

"I told you as of today we're through working together."

Polita turned to leave, but Dante said, "Not so fast." He calmed down. "Before I tell you what I've got to offer, I've got to admit that when I found out about Carmen's murder I thought you done it. I was sure of it. But now I've got a few doubts. Now I think someone might be after you. What I've got to offer you is protection. For a reasonable fee, me and Ramón will watch over you. We'll be your bodyguards. We've got a shitload of weapons. Even Tyrone and his gang across the street depend on us for firepower and ammo."

"I'm not impressed."

"Do I look like I give one fuckola if you're impressed or not?"

"I don't need your help. I've got friends."

"Who? I hope you're not talking about your bouncer friends at the café."

"Maybe."

Dante laughed, and Ramón grunted, which sounded like a laugh.

"You gotta be kiddin' me," Dante said. "You'd count on them for protection?"

"I can look after myself. I don't need anyone."

"Bullshit. A rookie like you won't last long in this city."

"I'm not afraid of you, that's for sure."

"What's those two bouncers' names anyway?" Dante snapped his fingers while thinking. "Allen and...ah...Steve. No, it's Seth. Funny. I remember one time Seth was hittin' on Kim at a party and I told him I'd blow his head off if I ever saw him around her again. He tripped all over himself trying to apologize to me."

"I'm sure he's afraid of some punk like you."

"Your bouncer friends are losers. Pretty boys. That's all. Smartass college boys workin' for minimum wage at a titty bar. They get their jollies hangin' around a bunch of half-naked women. All they're good for is to tell drunk customers to keep their hands off the dancers. They're in way over their heads if you expect them to help you."

"Leave me alone and you won't have to worry about them."

"Worry about them? Tell 'em to be good boys and go work on their muscles in their fancy gyms."

Dante returned to his car and resumed working under the hood. A boy from across the road chased after a baseball that stopped rolling near Polita.

Dante picked the ball up and tossed it to the boy, who caught it in his glove. "Attaboy, Manny. Good catch. Promise me when you play for the Marlins you'll give me your autograph."

The boy said, "OK," and Dante laughed.

While the boy popped the ball in his glove, Polita slipped her pistol into her handbag.

"Cute, ain't he?" Dante said. "I'd hate to see a kid like that get hit by a stray bullet. It happened to a little girl not long ago. She was walking down the next street over and a couple of dealers started a shootout. They missed each other but hit the girl. Right through the throat. This is one badass neighborhood where the cops ain't never gonna leave their squad cars unless they've got backup. Send your bouncer boys in here and they'll wish they'd never left their frat house."

Polita walked back to her car. She heard Dante curse loudly, and she turned, thinking that he was talking to her. He was sucking on one of his fingers from having struck it with a wrench.

"Motherfuck," Dante said. "Seems every time you come visit me I'm havin' to fix something that's broke. Last time you was here the a/c in my trailer wasn't workin'. Now it's the a/c in my car. What's next? It's gonna be one fuckin' hot summer for Dante, 'specially if he don't get his Rolex money. Man, I was plannin' on getting rid of this piece of shit, but certain people ain't paying their bills."

"That was between you and Carmen. I don't pay back other people's debts."

"Know what my mistake was? I put too much trust in Carmen. I kept getting her her drugs but she got way behind in her payments. I was runnin' up a huge debt of my own. And my creditors, shit, they don't like to be put off. Like Tyrone across the street - he puts a lot of pressure on me, man, and in turn I got to pressure you girls. Know what I mean?"

"I told you, that has nothing to do with me."

"It's got plenty to do with you. I can't even depend on Kim no more. You've got her turned against me. Carmen was fucked up with drugs. Kim has gotten greedy on me. And you, hell, I'm dealing with a woman who ain't got no morals."

"I didn't come to this shit hole for a lecture. I just want to know what you plan to do about my furniture you destroyed."

"Cash in that Rolex you're hiding and buy all the furniture you want. That is, if you can get a good price for it. Let me handle it and I can get you a better deal 'cause of my connections. I've even got international contacts."

"You don't have shit."

"Dante don't deal with pawn shops no more. My transactions are with big-time watch dealers. I can sell a Rolex in another country and have money in your pocket in three days. Max."

"I don't care about any of that. It's all bullshit to me."

"That wasn't your attitude before when I paid you for your stolen goods."

"You know, all you really did by tearing up my apartment was piss me off. I'll have to get some new furniture and look for a new place. But don't think you scared me."

"Who you think you're foolin'? You're scared shitless." Dante sniffed the air. "I can smell your fear. Smells like cunt breath. If it makes you feel a little safer, go ahead and believe it was me who broke into your apartment. I'd hate to know who's really after you. They must be real upset, don't you think?"

The handbag on Polita's shoulder was feeling heavy. She wanted to respond, but no words formed on her lips.

"Long story short," Dante said, "I want to help you for my own selfish reasons, 'cause if something bad happens to you like it did to Carmen, then I'll never see the Rolex. Now do you believe me? So I'll tell you what I'll do." He turned to Ramón. "Give her my Glock."

"Huh?" the surly Ramón said. He knotted his brow as if confused.

"I want you to give her my personal revolver," Dante said.

"No way. I don't like her. I won't give her jack-shit." Ramón shook his head obstinately.

"I know what I'm doing. Give her my Glock. Go ahead."

A hesitant Ramón, still mumbling half-articulated sentences, took a revolver from the trunk and handed it to Dante.

Dante bragged, "Like you saw earlier, me and Ramón have a small arsenal. Your muscle-head college boys are helpless when it comes to dealing with the likes of us. Since you don't want me and Ramón around, I'd rather you rely on this Glock instead of your pretty boys." He handed the revolver to Polita.

"With an extended clip, this weapon can fire thirty-three bullets in twelve to fifteen seconds."

"I don't want anything that belongs to you," Polita said. She refused to take the revolver.

"Don't make the same mistake Carmen made."

"I won't. Because I'll stay away from you."

Polita was about to open her car door when she felt Dante's hand on her. Startled, she turned around and faced him. Dante picked a loose hair off her blouse, and perversely he winked at her. Black grime was under his fingernails.

"Get your damn hands off me," Polita said. She started to reach for her pistol.

"Take it easy. Listen, I've got one other thing I want to say. I've got a homicide detective who's hot on my ass. One of those old-timers. A big spearchucker who won't take no for an answer. I don't know yet how he can link me and some others to Carmen. He makes me nervous. He's gonna get Kim to spill the beans on all of us. And soon he'll be coming after you with some questions. So we best get along. A word of advice. Watch out he don't ambush you somewhere you least expectin'. He'll work you over, get you all confused and tongue-tied. He'll try to get us to contradict each other. Before you know it, he'll have you turning us all in, like Kim's fixin' on doing. We've got to cooperate with him. If we do, I think he'll cut us some slack. But don't cooperate too much."

"I won't cooperate with you, that's for sure."

"Then I'll be back in prison, which Dante won't like. And you'll be right behind me. Know what I mean? We're in on this together, whether you like it or not."

"I don't like it."

"Then get used to it. Where you gonna be in case I've got to find you?"

"You won't find me at my apartment you trashed because I'm going to move real soon. Like in a day or two."

"So I can find you at the café?"

"If you do, it doesn't mean I'm going to talk to you."

"You dancin' tonight?"

"What's it to you? You plan on breaking into my apartment again when I'm at work?"

"So much for mournin' Carmen. A friend and associate of yours is murdered and you go dancin'. You know, you're one cold bitch. That won't look good if the detective sees you shaking your ass in front of a bunch of horny men."

"As if it's any of your damn business, I've got to work tonight because practically everything I own was broken or ripped to shreds by you and Ramón."

"Like I said, if it'll make you feel safer go ahead and think that."

Dante walked back to his car. He handed his revolver to Ramón, who put it back in the trunk.

Polita got into her car and drove to the end of the trailer park. Before pulling into the traffic, and without looking left or right, she took deep breaths while staring straight ahead. Both hands trembled so violently she could barely hold onto the steering wheel, and her heartbeat accelerated. If Dante hadn't lied to her, then who else could've broken into her apartment?

# 17

Friends and relatives greeted the passengers as they reached the concourse at Logan Airport. With no sign of his wife, Elliot went into the men's room and set his briefcase next to the sink. He stood before the mirror and examined the marks on his neck and wrists that continued to aggravate him. His sunburn disguised some of his neck wound; if Karen asked about it, he would tell her that it was a bite from some Florida insect. He knotted his necktie and rolled down and buttoned his sleeve cuffs.

Outside the men's room Elliot saw his son getting off the escalator. Jeremy, seven years old, was a miniature Elliot: he was big-boned, tall, pudgy, already with a little gut on him and the same light blue-green eyes as his father's. A moment later, Karen appeared walking up the stairway. She and Jeremy were dressed in ski jackets, jeans, and sneakers. Karen, laughing, put her arm around Jeremy's shoulder.

At the sight of Karen, Elliot started taking short, quick breaths. A hard knot formed in his throat, and he felt his heart racing. Perspiration soaked his shirt. With briefcase held tightly, he approached his family. Jeremy ran up to his father with raised arms, and Elliot stooped down so Jeremy could hug him. He then disengaged himself from Jeremy and straightened his shirt collar just in time to receive Karen's kiss. Searchingly, she stared at him for a few seconds without saying anything.

"I raced mom to the top floor and won," Jeremy said proudly.

"I saw that," Elliot said. He mussed his son's hair. "You beat her by at least two steps."

"I apologize for running late," Karen said. She pushed her jacket sleeve up and glanced at her Rolex. "I tried to get here early, but a front's moving through and the roads are slick. Look at your face. You're sunburned, and your nose is peeling."

He found it hard to endure Karen's stare. He nervously pulled at his tie knot, tightening it even more, and adjusted his shirt collar. He put his coat back on. He had to move, to do something to avoid her frontal gaze; after all, a moving target was harder to hit. So he headed for the escalators.

"I wanna carry your briefcase," Jeremy said.

"OK." Elliot handed him the briefcase.

"Why are you limping, Dad?"

"I stepped on some glass."

"Were you on the beach?"

"No."

"Then how did you step on glass? I stepped on a nail last summer, remember?"

"I sure do. I had to take you to a doctor."

"Were you barefoot when you stepped on the glass?"

"Yes."

"I haven't been barefoot outside since August," Karen said. She linked her arm in Elliot's. "It's been eight months. I can't wait for summer and to feel the grass under my feet."

He changed the subject and talked about the crowded airport. While he and Jeremy rode the escalator, Karen walked down the stairway. They met on the first floor. Elliot carried his son piggyback to the luggage center.

Karen said, "Jeremy, you shouldn't ask your dad to carry you when you know he stepped on some glass."

"Dad's strong," Jeremy said.

"I'm sure I can manage." Elliot's foot was throbbing.

"Dad, I've got a soccer game tomorrow."

"I thought this is baseball season."

"It's soccer too."

Elliot looked at Karen. "I should ask Jeremy's coach if he needs any help."

"I've been trying to get you to volunteer for two years," she said.

"I wanted him to play football, like his father."

"He's too young for that."

With his foot beginning to hurt, Elliot took his son off his back and held him by the hand.

"You don't know anything about soccer," she said. "You made fun of me when I told you I was going to sign him up."

"I think it's good that he's getting involved in athletics."

He noticed that she kept staring at his neck.

"Mosquito bite," he said preemptively. His comment kept her from lowering his collar.

"Hate to have seen the size of that mosquito."

"They're pretty big down there."

"I'll get the car while you're waiting for your luggage."

With Karen gone, he could breathe easier. He felt as though he had been holding his breath for the past few minutes. He and Jeremy watched the luggage pass by on the conveyor belt. Until Jeremy became restless, Elliot had forgotten that he was holding - squeezing - his son's hand, which felt small and warm, like a trapped sparrow. He released Jeremy's hand when he saw his luggage and called for a porter to load up his suitcase and golf bag. The porter followed them outside where they met up with Karen, whose green Land Rover was parked near a long line of taxis. The SUV was massive, with roof racks for her kayak and another rack at the rear for her mountain bike. A swirling wind blew from the main entrance to her vehicle, and the shock of cold air burned Elliot's cheeks. While he watched the porter load his luggage, he shrugged up his shoulders to protect his neck from the wind. Then he climbed into the warm Land Rover, and Karen circled the airport. Her headlights shone on the dirty plowed snow that was heaped along the street.

"Is that snow or sand?" he joked. He preferred the dark corner of the Land Rover to the bright lights inside the airport.

"I wish it were sand," she said. "I've seen enough snow this winter to last a lifetime."

"This will probably be our last cold front."

"I'm ready for some warm weather. I don't know why you left Florida so early to come back to this."

"I missed my family."

"I should follow your example and start going to business conventions in the subtropics. It seems mine are all in the North or the mid-West. Next time you go to Florida I'm going with you."

"I wanted you to come with me this time."

"That's what you said on the phone yesterday. I still don't remember you asking me. You seldom invite me anymore."

"You don't remember me asking you?"

"You must've mumbled it. I'm always excluded from your plans when it involves Wink or your other friends."

"I think I told you on the phone last night, but I have to return in another week or so to finalize a business deal with Dave Kornick." He didn't remember much about his phone conversation with Karen because that was when Carmen's Doppelganger had appeared at the hotel.

"Then include me this time. We can take Jeremy, or let him stay at mother's. I'm sick of this weather. It's been the same scenery for six months. Bleak and depressing. This is April and we're expecting more snow."

"You own your own company. You can go wherever and whenever you want to."

"It's not that easy for me to travel all the time."

While Karen made several calls on her cell phone, Elliot sat in his dark corner and watched her as the incoming headlights shone across her face. It occurred to him, for perhaps the first time, that she was aging. She was forty-five and kept her brownish-gray upswept hair its natural color. He noticed the slight sag to her chin and the tiny web of wrinkles at the corner of her eyes.

A half hour later they entered the town of Needham and then turned into their semi-rural neighborhood, Secluded Woods. They passed through the security checkpoint and drove down a winding tree-lined road. They had lived here since the third year of their fourteen-year marriage. The homes were large and luxurious, with wide rolling lawns, leafless hardwoods, and stone walls and picket fences.

She turned into their winding driveway and approached their stone Tudor, which set back on four acres. Ahead was a wooden bridge, under which a slow moving stream flowed across the rocks. The planks creaked as the Land Rover drove over them. The moon half-lit their property. Her headlights shone on a rabbit that was hopping across a patch of snow; it stopped for a moment, staring into the headlights. Jeremy aimed an imaginary gun at the rabbit and pretended to shoot at it.

"Jeremy, honey, stop doing that," Karen said. "Kids today, they have to turn everything into some violent fantasy. One day I want you to look at his video games."

"He's just playing," Elliot said. "When I was his age, I was probably pretending to shoot Indians."

"I want my child to be creative, not destructive."

She reached up next to the sun visor and pressed the garage opener. The garage door opened only halfway.

"I thought we had the garage door repaired last week," Elliot said.

"We did. That's the second time the door hasn't opened. Nothing seems to work in this kind of weather."

He got out of the Land Rover and pulled up the garage door. Karen parked, and Elliot and Jeremy carried the luggage into the house. Jeremy turned on the TV, but Karen came behind him and turned it off. While he limped upstairs, Elliot heard Jeremy whining to Karen about not getting to watch one of his favorite shows. In the master bedroom, he undressed and searched the walk-in closet for a sweat suit to wear. He turned off the closet light when he heard Karen enter the bedroom.

"Honey bunny, what are you doing in the dark?"

"Looking for something comfortable to wear."

"How can you see?"

"There's enough light from the bedroom."

"Then you have better eyes than I do."

She turned on the light in the walk-in closet and hung up her ski jacket. Awkwardly, he squeezed around her while keeping his neck wound turned from her view. With his back to her, he found a loose-fitting sweat suit and slipped it on; the hood easily covered his neck wound. She undressed. Naked, she gathered her clothes together. She was fleshy but not fat, her belly just a bit paunchy. Elliot admired Karen's rigid diet and exercise program, though she seemed to benefit little from it. Her tiny triangular patch of pubic hair - a mere dark strip between her legs - wasn't threatening. He kissed her on the lips while she was slipping into a robe.

"Aren't you hot with all that on?" she said.

"I wanted to wear something warm because I'm going in the garage to clean my golf clubs." Discreetly, he made sure the sleeves covered the scratches on his wrists.

"After you finish, could you check on Jeremy? I'm going to catch up on some paper work."

"I'll check on him now."

"How's your foot?"

"It's all right."

Karen put her arms around Elliot's neck and gave him a kiss.

"Jeremy's eyes lit up when you said that you were going to help coach his soccer team."

"I want to get more involved."

"We both need to."

"It wasn't that long ago when I was bouncing him on my knee." The pressure of Karen's embrace was pulling his sweatshirt down around his neck wound.

"He's still our baby. In a couple more years, though, he won't want much to do with us."

Elliot took Karen's arms from around his neck and put them around his waist. "I found something out at the airport tonight that kind of hurt."

"What was that?"

"I don't think Jeremy likes for me to hold his hand in public. I guess that's not cool for a seven-year-old."

"I'm sure he loves any kind of affection you show him. I enjoyed watching the piggyback ride you gave him in the airport. You were gone for only a couple of days, but he acted as though he hadn't seen you in months." She laughed. "But don't hold his hand when you're coaching him. That wouldn't be *cool* around his teammates."

"I wouldn't do that."

"Did you cut yourself shaving?" She stared at his chin.

"I nicked my chin pretty good the other morning."

Once again they kissed.

"My honey bunny came back from Florida all cut up," she said.

"Looks that way, doesn't it?"

He followed her into the study. She sat at her desk and turned on her laptop.

"I won't be long," she said. She peered at him over her half-moon reading glasses.

"I'll be with Jeremy."

When Karen wasn't looking, Elliot turned the thermostat down six degrees to sixty-four. His sweatshirt was uncomfortably warm. He stepped into Jeremy's bedroom and waited for him to come out of the bathroom. On Jeremy's dresser were two participatory soccer and baseball trophies. Elliot knew that his son was too big and slow and seldom got to play. Behind one of the trophies lay an open pack of chocolate peanuts. He ate a handful of them and fed one to Jeremy's hamster, which looked at Elliot through its cage at the end of the dresser. Jeremy came out of the bathroom.

"Where'd you get the chocolate peanuts?" Elliot said. "I know your mother didn't buy them for you."

"I got 'em at the airport when she wasn't looking and hid 'em in my jacket."

"Don't let her catch us."

"We'll get in trouble, huh?"

"Big trouble. Believe me, your mother doesn't miss a thing that goes on under this roof." Elliot ate another handful of chocolate peanuts. "We've got to cut down on these if we're serious about playing soccer."

"'Cause they make you fat."

"Which makes you slow. You've got to be quick in soccer." Elliot fed another chocolate peanut to the hamster. "When did you get him?"

"Yesterday. I named him Joey."

"I want you to show me one of your soccer DVDs. We'll play a couple of games, then it's lights out and time for bed."

Jeremy pulled out a DVD case from under his bed. He selected one and turned on the laptop. While he explained how to play the game, Elliot found it hard to take his eyes off his son.

# 18

Kim entered the dressing room of Café Sinsations and sat next to Polita on the sofa. With her high heels off, Polita was applying lotion to her feet after having danced for two hours without a break. Kim's visit surprised her. The color was gone from Kim's face; she was waxen, pale, stooped. A large bruise blossomed on her thigh. Two other dancers hovered in the dressing room as music blared in the background.

"That's a nasty-looking bruise," Polita said.

"Oh, that." Kim dismissed the bruise. "I must've bumped into something."

"Yeah, like Dante's belt buckle."

"He's never hit me once."

"Right."

"This ain't nothing. When I was a little girl, my daddy would use a razor strap on me. Momma would have to make sure I wore jeans half the time."

"You need to stay away from Dante."

"I'd leave him if he ever hit me."

"If you say so. Anyway, I thought you were staying away from here."

"I came to clean out my locker. I just finished talking to Miss Wanda. I told her I was quittin' 'cause of what happened to Carmen. I can't keep working here." She stared at Carmen's empty locker. "Miss Wanda told me a detective went through Carmen's things. It's probably that same detective who's been houndin' me since yesterday. You ask me, he's one of those highfalutin blacks who think he can talk down to me. I see his kind in here all the time. They're always smirkin' while they're paying me next to nothing to dance. Pretty soon this detective's gonna make me talk. He scares me."

"Be careful what you tell him."

"Dante figures if we cooperate, the cops'll go a little easier on us. That's what he told me to do."

"Whatever." Polita left the sofa for one of the makeup mirrors.

"The cops are gonna find out about us sooner or later."

"I can't let that worry me right now."

"You mad?"

"Just do what Dante told you to do. He should be an expert on talking to cops; he's been arrested enough."

They were quiet for a few minutes. Polita grabbed a brush and stared at her image in the mirror, which was framed with bright bulbs. She then undid her ponytail and loosened her hair, letting it fall to the middle of her back.

"Will you stay with me again tonight?" Kim said. She moved closer.

"Not if Dante is still hanging around you." Polita thought of her damaged apartment, the slashed bed, the broken furniture. She had nowhere to stay except at Kim's.

"I'll tell Dante not to come around when you're with me."

"I'll think about it."

"It's cold in here." Kim rubbed her bare arms. She then fidgeted with her cell phone. Tears welled up in her eyes. She sat next to Polita and clung to her arm. "I think someone's been following me."

"Why do you say that?" Polita stopped brushing her hair.

"I can feel it." Kim was crying softly.

The door opened, and Michelle, the broad-shouldered dancer, entered the room.

"This is the first time I've had a chance to talk to you about Carmen," Michelle said to Polita. "I feel so bad." Her eyes were solemn. "Me and Carmen didn't always get along. But once I got to know her, she was like a turtle, hard on the outside, but soft on the inside. I'll miss her. I'm sorry, you two were talking till I came barging in."

"You working the late shift?" Polita said.

"Yeah. I'm just not into doing much dancing after what happened to Carmen. I told Miss Wanda that I'll hang around and help out at the bar and the tables."

Michelle took her clothes off while staring at Polita. Naked except for her flip-flops, she stepped into the shower.

"She made it sound like her and Carmen was friends," Kim whispered. "Carmen had nothing to do with her. They got into it once, right here in front of Carmen's locker. I saw it. Michelle thought Carmen was saying bad things behind her back, and Carmen backed down to her. You blame her? Michelle's almost as big as our bouncers. We all think she had a sex change." She giggled. "We think her name used to be Michael."

"I was here when they were arguing. But it was the other way around. Michelle was the one who was crying. She accused Carmen of calling her ugly and goofy and that she was the ugliest woman here. Carmen got mad and told her she wasn't the one spreading rumors. So it was Michelle who backed down. I don't care about their argument. I want to know why you think you're being followed."

Kim wasn't listening to Polita; her eyes already dried, she was primping her spiky mohawk in front of the mirror. Her drained, haunted look changed to one of indifference and calm silence. She no longer made the appropriate frowns and signs of distress.

Polita put her brush and bottle of lotion in her locker while Michelle finished showering and dried off.

"How long you gonna keep working here?" Kim said. She was painting her eyelids green.

"I have no idea. Why?"

"I think once Miss Wanda finds out about us she's gonna fire you. I saved her the trouble by quittin' now."

"She's always been good to us."

"Don't matter now. Miss Wanda said when she hired us that if any dancer did anything illegal, she'd fire us. No questions asked. Dancin' here has already gotten one of us killed."

Polita slipped on her high heels.

"You should quit like I did," Kim said.

"This is all I've got. And I might as well work as many hours as I can since you think I'm going to get fired. Does it bother you that I'm still dancing?"

"No, not really. But, well... "

"Well what?"

"I mean, we just found out about Carmen yesterday." Kim finished painting her eyelids and went back to brushing her hair.

"That's weird, I just had this same conversation with Dante. He accused me of being a cold-hearted bitch for dancing on the day after Carmen's murder."

"When'd you see Dante?"

"Today. At his place."

"Why'd you go out there?"

"Because I had a few things to tell him. I'm surprised he didn't say anything to you about my visit."

"He didn't say nothing to me."

Polita took out some loose bills from a metal box in her locker and counted it. Sixty-four dollars. Kim, brush in hand, watched her. Michelle was several lockers down from them.

"Pitiful," Polita said. "Not even seventy bucks for almost the whole night. It's been awful slow. On a good night we can make over four hundred. Like you said, I shouldn't've bothered to come in tonight."

"See, that's what I was gettin' at. Carmen just got killed and you're complaining about how little money you made." Kim displayed a sudden, unexpected viciousness. Her eyes looked feverish, and her voice shook with anger as she jabbed her brush at Polita. "All you care about is yourself. You're the most self-centered person I've ever met."

"Don't shake that goddamn brush at me! If I told you why I've got to count up my puny tips, then you might understand why I'm out there 'shaking my ass' - to quote Dante. You can start by asking him."

"I'm talking about Carmen, not Dante."

"Then let's talk about Carmen. She wasn't a friend of mine. I knew her, I worked with her. But I was never her friend because she wouldn't let anyone get close to her. She was someone I knew who was murdered. It makes me sad when I think about what happened to her. You think I really enjoy dancing tonight in front of those creeps?" Polita crumpled the money in her hand and shook it. "Like I said, this job's all I've got. Right now I'm running on a high. I've got to keep moving. If I stop to think about everything that's happened in the last couple of days, I'd just crack. Yeah, I'd like to quit and just walk away from this shit. I just can't right now."

Polita threw the money into her locker and slammed its metal door shut. The sound made Kim jump. Polita noticed that Michelle was taking her time putting on her makeup.

"I go on in five minutes," Polita said. "I've got one more hour of this, then I can quit for the night. You know, when I was dancing tonight I started to block everything out of my mind. I didn't see one face out there. Those men watching me were just one big blur. I could've been dancing in an empty bar. I just listened to the music and tried to forget about everything. It kind of reminded me of this movie. Some prison guards were torturing this one man, and while they were beating him up, you know what he did? He imagined that he left his bloodied body and started doing something fun, like walking with his girlfriend on the beach. That's what I'm trying to do tonight. I imagined that I was out with a handsome man who loved me, while this other woman was dancing in front of a bunch of strangers. It made me deal a little better with work tonight."

Polita stopped talking when she sensed Kim's inattention. She watched as Kim transferred her makeup kit and clothes from her locker to her handbag.

"Like talking to the wall," Polita mumbled.

"Huh?"

"Nothing."

"I'm gonna ask Seth or Allen if one of them would follow me back to my apartment." The soft pain in Kim's eyes had returned. She was on the verge of crying.

"I can't figure you out. One minute you're angry, then you're OK, then you act scared."

"I didn't mean to get into another fight with you. I still want you to come over and stay with me."

"If you keep Dante away, I'll stay for a couple of nights."

"He won't bother you. I don't know why you're so worried about him."

"Because he's dangerous. I didn't want to tell you this, but someone broke into my apartment last night while I was staying with you. That someone took a knife to almost everything I own. That's the reason I went out to Dante's place today. I accused him and Ramón of doing it."

"What makes you think Dante did it?"

"You know what he's after."

"I don't think he'd do something like that."

Polita shook her head. "I learned not to argue with you when you're trying to defend him. All I know is I'm moving within the next couple of days. I've already told the manager at my apartment complex. I'll lose my deposit, but I've got to get out of there."

"If Dante didn't do it, who you think did?"

"It's time for me to go on." Polita glanced at the wall clock.

Kim followed Polita out of the dressing room. In the hallway, sitting on a float with cases of liquor stacked on it, Allen was staring at the floor. With an effort, he raised his eyes when

Polita stopped before him. There was anguish and tension on his face.

"You don't look good," Polita said.

"I can't say I feel like working tonight," Allen said. "Just thinking about what happened to Carmen has…" He shrugged and didn't finish his sentence.

"None of us feel like being here tonight. Who's guarding the fort while you and Seth are back here?" Polita noticed that Seth was stacking cases of liquor in the storage room.

"Mark's got the door. You know how he doesn't like to get his hands dirty. He's got us working back here since it's so slow tonight."

"Tell me about it. It wasn't worth coming in."

Seth carried two cases of liquor out of the storage room. Allen stood up and helped him stack the cases onto the float.

"Guess what?" Kim said. "This is my last night. I'm quittin'."

"Can't say that I blame you," Allen said.

"This place won't be the same without you and Carmen," Seth said.

"Before I go on," Polita said, "I've got a couple of favors to ask. Can one of you follow Kim home? She doesn't want to be by herself."

"I'll take care of her," Allen said. "I was going to ask Mark if I could have the rest of the night off anyway."

"I'll be leaving in about fifteen minutes," Kim said.

"That's about how long it'll take us to finish loading up the booze," Allen said.

"My second favor is if you two will help me move in the next couple of days," Polita said.

"You can count on us," Seth said.

"Give us a time and we'll be there," Allen said.

"Between Carmen, Kim and me," Polita said, "I think you two have moved us a half dozen times this year."

"We don't mind," Seth said. He reached out and held Polita's hand. "You doing all right?"

"Yeah. It's time for me to go on."

"I'm sorry about what happened to Carmen," Seth said, and released Polita's hand.

"It's been hard on us all," Polita said. She headed for the stage.

"I'll wait up for you," Kim said.

Polita stepped onto the stage. In a daze she danced to the music, keeping her distance from the customers by staying center-stage and avoiding the runway. After several minutes, she became nauseated and imagined herself vomiting seaweed all over again. She felt herself falling through clouds of cigarette smoke. The glare of the lights blinded her. Losing her balance, she slipped and fell on her rear. The impact almost knocked the breath out of her. Laughter sounded from the sparse audience. Embarrassed, she retreated from the stage and stepped behind the curtain. A pair of hands grabbed her, gently, and helped her to a chair.

"You looked like you were going to pass out the minute you got on the stage," Seth said. "You should go home and get a good night's rest."

"I might have to," Polita said.

"Drink this." Seth handed her a Coke. "It'll give you a little energy."

Polita nodded. She had an urge to brush her teeth.

"I've got to go," Seth said. "Mark's expecting me to relieve him at the door. You know how he is if you're late."

After Seth left, the deejay, Raul Mercado, came in to check on her.

"Need any help?" Raul said. "That was a nasty fall you took."

"I'm OK."

"Was that Seth who was just here?"

"Yeah. He was concerned about me."

Raul parted the curtain and looked at the still-laughing audience. He was lean and wiry, with slicked-down hair that was tied into a short ponytail. Various tattoos of demon-like creatures covered his arms.

"Well," he said, still gazing at the audience, "I'd better get back to my station. I figured that was Seth who followed you back here."

"Were you checking on me or Seth?"

"I guess both." Raul closed the curtain and looked at Polita. "I sometimes don't get very good vibes from Seth - or Allen, for that matter. They're supposed to be doormen but they sometimes try to act like tough guys."

"I've never seen either one of them get into a fight with a customer. Miss Wanda wouldn't allow it. And there've been times when I've seen some pretty drunk customers who should've been thrown out on their heads."

"If you say so. Let me know if you need anything."

After Raul left, Polita parted the curtain and watched him walk to his elevated station, next to a fountain and palm trees. He sat in a chair, glanced once at Polita, and, talking into his microphone, introduced another dancer.

She looked on as Seth took Mark's place at the door. She then noticed Kim mingling with some customers. A short time later, a man came out of the audience and whispered something to Kim, who nodded, whispered something back, and then followed him to the other side of the café. As they passed under some lights, Polita recognized that it was Wink. She had never met him, but she was at the café the day that he had introduced Carmen to Elliot. She also knew that he was a regular customer at the café.

Wink and Kim sat at a table in a dark corner where Michelle served them drinks. They seemed to be enjoying a relaxed conversation. Kim acted flirty, and from time to time she reached across the table and touched his hand. Fifteen minutes later they separated. Wink returned to a table where he had been sitting by himself, and Kim walked over to Seth, who was standing at the door, until Allen appeared. Allen took her handbag and left with her through the main door.

Polita closed the curtain and went down the hallway. Wink's visit with Kim had troubled her. She would have to ask Kim what she and Wink had discussed. Before she reached the dressing room, Mark called out to her.

"Polita," he said. "I saw you fall on the stage."

"If it's OK with you, I've got to take the rest of the night off. I haven't been feeling too good the last couple of days."

"Of course. By all means go home. Most of the employees seem a little lost tonight. Even Miss Wanda left early. Is there anything I can do for you?"

"I need about twenty-four hours of sleep."

"It would probably do you good to take some time off." Mark's mascara-lined eyes stared at her.

"I think I'll be OK to work tomorrow. I'm scheduled from six to midnight."

"If you don't feel like coming in, just give me a call."

She thanked him and opened the door to the dressing room.

With a hand on his waist, Mark said, "Let me know when you're ready and I'll walk you out to your car."

She went into the deserted dressing room and opened her locker, undressed, and got out her soap, shampoo and towel. In the steamy shower stall she stood under the warm rush of water. While shampooing her hair, she heard the dressing room door open. Someone entered and stopped near her shower stall. Hurriedly, Polita washed the shampoo out of her eyes but saw nothing except the steamed-up mirrors. Then she heard the person close the door and leave the dressing room.

She came out of the shower and swung her hair about. After twisting the water out of her hair and toweling off, she got dressed and put on her makeup.

The entire time she was in the dressing room she had avoided looking at Carmen's empty locker.

She walked down the hallway and stopped before Mark's office; his door was partially open and he was talking on his cell phone. She started to enter, then turned around and headed for the back door. She preferred to leave by herself.

Outside, the cars in the parking lot were greenly lit by neon signs. Several well-dressed men stopped talking when Polita passed them. She got into her car and drove away.

# 19

Propped up by two pillows, Elliot lay in bed in his flannel pajamas glancing through various financial newspapers. Karen, meanwhile, was in her walk-in closet changing into sweatpants and running shoes.

"Going for a run in this weather?" he said, peering over *Barrons.*

"It's too windy. It will be an indoor workout tonight."

"Good idea."

"What are you reading?"

"Is that a hint that I should be working out with you?"

"You've been absorbed with those newspapers for the past two hours."

Despite her being across the room from him, he kept the newspaper positioned where she wouldn't have a clear view of his neck wound.

"I was reading about how Obama and the Democrats are making the Republicans almost irrelevant in Massachusetts."

"We have always been rare in this state."

"To the point of extinction."

"Obamacare and the Democrats should be good for your business."

"Or put me out of business."

"I'm thinking about voting for him for a second term."

"I hope you're kidding. You've been a staunch Republican since you started your own business."

"I don't have time to debate politics. I'll be on the treadmill for the next half hour."

"Don't wear it out."

She disappeared down the hallway. With her gone, he lowered his newspaper and stopped acting like he was reading. He had met Karen at a Republican fundraising dinner in 1996. Less than a year later, they had married. It had been the second marriage for both of them, and neither of them had children from the previous marriage. Both of their businesses had prospered over their fourteen-year marriage. Times had been good for them, but he knew that unless he could clean up the mess in Florida, those years of domestic coziness might come to an end.

A sudden gust of wind snapped off one, then two, branches on an elm tree next to his bedroom window. He took his reading glasses off and got out of bed. The wind had been increasing for the past hour, but no snow had fallen. He glanced out the window, then took a step back when he thought he saw Carmen, expressionless, staring at him from the other side. Her smooth facial bone structure and creamy complexion glowed in the moonlight. Her eyes flashed red for an instant, like an animal's; then she vanished. He looked again and noticed that one of his distant neighbor's bedroom lights burned in the darkness.

He went into the bathroom and applied a Band-Aid to his neck wound. To further hide the wound, he straightened his pajama collar.

Back in bed, he resumed reading while listening to different sounds coming from inside the house. Across the hall, Karen worked out on her creaking treadmill. The clock ticktocked in the hallway. The hamster in Jeremy's bedroom played in its squeaking wheel. The sounds competed with each other: creak, squeak, tick, creak, squeak, tick. Wife and hamster running for their health. Now he wished he hadn't fed the damn rodent so much chocolate.

A while later Karen and the hamster stopped running. The only sounds came from the ticking clock. Karen entered the bedroom and took off her clothes. As was her habit, she gathered up her Rolex and necklace off the dresser and placed them in the top drawer of the nightstand. Elliot hid again behind the newspaper and took a deep breath peering above the page, his eyes followed the drawer opening then closing. To his relief, she didn't ask about his Rolex; instead, she was examining herself - critically - in the mirror, touching, poking, pinching, and squeezing different areas of her body. She turned this way and that for a different view, but no angle seemed to please her.

He was concerned about her excessive workouts. Trying to stay fit had become an obsession with her. She had converted one of the guest rooms into her own personal gym and had traded in her Lexus for the Land Rover to transport her mountain bike and kayak for camping trips to Vermont and Maine. For gifts on her birthday or for Christmas, her preference was exercise equipment instead of clothes and jewelry.

"You're looking as good as ever," Elliot said. He stared at her untanned body, her patch of pubic hair in stark contrast to her marble-white skin.

"I'd better not go to Florida next week. I would embarrass you in a bathing suit."

"I'm very proud of your appearance. How many women your age work out as hard as you do to keep in shape?"

"I'm not sure if that's a compliment."

"There are plenty of thirty-year old women who would give anything to have your figure."

"You're grasping for compliments."

"I'm being sincere. You've never looked better. And I admire your discipline. From the sound of your treadmill, I'd say you've been giving it quite a workout. Tomorrow, I'll spray it with WD-40."

"That's thoughtful of you. Did you check on Jeremy?"

"He's been asleep for over an hour."

She was quiet for a moment while gazing at him, her all-seeing eyes closely scrutinizing him. He raised his newspaper and pretended to read from it; he should've taken Wink's advice and had stayed in Florida for another couple of days.

"That looks like more than a mosquito bite," she finally said, lowering the newspaper with her forefinger. She then turned back his pajama collar to examine it better, touching around the Band-Aid. "It looks infected."

"Maybe the mosquito had rabies."

"Silly, I've never heard of a rabid mosquito."

"I also nicked it while shaving."

"You cut yourself again?"

"I must be getting palsy. But the mosquito bite was the size of a pimple."

"Why don't you use your electric razor?"

"Looks like I'll have to."

"I didn't know you still had those pajamas." She continued to stare at him. "They're so old they have holes in them."

"Since it's supposed to get cold, I thought I'd wear my warmest pair."

"What's with you?"

"What do you mean?"

"You're so bundled up tonight. You go from wearing sweat suits to pajamas while you're inside."

"I don't want to catch a cold."

"Are we changing sides tonight?"

"Your lamp is better to read by."

"Earlier, you could see in the walk-in closet without the light on."

"I'll change to my side when you're ready for bed." He had positioned himself on her side of the bed because that would prevent her from having a better view of his neck wound.

"You look stressed. I noticed that when I picked you up at the airport."

"I feel fine. If I look stressed, it's because our son overwhelmed me with too much soccer terminology. I'm confused with the fullback position and something called the sweeper. In football the fullback plays on offense, while in soccer he's a defensive player. I'll get it all straight. Jeremy's a whiz with that video game."

"I'm going to take a bath."

"Your side of the bed will be nice and warm when you return."

As she entered the bathroom, he breathed another sigh of relief. Restless, he got out of bed, went downstairs, and checked the locks. He moved his golf bag from the garage to a side room next to the kitchen.

Upstairs, he passed Jeremy's bedroom, and for a long moment he stared at his son's curled shape in bed. The hamster, inactive, watched Elliot from the corner of its cage. Gently, Elliot covered Jeremy with another blanket and kissed his forehead; his son's quiet breathing filled him with deep satisfaction and contentment. It felt good to be home. The hamster was still watching him, its nose testing the air. Perhaps it smelled something foul about him, or maybe it wanted another chocolate treat.

Back in bed, he held the newspaper in his lap but couldn't concentrate on reading. Through the partially open bathroom door he could see Karen taking a bath by candlelight. He knew that she was waiting for him. Her candlelight baths meant that she wanted him to join her. He turned the lamp off and moved to his side of the bed.

She called out from the bathroom, "Elliot darling?"

He lay still.

"Are you asleep?"

He stared at the dark ceiling.

"Honey bunny, where are you?" she said playfully.

He got out of bed and stood in the corner of the bathroom, in the shadows of the flickering, lavender-scented candles. She lay in the sunken circular Jacuzzi, immersed up to her breasts, with one foot raised to spread the soap suds. The hot mist clouded the mirrors. The bath water, fragrant with flowering herbs, filled the bathroom. On a tray next to the tub was a bottle of champagne and two gold-rimmed tulip glasses. A CD played Rachmaninoff's Theme on Paganini, one of Karen's favorites.

"You're so quiet," she said. In the candleglow her face had an olive complexion.

"I'm admiring you. You're a goddess."

"The last time you said that was during the fifth year of our marriage."

"And I regret that I haven't said it since. I said it earlier and I'll keep saying it: You've never looked more beautiful."

"That's because it's dark in here."

"Don't be so critical of yourself."

"Why are you standing way over there in the corner? Are you afraid to see me up close?"

"What did I just say about you being so hard on yourself?"

"OK, I'll behave."

He picked up one of the scented candles in its silver holder and blew it out. That left four lit candles. He took off his pajamas.

"You're making it hard for me to see you," she said.

"I can see you. That's all that matters."

"I can't reach the champagne." She was stretching her dripping arm toward the tray.

He uncorked the champagne and poured it into the glasses, handing one to her. As he lowered his fleshy hulk into the Jacuzzi, the sudsy water sloshed near the rim of the tub, almost spilling over. Once positioned, he and Karen clinked glasses.

"To my special love for you," he said.

"Oh, you're so sweet. You can be so romantic." She was all smiles.

He swallowed half his drink in one gulp. Then he lowered himself to where just his head was showing above the water. Karen, her breasts tipped with soap suds, leaned forward and kissed him. Her lips tasted of champagne. The candles burned low.

"Making love to you all these years has been the single most wonderful thing in my life," he said.

They embraced tightly. With his arms around her, he stared at the scratches on his wrists.

In the mirrors the candle flames flickered.

After their bath, they dried off and got in bed. In order to get hard he fantasized about Carmen and her tanned, shapely figure and thick bush. He was rough with Karen, his weight almost suffocating her. He pressed her against the bed, face down. She tried to turn her head at an angle to make some sort of eye contact with him. At times she seemed to struggle to free herself. Were her moans sounds of discomfort or pleasure, or both? Then he turned her over and watched her as she was on top. Crawling over him was Carmen, teeth bared, dark liquid eyes flashing.

# 20

Polita parked her car at Kim's apartment building. She locked the car, and, carrying her handbag, headed for the stairwell. The sky was black, starless. The streetlights radiated a weak amber glow. The parking lot was full of cars but no people, or so she thought. Out of the darkness came a voice that stopped her in midstride.

"Polita, do you have a minute?"

She peered into the parking lot without seeing anyone. The voice seemed to come from every direction. She thought she saw someone move between two parked cars.

"Who are you?" she called out. "Where are you?" She lowered her handbag from her shoulder. Inside the handbag, rolled up in a towel, was her pistol. "What do you want? Why don't you come out where I can see you?"

Across the parking lot someone approached her, materializing slowly out of the darkness. He was tall and thin and was whistling. He stopped once he reached the periphery of a streetlight nearest her maybe thirty feet away. He wore a Luxuria Resort and Spa uniform of khaki shorts and safari shirt.

"I know who you are because of Carmen," the man said, in a gentle, soft-spoken voice. "My name's Phil. I'm a bellhop at the Luxuria."

"You scared me."

"I didn't mean to."

She gripped her handbag. "I've got to go."

"What I have to tell you won't take long."

"You've been hanging around this apartment building for the past couple of nights, haven't you? I think I've seen you. Have you been following me?"

The bellhop was silent. Traffic hummed past them. A police siren sounded in the distance.

"I knew Carmen for, oh, about seven or eight months," Phil said.

"So? What's that got to do with me?"

"She told me she'd be at the hotel Sunday night with a girlfriend, either you or Kim, she wasn't sure which one. The two of you were to have a date with some CEO from Boston."

"I don't know what you're talking about."

"I caught on to what Carmen was doing at the hotel quite a while ago," he said, in his same soft voice. "We became friends, business partners, I guess you could say. I'd let her know when the hotel was having a convention, and when she'd arrange a date there, I'd keep an eye on her. I guess you could say I was her security. I've seen Kim with Carmen at the hotel before. And Sunday night was the second time I'd seen you there. But most of the time Carmen worked the hotel by herself."

"How'd you know I live here?"

"You don't. This is Kim's apartment. Carmen told me where you and Kim live and work. I've been at the café a number of times and have seen all three of you there."

"Why did Carmen tell you about me and Kim?"

"She said the three of you worked together, and that I might see you or Kim at the hotel from time to time. She wanted me to keep an eye on you, for security reasons, of course. You never know who you're dealing with these days."

"Why'd she need you?"

"I just told you."

"But she already counted on someone else."

"You mean Dante and Ramón? She depended on them for two things: to pay her for the Rolexes and to keep her supplied with drugs. She couldn't count on them for protection, at least not at the hotel. That's why she hired me."

"She never said anything to me about you."

"I guess I was her insurance, in case anyone was to double cross her. I wouldn't doubt if she had someone checking up on me. The last month or so she was really becoming paranoid. Maybe she sensed something bad was going to happen to her."

"She knew she could trust me."

"I'm not saying she didn't. She felt you needed protection, too, in case any man you were with got out of control."

A nervous strain had come into his voice. He put his hands into his pockets and then took them out again. Polita wanted to see more of this man's face, his eyes, but he remained on the darker side of the streetlight.

"I know what you must be thinking," he said. "If Carmen depended on me, then why did she end up dead? Well, she knew the risks. I work at the hotel, I have a job to do. I couldn't watch her all the time, and she knew that. I didn't know what went on behind those locked doors. All I could do was hang around the floor she was on, in case something bad happened. Know what I mean? We both carried our cells, but she never contacted me that night she was killed. You two were with that CEO for no more than forty-five minutes."

He paused, seemingly out of breath because he had spoken so rapidly. He had even stuttered a couple of words. In the ensuing silence, she took one step forward to get a better look at him. He took one step back and pulled something out of his pocket.

"The CEO you two were with that night was Elliot Anderson," he said, reading from Elliot's business card. He put the card back in his pocket.

"Why's that important?"

"You tell me?"

"I don't know. I lost contact with Carmen after we left his room."

"Are you sure?"

"Um…well, we went to the hotel's marina for a while."

"I know, I was in the lobby. Carmen signaled to me that everything was OK when she walked by."

"That's the last time you saw her?"

"No. I followed her to the marina. But I had to leave a couple of times. I remembered the last time I left. This one woman wanted me to carry her suitcase - actually, it was her makeup kit - to her room on the top floor." His voice suddenly had a tone of hostility in it. "Of course, our guests at the Luxuria expect us to kiss their pampered asses like we're their servants. Hell, I guess we are. We treat them like royalty, they treat us like shit. For all my trouble, that rich fat bitch tipped me one dollar. I shit you not. One fucking dollar – two quarters and five dimes - to carry her makeup kit from the pool deck all the way to the top floor. As if she couldn't carry it herself. I guess she would've tipped me a couple more quarters had I wiped her ass. She had so much jewelry hanging on her that she chimed when she waddled down the corridor. I thought to myself: Too bad I didn't have any of Carmen's knockout drops, I'd put them in that bitch's drink and make off with all kinds of jewelry. I wouldn't have to work at the hotel ever again. Yeah, I damn sure thought about it. Except I didn't really need any knockout drops to do it."

The bellhop became silent. Every few seconds he would shift from one foot to the other. His silence worried Polita more than his hostile tone had.

"That was the last time I saw Carmen alive," he said a little while later. "That fat-ass tourist who had me run all over the hotel with her makeup kit cost me at least fifteen minutes. By the time I made it back to the marina I didn't see you or Carmen. Someone must've gotten to her during that time. To think she got murdered while I was delivering that makeup kit. It's as if that fat bitch planned it that way."

"You have any idea who might've been following Carmen?"

"I sure don't. When I didn't see you, I figured everything was cool and that you both left, so I went back to work. I got off at eight in the morning. I didn't find out about her murder until I checked back in late at night."

"Dante knew she was at the hotel that night. Did you see him or Ramón?"

"I've seen them out there before, but not last night. The couple of times I've seen them they were all dressed up. Dante must've driven a rent-a-car and somehow got through the front gate. Even when those two dipshits are wearing suits, they still stand out like sore thumbs at a place like the Luxuria." He smiled. "They look like the Latino version of Laurel and Hardy."

"Did you see Kim at the hotel?"

"Not that night. When you showed up, I didn't expect her." His voice was no longer angry.

"Carmen told you to expect me or Kim. The only reason I went along was because Kim had to work. But she seemed upset that Carmen didn't include her. Plus she got off early that night."

"This might come as a surprise to you, but I did see that CEO at the marina."

She paused. "You mean the one who Carmen and me were with?"

"Yep."

"No way."

"I swear."

"When did you see him?" She was stunned.

"When I was returning from my errand with the makeup kit. We passed each other by the pool deck."

"But how? He'd just been drugged."

"That's what I thought. Sure surprised the hell out of me. He looked woozy, like he'd just left the party after having a few too many. That's one humongous fucker. Looks like a flabby old ex-jock."

"I told Carmen it wasn't a good idea to hang out around the hotel."

"She's done it before. She'd leave a guest's room, hang out in the lounge for a drink or two, then she'd disappear. She never seemed to be in any hurry."

"We had an argument because of that."

"I know, I saw that you two weren't getting along. Oh, guess who else I saw at the marina?"

"Who?"

"Mr. Anderson's two business buddies hanging around at the party. I guess he went looking for them but never found them. I've seen the three of them together since they checked in."

She thought of Wink having been at Café Sinsations tonight. "Was one of his friends around forty or so, always talking like a politician or a car salesman?"

"Yeah, that's him. That man never shuts up. Both his friends are still staying at the hotel. The CEO from Boston checked out today, two days before the convention was to end."

"Did you see either of his friends talk to Carmen any that night?"

"No. But remember, I wasn't around her all the time."

Polita was tired of standing. Her feet hurt.

"You know, Carmen was smart," he said. "Although she worked the hotel quite a bit, she never made it too obvious. She never flaunted her men. She never hung out for too long at any one place. And she could disguise herself real well. One time I walked right past her without recognizing her. Amazing what a wig or a different dress can do for a woman. But as careful as she was, I think there were a few employees at the hotel who were probably catching on to her act."

"I don't think she was being too smart the night she robbed that CEO."

"She made one mistake."

"And it cost her her life."

"Maybe she was getting too confident."

"You said there might've been other employees at the hotel who knew about her. Like who?"

"Maybe another bellhop, or a security guard. Someone who could cover a lot of territory. Well, I probably said more than I should've. I've got to go to work. These conventions keep me busy." He paused for a moment. "Oh, I almost forgot. There's one other thing I meant to bring up. Carmen had worked out a kind of payment plan with me. For my services, she'd make sure she took care of me. That Carmen, she wasn't tight-fisted with her money like those rich tourists are at the hotel. She was very generous. Problem was, she'd sometimes extend her IOUs. And, for whatever reason, she put off paying me for about a month or so. I was hoping, since I also kept an eye on you and Kim, that you'd reimburse me."

Polita gritted her teeth. Had it been Dante telling her this, she would've taken out her pistol and threatened him, but she was afraid of this man.

Finally, he stepped into the light as if to show his sincerity. For the first time Polita got a good look at his gaunt face, bloodless lips, and long-lashed eyes. He showed his gums when he smiled.

"I hope you understand the position I'm in," he said. "I know things didn't work out the other night with Carmen. I'm sorry about that. I truly am. But, like I told you, I don't think I'm the blame for that. I just couldn't be everywhere at once."

"How much are we talking about?" She tried to stay calm. She dared not argue with him. "I'm broke, and so is Kim. We haven't been in this business for long."

"You don't have to pay me all at once."

"Can you give me some sort of number?"

"Carmen owed me about five grand."

"Five…? I thought we were talking about a month…"

"More like two months."

After a long hesitation, she said, "I'm like you; what I make comes mostly from tips. I don't have that kind of money."

"You make money from the Rolexes and other gold jewelry that you steal, plus up to $500 an hour to entertain your executive friends. Seems to me you're rolling in the dough."

"I've only been doing this with Carmen and Kim for a little while."

"You already said that. Carmen did say you were pretty much a rookie. I'd settle for, say, four grand. Kim can split it with you."

"I've got to have some time..." Polita's voice trembled.

"I'm really running late. The royal guests at the Luxuria are waiting to be served. I'll be seeing you soon, Polita."

"Wait. I..."

Without saying anything further, Phil turned and walked away into the darkness. Polita soon lost sight of him. She waited for a car to start up and drive away, but the parking lot was quiet and dark.

She hurried up the stairwell and knocked on Kim's door. Outbursts of voices sounded across the marijuana-scented hallway. She heard cursing and children crying. Something crashed - a plate or a glass - against a wall. Kim answered the door while talking on her cell phone wearing a gothic getup of black clothes, black high-top sneakers, black lipstick, and black nail polish, all in stark contrast to her powered white face. Her spiky mohawk seemed sharper, more lethal, like a saw-blade. Polita was startled.

"You going to a party?" Polita said.

"What's it to you?"

"I...The way you're dressed..."

"What about it? You don't like it?" She snapped shut her cell phone in front of Polita's face.

"Forget it. Sorry I even asked."

"I was thinkin' about going out with some people I know."

"Good. Like I even care."

Polita went into the kitchen. Her mouth was dry. She poured herself a glass of water and took a long, quivering gulp. She drank so fast that she spilled it on her blouse. The water cooled her off.

Kim followed her into the kitchen. "Anything wrong?"

"Yeah. A lot's wrong."

"Like what?"

"About two minutes ago, right outside your apartment building, a man threatened to extort five grand from me. The asshole."

Polita's eyes were fired up with anger.

"What man are you talking about?" Kim said.

"You ever hear Carmen say anything about someone named Phil?"

"Phil? No... I don't think so... Phil who?"

"I don't remember if he told me his last name. He said he's a bellhop at the Luxuria."

"I don't know anyone who works there."

"He claimed that Carmen hired him for protection and that we have to pay what she owed him." Veins pulsed in her forehead. "Lately, everyone has been wanting to protect me, and I don't trust any of them. I don't need anyone's protection."

"Then don't pay him."

"That's what I wanted to tell him."

"You should've. I would've told him to fuck off."

"Sure you would've. Look how you let your punk boyfriend push you around. So don't go telling me how to deal with this other punk, OK?"

"He threaten you?"

Polita thought for a moment. "I'm not really sure. He looks almost like a choirboy. But there's something about him that scares me. Maybe it's his voice...or the way he looked at me."

"You gonna pay him what he wants?"

"I don't know what I'm going to do. Right now it looks like I'll have to come up with some cash. It's like that old saying, 'What goes around comes around.' I was trying to extort money from that CEO, and now it's happening to me instead. The shit just keeps getting deeper."

Polita found it unsettling to look at Kim's outfit. She avoided her and went around the apartment making sure all the doors and windows were locked. Kim followed her.

"I don't know why I'm checking the locks," Polita said. "Dante has a key to this place. He can get in whenever he wants to."

Kim got out some bed linen from the closet and put them on the sofa. Polita undressed and took off her high heels.

"I'll sleep on the sofa tonight," Polita said. She fluffed up a pillow. "I'm so tired I could sleep standing up. First thing tomorrow I've got to start looking for a new apartment."

"You probably don't want to hang around too long tomorrow anyway."

"Why, you expecting Dante?"

"I've got to see that detective tomorrow. I wouldn't doubt if he shows up here. I've been avoidin' him and he knows it."

"I'll be out of here at sunrise."

Kim started turning off some of the lights.

"I think I'll hang around here some," Kim said. "I'm not sure if I really want to go out with my friends after all. I was hoping they'd help me forget all the bad stuff that's been happening."

"I've got to ask you something before I go to bed."

"Go ahead."

"Who was that man you were talking to at the café?"

"Let me get you another sheet." Kim shifted her eyes from Polita to the closet. "That a/c vent is right under the sofa."

"I saw you talking to a man - alone - at a table."

"Oh, him. Yeah. He goes by the name Wink. He used to always ask for Carmen. She got tired of his act. Said he was full of shit. But she liked some of his rich friends he'd bring to the café."

"Was one of them the businessman from Boston?"

"Yeah."

All the air went out of Polita. Her shoulders slumped. "I knew the answer all along. I guess I was hoping he had a look-a-like. Carmen led me to believe that this man from Boston was at the convention by himself. And here Carmen robs him - knowing that his friend was with him at the convention. I don't know what to think any more."

Polita turned off the lamp and lay on the sofa.

"Polita, you mad at me?"

"I'm just tired."

In tears, Kim went into the kitchen and poured herself something to drink.

"What's wrong?" Polita said.

"Every time I think of Carmen..."

Kim couldn't finish her sentence. She came into the living room and sat in the dark. They were silent. Kim cried some more, exaggerating her sobs.

With no response or any kind of sympathy from Polita, Kim said, "I'm keeping you up with my cryin'. I'm just so upset." She went into the bedroom and closed the door.

Five minutes passed when Polita heard Kim on her cell phone. She put her ear to the bedroom door and tried to listen to Kim's hushed conversation. She thought she heard her giggling, but she couldn't understand what she was saying.

Polita returned to the sofa. She rolled over on her side and faced the wall. Her eyes were wide open.

# 21

Elliot sat up in bed and watched Karen disrobe in the walk-in closet. She slipped into a sweat suit and laced her sneakers.

"Honey, I'm going for a walk with Deb," she said. "Could you wake Jeremy up and help him with his breakfast? A bowl of cereal and toast would be fine. He has practice at ten."

"That means I'd better get ready," he said, but he lingered in bed.

"Because of the weather, they're practicing in the school's gym. If you're still serious about helping out, today would be a good day to talk to Jeremy's coach."

"Of course I'm serious."

"The loop that Deb and I walk takes about an hour."

"It's too cold to go for a walk. Come back to bed."

"Deb's on her way."

As she approached him for a morning kiss, he lowered himself in bed and pulled the covers up to his chin.

"Are you trying to hide from me?" she said, kissing him on the cheek.

"You wore me out last night."

"All I wanted was a kiss." She put on her wool cap and gloves. "See you in a little while."

Once he heard her close the front door, he slipped out of bed and stood by the window. Karen, her breath-plumes misting in the air, walked at a quick pace down their driveway. A weak yellow sunlight shone on the snow-covered lawn. At the end of the driveway, without breaking stride, she met up with her walking partner, and with jutting elbows and swaying hips, they made their way down the narrow two-lane road that curved out of sight.

Elliot dressed in his sweats and went into son's room. Jeremy, knuckling sleep out of his eyes, was already sitting up in bed.

"You're up bright and early," Elliot said.

"You coachin' today, Dad?"

"I'll ask your coach if he needs an assistant."

"What's an assistant?"

"That's someone who helps out the person who's in charge. Your friend, Ricky, his dad is my assistant sales manager."

"You've got a lot of assistants, don't you?"

"I have a few."

"You tell 'em what to do?"

"More or less."

"Why don't you tell my coach to be your assistant?"

"Because he knows a lot more about soccer than I do. Your father never played soccer, as you found out when we played your video game."

"But you played football in college. I've got your jersey. You were number sixty-one. You were a fullback."

"No, I played on the offensive line and blocked for the quarterback and the running backs. By the time you're in eighth or ninth grade, I hope you decide to play football."

"Mom doesn't want me to play football. Will you tell her to let me?"

"Your mother's the boss around here, and I'm her assistant."

"You played for the Patriots, didn't you, Dad?"

"In my dreams. I played at the University of Virginia. Remember, I was a Cavalier? Two knee surgeries ended my playing days, and now I have two creaky knees. Come on, it's time for breakfast. I'll meet you in the kitchen."

Elliot went downstairs and prepared breakfast. A few minutes later, Jeremy came down in his soccer uniform. They ate while talking about the kind of drills Jeremy did during practice. By the time Elliot had read some of the newspaper and had washed the dishes, Karen had finished her walk and came into the kitchen; her cheeks were florid from the cold.

"Are you guys ready to go to practice?" she said, taking off her cap.

"Yeah," Jeremy said.

"I'll take a shower and meet you in the garage," she said.

"I'll warm up the car," Elliot said.

She took off her jacket and gloves and went upstairs. While Jeremy got out his soccer ball, Elliot opened the garage door and started up his black Cadillac, then joined his son on the front lawn and kicked the ball back and forth. Low, gray clouds indicated more snow flurries. A meandering brook, which ran between his snow-coated stonewall fence and house, was almost frozen, as was the small pond in the middle of the front yard.

"Dad, you keep toein' the ball," Jeremy said.

"I'm kicking it right to you every time."

"But you're using your big toe. Coach doesn't want us doing that."

"Then how am I supposed to kick it?"

"Like this."

Jeremy demonstrated by kicking the ball on the inside of his foot; it rolled evenly across the light dusting of snow. Despite his sore foot, Elliot clowned around by trying to dribble the ball from left to right and almost slipped on the frozen lawn. Jeremy laughed at his father's silliness. The two kicked the ball around some more until Elliot got tired, at which time Karen showed up. She replaced the winded Elliot and practiced with Jeremy for a while. Excitedly, Jeremy tried to play keep-away from his mother.

Elliot backed the car out of the garage and got out to open Karen's door. As she was getting in, he took a hold of her by both arms and kissed her hard on the lips. His sudden display of affection surprised her.

"That was for last night," he said.

"We're running late." Smiling, she pulled her sleeve back to check the time. Sunlight reflected on her Rolex. "We need to be at Jeremy's school in fifteen minutes."

On their way to practice, Elliot made several calls to his office. Meanwhile Karen was telling Jeremy about the empty bag of chocolate peanuts she had found in one of his dresser drawers.

"I don't like it when you hide things from your mother," she said. "A little candy every once in a while is all right, but you over do it."

"OK, Mom," Jeremy said.

After Elliot got off his cell phone, Karen said, "Jeremy has an eating disorder. I'm going to make an appointment to have him see a counselor."

"Oh, hell, Karen. What kid doesn't have a so-called eating disorder? So he likes a few sweets."

"He inherited that from you."

"Yeah, I admit, I helped him eat half the bag."

"Then maybe that explains why you tossed and turned all night. You had all that sugar in your system."

"I don't remember having a hard time sleeping, thanks to the workout you put me through."

"Shh. Jeremy might hear you."

Elliot beamed.

"You did a number of unusual things last night," she said.

"Would you like for me to do them to you again?"

"Stop, I'm not talking about that. I heard you grinding your teeth. You've never done that before. I'm the one who has TMJ."

"You should've elbowed me, like you do when I snore."

"I did. But you kept grinding away until I had to shake you. Then later, you woke me by talking in your sleep."

He didn't say anything.

"You were actually having what sounded like an argument with someone," she said.

"You should've recorded it."

"I've heard you mumble in your sleep before, but nothing like last night."

"Make sure you wake me up if I disturb you that much."

"Why would I want to do that? I was trying to listen to your conversation." She smiled. "I'm just kidding. I did shake you again. This time you went downstairs and got some water."

"I went downstairs?"

"You don't remember? When you returned to bed, you mumbled something about the airport losing your luggage. I think you said it was your suitcase that was missing, but it was hard to understand you. You were having an anxiety dream."

He didn't reply. It was too hot in the car, so he turned the heat down and pointed the two vents that were blowing in his direction at Karen.

"Oh, I forgot to tell you one other thing you did," she said.

"What did I do now?"

"After I got up this morning, I had to pick up one of your pillows that you had thrown halfway across the bedroom. The pillow case was separated from the pillow and was all twisted up. I would hate to have been the person you were arguing with last night."

"Did you check yourself for any bruises?" He tried to make light of her comments.

"You had better not abuse me in your sleep. I hit back."

Karen, smiling, elbowed him.

He smiled, too, but uneasily.

# 22

Sleepless from having tossed all night, Polita got up from the sofa and dressed. She had gone to bed exhausted, but her late-night visit from the bellhop had kept her awake. To avoid waking Kim, she quietly gathered up her things and closed the door. Then she went down the stairwell and into the parking lot. The sun blazed everywhere, and the sun-glinting chrome and windshields from parked vehicles hurt her tired eyes. She got into her car and headed to her apartment.

At her doorstep, she found her cat curled up on the doormat. She cradled it in her arms and unlocked the door. As soon as she entered, the cat leaped out of her arms and returned to the doormat. She tried to coax it inside, but the cat scampered away. She kept the front door open and made a path back to her bedroom by pushing aside the overturned furniture, but the stench from the fish soon drove her out again. In the living room she sat on the floor in the middle of the damaged furniture and willed herself not to cry.

A tap on the front door surprised her; Seth and Allen were standing in the doorway.

"What happened in here?" Allen said. "Polita, are you all right?"

They both stepped inside, followed by Seth's brother, Paul.

"Paul's visiting me for a couple of days," Seth said.

"Hello, Polita," Paul said. "It's nice to see you again. I heard about Carmen. I'm sorry."

Seth took his sunglasses off to get a better look at the damage. Polita, legs folded under her, stared at her apartment.

"We just left Kim's," Seth said. "She told us that we'd probably find you here."

Allen helped Polita to her feet. She felt moisture on the back of his shirt; he was perspiring heavily.

"I'm not a very good homemaker, am I?" Polita said.

"Who did this?" Seth said.

"Why would someone want to destroy your furniture?" Allen said.

"It's a long story that I can't get into right now," Polita said.

"Did you call the cops?" Allen said.

"No." She sighed. "It's just a feud I'm having with someone. He did this to me, and I'll probably get my revenge by burning his place down."

She tried to smile as Seth exchanged glances with Allen and Paul. In his early thirties, Paul was short like Seth but not as broad and muscular. He wore camouflage pants, a black T-shirt and moccasins. Every time Polita saw him, whether at the café or at his lodge in Everglades City, Paul was dressed very informally. Always quiet and reserved, he was a successful real estate developer but looked like a local outdoorsman with his short-cropped beard, shoulder-length hair, and sun-browned complexion.

"What's that smell?" Seth said.

Polita answered, "Ah...just some garbage."

"Where do we begin cleaning up?" Allen said.

Polita closed the bedroom door. "How about right here? I'll do the bedroom by myself."

"This looks like something more than a feud to me," Seth said. He held Polita at arm's length and looked into her eyes. "Tell us who did this."

To keep them from pressuring her, Polita said, "If I tell you, promise you'll keep it a secret? It was one of Dante's friends."

"Dante?" Seth said. "Kim's boyfriend?"

"Yeah. One of his friends thought I was holding out on him. It was over some dope."

"For some dope he'd do this?" Seth said.

"They take their drugs pretty serious around here."

"It's got nothing to do with Carmen?" Allen said.

"No. Nothing at all."

"Was it that ugly goon who hangs around Dante?" Seth said.

"You mean Ramón?" Polita said. "It wouldn't surprise me. Anyway this doesn't leave my apartment. Since it involved drugs, I could get into some trouble. I'd rather just clean up the mess, move someplace else in a couple of days, and start all over."

"What's to keep him from doing this again?" Allen said.

"They'd have to wait till I buy some new furniture, wouldn't they?"

All four of them glanced around the apartment.

"Well, this place isn't going to get clean itself," Allen finally said. "Should we go ahead and move some of your furniture – what's left of it – to your new apartment?"

"I'm moving to Ocean Way, but I won't know which apartment number till tomorrow."

"Then we'll move you tomorrow," Allen said.

"I don't know if Kim has told you, but Carmen's funeral's tomorrow," she said, looking downcast. "I don't want to move till after that."

"Of course," Allen said.

"Some of this furniture's salvageable, so we'll leave it until you're ready to move," Seth said. "The stuff that's not, Allen and I can take to the dump."

Leaving the three men to work in the living room, Polita took a plastic garbage bag and went into her bedroom. She scooped the fish and the seaweed off the mattress and tossed it into the bag. The smell made her dry heave once. She tied the bag and took it outside to the dumpster, where she threw it away. Almost immediately, flies swarmed over the garbage bag

# 23

Elliot and Karen were spending the night alone. After soccer practice, she had allowed Jeremy to stay overnight with one of his friends. Elliot had influenced her decision since he preferred to have her alone if he was going to tell her about what had happened to him at the hotel. The day passed, however, without his having mentioned anything about the call girls.

He lay in bed with his flannel pajamas on, reading *The Wall Street Journal*. She entered the bedroom, her nightgown flowing lightly behind her, and he watched as she stood pigeontoed in front of the mirror while applying face cream. Then she went about the bedroom, tidying up and fretting over the various familial pictures on the dresser; it was simply in her nature to decorate and piddle whenever the mood came over her. Such simple things moved him.

A half hour passed in a comfortable silence. She was straightening up her bedside table by rearranging the pink box of Kleenex, her TMJ container, her reading glasses, a bottle of water, and her vaporizer. While she cleaned out one of her dresser drawers, she transferred her Rolex and jewelry from the bathroom counter and placed them in the nightstand drawer. This brought Elliot straight up in bed as he stole slant-eyed glances above his newspaper at her nearby activity.

"Honey Bunny, hand me your watch and I'll put it away for you."

Elliot's Adam's apple contracted once. He started to grit his teeth.

"It's in my briefcase downstairs," he said.

"Since when did you start leaving your watch in your briefcase?"

"The wristband came loose again when I was playing golf in Florida. I'll drop it off at the jeweler's tomorrow." He noticed by holding the newspaper out in his lap that his scratched wrists were visible to her.

"I meant to ask you about it last night when I didn't see it."

He set the newspaper down and put his hands under the covers. When she climbed into bed, he turned off his lamp. She turned her lamp on.

"Why do you keep turning off all the lamps?" she said.

"I thought you were ready to go to sleep."

"Not yet. I asked you back in February or March if you wanted me to take your watch to a jeweler. You've only had it for four years and it's already coming apart. For a Rolex, that's ridiculous."

"Well, it's very accurate with the time."

"I would hope so."

"I've just been a little rough on the wristband."

"Rough? What do you do, work under a hood of a car all day?"

"It just fits too tightly on my wrist and needs to be adjusted, that's all."

"Is it tight because someone has been gaining weight?" She pinched his waist, tickling him.

"Gain weight in my wrists? Come on." He squirmed free of her hand. "I'll take care of the watch tomorrow."

"That's what you said two months ago."

"I'll get it done this time. And I promise to start losing some weight in my wrists."

"Don't be grouchy now." She stared at the Band-Aid on his neck. "You should give that cut a chance to breathe so it can heal."

"I will." He touched the Band-Aid to make sure it covered most of his wound.

"Then why don't you take it off?"

"I will, in a little while." He kept touching the Band-Aid.

"Are you sure it was a mosquito?"

"Maybe it was a spider."

"Probably a tarantula."

"You're funny. What can I say? I was in the subtropics. Things can just jump out and bite you down there."

"Sounds like you're trying to talk me out of going next time."

He told himself, *Now's a good time to tell her the truth about the Rolex. Get it over with. She's going to find out the truth eventually. Just spill the beans.* But all he said was, "You look very pretty."

"Thank you. I've been enjoying all of your compliments."

"I think Jeremy had a great time today. He was all smiles."

"That was because of his new coach. He was the happiest kid out there. And I was the happiest of the mothers. By the way, I noticed you were still limping some during practice. How's the foot?"

"Better. I shouldn't have kicked the ball around the front yard. Horsing around made it a little sore."

She took her bite guard off the bedside table and adjusted it in her mouth.

"I guess that's a hint that we won't be making passionate love tonight," Elliot said.

"That's never stopped us before."

Switching off her lamp, she snuggled up next to him. Her cold ankles brushed against his feet.

A whitely-glaring moon through the window gave the room its only light.

She kissed him on the cheek. "Do you love me?"

"More than you'll ever know." A desperate tone came into his voice.

"Could we just hug tonight?"

"I had planned for something a little more erotic than hugging."

"I'm tired, honey bunny. You were a little rough with me last night."

"That's what you said on our way to Jeremy's soccer practice."

"It felt like we had a wrestling match."

"A wrestling match? I was hoping you'd say that I made love to you with extraordinary passion."

"I think you did leave a few bruises."

"That's called tough love."

"Just hold me."

"Whatever you say."

She fell asleep in his arms.

He lay still for a long time and listened to her breathe against his chest.

His thoughts eventually turned to Miami and to Carmen's naked body. He found himself becoming hard, but with Karen holding onto him, he resisted the urge to touch himself.

# 24

Polita and Kim were sitting next to each other at Carmen's sparsely attended funeral in a wood-framed Catholic church with Venetian-blind windows. Tears in her eyes, Kim gazed at Carmen's casket. Polita, hands folded in her lap, observed Carmen's parents and teenaged brother sitting in the front pew. The mother - small, dark-haired, bespectled - leaned forward, one hand holding a rosary and the other holding a Kleenex to her eyes. The father stepped forth and placed a wreath of flowers on his daughter's casket. Mr. Rafael was thin with short-cropped graying hair. He touched the casket, caressing it. He remained there for a long time, head bowed in prayer. He then sat next to his wife.

A few of Carmen's relatives were seated next to her family. Seth's and Allen's wide-shouldered frames took up almost the rest of Polita's pew, while Miss Wanda and Mark sat two rows behind. Miss Wanda wore a black dress and her hair was partially pinned up under a hat. Mark kept touching the knot in his tie with slim, restless fingers, his mascaraed eyes staring at the casket. Seven or eight Café Sinsations dancers – all wearing conservative dresses - were sitting next to each other in a middle pew. The towering Michelle stayed to herself in the corner of the church. Across the aisle from her was Dante, looking humble in his wrinkled dark blue suit. Behind him was a stocky black man in his late fifties with slightly-hunched shoulders. Two funeral directors stood at the back.

The priest was a short, gray-haired man with wire-rimmed glasses. His high forehead, not quite balding, shone from the ceiling lights as he eulogized Carmen's modest accomplishments: "She graduated from high school with good grades. She sang in the school choir and was popular with her friends. She was a devoted big-sister to her younger brother and a loving daughter to her parents. She dreamed of being a singer. She loved animals." The priest spoke of Carmen's hard-working parents. The mother, stooped over, buried her face in her hands. The father, sitting straight and firm, tried to show a stubborn, disciplined grief, but his tortured eyes betrayed him.

In a soft, compassionate voice, the priest continued, "With today's temptations so many of our young have become lost souls, and only God can save them. And He will accept them back if they have faith in Him." He read from Mark, chapter four, verse 35-41: "'He woke up and rebuked the wind, and said to the sea, Peace! Be still! Then the wind ceased, and there was a dead calm.'" As he said those words, he stared at the motley collection of mourners. At Polita and Kim. At Seth and Allen, whose suits were too small and ties were too tight. At the nervous-looking Dante. At Miss Wanda and Mark. At the tearful Michelle. At the dancers, whose tearstained faces smeared their gaudy makeup. And for a brief moment he stared at Carmen's casket, as if trying to fathom her criminal behavior. "When our young find themselves in stormy waters, they become lost and frightened. No one seems to hear their cries for help. Calm your storm. Find peace in God. He will hear you. Allow Him to guide you to safer shores. If you feel you're sinking, if you feel you're descending into darkness, reach out and His helping hands will find you. You will find comfort and safety in His embrace."

Carmen's parents tried to stifle their sobs. The father's shoulders lost their firmness and began to slump. His chin rested on his chest. His sobs turned to moans. Then an uncontrollable attack of weeping overcame him. Carmen's brother, who resembled her with his raven hair and slim build, sat motionless and was stunned by his father's hysterics. Tears flowed down the mother's cheeks. She hugged her son, as if to protect him from having to witness his father's pain.

Choked with sorrow, Polita closed her eyes and tried to tune out the father's wails of anguish. After a while several relatives led the father out of the church. He was shaking his head and kept repeating, "No, no, no. Not Carmen. She was my beautiful little girl."

As the priest led them in prayer, the mourners clasped hands with those nearest to them. Polita held hands with Kim and Seth; his grip was so firm that it caused her some discomfort. When it came time to release hands, Seth, his head still bowed and eyes closed, continued to hold onto Polita's and absently massaged it. She finally squeezed her hand away from his.

The mass ended, and the pall-bearers carried the casket out of the church. Carmen's mother and her relatives followed the casket in silence, their arms linked. On the church's front steps Carmen's weeping father, standing unsteadily, was assisted by his son who was holding him by the arm. The mother groaned and wrung her hands. The priest joined Carmen's family, and they excluded themselves from the Café Sinsations crowd.

Presently Miss Wanda gathered her employees around her, offering them encouragement. Kim held Miss Wanda's hand and listened forlornly. Seth's eyes were moist. Only Allen showed no emotion; his gaze was neither afflicted nor even sympathetic as he stared at Carmen's casket being loaded into the hearse.

Polita heard almost nothing of what Miss Wanda was saying. Instead, she watched as Dante was talking to the black man near the funeral motorcade. Dante then got into his car and drove away. The black man leaned against a car and observed the mourners. No one else among the Café Sinsations crowd seemed to notice him.

The priest continued to console Carmen's family.

The clouds were golden with tropical sunshine.

Michelle, who had been standing by herself, approached Miss Wanda and the dancers.

"I cooked up a bunch of food," she told them. "So if anyone wants to come by my apartment after the funeral, there'll be plenty to eat."

"I'll drop by later," Miss Wanda said on her way to her car.

No one else spoke to Michelle. She left for her car, alone.

"She almost scares even me," Allen said to no one in particular. He studied Michelle as she got into her car, looking uncomfortable in an almost comical way as he tried to twist his thick neck from the tight grip of his stiff shirt collar. "I don't know why she works at the café. She can barely support herself with the puny tips she makes. Hardly anyone ever requests her, unless they're really weird. She should've stayed a man. I know why Miss Wanda won't fire her, because she's got a soft spot for misfits."

"Then that must include all of us who work there," Polita said, irritated at Allen's comment. "I don't think this is a good time to be trash-talking anyone."

Allen, staring at Polita, became quiet for a moment.

"Yeah, you're right," Allen finally said. "I'm sorry." For the first time he showed some emotion by looking humbled. "I shouldn't've gone off on her like that. I guess I'm just angry about all this. I don't know why I had to take it out on Michelle. She's got a good heart."

"All of us are upset," Polita said. She held Allen's hand.

Allen said nothing further. He looked relieved because he had taken off his coat, loosened his tie, and rolled up his sleeves to his forearms.

Carmen's family walked past the dancers, ignoring them. The father had wept for so long that his eyes looked like wounds, red and swollen.

"It's time to head for the cemetery," Seth said.

As Polita and Kim walked to Polita's car, the black man approached them. Kim, too absorbed in her grief to look up, almost bumped into him.

"Miss Ellis," the man said. His burly, thick-chested frame towered over the women.

Dabbing tears, Kim looked up. Her face was blank.

"Remember me?" the man said. "Detective Hawkins." Although he spoke to Kim, his gaze focused on Polita. He was courteous and offered apologies to both women. "I'm sorry to bother you at a time like this, but I wanted to ask you a couple of quick questions. Who was the tall woman who was just drove off?"

"Who?" Confused, Kim looked around.

"Her name's Michelle," Polita answered for Kim.

"Does she work at the café?" Detective Hawkins said.

"Yeah," Kim said.

"I haven't seen her before."

"She's worked there for a couple of years."

"They're the bouncers, aren't they?" Detective Hawkins watched as Seth and Allen got into Seth's Jeep.

"Yeah," Kim said. "The tall one's Allen."

"Oh, right. I recognize him now. The other is Seth?"

"Yeah."

The detective nodded. He spoke in a gruff voice, and behind his rimless glasses his eyes were piercingly intense. He had a thin, gray mustache and gray-flecked hair.

"You must be Polita Flores," Detective Hawkins said.

"That's me."

"Dante pointed you out to me. You're a hard woman to reach. I've missed you the couple of times I've been by the café. I've called your home and cell numbers at least a half dozen times. I even stopped by your apartment once."

"My voice mail messes up from time to time."

"Then that explains why you haven't returned my calls." His voice lost its relaxed tone and became more abrupt. "Miss Flores, it's real important that I talk to you." He turned to Kim. "And I need to finish our conversation from the other day."

"I've got to go to Carmen's funeral," Kim said.

"I know this is a bad time. Maybe tomorrow, in my office?"

"I guess so," Kim said, wiping her eyes with a Kleenex.

"Miss Flores, what's a good time for you?"

"I don't know. I'm just trying to make it through the funeral."

"I understand. How about tomorrow?"

"Sure. Why not?" Polita looked everywhere except at the detective.

"Three? Four?" The detective was insistent.

"Make it four."

"I need all the cooperation I can get from you two and your friends," the detective said, more to Polita than to Kim. He stared at Carmen's parents. "Maybe we can help ease their suffering some. God only knows I've seen enough funerals." He returned his gaze to Polita. "I know you're gonna do everything you can to help me."

"I'll try."

The detective handed each woman his calling card, then walked to his car.

# 25

Plushly cushioned chairs surrounded a mahogany conference table. Elliot, his vice president of operations, and his account executive sat in three of them while they discussed the company's need to hire five additional sales reps and eight technicians and to increase their fleet of delivery vans from sixty-one to sixty-five.

"So, the bottom line is that we're looking at hiring thirteen new employees," Elliot said. "That'll be a total of seventeen employees – not counting six part-timers - we've hired since the end of last year. And economists are calling this the Great Recession. We must be doing something right. Almost every employer I know is letting people go." The clock on his desk said three-thirty. "Gentlemen, if you'll excuse me, I have to get ready for practice."

The two men seated across from him looked at each other with amused expressions. Earlier, Elliot had changed from his suit into his sweats.

"Are you training for the Boston Marathon?" Tim Erickson, vice president of operations, said. He was a heavy-set man with bushy eyebrows.

"Not in this lifetime," Elliot said. "I'm a Clydesdale, not a greyhound. I want you both to know that I've started a kind of second career. I'm now a coach. For probably four hours a week I'm the assistant coach for my son's soccer team. Karen should be dropping Jeremy off in a few minutes." He looked at Steve Snyder, his account executive, whose glasses and semi-bald head reflected the lights. "I want you to use the next two weeks to screen all the applicants for our new positions. I'm thinking of three sales reps instead of five. We want to be a little careful in this economy; I don't want to over-hire. Have a short list by then so we can start making our decisions. Tim, check into the vans. I haven't been too happy with Stratton's Chevrolet, and let old-man Stratton know that. Tell him I'll take my business elsewhere if he doesn't improve his leasing agreement. Check with some other dealerships and see what you can come up with. And Steve, our merging with Dave Kornick in Florida should be a done deal. Go ahead and get the legal stuff started."

Elliot's associates left his office. While he waited for Karen, he glanced through one of Jeremy's soccer books on various practice drills and wrote down several that he would try that afternoon. Fifteen minutes passed. He wondered why he hadn't heard from Wink. His thoughts turned to the hotel in Miami and to its moss-draped trees. He could smell the deep sweetness of the abundant flowerbeds and the salt air off the bay.

His secretary entered his office while he was again checking his cell phone for any messages from Wink. She handed him some papers to sign. Slim and long-legged, Cindy Reese was in her late thirties. She was thrice-divorced and had a six-year-old boy. Elliot knew that she had numerous tattoos from having seen her at various sporting events, but his dress code at work required all employees to keep them covered. He once suggested to his vice president of operations that at least half of his six hundred employees under forty had tattoos or body piercings. It no longer disturbed him as it used to, and it didn't surprise him when he saw some of Carmen's and Polita's body art.

"I've got you down for soccer practice in a little while," Cindy said.

"I'm almost ready." He handed her the signed papers.

"Are you in a league?"

"Me, play soccer? No, I'm helping to coach Jeremy's team."

"I thought of signing my son up."

"You should. On the practice field I saw kids from almost knee-high to probably high school. Jeremy loves the sport."

"All I've ever heard you talk about sports-wise are the Pats, Celtics, and the Red Sox."

"I'm getting to where I like soccer. I'm caught up in Jeremy's enthusiasm."

After his secretary left, he turned his creaking leather wingback chair around and looked out the third-floor window at the raw, gray afternoon. The cloud cover was low and dense, and the snow-bright landscape shone like a mirror. He watched some of his employees working on the loading dock where his trucks and vans were coming and going. On each side of the vans and trucks read:

ANDERSON HEALTHCARE
BRINGS HEALTHCARE TO YOUR HOME

- HOME MEDICAL EQUIPMENT
- HOME OXYGEN THERAPY &
  RESPIRATORY MEDICATION
- HOME IV THERAPY

Impulsively, he called Wink's cell number. He waited by rocking in his chair. Wink answered and they exchanged greetings. Wink was so loud that Elliot had to hold the cell phone away from his ear.

"I don't mean to interrupt you," Elliot said, while Wink was trying to tell him one of his golf stories, "but I wanted to know if you've found out anything."

"I went back to the café last night," Wink said. "I'm still gathering information on this Polita."

Polita's image crossed Elliot's mind. He pictured her full-lipped mouth and high cheekbones, her dark eyes, her tanned, healthy skin, the streaks of blue in her hair.

"What did you find out about her?" Elliot said.

"I didn't stay long. In fact, I've got to stop going to the café. I found out that one of the dancers told the cops that I was one of Carmen's regular customers. So now I've got an appointment to see a detective, tomorrow, I think. Or maybe the next day. Who knows? Who cares?"

Elliot was motionless. His leather chair did not creak once. Thirty seconds passed before he finally moved by changing hands with the cell phone. The chair creaked slightly.

"Jesus," Elliot exhaled.

"I'm not the least worried."

Elliot sat heavily back in his chair and stared out the window. Sleety rain began to fall on his vehicles and across the loading dock.

"What are you going to tell him?" Elliot said.

"That I used to patronize the café maybe two or three times a month. You know me, I'll tell him some cockamamie story. And that I knew some of the dancers, including Carmen. So what? I won't mention your name, unless of course I have to."

"Go ahead and mention my name. What the hell. It's time to come clean. Being around Karen has been a real pressure cooker. I just haven't had the courage to tell her. I keep putting it off because I'm hoping for a miracle."

"Don't tell her yet. Let me get a feel for this detective. Be patient. I know you get tired of me saying that, but I think we're going to get a big break."

Wink's tone was casual.

"Will you call me after you talk with the detective?" Elliot said.

"You know you can count on me, pardner."

Elliot tried to hang up, but Wink insisted that he finish the golf story he had begun. Patiently, anxiously, Elliot listened to his story while he drummed his fingers on the desk. After they hung up, he looked for Karen's Land Rover to show up in the parking lot below. He lacked any energy to stand. He leaned his head wearily against the back of the chair, and it creaked with each deep breath he drew.

A short time later, a loud knocking sounded on his door, and his son appeared in the office.

"I'm here," announced Jeremy. He was holding his gym bag.

"Where's your mother?"

"She dropped me off downstairs. She had to go to a meeting or something."

"Well, I think it's time for practice."

Beaming, Jeremy said, "I can't wait."

Elliot and Jeremy took the elevator to the first floor, left the building, and got into the car.

On their way to practice Jeremy said, "Mom told me to tell you two things."

"And they are?"

"One is to take your watch to the jewelry store."

"OK."

"Don't forget."

"I won't. What's the second thing?"

"Um…I forgot."

"Maybe you'll remember it later."

"I'll try."

Elliot glanced at his wrist, which felt weightless without his watch. He turned into a strip mall and parked at a sports store. He and Jeremy went down one aisle after another picking out all the equipment they needed. Then they drove to Jeremy's school.

The head coach, a young anorexic-looking man with a goatee, divided up the boys, the offensive players with him, and the defensive players, including Jeremy, with Elliot. At the far end of the gym, the boys formed two lines behind Elliot, who started them out with dribbling and passing drills. Within the first few minutes he could already determine who were the more athletic and coordinated boys, and Jeremy was not among them. He picked two of the more skilled players and told them to demonstrate to the others the proper technique of trapping the ball. Since their attention spans wandered every couple of minutes, Elliot would blow his whistle and change drills to keep them interested. Jeremy laughed as his father excitedly went around and high-fived every kid on the team.

# 26

Polita entered the main doors of the Miami-Dade County police station and approached a large Plexiglas window behind which a female security guard was sitting at a desk.

"I'm here to see Detective Hawkins," Polita said.

"Your name?" the guard said.

"Polita Flores."

"Step over there."

The guard motioned for Polita to enter a checkpoint. Another guard then told her what to do, and she obeyed, taking off her boots and placing them and her handbag in trays on a conveyor belt. While her items passed through a scanner, she was searched from head to toe by the security guard. She stepped forward, grabbed her handbag, put her boots back on, and sat in one of the several dozen or so vinyl chairs in a crowded waiting room. A custodian rolled a mop-bucket to an area near Polita where someone had urinated on the floor.

Five minutes later, the security guard behind the Plexiglas summoned Polita to stand next to a locked door. A buzzer sounded, the door opened, and Detective Hawkins appeared. His glance indicated disapproval of her attire. She wore stone-washed, skin-tight recycled jeans with raveled edges and rips, which partially revealed one of her ass cheeks. A braless camisole and the jeans tucked into paratrooper boots completed the ensemble.

"Follow me," he said.

On their way down a cinderblock, windowless, brightly fluorescent-lit hallway, Polita stopped at a soft drink machine and deposited a dollar bill into the changer. Across from the machine, several police officers stopped talking and watched as Polita leaned over to get her drink. They smirked as she twisted off the top of a Diet Coke and took several sips. Frowning, Detective Hawkins waited.

Her long hair swung back and forth as she followed Detective Hawkins down another cinderblock hallway, passing offices obscured by Venetian blinds. She followed him through a bustling crowd of police officers and manacled prisoners. They continued on under more harsh fluorescent lights and into yet another windowless slab of concrete. She felt as though she were in a bunker. Finally, they entered an interrogation room with a wooden table and three metal chairs. Windowless concrete walls surrounded a tile floor. A female police officer in her late-twenties entered the room and closed the door. She spoke to the detective while placing a tape recorder and three bottles of water on the table.

"Officer Rojas will be sitting in on our discussion," Detective Hawkins said, turning on the tape recorder.

Officer Rojas stared straight at Polita and said nothing. The three of them sat at the table, Officer Rojas and the detective across from Polita.

"I'm sure Carmen's murder has been very hard on you and Kim," Detective Hawkins said. "Did you make it through the funeral all right?"

"It was the first funeral I've been to where someone I knew was murdered."

Detective Hawkins nodded. He leaned back in his chair and glanced through a folder. His badge was pinned against his shirt pocket, his white long-sleeved shirt was rolled up to his elbows, and his tie was loosely knotted. His clothes looked slept in. Polita knew that his relaxed demeanor was a tactic to disarm her.

"Before I ask you some questions about Carmen," Detective Hawkins said, "why don't you first tell me a little about yourself."

"Like what?"

"Start from the beginning."

"There's not much to talk about."

"Everyone's got a story."

"Well, I was born in Miami. When I was in first grade, my family moved to Tampa. After I graduated from high school, I worked at different jobs."

"Such as?"

"I was a waitress and a florist. Then I got a job as a secretary at a travel agency. I also took some college courses."

"Where?"

"Tampa Community College."

"Did you graduate?"

"I need about fifteen more hours for my A.A. I plan to go back. I had a 3.2 GPA."

"How'd you end up back down here?"

"I wanted to get away from home, to live somewhere different."

"How long have you been a stripper?"

She paused for a moment. The detective waited for her to answer his question. His domed forehead shone under the fluorescent light. The female officer looked at the detective with calm regard.

"With the economy and all, I was making next to nothing at my other jobs," Polita said. "So I became an exotic dancer at the Gold Coast Lounge. I quit after about four months. The owner there was a creep. I've been at Café Sinsations for almost a year."

"That was where you met Carmen?"

"Yeah. Her locker was next to mine."

"You were friends?"

"Kind of. I mean, we did some things together. But we were, like, never really close. Carmen was the loner type."

"What kind of things did you and Carmen do together?"

"Well, like I said, I saw her at the café a lot because our lockers were next to each other. We went to some parties together, and to some baseball games."

"Was Kim good friends with Carmen?"

"They were roommates for a while. Kim probably knew her better than anyone."

"Was Kim with Carmen the night she was murdered?"

"They worked the same shift that day."

"You and Carmen were at the Luxuria the night she was murdered, is that correct?" Detective Hawkins glanced at his notes.

"We went to a party there."

"How'd you know about the party?"

"Some businessman invited Carmen."

"Who?"

"She didn't tell me."

"Do you know a man by the name of Charles – or Charlie - Lampron?"

"Never heard of him."

"He used to be a regular at the café. He always requested Carmen to dance for him. Tipped her big bucks. He also owns a yacht that was docked at the hotel that night. It was one of the party boats."

"Like I said, I never heard the name."

The detective and the police officer glanced at each other. Officer Rojas observed the detective more than Polita; square-shouldered, she sat with extraordinary posture and composure. She had dark hair, a round face, and the hard, inquisitive eyes of a seasoned cop. Her revolver and other hardware on her belt made her appear thick-waisted.

Detective Hawkins leaned over the table and hunched up his shoulders as if he were ready to pounce. He looked neckless. For the first time he regarded Polita gravely, and his sudden intensity made her uneasy. She sipped her soft drink. The three bottles of water remained unopened.

"Am I supposed to have a lawyer?" Polita said. She touched one of her dangle earrings.

"I'm gonna be upfront with you, Miss Flores, because I expect the same," Detective Hawkins said, looking Polita straight in the eye. "Can we agree on that?"

"I'm being upfront with you."

"I told both Dante and Kim that if they cooperate with me then I might - just might - give them a break or two. You've never been to jail before, but that's where you're fixin' to go if you think you can sit there and lie to me." The detective's voice turned deep and forceful. He dropped all pretense of courtesy. "I found out about the prostitution ring – this so-called escort service - that you and Kim and Carmen were involved in. But for now, I'm not that interested in all the illegal things that your little gang did together." He paused dramatically. "I'm in homicide. I want to find out who murdered Carmen. I've got four detectives on my team and we're workin' on nine homicides. This city has about one murder a day. That's a lot of murders to work on. That's a lot of long hours me and the detectives have to put in. We're stretched awfully thin. So don't try my patience, because I've got very little of that to go around. I don't have time to play games with you and your gang of thieves."

Polita and Detective Hawkins stared at each other. Somber and erect, Officer Rojas glanced at each of them. After a while Polita finally looked away from the detective. A fluorescent haze descended over her.

"We're gonna level with each other, right?" Detective Hawkins said. "If not, go hire yourself a lawyer because you're gonna need one. A damn good one." He gave another dramatic pause. "You'd better pay good attention, because I'm not gonna repeat myself – there's almost too many charges to read off. I've got them all written down in case your lawyer wants to have a look. I could have you arrested on suspicion of menacing, for second-degree assault and criminal mischief. Not to mention for the obvious charge for prostitution. For credit card theft. For fraudulent use of credit cards. For grand theft. For strong-armed robbery. For - "

"Strong-armed robbery? I never used a gun. And I - "

"Doesn't matter. By slippin' knockout drops in your johns' drinks you were using force. Your victims were in no position to defend themselves. But let's save that for later, Miss Flores. I had a number of reasons why I brought up Mr. Lampron's party boat."

"I told you I don't know who he is."

"All right. Say you're telling me the truth."

"I am." Unnerved by the detective's accusations, Polita had forgotten about the drink in her hand and almost spilled it. She set the drink on the table. "I never heard of a Mr. Lamp..."

"Lampron. Mr. Charles Lampron got back from the Bahamas today. He heard about Carmen's murder. He also found Carmen's handbag on his boat and returned it to us. In her handbag were some of Carmen's things." The detective took a small black book from his folder and held it up for Polita to see. "Are you familiar with this book?"

"I don't think so. Carmen was always texting on her cell or flipping through little books like that. She never let anyone look through them, at least not me."

"This was Carmen's appointment book. Or, as we cops call it, a trick book. You have one, I'm sure."

"I swear I don't. Carmen set up everything."

"Hmm. Well, Carmen documented everything about her johns. Their names. The places where she met them. The dates and the times. In fact, Carmen was even more sophisticated than keepin' just a little old trick book. Hell, she kept her escort service on her laptop. She had her own website. This woman brought the world's oldest profession - your profession too, Miss. Flores - into the Information Age." The detective handed the book to Polita. "I want you to look through it. Go ahead. Your initials are in it three times. I think I counted five or six of Kim's. The last entry Carmen made had you in it. What I find fascinatin' about that little book is that it reads kind of like a diary. I've already talked to Kim and Dante about it. Kim's not saying a whole lot right now, but Dante is. He's been cooperating by interpreting the different codes that Carmen used."

"I don't understand any of this." She glanced through the book.

"Here, I'll be more than happy to help you. The asterisk next to each name means a hit. A hit, Miss Flores, means that knockout drops were used and that credit cards, jewelry, and money were taken. Each stolen item has its own initial. A double asterisk means a Rolex was stolen. And so on. It's not very complicated. Are you sure you're not familiar with any of those codes? Or am I telling you something you already know?"

"Dante and Carmen ran the operation. This is her handwriting, not mine."

"Dante admitted that this trick book served as an accounting system that he and Carmen used. He admitted that he was the middleman for the Rolexes and for whatever jewelry y'all stole. Am I leaving anything out, Miss Flores? Has Dante been cooperating with me, or has he been wasting my time by lyin' to me? Because if he has, I'll make sure he pays for it by doing a lot of time in prison. Including anyone else who wants to play games with me. Am I clear on that?"

Polita gave a weak nod for an answer.

"Talk to me. Don't nod. This tape recorder can't hear nods."

"I'm not playing games with you."

"I certainly hope not. You see, Miss Flores, I know what you're thinking. You think we're playing games with you."

"I didn't say that."

"But you thought that. You think we're playing the good cop bad cop here. Hell, Officer Rojas and I are both good cops. Ain't no one playin' bad cop in this room. Don't have to. You've watched too many cop shows. I tell it like it is."

"I'm not sure I follow you." Polita was confused. She sensed that the detective was perturbed for some reason, was going off on a rant. She glanced at Officer Rojas, who quietly continued to observe her and the detective.

"I was talking about Dante."

"Oh. OK. I guess I lost you."

"I told you to pay attention."

"I'm trying to." She could hear the hum of the fluorescent lights. "What do you want me to say about Dante?"

"Why don't you answer your own question?"

"Um... I think he'll make sure he turns us in if it means saving his own ass. That's the only reason he's cooperating."

"I kind of figured that. And I suggest you follow his example."

Polita handed the book back to Detective Hawkins.

"Come straight with me, Miss Flores. How many johns did you rip off?"

"What's that got to do with Carmen's murder?"

"How many?"

"Three, like the book said. All of them were with Carmen. I was too nervous to work by myself."

"How about Kim?"

"Probably six or seven, like the book says."

"How many johns did Carmen rip off?"

"I don't know. A dozen. Maybe more."

Detective Hawkins sat back in his chair and smiled broadly. His teeth were a block of grinning white.

"They're all damn knockout artists," Detective Hawkins told Officer Rojas, who only blinked. He chuckled. "Y'all could've opened up your own jewelry store."

A long, wordless moment passed between Polita and Detective Hawkins. For the first time Officer Rojas moved in her chair. She cocked her head slightly toward Polita.

"You were with Carmen the night she was murdered," Detective Hawkins said. "Tell me about that night."

"I was with her at the party."

"That was after you'd stolen the Rolex from -" the detective opened to the last entry in the trick book – "Elliot Anderson, a businessman from Boston."

"After we spent some time with him in his hotel room, we then went down to the marina."

"You sure you never heard Carmen say anything about Mr. Lampron, the owner of the yacht?"

"You keep asking me that."

"It's important for me to develop a time frame of what Carmen did that night."

"She told me she wanted to meet someone, but she never said who. She was supposed to go with someone to the islands. I just wanted to leave the marina."

"What was your hurry?"

"We'd just robbed a man at the hotel."

"That's the answer I wanted to hear." The detective's eyes were still and intent. "I think you're gonna cooperate with me after all. That means we'll find out real soon who killed Carmen. It's just a matter of time. Tell me something, how did you three women decide on which johns to rip off?"

"Carmen didn't want to hit the locals. She targeted tourists and the executive-types at business conventions. Although the last month or so she started to get careless."

"How?"

"I think she started to hit some of the locals. The more she got into drugs, the more desperate she got. She didn't care who she hit."

"Was it drugs that got her into prostitution?"

"It was one of the reasons."

"How about you and Kim? What reasons did you have?"

"You said you were concerned with Carmen's murder."

Detective Hawkins didn't reply. He studied Polita for a long time.

"Look, I was stupid to get involved with Carmen and Kim, and especially Dante," Polita said, her voice wavering a bit. Shamefaced, she looked away from the detective. "Don't get me wrong, I don't blame them for what I've done. It was my decision." She tried to hold her voice even. "You know, I went into this call-girl thing with Carmen and Kim thinking I was above it all. I wanted to be classy. I had rules. Only recreational drugs. Wine or champagne, but no hard liquor or beer. Condoms had to be used. There'd be no rough stuff. Good thing I didn't last long in this business. I would've bored the men with all my rules." Blinking back tears, she added, "Who was I trying to fool? You're looking at a real classy woman, aren't you?"

"Drop the weepy act," Detective Hawkins said. He bored into her with his eyes. "I'm not buying it. You had rules? You tried to be classy? Who you tryin' to fool? You won't get my sympathy. You used strong-armed tactics by poisoning your victims who had dicks for brains. You robbed them of jewelry, credit cards, thousands of dollars. You're a thief. You were in a predatory partnership with two other women – and one of them got murdered. And you'd still be rippin' off johns if your partner in crime hadn't gotten herself killed. You disgust me. I should lock you up right now."

Detective Hawkins's outburst made both Officer Rojas and Polita reposition themselves in their chairs. Officer Rojas was the first to uncap one of the water bottles and take a sip. Detective Hawkins set his glasses on the bridge of his nose and rubbed his washed-out tired eyes with his forefinger. Officer Rojas, sitting as straight as a board, stared directly into Polita's eyes.

"You asked about Carmen," Polita said. "I'll tell you what I know about her. Dancing gave her the opportunity to make more money. And she was an exhibitionist. She craved attention. It gave her a feeling of power. And like I said, I think it was the drugs that made her desperate enough to get involved with Dante. He knew he could use her. And she could use him. They worked real good together. He couldn't depend on Kim or me because we were too scared."

"Why did Carmen start hitting the locals?"

"Her days in Miami were numbered. She talked about moving to other cities. Atlanta. Houston. LA. She rented a furnished apartment, so all she had to do for a quick-get-away was pack her clothes. I don't know if this meant she wanted to take her act to another place, or if she wanted to put her past behind her and start all over. My gut feeling is that she was trying to get away from all the sleaze. She was scared just like me and Kim."

"Scared of who?"

"I don't know. Maybe she was running away from herself. She knew she needed help. She had a certain rage in her. Deep down she hated herself." Through tears, Polita said, "I know, because I'm feeling the same way."

"Spare me the tears. You ever think about becoming an actress? Because you're good. Either that or it sounds like you've been watchin' too much Dr. Phil." Detective Hawkins held up one hand and looked at Officer Rojas. "That was some good acting or psychobabble. Or both." He returned his eyes to Polita. "Don't give me another poor-little-me speech. You should hate yourself for what you three women did." A withering, incongruous silence passed during which he flipped through some papers in the folder without taking his eyes off Polita. "Plus, I don't buy this scared act. You were in complete control of what you were doing. Your victims were helpless. You may as well have put a gun to their heads. Or to their dicks. They were the ones who should've been scared." He paused for another moment, then added, "By the way, whatever happened to Mr. Anderson's watch? This fancy Rolex that I keep hearing so much about?"

"Carmen had it last."

"It was never found in her purse or her handbag. We searched the yacht, the hotel, the marina. The entire area. But no Rolex. Maybe she was robbed herself."

"Who would kill for a watch?"

"It was a Rolex."

"Still."

"You want to know what criminals will kill for?" the detective said. "Officer Rojas and I could tell you. Just last week a teenager was gunned down for his fancy basketball shoes. A panhandler who worked Fourth and Seabreeze was stabbed to death because his corner averaged ten bucks a day more than his killer's."

Polita remembered the panhandler from the other day who had told her to be careful.

Very erect in her chair, Officer Rojas said, "A couple of weeks ago I was at a crime scene where a tourist had his brains blown out for pocket change. The killer was upset because his victim didn't have enough money on him."

Polita focused on the officer's dazzling white teeth as she spoke. The officer resembled Polita in complexion, was a few years older, and was probably Cuban-American.

"The night after Carmen was murdered two fast-food workers were shot for less than a hundred bucks," Detective Hawkins said. "One of them died, a high-school kid. That's what we deal with on a daily basis, Miss Flores." He narrowed his eyes at her. "So you tell me. Do you think someone could kill for a Rolex?"

Another weak nod for an answer.

"I didn't hear you," Detective Hawkins said, moving the tape recorder closer to Polita. "You're gonna have to speak up."

"I guess so."

Detective Hawkins grew impatient with Polita's hair-tossing, her sighs, her bored expression.

"You still payin' attention?" the detective said.

"Yes, sir."

"Seems like you've got something else on your mind. Maybe you find me and Officer Rojas boring."

"No, sir, I don't."

"How much cash did Carmen have on her?"

"At least four-hundred dollars."

"That's how much you took out of Mr. Anderson's wallet?"

"I don't remember the exact amount."

"Any credit cards?"

"No."

"Why? You stole them on your other johns."

"This one made me nervous. I kept dropping his wallet."

"What made you nervous? Sounds like you were becoming a real pro at this. I bet rippin' off johns was second nature for a knockout artist like yourself."

"Carmen started to freak me out when she couldn't get his watch off. She was scaring me."

"Scaring you? But you were the other thief. I'd think the one who should've been scared was this Mr. Anderson."

"She broke a bottle and threatened to cut him. I didn't want anyone to get hurt."

"Didn't you drug him? Wasn't he immobilized?"

"Yeah, we drugged him. But he kept trying to move. And Carmen was acting crazy. That's another reason why I wanted to get away from her that night. We went to the marina for a little while, then I split after she gave me half the money. She kept the Rolex to give to Dante."

"She didn't give you the Rolex?"

"No."

"I'm curious. Why do you think Carmen included you and Kim in this escort service? She could've kept all the business to herself and Dante, if she even needed him."

"I've wondered about that myself. But I guess an escort service means more than just one call girl. Part of me thinks she got us involved to cover for her. If we got caught, she had plans for an escape."

The detective studied the trick book for a while. Officer Rojas gazed at her hands in her lap.

"I'm sure every john in this book would like to've gotten his hands on Carmen," Detective Hawkins said. "And on you and Kim." He tapped his fingers on the book for a while. "What other enemies did Carmen have?"

"I don't know if she had any enemies, besides the ones in that book."

"No jilted ex-boyfriends?"

"Carmen? Boyfriends? She was a call girl. She wasn't the touchy-feely type."

"Did any customer at the café show any special interest in her?"

"She was probably the most popular dancer. A lot of men requested her."

"That's what most people have been telling me. Did she ever complain about any of the employees at the café?"

"Not that I know of."

"No problems with the bouncers, bartenders, deejays?"

"I don't think so."

"Did any dancers show signs of jealousy because of Carmen's popularity?"

"I heard some gossip, but it was mostly women talking. Nothing serious."

"How about you? Were you jealous of her?"

"For all I cared, she could've had the spotlight on herself."

"In my line of work I've seen women turn on their female friends with such viciousness it's scary, even worse than when men turn on each other."

Detective Hawkins glanced at Officer Rojas, who gave him a slight nod.

"You said she was once roommates with Kim," the detective continued, looking again at Polita. "Did something happen to separate them? Did Kim have anything against Carmen?"

"Kim once suspected Carmen was fooling around with Dante. Exchanging sex for drugs, that sort of thing. But I think Kim got over it."

"Her trick book indicates that she used the Luxuria to meet most of her johns. Did she ever mention anything to you about any of the employees there?"

Polita thought of the bellhop's face blending with the darkness in the parking lot.

Detective Hawkins repeated his question, "Did Carmen mention anything about any of the employees at the hotel?"

"I don't think so."

"You never saw her talk to any of the employees? She must've had a contact there."

"I never saw her talk to anyone."

Detective Hawkins paused for a moment. His fingers tapped on the trick book. Polita could feel Officer Rojas' eyes on her. The detective uncapped a bottle of water and took a few sips.

"Was there anyone at Carmen's funeral you were surprised to see?" Detective Hawkins said.

"No, not really."

"Do you know Carmen's father?"

"No. But I've seen him twice. Once at the café and then at the funeral."

"Some of the employees I interviewed at the café said that Carmen's father came in one night and threatened her."

"I was there when it happened. It was an angry father coming to rescue his troubled daughter. My mother almost did the same thing to me."

"Were you surprised to see Dante at the funeral?"

"No. He only showed up because he felt he had to. I thought Ramón, his friend, would've been there. But Ramón doesn't have much to do with anyone."

"I've talked to Ramón too. He knows he's in big trouble with me. He comes across as slow-witted."

"Don't let him fool you. He's smarter than he acts."

"I hope I don't let any of you fool me." Detective Hawkins paused to see what affect his comment had on Polita. She glanced at the table. "This Dante and Ramón, they've been in trouble with the law since they were in middle school. They're ex-gangbangers with a rap sheet a mile long. Was Carmen afraid of them?"

"Probably."

"You think Dante is dangerous?"

"I think all men are dangerous."

Detective Hawkins took off his glasses and massaged the bridge of his nose with his thumb and forefinger. His red-veined eyes gazed at Polita for some time. He placed his glasses back on.

"Dante thinks you robbed Carmen," he said.

"I'm sure he also told you that I killed her."

"He mentioned it, yeah. Did you?"

"No, I didn't."

Detective Hawkins took his time by uncapping a small white plastic container, took out what looked like two diabetic pills, put them in his mouth, and sipped some water.

"The two bouncers at the café, Allen and Seth, how did they get along with Carmen?" he said.

"They got along OK."

"Was she involved with either one of them?" He checked his notes.

"She and Allen went out a few times. But Carmen wasn't serious with any one man. I guess that's obvious."

"Allen didn't work the night Carmen was murdered. Seth worked but got off early."

"Am I supposed to say something about that?"

"It's something to think about." Detective Hawkins turned a page in the folder and read for a minute or two. "It says here that Allen is nicknamed 'Alien.' Why's that?"

"It's a harmless nickname, and I guess Alien sounds a little like Allen. He acts kind of crazy at times, or used to. He was into steroids at one time, so maybe that explains it."

"Steroids supposedly induce rage in some users. You ever see him lose his temper?"

"Not really. I've seen him deal with some drunks, but he always handled himself OK. Miss Wanda would fire any bouncer who tried to bully any of the customers."

"Don't you think it's a little unusual for Allen, in his late thirties, to work at a strip joint? That's his only job. At least Seth's a full-time student."

"For a lot of us who work at the café – dancers, bartenders, bouncers – that's the best we can do right now. Some of the employees at the café have good educations, though. One of our bartenders is a laid-off engineer. One of the dancers lost her job as a sales rep who went to some fancy college."

"Makes me happy to hear how good y'all are doin' at a strip joint."

"Most of us are just trying to get by."

"A lot of people are struggling, Miss Flores, but they don't work at strip joints. And they damn sure don't turn to crime."

Polita shrugged.

Detective Hawkins read from a folder. "Says here that Allen was once arrested for felonious assault and resisting arrest. He was also arrested for aggravated stalking."

"What can I say? He's always been nice to me. I guess we all make mistakes."

"Did Carmen get along with the owners of the café?"

"I don't think she had any problems with Miss Wanda or with Mark. You couldn't ask for a nicer boss than Miss Wanda. Some of us would get upset with Mark when he wouldn't always give us enough hours. But as far as working for them, I never heard of too many complaints. Most topless lounges rip you off by making you buy from them, everything from stockings to costumes at high prices. But the café doesn't do that. They treat their dancers real fair."

Detective Hawkins gathered up his loose papers and the trick book and put them in another folder.

"I'm in a little bit of a dilemma," he said, more to Officer Rojas than to Polita. Then, after another pause, he placed his handcuffs on the table and looked directly at Polita. "Do I put you in jail now, or do I wait? I may end up with egg on my face, but I think you'll help me more with my investigation if you're out on the street than sittin' in jail. It's all about cooperation. If you're an asset to my investigation, I'll try to keep you out of jail – for the time being. I'll never promise anything in exchange for your help. But let's just say I can be more lenient. None of your charges will be swept under the rug.

That ain't never gonna happen. Ultimately, you're gonna have to face up to what you did."

"I know that."

"You keep working with me on this, and we'll be doing each other a big favor." Detective Hawkins' voice was stern and unequivocal. "You're on the hot seat, Miss Flores. I can arrest you anytime I want to. Don't forget that."

"I understand."

"I hope you do. I don't want you going anywhere. No trips out of Florida. No disappearing acts. I want you to call me every day. Once in the morning, once in the evening. You follow me?"

"Yes, sir."

"If you forget, I'll come lookin' for you. Remember, I don't want egg on my face. You gonna make me look good by cooperating, aren't you?"

"I'll try."

"You'll have to do better than try."

"I'll help you the best I can."

"By helping me you'll be helping yourself." He paused. "Of course, I can't rule you completely out as a murder suspect."

"I understand that."

"If I need some information on Dante, would you be interested in wearing a wire?"

"Yeah. Sure."

"One other thing. Next time you come in here I want you dressed like a young lady. I don't want you wearing something that shows half your ass. And no hooker heels. I want you to treat this room here like you're in my office, and no one comes into my office lookin' like that. We're gonna change your ways, aren't we?"

Polita nodded.

"Remember what I said about noddin'?"

"I'll do whatever you say."

"Good. Next time I see you, I want you to look like you're going for a job interview at some respectable business. If you come in looking like this again, I'll have you wearing an orange jumpsuit and shackles. And I don't want to hear any excuses about how bad the economy is and how you can't find a job. There're plenty of good folks out there looking for work. And I want you standing in line with them with an application in hand. Understand?"

"Does it even matter?"

"Does what matter?"

"I mean, I'm going to jail. Who'll hire a felon?"

"You planning on doing life?"

"No. But…"

"You'll have to get out of jail sometime. Besides, it'll take months, maybe over a year, before you go to trial. I take it you've got bills to pay."

"Of course."

"Then find a job. Any respectable job will do. That might impress a judge. And another thing. Don't come in here trying to put on this tough act. Change that attitude of yours, or I'll send you home. Or to jail. You and Kim and the rest of your gang did a lot of damage in this city. I'll make sure you pay for it if you do me wrong. Understand?"

"I plan to cooperate with you."

"We'll continue this conversation some other time." He handed Polita his calling card.

"You gave me your card at Carmen's funeral."

"Then have two, just in case you lose one. I don't want to hear any excuses why you didn't call me."

Detective Hawkins collected his handcuffs off the table and walked out of the room.

Polita looked at Officer Rojas. "Is it OK to leave now?"

"We don't have you in custody yet."

"So that means I can go?"

Officer Rojas nodded while checking something on the tape recorder. Polita slid her chair up to the table and left the room.

# 27

Elliot was in the kitchen and ready to leave for work when his cell phone rang.

"I tried your office but your secretary said you wouldn't be in until after ten," Wink said.

"I prefer you call my cell."

"Sure. What's up?"

"I have to take Jeremy to get a physical. Then I'll drop him off at a friend's house for an hour or two."

"Is Karen home?"

"She had a meeting in New York and won't be back until tonight."

"Well, things are really heating up down here."

"I hope you're talking about the weather."

"We still have a heat wave hanging over us. This is only April and it's humid as hell."

"I know you didn't call to give me the weather report. How did it go with the detective?"

"It was a quite an eye-opener. It turns out that Carmen and a couple of dancers at the café ran an escort service. The detective even showed me Carmen's trick book."

"Trick book?"

"You have lived a sheltered life, Elliot. Some call girls keep a trick book with their johns' names. You do know what a john is?"

"Of course I know what a john is. Was my name in her book?"

"The very last one. What's worse, there was a story in *The Miami Herald* about the book. Front page."

"Was my name in the paper?" Elliot breathed into the phone.

"No johns were, but the three women - Carmen, Polita and Kim – had their names all over the place. And once the local tabloids get their hands on this trick book, they'll have a field day. It'll be a massacre. Rumor has it that there are some local celebrities in it, the usual that show up on things like this - professional athletes, political and business bigwigs, maybe even a high-profile minister. Your guess is as good as mine. I know one thing: Dave's a nervous wreck over this. He's supposed to see the same detective today."

"Why does he have to see a detective?"

"It so happens that his name was in the trick book."

"It was? Then he lied to me. He said he was never with her." Elliot called out to Jeremy in the hallway, "Son, make sure you brush your teeth."

"He told me he arranged to have sex with Carmen a week before you came down. But an emergency came up, so he canceled his appointment. After that happened, he got cold feet and never followed through with it. Nevertheless, Carmen left his name in her book."

"Did the detective say anything about the Rolex or the DVD?"

"He was tight-lipped about a lot of things. Most of his questions had to do about my visits to the café."

"Did he ask anything about me?"

"Get a load of this," Wink said, ignoring Elliot's question. "Carmen wrote next to each name in her book where the trick was performed, the time, date, and the kind of sex each john preferred, even though she seldom if ever fucked one. She even kept their business cards filed in the back of the book."

"Did she have mine?"

"Both yours and Dave's. She was quite a businesswoman."

"Don't kick the ball in the house," Elliot told Jeremy as he watched him play with a soccer ball in the hallway. He gripped the cell phone tightly.

"Guess what the *Herald* calls Carmen and her friends?"

"What?"

"Guess."

"Damn, Wink. I can't even think straight right now. Just tell me."

"They're called 'The Rolex Bandits.'"

"How fucking cute."

"They stole over a dozen Rolexes among them, so you don't have to feel alone any more. Their methods were the same as they used on you. They'd drug their johns, then take whatever they could get their hands on. Carmen had me fooled, the little whore. She put up a good front. She damn sure made me feel like an ignoramus."

"You make it sound as though she were a naive schoolgirl. She worked at a strip joint, for christsake. You knew she turned tricks; that's why you introduced her to me."

"Oh, I knew she was a shrewd one. And I knew she would fuck a customer or two if the price was right. But I never knew she ran a call-girl racket that ripped off her johns. She ran quite a sophisticated operation."

"I wonder why I haven't heard from the police."

"You will."

"I will? Do you think the same detective will come up here to see me?"

"I'm sure someone will contact you, since your name is in the trick book. The detective asked me about you and Dave. I tried to keep the heat off you guys. I told him I'm the one who got you involved in all this."

Elliot told Jeremy again to put the ball down and to brush his teeth.

"The detective who questioned me was relentless," Wink said. "He's an older black guy. With all the black-on-black crime, I suppose it makes sense to have more black homicide detectives. I don't think he gives a damn about Carmen's murder, unless it involves someone who's prominent in the community."

"What should I say if I'm contacted about my name being in that damn book?"

"My best advice is to keep quiet and hire an attorney to handle everything for you."

"Then he'll really think I'm hiding something."

"Who cares what he thinks? If he tries to talk to you, just ignore him. Don't give him a chance to confuse you."

"How would he confuse me?" Elliot watched as Jeremy walked past the bathroom for the third time without going inside. He said sternly, "Son, I'm not going to tell you again to brush your goddamn teeth." Then he spoke into the phone again. "I'm back. Jeremy interrupted me. What did you say?"

"I was going to ask about your wrists."

"They're still scratched a little."

"There you go. A detective might want to look at them. He could come right out and ask you, or he could sneak a look. We both know that she scratched you while trying to unsnap your watch."

Wink abruptly stopped talking.

"What's wrong?" Elliot said, alarmed by the sudden silence.

"Ah…Nothing."

"Why are you so quiet?"

"I was just wandering about what a detective might say about your scratched wrists."

"I'll have to tell him how my skin really got under her fingernails."

"Don't ever mention *anything* about your wrists. If you do, then the detective can probably get a warrant for a DNA test, and you don't want to mess with that. Since you were Carmen's last john, I wouldn't doubt if the cops have already combed your room at the hotel for any hairs that they could use in their lab work."

"Do you think the cops were in my hotel room?"

"I'm pretty sure that was probably the last room she was in before she was murdered."

Elliot thought for a moment. "She was underwater for quite a while. I wonder if that would make it hard to determine the DNA of my skin under her nails."

"Either you or Dave asked me a similar question about fingerprints on a golf club that was underwater. I don't know. I'm not a lab technician."

"I guess none of it really matters."

"All this is going to blow over." Wink sounded so confident, so smooth. He even laughed a little.

"You said things would get better when I was at the hotel. But it keeps getting more complicated."

"In a way, I think the trick book works in your favor."

"How? I was the last name in it. I was the last – I hate the word 'john' - to see her alive."

"I realize that. But there were other people who saw her after she left your room, like her partner. This Polita...the more I think about her involvement in all of this...She's beginning to scare the bejeesus out of me."

"But I told you, she tried to help me when I thought I was having a heart attack."

"I doubt she helped you out of any kind of mercy. She knew if you died of a heart attack during the robbery, she would've been charged with murder. She was covering her own ass, not trying to save yours."

Elliot remembered Polita pressing the warm washcloth against his forehead.

"There were other witnesses who saw Carmen at the marina," Wink said. "So you weren't the last person to see her."

For a moment Elliot imagined that he was back at the hotel and could hear the waves lapping against the seawall, could smell the flower-filled gardens.

"Are you positive that you and Dave didn't see her at the marina?" Elliot said.

"We didn't, but others did."

"How do you know that Dave didn't return to the marina when you weren't around?"

"He told me he didn't."

"He could be lying. I'm not sure if I can trust him. And here I am about to do a major business deal with him."

"Come on, El. The three of us have got to work together on this. That's the first tactic the cops will try to use on us if we let them, to divide us. Dave's in a bind, so you've got to cut him some slack."

"*He's* in a bind? How about me?" Elliot thought for a moment. "I wish I'd been somewhere in the middle of her trick book. At least my name would've been more hidden. Being the last one makes my name stand out in bold letters."

"Look at it from the positive side."

"You can find something positive in all this?"

Jeremy finished brushing his teeth and stood next to Elliot, pouting because his father had yelled at him. Elliot wiped Jeremy's running nose, said he was sorry he had raised his voice, and told him to wait for him in the living room.

"If there was no trick book," Wink said, "then you would be standing out by yourself. But now the detective has to work with more johns. More motives. You can bet he's checking out every name in that book. He'll probably play hardball with all of them. All he has to do to get them to talk is say he'll leak their names to the media."

"What you're telling me is misery loves company."

"Exactly. Just ask Dave. He's worried sick that he'll have to go through the entire humiliation again."

"I still get this terribly lonely feeling that I'm all by myself."

A silence fell between them. In the long pause, Elliot watched as Jeremy approached him. Jeremy's eyes had welled up with tears.

"Son, I need you to wait for me in the living room," Elliot said. "I'm having a very important conversation. I love you. I didn't mean to yell at you. Run along now. I won't be long."

Jeremy returned to the living room.

"I'm back," Elliot said. "Jeremy has been driving me crazy."

"I told you when you were at the hotel that I'll see you through this to the end. You know you can count on me. I'll keep in touch. Remember the two things I told you: don't say a word to anyone, and hire an attorney."

"That's comforting to hear."

"Don't let a detective intimidate you." Wink paused for a moment. "When you think about it, detectives don't want the public to know this, but most murders go unsolved, especially when they involve prostitutes and transients. We talked about that at the hotel. Now the detective I dealt with, he comes across as a tough, no-nonsense type, but I'm not sure if you'll have to deal with him or with someone up there. Just be careful."

"Thanks for the advice."

"By the way, Dave gives his regards. He wants you to call him. He's waiting on your decision about the merger."

"I like his business model, but I'm not so sure I like dealing with him."

"Don't let his personal shortcomings interfere with your business decision. You're both decent men who got caught up in a little mischief."

They hung up. Elliot went into the living room and told Jeremy he was ready to leave. Jeremy was talking about soccer, but Elliot was too preoccupied and went into the garage without hearing a word his son was saying.

# 28

Polita arrived at the café through the rear door. Several dancers passed her in the hallway without speaking to her. As she opened the door to the dressing room, Mark stepped out of the office and approached her.

"Polita, the boss sent me to get you," Mark said.

"OK." Polita adjusted the handbag on her shoulder and followed him down the narrow hallway. Dim, flickering fluorescent lights cast shadows across their faces. When they entered Miss Wanda's office, they found her behind her desk, talking on the phone and making notations on a legal pad. Polita and Mark sat on the sofa. Mark, his hands folded primly, looked down critically at his fingernails. After a serious conversation that lasted another minute or two, Miss Wanda hung up and glanced first at Mark, then at Polita. Polita noticed that her picture, along with Kim's and Carmen's, had been removed from the wall.

"Polita, I called you in here because I'm going to have to let you go," Miss Wanda said. Her voice was deep and hoarse. She looked more sad than stern.

"I came in tonight knowing you had to fire me," Polita said.

"For the past couple of days this place has been swarming with cops and reporters." Miss Wanda tapped her long fingernails on a newspaper on her desk. "The story about you and Carmen and Kim has really hurt the café."

"I feel bad that I've done this to you. You're the best boss I've ever worked for."

"The public now thinks that the café is the hub for a drug and prostitution ring. I should've fired Carmen three months ago. I knew she was having problems, but against my better judgment I kept giving her more chances. Maybe one reason I didn't fire her was because she was good for business. But every dancer knows my rules: Drugs or prostitution will cost you your job. I've been in this business for a long time, as both a dancer and an owner, and I know the temptations."

"I made some stupid mistakes."

"As you know, my dancers can make a decent living without resorting to anything illegal. Some of my dancers are mothers, college students, secretaries, saleswomen - they come from all walks of life. I try to run one of the best lounges in Miami. Although the café has a pretty solid reputation, I still have to deal with some bad press from time to time. What we do here isn't for everyone, but for those who enjoy tasteful adult entertainment, the café has something to offer. That's why you see a lot of professional men here. But once a place like ours is associated with drugs and prostitution..."

"I don't think Polita needs to hear a lecture," Mark said.

Miss Wanda's eyes locked on his in a cold glare.

"I mean," Mark tried to explain, "Polita has been through a lot the past week. She needs to hear some advice, some encouragement, not..."

Miss Wanda stared Mark to silence. He grew restless and groomed his thin mustache with the tips of his fingers. His always manicured hands, Polita noticed, were raw-looking and his fingernails were chewed and blistered.

"I really appreciate what you've done for me," Polita told Miss Wanda. "I blew it. I made pretty good money, and you were always very fair."

Miss Wanda was still staring at Mark, whose face had hardened into an expression of contempt as he returned her stare.

"I want to ask you something, Polita," Miss Wanda said. She took her eyes off Mark. "I'm letting you go but I'm not throwing you to the wolves. I'm concerned about your safety. And even though Kim has already quit, I'm also still concerned about her. I asked Kim, and now I'll ask you. Have you ever felt threatened, in any way, by one of our customers? If so, I want to know and I'll point him out to the cops. In this kind of business, there's always going to be some weirdo who'll try to harass the dancers."

"I can't think of any customer who's ever threatened me."

"Kim said that no one stood out in her mind. I'm also aware of her boyfriend, this Dante. The detective told me he's bad news."

"He's a pissant. I keep my distance from him."

"Kim also told me that your apartment was broken into."

"Several apartments have been broken into where I live."

"But yours happened the day after Carmen was murdered."

"I'm sure it has nothing to do with Carmen. I'm moving to a new apartment tomorrow, anyway."

Miss Wanda's eyes were full of soft light. Polita glanced at Mark, who continued to glare at Miss Wanda.

"Hon, I'm not mad at you," Miss Wanda said. "I'm disappointed in what you did. When I was your age, I did some very foolish things, too. I'll miss the three of you. I got too close to Carmen. She was special, for a while at least. She was one of the most popular dancers who ever worked here." Miss Wanda dropped her eyes for a moment, swallowed hard, and then looked back up. "I've told you I've been in this business for a long time, longer than I'd care to admit. I've seen bad things happen to some of my dancers. I hope you and Kim have got enough sense to do something better with your lives."

"This is probably it for me. I'm sick of the noise, the smell of cigarettes and booze. I'm sick of the sound of guys laughing." Polita stood up. "I'll clean my locker out now."

"You and Kim have some tough times ahead because of this Rolex thing, but if you cooperate with this detective's investigation, I really think you'll get a break or two." Miss Wanda's voice was warm and reassuring. "If there's anything I can do to help, let me know. I wish you the best."

Polita thanked her and walked out of her office. She entered the dressing room where Michelle was standing next to Polita's locker and attaching press-on tattoos to various parts of her body.

"One of the dancers told me you were in Miss Wanda's office," Michelle said. "Is everything all right?"

"I've been fired. I'm sure every dancer is happy to hear that."

"I'm not."

Polita started to unlock her locker but found that it was already open. She assumed she had forgotten to lock it the day before.

"Kim told me you were moving," Michelle said.

Polita was preoccupied with looking through her things. Nothing had been stolen.

"Have you found a place yet?" Michelle said.

"I've already put a deposit down for a one bedroom at Ocean Way Apartments."

"I know where that's at. I live a few blocks from there."

Polita took her things from the locker and stuffed them into her handbag.

Michelle said, "Would it be OK if I drop by to see you? We'll be living so close to each other."

"Sure. Come over whenever you feel like it."

Polita finished cleaning out her locker, said good night to Michelle, and left the dressing room. Mark, rubbing his hands with moisturizing lotion, was waiting across the hallway.

"I wanted to talk to you when you were in Miss Wanda's office," Mark said, "but the boss wouldn't let me." For a few seconds he stared down the hallway at Miss Wanda's office door. "What are you going to do for an income?"

"I'll look for a waitress job or maybe work at a florist shop. I'll find something. Of course, it won't help when I end up with a felony or two next to my name."

"I'll ask around. I have some contacts. Do you need any money?"

"I pretty much live paycheck to paycheck. I'll be all right for a while.'"

"I wish you'd let me help you. I don't want you to leave with hard feelings.''

"You're the ones who should be mad at me."

"I'm upset with Carmen. She went around here thinking she was above everyone else, but you and Kim were different." He pulled a paper clip of money out of his pocket and counted five one-hundred dollar bills. He glanced at Miss Wanda's office door, then folded the bills and squeezed them into Polita's hand. "Here. I want you to take this. It's not much, but I can get you plenty more."

"I can't take this."

"Consider it severance pay. Please, take it. But don't tell anyone, especially the boss. Maybe one day you can return the favor."

Polita pocketed the money. She was about to thank Mark when Miss Wanda stepped out of the office.

"I've sent for Allen to walk you out to your car," Miss Wanda said. She ignored Mark. "Please take care of yourself, Polita. Don't be surprised if you and Kim start getting hounded by newspaper and TV reporters. I've got one in my office now."

Mark waited until Miss Wanda closed her door. He acted nervous. His eyes glanced back and forth from the office door to Polita.

"I don't think she saw you," Polita said. "Why don't you take it back? I don't want to get you into any trouble."

"It's my money, not hers." Mark seemed to pout. "This place is almost mine anyway. In another year it will be; you wait and see."

Allen appeared in the hallway. He started to approach Polita but stopped when he saw Mark.

"I can escort you to your car," Mark said.

"You're busy," she said. "Let Allen do it."

"I'll keep in touch with you," Mark said. Then he walked past Allen in the hallway.

Allen opened the rear door for Polita. He was quiet and distracted.

"You don't have to walk me out to my car," Polita said. "I was just fired anyway, so I've lost that privilege."

"Miss Wanda asked me to. She's worried about you."

It was the first time that Allen had acted cold to her. They walked outside. The neon-lighted parking lot revealed a man leaning back against his car. He was either urinating or masturbating. He noticed Allen and zipped up his pants.

"Get the hell out of here!" Allen yelled as the man walked away. "I'm tired of this place and all the perverts who come here."

"You're mad at me, aren't you?" Polita said. She stopped in the parking lot and held her handbag before her.

"What makes you say that?"

"Because of the silent treatment you're giving me."

"I didn't know what was going on till I heard about y'all on the news. It shocked me to think that y'all did that kind of stuff."

"Yeah. Well, we did. What can I say?"

"It makes me want to hate Carmen."

"If you hate her, then you must hate me too."

"I didn't know Carmen had this... evil side."

"You think I'm evil?"

"I didn't say that. Y'all did some bad things."

Polita abruptly turned away and opened her car door. Allen stopped her by grabbing her arm.

"Let go of me," she said.

"I didn't mean to grab you that hard." He released her arm. "Don't leave mad. I've just been in a real bad mood because of what's been going on here. And what's made it even tougher, I've had this detective hounding me. As if I've done something wrong just because I knew Carmen."

"I've got to go."

"Polita..."

"Bye."

Allen stepped back from the car when Polita turned on the ignition. His broad shape flickered under the neon lights. Without looking at him, she drove out of the parking lot.

# 29

When Elliot returned home after work, he found Karen in the bedroom hanging up her clothes.

"What time did you get in?" he said.

"Oh, maybe a half hour ago."

"How was New York?" He kissed her on the nape of her neck.

"It was hectic but productive. Where's Jeremy?"

"I let him stay for a while at Paul's. I told him I'll pick him up at eight."

"On a school night?"

"He said he didn't have any homework."

"He'll always tell you that."

"Teachers give homework to first-graders?"

"They do at his school. I sit down with him every night for at least an hour or so."

"I'll make sure he opens up at least one book before he goes to bed."

He had talked Jeremy into staying at his friend's house so that he could tell her about his troubles in Miami without his son having to witness a fight.

Karen, in her bra and panties, turned completely around and faced him. He couldn't look her in the eye. He was uncomfortable and wanted to take off his tie and suit jacket, but then that would give her a chance to examine his neck wound.

With a smile she said, "Usually when you find an excuse to get Jeremy out of the house, it's to make love to me."

"I noticed you've got some logs burning in the fireplace. You beat me to it." He tried hard to smile but couldn't. His face was rigid, expressionless.

"We haven't done any smooching in front of the fireplace for a long time."

"It has been a while."

He embraced her and kissed her on her lips, neck, shoulders. She returned his affection. Then, holding both her hands, he stepped back and looked at her. He felt moisture on the back of his neck. He drew a long deep breath.

"Well," she said, "are we going to camp out by the fireplace or what?"

"Karen, I have something to tell you," he said gravely.

Immediately her smile faded. Her grip on his hands weakened.

"What is it?" she said.

She released her hands from his and stepped backwards. Her gaze was cautious. She then took her housecoat from a hook on the door and put it on. He gestured at the sofa, and they both sat down. She moved away from him, leaving a large space between them. He had rehearsed this countless times, but he was speechless and couldn't meet her gaze. Her eyes looked defiant one moment, and then wounded and confused the next. Sitting erect, with hands folded on her lap, her face raised slightly as if expecting a blow, her calm dignity moved him; never before had she looked so attractive to him.

"I think I've gotten myself into a little bit of trouble," he said. He took an even deeper breath. A scratchy sound came from his throat. "I want you to hear it from me - now, not later. And not from someone else."

"What kind of trouble?" Her complexion slowly drained of color.

He stared at his shoes.

"Damn it, Elliot. You're acting like Jeremy when he gets into trouble and we both have to tell him to look us in the eye. Now look at me."

He lifted his eyes from the floor and tried to look at her. "It happened when I was in Miami."

"Who did you fuck?"

"No one."

"You're having an affair."

"No…it's nothing like that. But you're going to hate me after I tell you what I did."

"I'll decide when to hate you."

"I almost got involved with a call girl."

"A call girl? Almost? What do you mean?" Her posture stiffened with each question.

"Ah…well, yes, it was a call girl."

"You paid for a whore. Is that what you're stuttering to tell me?"

At first her face was a perfect blank. Then, slowly, her eyes seemed to pulse. She stood up, distancing herself even farther from him.

"She wasn't just a whore," he said. "She was a - "

Karen spit out the words, "I don't care what you call her! A *call girl*! A *whore*! A *prostitute*! A *hooker*! They're all the same to me!"

She glanced around the room - at his books on the end table, at the lamps, at the pictures on the dresser - perhaps looking for something to throw. Her hand was actually touching a hardback book. He was ready to duck in case a carefully aimed missile came at his face, but she didn't pick up the book. She stared at him, her tiny black pupils hardening. She was so angry her lips whitened to match her complexion. The muscles in her jaw visibly tightened.

"How was she?" Karen said. "Was she a good whore? Did she fulfill your sick fantasies?"

"If you'd be quiet for a minute and quit interrupting me I'll tell you what happened."

Her eyes flaring, she lashed back in enraged disgust, "Don't tell me to shut up!"

"I didn't tell you to shut up!"

"Don't you yell at me!"

"I'm not yelling!"

"Yes, you are!"

He tried to keep his voice calm. "There, is that better?"

"Oh - what a hateful, sarcastic tone that is! I'd rather you just go ahead and scream at me!"

"What the…?"

"So now you're going to start cussing at me? Here comes the verbal abuse!"

"I didn't say one cuss word. You won't even let me finish."

"I know what happened next so you don't have to finish telling me."

"You haven't let me get one word out so I could explain what happened."

"I don't want to know how you lusted after her. How you ravaged her. You make me sick! Paying to fuck a *whore*!"

"Nothing happened between us."

"Liar! So what do you think you gave me? AIDS? Genital herpes? Gonorrhea?" She seethed with anger. "Maybe all of the above?"

"Would you listen? I told you we didn't do anything. You don't have to worry about any diseases."

"What do you mean you didn't do anything?"

"I couldn't perform."

"You couldn't get a hard-on? Is that what you're trying to tell me? We know you're not impotent."

"She drugged me. We were drinking a glass of wine and - "

"You bought a bottle of wine for a *whore*?"

"Dammit, Karen, let me finish."

"I warned you about screaming at me!" She clenched her fist, poised to strike him.

"I'm not screaming." He felt the heat from her outraged eyes. Once again he stared at his shoes. He rubbed his temples. "She was the one who brought the bottle of wine to my room."

"Oh, but of course she would. I forgot, she's supposed to be classy and sophisticated. Any *whore* who pours wine before she fucks must be high class."

"The wine thing was all a part of her scam. She slipped something into my drink. Then they robbed me."

"*They*?"

"Yes…They. There were... two of them."

"*Two*?" Karen's blood-filled eyes got redder. Disgust contorted her face. "You greedy bastard! One whore wasn't enough for you! You had to have *two*!"

"I didn't know where the other one came from." Elliot returned his eyes to Karen. He wanted to be ready to protect himself if she were to strike him. "The other one just happened to show up. They must work in pairs to take advantage of their clients. They're predators."

"And you were the little helpless victim. You certainly didn't object when the other one just so happened to show up, did you?"

"I fell for their scam."

"You sure did. You got caught with your pants down, didn't you?"

"What can I say?"

"What can you say? How about admitting you're pathetic?"

"Yeah. I guess I am."

"Don't agree with me."

"What am I supposed to do?"

"They stole your Rolex, didn't they? That's why you lied to me about not having it."

"Yes, they stole the Rolex and some money."

"I bought you that Rolex for our tenth wedding anniversary."

"I'm aware of that."

"Thank you for remembering." She paused for a moment, narrowing her eyes at him. "You mean to tell me that a man your size - all six foot-three and almost three-hundred pounds - couldn't defend himself against two little whores?"

"I told you they drugged me. It was hard to try to fight them off when I couldn't even make a fist."

"Don't look at me for sympathy. You asked for trouble and you found it."

"Something else happened after they left my room. I know I'm innocent and I really shouldn't have to worry."

"Are you talking to me or to yourself?"

Elliot paced the bedroom. Karen sat back down and stared at him.

"The next morning," he said, "one of the call girls was found dead."

"Was your Rolex worth killing her for?"

"I'm trying to be serious." He stopped pacing.

"I am serious. Why did you kill her?"

"The police think she put up a struggle before she was murdered because someone's skin was found under her fingernails." He took off his suit jacket and rolled up his shirt, showing her the marks on both wrists. "They don't look too bad now. Just a few red marks. But when she scratched me up they were almost gashes that were deep enough to draw blood."

"What does your back look like? Did she claw you there as you were fucking her?"

He made an audible sigh. "That's not where she scratched me."

"I'm way ahead of you. Her killer's skin is under her nails. My whoring husband is a murderer. What's stopping the police from arresting you?"

"Goddamn it! Will you quit treating this like a joke?"

"It is a sick joke to me! You're a sick joke! And how many times do I have to tell you to quit your damn cussing at me?"

"I didn't...kill her."

"You didn't say that with much conviction. Or emotion. If you want a jury to believe you, you'd better make it sound better than that."

"She clawed me while trying to take off the Rolex. You know yourself how hard it was to unsnap."

"Since when did you wear two Rolexes?"

"I guess she scratched up my other wrist for the hell of it."

"You guess? Again, no jury will believe such lack of conviction."

"She also broke the wine bottle and threatened to cut me."

Karen laughed. "I think you asked her to get rough with you. It turned you on to be dominated. You hired a dominatrix – two of them - to abuse you. My fat-ass husband begged to be pushed around and punished by two whores."

"I kept passing out. I think she would've seriously injured me...probably would've killed me...had the other woman not intervened."

"Then it's a good thing you hired two whores. Maybe you should send the other one a thank you note."

"I'm tired of your smartass remarks."

"Get used to them!"

Elliot slouched down on the sofa. Immediately, Karen got up from the sofa and sat in a chair the farthest from him. There was a lull, an intense silence, between them. She studied the furnishings as if calculating what possessions she might take in a divorce. Then she glared at him.

"Would you tell me if you killed her?"

He answered her with another deep sigh. He sat still with head bent, silent, staring fixedly at nothing.

"I really do think you murdered her. You have an explosive temper and can be violent at times."

"Oh, stop being so dramatic. In over fourteen years of marriage I've never laid a hand on you."

"That's a lie. Remember that time when you accused me of having an affair? I came in late one night and we got into an argument. You grabbed me by the coat and slammed me against the wall. Fortunately, it was winter and I had my heavy coat on with a thick hood. Even you admitted that had it not been for that hood to cushion the blow, you could've killed me."

"I never said it could've killed you. And I never slammed you. I pushed you."

"You knocked me out. I had a concussion."

"I didn't knock you out. You had a slight headache for about an hour. That happened before Jeremy was even born. Why are you bringing up an argument that happened nine, ten years ago?"

"Because a prosecutor might ask me about your violent temper. And I would be happy to tell him. You had better use all of your connections and hire the best possible criminal attorney."

"It just warms my heart to know that I can count on my wife to give me some moral support in case I need it."

"What you did was immoral. And don't refer to me as your wife anymore."

"What do you mean by that?" He raised his heavy eyes and looked at her.

"After what you did, do you think I could still love you? Trust is very important to me. You've broken that trust. You're nothing to me."

"Thanks a lot for standing by me when I'm facing the worst crisis of my life."

"Me? Support you? For what you did? I would be there for you if you were battling cancer or lost one of your parents. But not for this. I won't be one of those humiliated wives who stand by their disgraced, lying, cheating, whoring-around husbands."

Karen went to the closet and changed into a pair of jeans and a sweater. Back in the bedroom, she slipped on her running shoes.

"You have a lot in common with that ex-governor of New York besides having his first name," she said as she laced her shoes.

Confused, he could only release another sigh.

"Remember Eliot Spitzer?"

He sighed again.

"He also had a secret life with hookers." After he didn't respond to her comment, she continued, "I know you remember ex-Governor Eliot Spitzer, don't you, Elliot?"

He stared at her with tired, reddening eyes.

She finished lacing her running shoes and returned his stare. "He became governor in '07 or '08. Something like that."

"Who cares?"

"I care. Because I'm trying to make a point."

"Then make it."

"Don't rush me." She stood and stretched some. "Governor Eliot Spitzer. Everyone thought he was going to be the next great thing. Maybe the next president. Possibly our first Jewish president. But he had some dark secrets, didn't he? He resigned as governor one year later, disgraced and humiliated. Do you want to know some of the reasons why he got involved with prostitutes?"

"I could care less, but I guess you'll tell me."

"He said it was hubris. Do you know what I think? I think it was because he had a dick for a brain. Like you. He was ready to throw away a beautiful family and a great career for a piece of ass. Like you."

"If I remember, his wife forgave him."

"And she was a fool."

"Hillary forgave Bill."

"Another fool."

"You should look up the definition of *forgiveness.* Or *love.* Sometimes spouses make mistakes."

"Since we're having a vocabulary quiz, you should look up the definition of *adultery.* Or *betrayal.* Or *prick.* How about *asshole?*"

"I'm all of those, I admit. I guess it would be too much to ask if you could hate the sin but not the sinner."

"You're right – it would be too much to ask." Karen started to walk out of the bedroom but did a quick about face. "I forgot to ask you, where was your drinking and golf buddy, Mr. Wink Ferrell, during your whoring around?"

"Beats me."

"I'm sure he had something to do with this."

Elliot was silent.

"I bet he was supposed to have been with that other whore," she said. "You don't have to act like a macho-man by playing silent to protect your friend. I've known Wink since we've been married, and he would screw you over in a heartbeat. And you know that. That bastard wormed his way into our life a long time ago. Even when he moved over a thousand miles away, I can still feel his presence. He's a loser. A moocher and a schmoozer."

"It took you this long to show me your true feelings about him?"

"You know that I always thought he was a fraud. He's one of the most insecure men I've known. He always has to perform, to be the center of attention. Mr. Slick thinks he's a real lady's man and a comedian. Does he still put on his trademark winks, eye-crinkling smiles, back pats, and shoulder grips?"

"That's Wink."

"Then tell me, what was his role in this sordid affair?"

"He and I met her at a lounge."

"I knew it!" Karen clapped her hands once. "I knew he had something to do with this. Was this a lounge at the hotel?"

"No."

"Where was it?"

"It was in Miami."

"I figured that much. What was the name of this lounge?"

"What difference does it make?"

"I would like to know."

"It was called Café something."

"Café what? You know I'll find out."

"I think it was Café…"

Angry and insistent, Karen demanded to know. "Café what?"

"Would you let me think? It was… Café…Sinsations."

Karen shook her head. "But of course. How original. Well, was she sinful?"

"She was a dancer there."

"I'm impressed. In other words, she was a stripper. Both of them were. They were – what do they call them? - pole dancers, I bet. You picked them up at a strip joint. And I'm sure it was a classy place, wasn't it? And they were classy pieces of ass, weren't they?"

He gave her another deep sigh for an answer.

"How many women have you seduced - or paid for - since we've been married?"

"None. This was the first time."

"You're lying. I remember when you hired that saleswoman right out of college a few years ago. I'm sure now that you fucked her. The only reason you're telling me about these two whores is because you got caught."

Elliot winced. His infidelities had consisted of several brief affairs and three different call girls, not including Carmen and Polita.

"You don't have to blame Wink for any of this," he said.

"You would like me to though, wouldn't you? I blame you, not him. But it was Wink who helped get you into this mess."

Karen walked out of the bedroom and started down the stairs. Elliot followed her.

"Where are you going?" he said.

"As far away from you as possible." She reached the last step and turned around. Her eyes were full of hate and sadness. "How old were these whores?"

"I don't know." He ran both hands through his hair.

"Were they teenagers?"

"Of course not. They were probably…I don't know…in their thirties, I guess." He knew they were much younger, but he wasn't going to admit it to her.

"Well, I'm going to pick up my son, *coach.*"

"I'll pick him up."

"I don't want my son around you, *coach.* When I get back, I want you out of this house."

"I'm staying where I am. I don't want you saying a word about this to anyone. And I want you to try to act normal around Jeremy. I don't want him to think we're fighting."

"Whatever you say, *coach.* So you want us to put on an act in front of our friends and our son? All of this was a game, wasn't it, *coach*? After you were with the whores in Florida you came back here trying to act like the model family man. Just like Governor Spitzer tried to do. I was a little suspicious when you cut short your Florida trip. Is that where you saw all your whores, at these so-called conventions? You go to at least a half dozen a year, so no telling how many whores you've had. I guess that's what some husbands do when they're away from their wives and children – they pick up strippers. So all those so-called baseball and football games you went to when you were away were really strip joints. Am I an idiot or what? I sensed something was wrong when I picked you up at the airport. But you were so smooth with your talk about how much you loved me. No wonder you and Wink get along so well. His bullshit and sleaziness has finally rubbed off on you."

Karen marched through the house, went into the garage, and started up her Land Rover. Elliot plopped in a chair in the living room and stared at the logs burning in the fireplace. He listened to her pulling out of the driveway. A log fell and ignited mini explosions.

An hour later, he was still staring at the fire.

# 30

Polita was in her kitchen, wrapping plates and glassware with newspaper, when Seth knocked on the half-open door.

"Your movers are here," Seth called out. His brother Paul was with him.

"I'm in the kitchen," Polita said.

Seth walked up to her with a smile and gave her a pat on the shoulder. Paul also said hello.

"Allen's on his way with the U-Haul," Seth said. "I drove my Jeep in case we need it. Paul wants to help."

"I won't be able to stay for too long," Paul said. "Unfortunately, I have an appointment in Everglades City."

"I appreciate any help you can give," Polita said. "I'm surprised Allen's helping me move. I got into an argument with him last night."

"Seems like Allen has been arguing with everyone," Seth said. "He quit at the café last night."

"What happened?"

"He quit for a number of weird reasons. He said the second-hand smoke at the café would give him cancer; he wasn't getting along with Mark; working there made him immoral; and last but not least, he said he quit because he found Jesus."

"Since when did Allen become so religious?"

"He told me that the café was poisoning him both physically and spiritually; those were his words. After he tried to convert me and some of the dancers, he almost got into a fight with a customer, who was just a harmless drunk. Miss Wanda got onto him for being too aggressive with the poor man. She told him she didn't hire thugs. That's when he quit. He even mouthed off to Miss Wanda. I had to get him away from everyone so he'd cool off. I bet he hasn't said more than five words to me all morning, so don't expect him to be all smiles when he walks in here. By the way, wait till you see the new tattoo he just got on his left hand. It says *Jesus Wept – John 11:35*. It matches perfectly with his right hand that has the devil on it. How weird is that?"

"That's his *Alien* tattoo," Polita said.

"Same thing."

Seth shrugged, and then he and Paul took the boxes Polita had taped and stacked them in the corner of the kitchen.

"Among our little group," Seth said, "I'm the only one left at the café. You, Kim, and now Allen, are all gone. After this past week, I should quit and get on with my life."

"I'd say you're doing a lot with your life, since you graduate this summer. The café is just a part-time job for you. You'll go on to better things." Polita looked at Paul. "You're very lucky. You've got a big brother to look after you."

"You know I'll keep an eye on him," Paul said. "I've been getting onto him about his homework since grade school. Polita, what do you plan to do?"

"You mean, once I get out of jail?" She looked away from both men and taped another box.

"You haven't been arrested for anything," Seth said.

"The cops are just using me right now to help with their investigation. My time's coming." She leaned against the kitchen sink and observed Seth and Paul as they stacked the boxes. "Why are you two helping me?"

"Because we're your friends," Seth said. He and Paul stopped working momentarily.

"But you've heard of all the bad things I did."

"That doesn't stop us from liking you."

"You're invited to come out to my place next week," Paul said. "You said you enjoyed it last time you were there."

"I had a lot of fun," she said.

"Then I expect to see you," Paul said. "I'll give Seth the date and you'll be able to escape Miami for a day, or stay several days."

They went back to work. A few minutes later, in silence, Polita and Seth glanced at each other and smiled.

Allen entered the apartment wearing a weightlifter's belt and an iPod.

"Here's the other half of the work crew," Seth said.

"The U-Haul's parked by Seth's Jeep," Allen said, entering the kitchen. "Let's go ahead and load up the big stuff first."

"Thanks for helping," Polita said.

Allen turned off his iPod and gazed at Polita, Seth, and Paul with a grim expression.

"I told you I'd help," he said in a gruff voice.

"You can always depend on Allen," Seth said.

"Seth and I are going into business as movers," Allen said. His serious expression changed to a wide grin. "Our motto is 'Weak minds but strong backs.'"

Seth and Allen then stripped off their shirts and began mock-posing as bodybuilders. Polita and Paul laughed at their clownish behavior. Allen possessed a thick upper torso - with a bit of a gut - and matchstick legs, while Seth was triangular waist to shoulder but was bowlegged and heavy in the rear. They looked ridiculous in their exaggerated poses.

After a few minutes of fun, Seth and Allen got serious and started moving the heavy pieces of furniture out to the truck. Meanwhile, Polita and Paul loaded up her car and Seth's Jeep with her clothes and smaller possessions.

"Before I leave," Paul told her, "I've something for you." He opened the door to his BMW, took a wrapped gift from his front seat, and handed it to her. "I hope you like it."

Polita unwrapped the gift. It was a framed picture of herself, Kim, and Carmen that had been taken on the dock of Paul's hunting lodge in Everglades City. The three women had their arms around each other and were smiling.

"I have another picture of Seth and me with you three women at the lodge, but it didn't turn out as well," he said. "That's the only picture I have of Carmen."

"This is very thoughtful of you. You don't know how much I appreciate this." For a while she stared at Carmen's bright smile. "Until now, I didn't have one picture of Carmen. I'll always keep this."

"I know I didn't help much, but I've got to head back to Everglades City."

"I appreciate your support more than anything."

"I expect to see you at my place in the next week or so."

Paul gave Polita a hug, and he shook hands with Seth and Allen. He then got into his car.

Paul smiled at Polita. "Keep an eye on Allen and my little brother."

"I will," she said.

She waved at Paul as he drove away.

It took them less than an hour to empty the apartment. Seth was handing the last of the boxes to Allen, who was in the truck, when a box gave way and dishes crashed onto the pavement. Polita cringed.

"I can't believe this happened," Allen said.

"It's my fault," Polita said. "That's one box I didn't tape too good."

"Your movers are weak-minded, all right," Seth said, laughing. "I don't know if our business covers all the dishes we break. I'll ask our president." He looked up at Allen in the truck. "Mr. President, do we have insurance on the stuff we damage."

"Dumbass Seth didn't give me a chance to grab the damn box," Allen said. He took off his iPod and tossed it inside the truck.

Allen's outburst surprised Polita.

"Allen's just playing with us again," Seth told her.

"The hell I am!" Allen said.

"You are joking, aren't you?" Seth's long-held smile slowly faded.

"Fucking around with those boxes could've gotten one of us hurt." Allen glared down from the truck.

"Don't get so bent out of shape," Seth said. "Listen to that language of yours. Some born-again Christian you are. Thanks for the sermon last night at the café when you told us we're all damned and are going to hell. Too bad you don't practice what you preach."

Allen jumped down from the truck and stepped up to Seth, his face and eyes suddenly a dark red. The cords in Seth's neck tightened as he looked up to the taller Allen.

Through clenched teeth Allen said, "I'll kick the everliving shit out of you."

"Stop it!" Polita said.

She squeezed herself between the two men. Allen breathed heavily through his splayed nose. Silently enraged, Seth stared into Allen's eyes. One of Seth's facial muscles gave a funny twitch.

"I crammed too many dishes into some of the boxes," Polita said, her voice quivering. The situation had clearly shaken her. "You two are friends. Please don't argue over something like this."

Neither man moved. Allen's eyes were remote and unfathomable, and the vacancy of his gaze disturbed Polita. Seth held his ground. He even stepped closer to Allen, both fists clenched.

"Don't," Polita pleaded.

Allen mumbled to himself while unbuckling his weightlifter's belt, continuing to gaze blankly at Seth. He took several deep breaths, then turned and climbed back into the truck. As Allen rearranged some boxes, Seth continued staring at him. That same facial muscle of his made another twitch. He then turned, glanced once over his shoulder, and walked back to the apartment.

Near the verge of tears, Polita absently picked up the broken dishes. In a little while Seth returned with a broom and a knife. He cut up the busted box into a smaller piece of cardboard, then swept the broken glass onto it and carried it to a nearby dumpster. Allen, sitting on the tailgate of the truck, fidgeted with his iPod.

Polita and Seth returned to the apartment. She took some dirty clothes and started stuffing them into a pull-string laundry bag.

"I'm so stressed out I can hardly breathe," Polita said.

"I shouldn't have blown up like that," Seth said. He returned the knife to his pocket.

She pointed outside. "It was *him* who blew up over nothing."

"I kind of started it. I was the one playing around by throwing boxes at him." Though Seth sounded humble, his eyes burned.

"He had no right to act like that."

"I've seen Allen blow up once or twice, and it's not a pretty sight. I'll never know how he lasted at the café for over four years without ever hurting someone. He's a good guy, but that bully comes out every once in a while."

From the doorway in the kitchen, Allen, huge, towering, was staring at Seth, whose back was turned. Polita watched the hulking figure as she held her laundry bag. Afraid of another confrontation, she backed away without taking her eyes off him. Seth turned and saw Allen, who approached him with an extended hand.

"I lost my cool," Allen said. He shook hands with Seth.

"I was afraid I was going to have to run from you," Seth said, uneasily. "You start looking like the Hulk when you get mad. That's when Allen becomes Alien."

"I promise something like this won't happen again," Allen said to Polita.

Shaking, Polita looked away from him.

"In the last day or two I've jumped on three of my favorite people," Allen said. "Last night I got into an argument with Polita and Miss Wanda, and today I jumped all over Seth. I just feel so bad, and angry, about what happened to Carmen. I can't get her out of my mind."

"I know how you feel," Seth said.

"We're all upset," Polita said. "All I care about right now is getting out of this apartment."

Polita took a box of cleaning supplies and went into the bathroom to clean the tub and sink while Allen swept around the front door and Seth vacuumed the living room. When she came back into the kitchen, she noticed that the picture Paul had given her of Carmen was on the counter. With no one looking, she grabbed it and threw it into the trash.

In the bathroom, she got on her knees and began to scrub.

# 31

While Elliot was getting dressed to take Jeremy to soccer practice, he heard Karen stacking dishes into the dishwasher. He was in one of the guest bedrooms where he had slept the previous night. He and Karen had not spoken to each other since their fight yesterday. When they had passed each other, Karen had stiffened.

He went into the kitchen where Karen had turned on the dishwasher and was wiping off the counter. When she noticed that he was staring at her, she left the room and started up the stairs. He followed her.

"How long do you think I'll be staying in the guest room?" he called out to her, his voice tinged with sarcasm.

Halfway up the stairs, she stopped.

"I'm glad you think this is amusing," she said. She spoke with her back turned to him.

"I don't think there's anything about this that's funny. I'm interested in getting our sleeping arrangements straight. You know I'm comfortable only when I'm sleeping on my king-sized bed."

"You can count on staying where you are for a while."

"How long is a while? A couple of nights? A week?"

"Until you make arrangements to find another place to live."

"I told you I'm staying put."

"That's what you think." She turned and faced him. The coldness in her eyes intensified their bluish hue. "I don't want you sleeping in the same bed with me because I don't love you anymore."

"That's fine with me. Go ahead and kiss fourteen years of marriage goodbye because I made one stupid mistake."

"You also scare me."

"Scare you? I'm your husband."

"The only thing we have in common is a son."

"You can count on me sleeping in my bed tonight."

"I'll call the police."

"For what, sleeping in my own bed?"

"For sexual harassment. For stalking me."

"I'm stalking you in my own house?" He laughed. "I know you can't be serious."

"I'm very serious. You come anywhere near me and I'll call the police."

She turned and walked up the stairs. He returned to the kitchen and shared a soft drink with Jeremy. A short time later, Karen came into the kitchen and told Jeremy to have fun at practice. She went into the garage and started up her Land Rover.

"Hurry up," Elliot told Jeremy. "We're running late."

"Daddy, are you and mom getting a divorce?"

"What?" He was surprised that the word 'divorce' was in his son's vocabulary.

"Mom's been in a bad mood."

"Has she said anything to you?" He heard Karen drive away.

"She's been real quiet."

"We had an argument. We've had them before and made up. Have you ever had an argument with one of your friends?"

"Yep. Me and Timmy got into one yesterday."

"See. Even the best of friends don't always agree. You don't have to worry about your mom and dad."

Elliot and Jeremy loaded up the car with soccer equipment and started pulling out of the garage when a white Saturn turned into the driveway and came to a stop nearby. His two female housekeepers got out of the car, waved to him, then proceeded to retrieve some cleaning supplies out of the trunk. Another vehicle, this one a black truck, pulled into the driveway and parked next to the Saturn; it was Elliot's three painters, a father and his two sons. Elliot backed out of the garage and was turning around when yet another white car pulled into the driveway and parked. Detective Hawkins and another man climbed out and approached Elliot.

"May I help you?" Elliot said, rising out of his car.

The men introduced themselves to him and showed him their badges. Hawkins' partner was a Boston detective named Pierce with silvery hair and broad shoulders. He was so pale and white that he blended in with the dusting of snow on Elliot's property.

"I think you know why I'm here, Mr. Anderson," Detective Hawkins said. He adjusted his glasses. "If you don't mind, I'd like to ask you some questions."

"I'm afraid this isn't a good time," Elliot said. "I'm taking my son to soccer practice, and I'm running late."

Elliot was surprisingly composed. His voice sounded clear and even. Jeremy watched everything from the back seat of the car.

"Beautiful home," Detective Hawkins said as he looked past Elliot. "Your neighborhood has a lot of that New England charm. The big homes, the rolling hills, the winding streams. This area has a real woodsy feel to it. And look at all those hardwoods. Bet it's just beautiful here in the fall. No doubt some of these homes were built before the Revolutionary War. In Florida, most of the neighborhoods are so brand-spankin' new, and everything's so flat. Hell, our landfills and golf courses are our biggest hills." Detective Hawkins chuckled at his own joke. "I'm sure you noticed that when you were in Miami a few days ago."

"Sir, I'm really running late."

"I'm sorry. I'll get to the point."

Everything about the detective - his speech, his movements – seemed deliberate, even slow, except for his quick eyes, which studied Elliot furiously. Elliot made sure the sleeves of his jacket covered his wrists. He noticed that his housekeepers stole glances at his visitors, and then they went inside. The other detective silently observed Elliot.

Detective Hawkins said, "Mr. Anderson, I wanted to ask you some questions about Carmen Rafael. As you know, Carmen was murdered at the Luxuria while you were staying there. Probably no more than thirty, forty-five minutes after she left your room. Any information you can give me about that night you were with Carmen, I'd sure appreciate it."

"Sir, I've got a son who I'm sure can hear just about every word you're saying."

"I don't want anyone to be uncomfortable. Would you like to follow us downtown, where we can talk in Detective Pierce's office?"

"I told you, I have soccer practice to take my son to."

"I could talk to you after practice. I'll be staying in town for a while."

Elliot was silent.

Detective Hawkins had a habit of pushing his glasses against the bridge of his nose.

A wind moved through the leafless elms that lined the driveway.

"I'd also like to know about the woman who was with Carmen that night," Detective Hawkins said, lowering his voice. "The other one who robbed you, Polita Flores. I'd appreciate any information you can give me on her. Carmen and Polita had robbed a number of johns." He shrugged his big shoulders. "Maybe we can get you to press charges so you can get your Rolex back. None of the other johns seem to want to talk to us. They just clam up, as my momma used to say."

"I don't like being called a john," Elliot said. "I think of a toilet when I hear that word."

"Just cop talk, Mr. Anderson. Nothing personal. You were a victim. These women victimized a number of men, like yourself."

Elliot didn't reply.

"Mr. Anderson, you were seen later at the marina that night. Did you see Carmen or Polita while you were there?"

"I was too groggy to remember anything."

"But you weren't too groggy to leave your room and walk down to the marina?"

"I was looking for a friend."

"Was that Mr. Ferrell?"

"Yes."

"Mr. Ferrell used to work for you, is that right?"

"He did."

"Was it Mr. Ferrell who set you up with Carmen at Café Sinsations?"

Elliot was silent. Jeremy opened the car door, but Elliot motioned for him to stay inside.

Detective Hawkins was persistent. "Mr. Anderson, I'm got to level with you. This whole thing's gonna get ugly. In Miami, the media are pressuring us to publish those names in Carmen's trick book. Wouldn't surprise me one bit if this story even goes all over the country once the tabloids get into the act. Mr. Anderson, I assume you've heard about Carmen's trick book? I'm sure Mr. Ferrell is keeping you informed of things."

"Sir, I don't mean to be rude. I know you've got a job to do, but I don't have anything else to say. You'll have to talk to my attorney."

"I might have to, Mr. Anderson." Detective Hawkins handed Elliot his and Detective Pierce's calling cards. "If you can't reach me, call Mr. Pierce and he'll get in touch with me. I hope we can talk next time when you're more comfortable."

"I don't have anything further to say about any of this."

"You know," Detective Hawkins said, his eyes once again taking in the scenery, "I'd like to do the opposite of what other people do when they retire. I want to move up here, to one of the New England states. Miami's just wearing me out. I'm getting too old for all that humidity down there. So what if it gets cold up here. If you're retired, you can stay inside and watch everyone else go to work in the snow. The only thing I'd miss is playing golf year round. You just can't play a whole lot up here like you can in Florida. You play much golf, Mr. Anderson?"

Elliot was mildly annoyed at the detective's voice, which had a teasing undertone.

"I'm usually too busy running a business and taking care of my family," Elliot said.

"I'd like for us to sit down and have a little chat, Mr. Anderson. Let me know when you feel like talking. Just give me a call. OK?" The detective rubbed his hands together. "Sure is cold with that wind. While I'll be staying here for another day or two, I think I might drive around and check things out. Yeah, I think I could retire up here. I'd just have to get used to the weather."

Elliot said nothing and returned to his car. He watched the white car turn around and head down the driveway.

"Who were those men, Dad?" Jeremy said.

"Oh, they were just looking at the house. Let's go to practice."

"OK, I'm ready."

Elliot pulled out of his driveway and drove down the winding road. For the next couple of miles he saw no sign of the detective's car. He then turned to his son and started talking about soccer.

# 32

Polita finished decorating her new one-bedroom apartment by watering the potted plants and hanging flowers, which Seth and Allen had bought her as house-warming gifts. It was on the ground floor in a two-story, U-shaped cement-block complex. A narrow parking lot and a street were in the front, a drainage culvert and highway overpass in the back, so the sound of traffic surrounded her. Overhead, a high-voltage transformer hummed. Neon-trimmed motels across the street glowed in the night. Across from the motels were a flea market and a used car lot.

She sat on her new sofa with legs crossed and a notepad in her lap. Her cat lay on a cushion next to her. She was figuring out how much she had spent on her new furniture when a knock sounded on the door. It was Kim, dressed in a sarong skirt and a bead-shell necklace. Polita showed her through the apartment.

"You should be an interior decorator," Kim said. "You have a special touch when it comes to decorating."

"I'd get you something to drink, but I haven't had a chance to buy groceries."

"I'm OK. I like your new furniture."

"It's not much. My move here has just about wiped out my savings. Know anyone who'd want to buy my Mustang? I can't afford the payments anymore."

"I'll ask around. I know where we can get some quick money."

"Doing what? If we screw up again, we've got a detective who'll lock us up in a heartbeat. This place might be a dump, but it sure beats prison."

"We can make $500 each for one hour of dancing at a party, a thousand if we dance for two hours."

"What kind of party are you talking about?"

"A bachelor's party. It's all legit. We wear bikinis. Nothing comes off. We'll pay Seth or Allen to be there with us. And the man who's setting it up said he knows a friend who's also getting married next week, and he wants to hire him some dancers. I need the money bad. That's a thousand bucks each. Cash. Minus a hunnerd or two for Seth or Allen."

"My dancing days are over."

"Me and Carmen danced at a couple of parties. Allen was with us in case there was any trouble. We had fun. It was easy money. And most of the men behaved real good."

"I don't think you can depend on Allen anymore."

"Then I'll call Seth. I don't know about you, but I'm doing it. I couldn't tell you how many job applications I filled out today. Nobody's hiring, unless you want a shit job flippin' burgers or waitin' on tables."

"We waited on tables at the café."

"Yeah, but there's a big difference between the café and something like the Waffle House."

Polita stood up. She looked for her cell phone.

"I forgot to call the detective," Polita said. "He makes me check in with him twice a day. He wants me to get a real job, and the Waffle House might be the only place where I can find work."

"That detective can't make you get a job."

"I don't know if you heard me earlier, but he's going to lock us up sooner or later."

"And he knows we can post bond and be out on the street. That ain't gonna help his investigation none, and he knows it. Like I said, dancin' is legit so long as we keep our clothes on."

"I want to stay on his good side and enjoy a few more days of freedom." She continued to look for her cell phone. "I must've left my cell in the car."

"I've got to go, anyway."

Polita opened the door and they walked down a short hallway that was lit by a dim, bare bulb. They approached Kim's car. A cloud covered the dull-colored moon.

"Let me know if you want to dance at the party," Kim said, raising her voice above the sound of traffic. "If you don't, I'll ask someone else. You know, it's almost nine-thirty. Normally we'd be dancin' at the café right now."

"I don't miss it."

"I miss the money." Kim opened her car door. "Did I tell you I had a couple of reporters call me?"

"For what?"

"They want to know who's in Carmen's book."

"You know of any names?"

"Nope. Do you?"

"She always kept me in the dark about most things."

"Me too. You'll probably be hearing from some reporters. Dante said there might be some big money in this for us. He said there's no such thing as bad publicity, 'cause you can always cash in on it."

"Like I said, I don't want to do anything to get that detective mad at me."

"I'll be seeing you."

Kim got into her car and drove away. Polita walked down the sidewalk in the direction of her car when headlights from a parked car came on and shone in her eyes. She was momentarily blinded until the headlights flashed off.

"Polita," a man called out as he exited the car.

She immediately recognized the voice; it was Phil, the bellhop from the Luxuria. For a moment he hung back, maintaining a shadowy, lurking presence. She stood motionless, waiting for him to make a move. Finally, he strolled over to her, hands-in-pockets. She hardly recognized him; instead of the handsome khaki uniform he had worn before, he had on wrinkled cargo shorts, a stained *Miami Heat* T-shirt, unlaced Nike hightops without socks, and a red bandanna that was wrapped around his head. His clothes hung loosely on him. Instead of being neatly groomed, he looked gaunt, grim, with two day-old whiskers. His eyes were bloodshot and protruding.

"I see that you moved," he said.

"Yeah." She ran her tongue over her lips. Her mouth suddenly felt very dry. "It was a lot of work."

Almost a minute of silence passed between them. In the hazy yellow light of the moon, she saw his eyes looking her over. Across the street, several defectively lit letters flickered in the neon sign that advertised ENRIQUE'S USED CARS.

"You didn't tell me you were moving," he said.

"I didn't? I thought I did the other night. So much has been going on this past week." She was stammering.

"I tried to see you yesterday at your other apartment, but you were with your bouncer friends. I wanted to talk to you alone." He took his hands out of his pockets. "Seems like I'm always meeting you in dark parking lots. I feel like a spy."

She noticed that he was gazing behind her in the direction of her apartment.

"I've got to talk to you about what we agreed on the other night," he said.

"I'm still working on getting you the money. I think I can come up with at least half of it real soon."

"How soon is soon?"

"Maybe as early as tomorrow night."

He fell silent. Another cloud blocked the moon. Darkness covered them. He stepped closer to her. Nearby two men were leaning against a car, talking. The cloud passed.

"I want to talk to you where no one can hear us," he said. "Like I said, I'm tired of dark parking lots and alleys. They make me nervous. You probably don't believe me, but I was one of those kids in middle school that if you just said boo I'd piss in my pants. Seriously. I was a real scaredy-cat when it came to dark places."

"They're not paying any attention to us." She glanced at the two men, who were drinking from the same bottle of wine. "We can talk here."

"Goddamn winos. The way things are going in my life, that'll probably be me in a couple of years."

For a moment Phil gazed again in the direction of her apartment. Polita knew she had to keep him outside. She thought of asking one of the men for a cigarette.

"I don't like it here," he said, sounding agitated.

"They won't hear us."

He now stared directly at her apartment from under his brows. He looked angry.

"If you want," she said, "we can talk in your car."

"I prefer your apartment."

She stood flat-footed, unable to move. She again glanced at the two men. They were too absorbed in their own conversation to notice her.

"I want to talk now," he said firmly.

Polita obeyed, and they went into her apartment. She picked up a water bottle from an end table and held it. He locked the door behind them and closed the window blinds. She stood in the middle of the living room, too nervous to think.

"Nice furniture," he said, circling the living room and touching Polita's sofa and two chairs. "I'm impressed. For a prostitute, you've got good taste. But I'm a little confused."

"Confused? About what?"

"I thought you said you were hard up for money, yet I'm looking at some expensive furniture. Cool looking flat-screen TV. Must've cost some big bucks."

"I charged it all."

"I bet you charged a lot of things with all those stolen credit cards. What I don't understand is that you bought all this nice stuff, yet you'll soon be going to prison. How are you going to pay for all this once they lock you up? I mean, you're probably looking at three to five years. Maybe half that if you keep cooperating with the cops. However, if they end up pinning Carmen's murder on you, you'll be put away for a long, long time."

"I'll get you your money. I promise."

"What are you planning to do, knock out some more CEOs at the Luxuria? Or maybe you're hoping to win the Florida Lottery. You know, I might have an opening for you. I've got a female friend who kind of double dips at the Luxuria, but I think she's getting burned out. You think you might be interested? One of her jobs was similar to the one you were doing there. Know what I mean? That might be a quick way for you to pay back your debt."

"I'm not sure..."

"Think about it. I'm fixing to get rid of the one who's there now. I can't always depend on her. She's becoming a little too independent to suit me. A little too high maintenance."

Polita watched Phil circle around and around the room, touching everything he came into contact with. His eyes were blinking rapidly, and he was always mumbling or talking. His erratic behavior reminded her of Carmen's. She chewed her lower lip hard.

"Boy, you do have expensive tastes," he said. "Women like you want to enjoy the finer things in life, don't you?"

"I guess."

"You guess. You think you're too good for someone like a bellhop, huh?"

"It's hard for me to get my hands on some cash right now. But I can get you a Rolex."

He stopped walking around the room. His lips seemed ready to smile.

"Now where would you've gotten a Rolex?" he said.

"Carmen gave it to me that night at the hotel."

"She just gave it to you? Just like that. Yeah, right."

"Honest."

"You sure you're telling the truth? Cross your heart and…hope to die…"

"I'm telling you the truth." She took one step back from him. "Carmen gave me the Rolex."

"I know better than to believe that. Anyway – whoopee – a Rolex? What do you expect me to do with a Rolex, wear it? It'd look real good on a bellhop."

"The street value alone is probably worth twenty to twenty-five grand. We could split the money. All we need is a middleman. I can't use Dante because he's not supposed to know I've got it."

Polita had spoken rapidly. Her mouth was still very dry.

"It's too risky dealing with stolen jewelry," he said. "I want cash."

"You don't know someone who could help us? I just don't want to deal with Dante."

"Come to think of it, I might know someone." He shrugged. "And then I might not."

"I'm sure we can work something out."

"I'm sure you'll work something out real soon."

He slowly approached her.

"Please don't hurt me," she said. Her pistol was in the bedroom.

"Take your shirt off. I've seen you dance at the café a couple of times, but it was from a distance. I couldn't tell if you had store bought tits or if they're the real deal. Half the dancers at the café have fake ones. It's simply amazing what implants can do for a woman's ego. Some women think the eyes of the world are on their cleavage, don't they?"

Polita didn't move. Up close, under the lights, it looked as though Phil were wearing eye shadow and a thin layer of lipstick.

"I told you to take your shirt off. That shouldn't be hard for a stripper like you to understand. You do it all the time - in front of complete strangers. You should feel comfortable around me.

You know me, I'm your friend." A knife appeared in his hand as if by magic. "Do as I said."

Hands trembling, she slipped off her blouse and undid her bra. She stood before him, eyes downcast, as he stared at her for a long time without blinking. She was on the verge of tears. Her entire body shivered once. He took off his T-shirt. His sleekly muscled body was hairless and glistened with sweat. He held her blouse up to his face, smelling it. Then he dropped it on the floor. His breathing was rapid and shallow. Awkwardly, he fondled her breasts. She shrank back from his touch. His face came closer to hers.

"Stop moving," he said.

Slowly shaking her head, she said, "I don't..."

"I said quit moving."

He was panting, as if he had asthma, his raspy breaths the only sound in the apartment. She raised her water bottle to deflect his kiss, but he slapped it out of her hand.

"If you fucking move one more time, I'll…" He stopped talking. Delicately, he traced the outline of one of her neck tattoos with the cold blade of the knife. She shivered from its touch. He then ran the blade between her cleavage and across each nipple. "I'll be damn, those are real honest-to-goodness tits all right. Nothing fake about those knockers. I can see why men would pay to look at them. And for a small fortune, the lucky CEO-types who get to tit-fuck them."

With one hand he placed the knife at her throat and with his other he gripped the back of her hair, tugging it downward. Swallowing hard, she stared at the ceiling, her throat completely exposed. He took the knife and guided it around her neck in a gently sawing motion. She closed her eyes, expecting to feel or see blood. She felt no pain, only a tickling sensation. As the knife made its way to the back of her neck, she thought she heard him repeat in a child's voice, "La-di-da. La-di-da." He then released his grip. When she opened her eyes, she noticed that he was staring at three long locks of her bluish hair.

So expertly had he cut her hair that she barely felt him do it. Neatly, he folded the locks of hair and tucked them into his shirt pocket.

"A souvenir," he said, winking.

He then tried to embrace her, but it was with absent dispassion, a timid, slithering kind of caress. She felt his breathing along the side of her neck. His deep, warm breaths had replaced the cold steel of the knife. She tried to keep her eyes on the knife, but he kept it from her view. His course, cat-like tongue ran over her mouth, neck, breasts. His bristly chin scratched her. Up close, she could see his nostril-hairs and the fillings in his teeth. She arched her back and, not wanting to provoke him, gently pulled away.

He stepped back from her. His eyes were brimmed with tears. He held the knife behind his back.

"I'm not too good at this," he said, shyly. "Why'd you ask if I was going to hurt you?"

His sudden change of behavior, from aggressive to almost submissive, confused her.

"Your knife..."

"What about it?"

"It scares me."

She eyed her nail file, which she had left on the end table only a few feet from where she stood; that was her only accessible weapon.

"You don't trust me?"

"I don't know you. I..."

"You don't know me?" He giggled. "You've fucked men who you didn't know because you're a whore."

"But...um...There've been only a couple of men who've paid to be with me. But they hardly touched me. They were drugged and couldn't do anything."

"So that makes you feel better about yourself?"

"No...I..." Her eyes glanced from the nail file to his leering face and back again.

"And you let any stranger in this city watch you dance practically naked. Who're you trying to fool?"

"Dancing was just a job to try to make ends meet." Her voice was low and resigned. She was waiting for him to reveal the knife.

"You moved here to hide from me, didn't you?"

"I didn't, I swear."

"I think you did." He became quiet for a while. His eyes studied the walls of the apartment. He continued to conceal the knife.

"I moved because someone broke into my last apartment."

"Why do you live in such high-crime areas?"

"It's all I can afford."

"After you finish doing time in prison, who do you think will want to hire you for a job?" he suddenly said.

"Huh?"

"I was just thinking about the job I offered you at the Luxuria. That might be your only job opportunity when you get out of prison. But never mind. I'm just talking to myself."

He continued to gaze at Polita's decorations. His breathing returned to normal. He seemed strangely composed, at least for the moment. He sat on the sofa's arm, purposefully putting too much weight on it.

"I wanted to be an engineer once," he said, dreamily. "Maybe one day I'll go back to school and finish up. I was real good in math. I was always one of the smartest in my class. I lack maybe twenty-four hours from getting my degree."

While he continued to talk to himself, Polita picked her blouse off the floor and slipped it back on. She moved another step closer to her nail file.

"I've been out of college for about five years now," he kept babbling. "My friends have all graduated. They don't say it, but I know they think I'm a loser. I mean, I'm a bellhop. The Luxuria dresses me up like I'm going on a safari, like I'm a fucking monkey in a cute little costume who's supposed to smile and wait hand and foot on our privileged guests."

As she started to reach for her nail file, his eyes snapped out of their trance-like state and looked at her.

"What are you doing?" he said, getting off the sofa's arm.

"Um. Nothing."

"Who said you could put your shirt back on?"

"You were telling me about college."

"So? I didn't give you permission to get dressed."

Polita tried to block Phil's view of the nail file by standing in front of the end table. With the knife still held behind his back, he approached her, but then he became distracted again. His eyes lost their focus on her and took another flight around the apartment.

"I'll take the Rolex, if that's all you've got," he said. "I think I can find someone who's got contacts in the jewelry business."

"I'll do my best."

"I knew you had the Rolex all along. You never fooled me. You wanna know why?" The aggressive posturing returned, and a strange spark flickered in his eyes. "Because I think you had something to do with Carmen's murder. Hey, but that's OK. No one cared about her anyway. Just another call girl. She was out of control. She was going to bring us down with her. Shit, she still might."

"I had nothing to do with her murder."

"Like, you're going to admit you did it?" He smiled confidently. "I know more of what's going on at that hotel than all the security people and the managers combined."

She glanced at her nail file.

"When can you get me this Rolex?"

"Tomorrow night." She stepped back so that her legs touched the end table; in a split second, when his eyes started to drift again, she could grab the nail file and lunge toward him.

"What time tomorrow night?"

"How about nine o'clock."

"I'll park where I was tonight. Look for me. I'll flash my headlights on twice."

"I think I'm being followed. The cops are watching me and Kim real close. And Dante, he's also watching me." She doubted if the police were following her, but she wanted him to believe it.

"If you tell the cops about me, I'll tell them what I saw you do to Carmen at the marina. You know, you've got one badass swing when it comes to a golf club. You're fucking vicious. Blood just gushed out of the top of her head. Good thing the music was loud or everyone at the hotel would've heard Carmen's skull split right down the middle. *Splat.*"

He produced the knife from behind his back and curled his lips. He used the blade to errantly poke tiny holes in Polita's sofa.

"You were in my other apartment, weren't you?" she said, her hands reaching for the nail file. She never took her eyes off his knife. "You went through my apartment looking for money and maybe the Rolex."

"Maybe. Maybe not." He smiled grimly. "What's it to you?"

"My furniture was damaged. It cost me a lot of money."

"Tough titty."

The bellhop slipped his knife into his shorts and turned for the door. Polita watched his every move.

With his back to her, he said, "By the way, a nail file would be very unreliable. Too blunt. You'd have to make sure you hit the carotid artery and got it in deep and ripped hard to do any good. Sure would be a mess to have to clean up. Jeez, all that blood; it'd be everywhere, even on your nice furniture. Stick to using a golf club."

She withdrew her fingers from the nail file.

Before she could say anything, he closed the door and disappeared. She locked the door and peered through the living room curtains until he pulled out of the parking lot. For a few minutes she leaned against the door, trying to compose herself.

She could still feel his panting breaths on her face.

# 33

Elliot finished telling his attorney about his problems in Miami and about Detective Hawkins' visit to his home the day before. Sitting behind his mahogany desk, Jack Hartigan, the attorney, stared at his client through heavy-rimmed glasses.

"Everything you told me is accurate?" he said, taking off his glasses.

"I think so."

"You have to do better than that."

"As I told you, I was drugged, so I'm not sure if I've got every detail exactly right."

"May I see your wrists?"

Elliot started to roll up one of his sleeves.

"That's what I don't want you to do," the attorney said, slapping his desk.

"But I thought you just said you wanted to see them."

"I was testing you. I don't want you to show your wrists to anyone, even to me."

"The marks on them are practically gone."

"I don't care. Correct me if I'm wrong. You said you showed your wrists to your friend in Miami and to your wife."

"Yes."

"That's two too many. But I'm not worried about your wife."

"I am."

"What you've told your wife is confidential. But I don't like the idea that you've shown your wrists to your friend."

"You don't understand my wife. She's ready to turn me in to the police." He could still feel Karen's hot-eyed stare.

"We'll worry about your wife later. Did the detective ask to see your wrists?"

"No. He kept asking about the dead call girl. Also, he wanted me to press charges against the other woman. He said if I did that, I might be able to get my Rolex back."

"Mr. Anderson, this detective didn't travel over a thousand miles to do you a favor by trying to find your stolen watch; your Rolex is his excuse to talk to you about the dead call girl. He's looking for evidence for a prosecutable case. I don't want you to make any statements to anyone, especially to him. Do you understand?"

"Yes."

"I don't want you to talk to cops, reporters, or friends. Avoid contact with anyone from Florida." He looked at his notes. "This Wink and Dave, they're not your friends anymore."

"Wink has been keeping in touch with me about what's going on in Florida. And I plan to finish a business deal with Dave sometime soon."

"Don't depend on this Wink for anything. We'll rely on the Internet for our information. As for any business deals with your other friend, I would advise you to send one of your assistants to Florida."

"I should be there for the closing."

"Mr. Anderson, your skin is probably under the fingernails of a murdered woman. That should be enough to keep your ass right here in Boston."

The attorney spoke in a growl. In his fifties, he was blunt-featured, crew cut, and abrasive. He hadn't revealed a smile or a frown.

"If I do go down there," Elliot said, "can the detective harass me?"

"I'll call him to let him know that I'm representing you, but I won't tell him that you're going to Miami. He can't ask you anything until he talks to me first."

"Actually, I'll meet Dave in Naples this time, not Miami."

"Hell, take the trip. In a way it looks good that you have nothing to hide by going back to Florida. All I'm trying to say is that nothing can go wrong by staying in Boston and Needham. Stay here and spend time with your family and run your business. Play it safe. But if you go back to Florida, talk business only. You've never heard of any call girls. You're deaf and dumb if anyone asks about them. And if this detective ever contacts you, whether it's here or in Florida, you tell him to direct his questions to me. In writing. Let me do the talking. That's what you're paying me for."

"I understand."

"I am glad you do, Mr. Anderson." The attorney paused for a long time. "Maybe we're being too obsessed with these marks on your wrists? So what if the skin under that dead call girl's fingernails belongs to you? After she drugged you, she got kinky and clawed you and tried to cut you up with a broken bottle. The other call girl witnessed that, not that we ever want to count on her. Yes, you were seen at the marina later that night. Yes, your name is in the trick book. But none of this is probable cause for an arrest. Nor is it probable cause for a warrant for a bodily search for your fluids to check your DNA. Mr. Anderson, we're about the same age. Did you ever watch any of the O.J. Simpson trial?"

"Some of it."

"If anything, his trial educated the public about the law. It showed the shoddy police work and the faulty forensics."

"I'm just worried. I didn't cooperate with the detective. I think I got him mad at me."

"I don't want you to cooperate with him. You have nothing to say to him. However, let me warn you; if you consent to any of his questions, you are fair game, Mr. Anderson. If you lie to him, and he can prove you wrong, then he might have something on you. He couldn't use it in court, but he might think you have something to hide."

"The detective did give me a subtle threat."

"Oh? He threatened you, did he?"

"He told me there are a lot of reporters – local and national - who are after the trick book. He hinted that he might leak names to the media if it'll help his investigation."

"Don't let him intimidate you." The attorney waved off Elliot's comments. "Sounds as if he's after headlines. An ambitious detective or Assistant State Attorney is likely to welcome some publicity for himself. If there are some local celebrities in that trick book, then he will probably pursue his leads more aggressively. He'll maybe even get his fifteen minutes of fame on CNN."

"It was just the way he looked at me."

"What do you mean, Mr. Anderson?"

"Well, he made me feel as though I were the criminal, and the murdered call girl was the victim. I realized that she turned out to be a victim herself, but I didn't..."

"Forget her." The attorney shook his head and held up his hand to stop Elliot from speaking. "You were the victim, Mr. Anderson. Repeat after me. You were the victim."

"I was the victim."

"Say it again."

"I was the victim."

"If you have to, Mr. Anderson, I want you to repeat those words in your sleep. The two call girls who robbed you and who threatened to kill you were the criminals, not you."

Elliot corrected the attorney by saying, "It was just one call girl who threatened me. The other one tried to help me when her friend came at me like a damn banshee."

"The one who lost control threatened to kill you, Mr. Anderson. And I don't give a damn about the other call girl. Don't defend her."

"I'm not. I'm just..."

"You are just what, Mr. Anderson? You could very well get yourself implicated in a murder. Don't show any sympathy for your attackers, or the cops will nail your ass. You don't know this other call girl" – he consulted his notes – "this Polita. For all you know she may have killed her partner. This detective got to you, Mr. Anderson. He has got you doubting yourself, making you think that you are the criminal. You see, Mr. Anderson, our criminal justice system has been turned into a kind of Alice-In-Wonderland fantasy. In our system, the criminals portray themselves as the victims. With their endless excuses, they can make a bunch of nonsense and bullshit sound sensible. Using this kind of logic, it's the victim - someone like you - who causes the real criminals to behave like they do. Give a criminal an excuse - poverty, broken family, child abuse, drugs - and he cannot be held completely accountable for his crimes. The abuse excuse. Then he – or *she*, the criminal - becomes the victim and the real victims like you will pay. So get your ass out of this rabbit hole and come to your senses."

A twitch, a slight movement of facial muscle indicated a brief smile on the attorney's face.

"I see your point," Elliot said.

"I hope you do, Mr. Anderson. I can't stress it enough to you. Our society is full of crybabies claiming to be a victim of some injustice. And I admit, we lawyers create victims out of everybody. I realize I keep going back a little in time, but remember the L.A. riots? On videotape the entire country saw a man smash a brick - a cinderblock - over a truck driver's head." The attorney demonstrated by raising his hands over his head.

In one violent motion, with eyes bulging, he threw his hands downward and made the sound of an explosion, presumably of a cinderblock. "The jury decided that the brick thrower was not a criminal but a victim who just got caught up in some kind of mob frenzy - the mob made him act that way. Mr. Anderson, don't fall for that kind of bullshit."

"I won't."

"You still look confused about something. What is it?"

"It's the DVD of me with the call girl."

"What about it?"

"What should I do if the detective gets his hands on it?"

"Forget about it. We'll make that DVD work to your advantage, if it even comes to that."

"To *my* advantage? How?"

"It will show that you were a victim of a robbery, made defenseless by knockout drops that were used by experienced call girls with the talent for flimflammery. It will show the helpless condition you were in. How could a victim who can't keep his eyes open suddenly come to, then track down and murder, a woman thirty minutes later? How? If the detective calls you about the DVD, let me handle it. I'll be the only one who does the talking for us, Mr. Anderson. Don't ever forget that. If some mysterious voice calls you late one night and wants to blackmail you, simply hang up. Your wife already knows what happened, so there is no need to hide anything."

"If a blackmailer calls my house, my wife would buy the DVD to use against me in a divorce. She'll clean me out." Elliot smiled, but his attorney remained stoic.

"If you can't adhere to any of my advice, Mr. Anderson, you will have to find another attorney to represent you."

Elliot coughed. "I'll do whatever you recommend. I have complete trust in you."

The attorney nodded.

Elliot fidgeted a little. "By the way, my friend mentioned that I could be charged for soliciting and paying for sex. I was wondering…"

"Are you referring to" – another quick glance at his notes – "Mr. Wink Ferrell?"

"Yes."

"I told you earlier, you don't have any friends when it comes to what happened in your hotel room. Trust no one."

"Wink did say, however, that this soliciting thing could…"

"Is this so-called friend of yours an attorney?"

"No. He's a sales rep who used to work for me."

"Don't listen to a word he says. He doesn't know what he's talking about. I'll tell you what you need to know about soliciting and paying for sex, and right now, there's not a thing you need to know. All of that is very minor compared to the murder of that woman."

"OK. Well, I don't have any trouble with anything you've told me. My concern is with my wife. She's very angry and irrational right now. She's a bunch of hows and whys. How could you? Why did you? She hammers me constantly. That's all I was trying to say before I started talking about Wink."

"Only you can save your marriage. I'm afraid I cannot help you there."

# 34

The moon dissolved behind a large cloud, and an unseasonably cool breeze lifted the curtain in Polita's kitchen window through which she had been looking for the bellhop's car. Seth's Jeep was parked near a dumpster at the far corner of the parking lot: she had asked him to help her keep watch.

She passed the time by filing her nails. The TV played in the living room, but she wasn't watching it. She looked haggard and hollowed.

She continued to wait. Only four cars had left the parking lot since she had been at the window; none had entered. The bellhop was forty-five minutes late.

She opened one of the kitchen cabinets and cleared away some dishes. From a Tupperware container she took out the Rolex and slipped it into a pocket in her baggy shorts; in her other deep pocket, wrapped in cloth, she concealed her pistol. Both the Rolex and the revolver bulged slightly, but not enough to alert the bellhop. She went outside and walked up and down the sidewalk, avoiding Seth's Jeep. The traffic, as usual, was heavy, but still no cars turned into the parking lot. She wondered what was keeping the bellhop. Maybe he had decided against the Rolex, had concluded that it would be too much trouble.

Somehow she knew he was out there, lurking in the dark.

The moon, free of clouds, shone brightly. On the horizon lightning lit up the sky. Suddenly, a headlight from a parked car flashed twice. Polita walked toward the car; it was the bellhop, but he was in a different vehicle than last time. She had been looking for a white Honda Civic, but this was a black Kia with one headlight out.

How long had the bellhop been parked here? He sat reclined in his seat, his head barely visible. It looked as if he were taking a nap. She stepped up to his door. No interior lights or dashboard lights were on in his car. He remained reclined, his hands clasped behind his head. He wore his hotel uniform and had the same clean-cut look from their first encounter. She took the Rolex out of her pocket and handed it to him.

"It's all yours," she said. "It should be worth a lot of money."

"Sweet. Ka-ching, ka-ching."

To get a better look, he sat up straight. In his palm the Rolex shone as if phosphorescent. She felt the weight of her pistol in her pocket.

While examining the Rolex, he said, "So this is what got Chechoter killed. All because of something that tells the time. What a shame. Of course, look at you or me. Someone could rob us right now – maybe even kill us - for the same thing."

"That should be more than enough to cover what Carmen owed you."

"Stolen jewelry is still so iffy."

"We made a deal."

"But deals can be broken, especially if one side thinks there's something fishy going on."

"There's damn sure nothing in it for me."

The bellhop hesitated for a moment, then locked the Rolex in the glove compartment. He looked at Polita. His eyes went into her, searching. His gelled hair was slicked back, as if he had just come out of the shower.

The breeze picked up and swirled around her. The air smelled of rain.

"You've let me down," he said.

"What now? We agreed on the Rolex. It's worth three times what Carmen owed you. Maybe more."

"You don't trust me, and that disappoints me more than anything. I really wanted to like you." He turned on the ignition. "I just wanted to be your friend."

"I don't know what you're talking about." She stared in his car to see if he had his knife.

"I told you not to tell anyone about me."

"I haven't."

"Polita, Polita." He shook his head. "You have a friend in that Jeep over there who knows all about me."

She found herself too stunned to speak. She glanced at the Jeep.

"I guess you forgot that I knew about your bouncer friends," he said. "I've seen them at the café, and I watched them move your furniture. Something told me you'd invite one or both of them over tonight. Maybe you had planned to *rob* me."

"That's not true."

"Or maybe you wanted him to hurt me. And he'd steal the Rolex from me and you two would split the money." In a wounded tone, he added, "He could break a skinny wuss like me in half. Both your bouncer friends are such big, strong men. I think one of them is even nicknamed Alien because he's so scary and mean."

"That's not why I asked him to park there."

"Now, now. Let's be honest."

"I swear, he doesn't know anything about you."

"Then why is he hiding over there in the darkest part of the parking lot?"

"He's not hiding."

"So I guess he parked near the dumpster for the view?"

"He's a friend of mine. That's all."

"Is he your lover?"

"No. I asked him to park there because, um, I don't know you."

"There you go again, saying you don't know me. We had this conversation last night. That's so weird for you to say, being the whore that you are."

"But you...scare me."

"I scare you? When I came to visit you last night you were ready to stab me with a dull nail file. I'm the one who should be scared shitless, knowing what you did to Carmen. If I'm not careful, I might be your next victim. Yeah, I might end up with a golf club slicing through my brain. Or a nail file stuck in my neck. You don't play around, do you? You know, Polita, you really didn't have to do that to Carmen. I realize that arguments can get out of hand, but violence was totally unnecessary that night. Speaking of deals, Carmen would've worked out a deal with you. Don't you believe in something called 'principled compromise?' Why did you have to use violence? Why, Polita?"

"Look, he doesn't know your name or where you work."

"You didn't tell him about the Rolex?"

"Not a word."

"It doesn't matter." That smile was still there. An odd, wicked smile. "Seth *was* the short, stocky one, *wasn't* he?"

His question sent a chill through Polita.

"What's wrong, Polita, you forgot how to talk? Your mouth's open but no words are coming out. You might want to go over and check on him. I kind of surprised him - he didn't know what hit him. Never forget how important the element of surprise is, especially when you're dealing with a stronger foe. I'm so sorry I had to do it. Boo hoo. I feel your pain."

Phil, still grinning, made a slit-throat sign with his finger. Then he rolled up his window and pulled out of the parking lot.

Breathless, Polita hurried to Seth's Jeep. Her legs felt rubbery, and she was already winded before she made it halfway across the parking lot. She grew weak. She couldn't see Seth in the driver's seat. The corner of the parking lot seemed to get darker, and the Jeep farther and farther away. By the time she reached the Jeep, Seth had opened his door. She stopped once she saw him.

"Polita," Seth said. "What's going on?"

She took several deep breaths, despite having run only a short distance.

"Was that him in the dark car without a headlight?" he said.

She nodded, panting.

"I wasn't sure," he said. "You told me to look for a white Honda."

"He tricked me." She held her hand next to her heart and swallowed hard. "He drove a different car. And he knew you were here."

"How? You stayed clear of my Jeep."

"He saw what you drove when you helped me move. He got here before you showed up and checked out the parking lot. No telling how long he was parked here. He made me believe that he surprised you, that maybe he even hurt you."

"Who is this creep? What does he want with you?"

"It's nothing."

"Maybe I should hang around in case he decides to return."

"I'll be OK. He won't be back."

She watched the traffic go by.

"I was hoping you would invite me in and let me stay with you for a while," he said.

"I don't think now's a good time. I feel sick."

"Call me if you need me. I'll be at my apartment studying all night for a test. I could use a break."

Seth touched Polita's shoulder, giving it a firm grip to reassure her, and then he returned to his Jeep. She watched him leave the parking lot, then rushed into her apartment and locked the door behind her. She passed the sofa, stopping once to rearrange a pillow to better hide the knife marks that the bellhop had left. When she flipped on the bathroom light, a cockroach fled from the bristles of her toothbrush. Disgusted, she threw the toothbrush into the trash, turned on the faucet, and washed her face. Her burnt, empty eyes were holes in the mirror.

Hearing thunder, she went around the apartment and closed the windows. A steady rain fell. Rivulets of water ran down the windows. The lights in the apartment flickered, then went out after a bolt of lightning flashed. The entire apartment complex was without power.

She took a pillow off the sofa and, hugging it, stood in the corner of the living room. She was cold, and her teeth chattered. Every few seconds or so headlights from passing cars swarmed over the ceiling.

The storm and the darkness of the apartment didn't worry her, nor did she fear the return of the bellhop. Instead, she found herself sinking into a bottomless despair. A sick, gray emptiness enveloped her. Tears spilled down her cheeks, and deep sobs shook her body. She closed her eyes tight to try to keep from crying, but she couldn't control herself.

Arms around the pillow, she slid to the floor in a heap. She fell apart, wailing, "What the fuck have I become?" She wept from the depths of her body. She felt a terrible isolation, an utter loneliness. The living room windows misted, blurring the sickly glow of neon lights from the motels and the used car lot and intensifying her despair.

Her three Rolex victims appeared before her: the shy businessman who had bragged about his children while undressing; the talkative and nervous elderly tourist; and Elliot's terrified eyes when Carmen had threatened him with the broken bottle.

She thought of Carmen. She heard a dull splash in the bay, and Carmen sank in a slow spiral, arms outstretched like wings, blood flowing from her head, her wide-staring eyes fixed upward, the spooling black water sucking her to the bottom.

The storm blew over. A short while later the lights in the apartment came back on. Faintly, she heard the sounds of other tenants as a commotion broke out in the stairwell above her apartment; she could make out the squeak of sneakers, a blaring radio playing hip-hop music, shouting, doors slamming. From the wet street came the swoosh of traffic.

In the corner of the room, she sat in her emptiness and gazed at the blinking neon lights.

A few minutes later she slowly stood up. The pillow she was holding fell to the floor. She pulled the pistol out of her pocket and placed it on the end table. Her thoughts turned to the bellhop. She pictured his smug smile, his shifty eyes. Shaking with rage, she screamed, "I'll kill the *fucker* if I ever see him again!" She picked up the pillow and slammed it repeatedly against the wall. When she became exhausted, she sat back down on the floor, leaned against the wall, and stared vacantly at her damaged sofa.

# 35

After a sales meeting in the conference room, Elliot was returning to his office when Dave Kornick called him on his cell phone.

"Elliot, how's everything in Boston? I guess the weather has kept you indoors. I just played eighteen holes. Shot a seventy-eight. Wink was supposed to have joined me but had to cancel at the last minute. Well, when are you coming back down to finish business?"

Elliot entered his office and closed the door. Dave's voice, he thought, was filled with false enthusiasm.

"Elliot, are you still there?"

"I'm listening."

"You're awfully quiet. I hope our business venture is still on."

"I'll be down soon."

"I'm looking forward to seeing you again. I want you to be a guest at my home."

"I can make arrangements to stay at a hotel."

"No. I insist that you be my guest."

"Dave, I can't. My attorney told me to make this a business trip only. He looks and acts like a drill sergeant, and he gave me orders. I've got to be real careful."

"Sure. I understand. Wink told me about the detective showing up at your place. The ballsy bastard. He saw me once, but I didn't say more than hello and goodbye to him. I also hired an attorney. It's been pretty tense down here."

"I can imagine." Elliot sat at his desk and stared at the wall in front of him.

"Yeah, it's been rough on us all." Dave's voice lost its energy and sounded tired and hoarse. He sighed deeply into the phone. "Wink told me that he's been keeping you informed about these Rolex Bandits."

"According to Wink, it's the talk of Miami."

"Goddamn tabloid journalism. The media down here can't get enough of it. The local talk-show yokels are having a field day. Pretty soon it'll probably be on CNN and Fox News." Dave's voice grew stronger the angrier he became. He was *goddamning* everything. "There's practically a murder every day in Miami and the goddamn TV news doesn't spend more than a few seconds on each one. But let one call girl get killed who kept a trick book, and every goddamn reporter wants to get his hands on it. Right now there's speculation that one of the johns plays on the Miami Dolphins. They're more interested in finding out who the johns are than who the goddamn murderer is."

"That's what Wink said."

"Goddamn. Just the other day one of the local yokels spent an entire show talking to a goddamn panel of experts about why the overwhelming majority of johns turn out to be married men. Another talk show interviewed yet more experts on why some women turn to prostitution. There's no end to it. It's a goddamn feeding frenzy. Turn the TV on and listen to the experts. Tomorrow there's a show that'll have interviews with three arrested johns from a prostitution sting."

"I've heard the word 'john' more in the past week than I have in a lifetime."

"Goddamn, you're right there." Dave paused to catch his breath. "Even the Luxuria is getting a lot of bad publicity. There's a rumor that some of these high-class resorts in Miami, and even here in Naples, look the other way when call girls show up to entertain their guests."

"Sounds like the Luxuria was running its own economic stimulus plan."

"Yeah. Whatever." Dave wasn't amused at Elliot's comment.

"I was surprised when Wink told me that your name was in the trick book." Elliot tried to sound concerned, but he found some comfort in the agonizing tone in Dave's voice.

"Can you goddamn believe that? There's something like a dozen of us in that book."

"By the time the tabloids are through with us, they'll be calling us the 'Dirty Dozen.'"

"We're all sweating pellets about having our names in the news."

"I thought you told me that you were never involved with her."

"I wasn't. I never touched this goddamn Pocahontas, this Sacagawea. Or was it fucking Crazy Horse?"

A faint smile appeared on Elliot's lips. "Crazy Horse was a male warrior who fought General Custer at Little Big Horn; I know at least that much Indian history."

"For all I care, she should've called herself Crazy Cunt. If Wink hadn't kept talking me into going to the café every time I was in Miami, none of this ever would've happened. I don't know why she left my name in the book. God damn it to hell."

Elliot's smile faded. "I know one thing: I'll forever be looking vulnerably up at her flaming bush."

"Cocksucking whore."

"What have you told your wife?"

"I listened to you when you told Wink about how you were going to handle it with your wife. I thought you had the best advice: Get it all out in the open and be as honest as possible. So I told Ashley everything."

"Too bad you took my advice. Considering what my wife wants to do to me, I'm the last person you should've listened to. So I guess your wife wants a divorce."

"Actually, she supports me all the way."

"She what?"

"She's been a saint."

"A saint?" Elliot tried not to sound disappointed. He remembered the blood climbing up in Karen's face when he had confessed.

"When I told Ashley what happened, I expected the absolute worst. This was, after all, the second time in five years that I had to tell her about another woman. But she ended up blaming herself."

"What in the hell did she blame herself for?" Elliot tried again to hold back his disgust.

"She said it must be her fault that I had this need to see other women. Seems she has some secret desire to flagellate herself over this. I don't know."

"You've got to be kidding me."

"I'm serious. The only thing she asked me to do was for both of us to start going to a marriage counselor. I signed up for that right away. Goddamn sure beats going through an expensive divorce."

"Tell me about it."

"She said she would support me as long as I showed the effort to make our marriage work. Now how hard is that?"

"If only my wife could be so forgiving."

"Wink told me that your wife is not someone to cross."

"As I expected, she exploded when I told her about the call girls. We've been able to make it through some bad arguments, but this one is something else."

"She'll get over it."

"I'm not so sure."

"Tell her you felt unloved."

"That would explain why I paid for two call girls? Karen would laugh in my face. Or spit in it."

"How important is your marriage to you?" Dave's voice was sounding relaxed.

"I didn't realize how important it was until all this happened."

"That's the way it usually works, isn't it? You don't realize how much you love your wife until she walks out on you."

"I have only myself to blame."

"Then tell your wife that." Dave's voice had completely lost its anger. "Take the humble approach. Tell her you'll go to a marriage counselor. Admit that you have a problem and you need help."

"What problem would that be?"

"It's the nature of the beast. You're a womanizer. You can't control your sexual drive. We both risked destroying our marriages just to have a little lust in our lives. Ash condones my past behavior as a loveless promiscuity. She dismisses my affairs as having no real significance."

"Would you condone that kind of behavior from her?"

"She never brought up any of her sexual secrets. The point is, she knows some of the Latino couples who work for me. She learned that it's a Latino custom for married men to see prostitutes and still remain fiercely in love with their wives. And their wives, in general, seem to tolerate it."

"If I told Karen that, she would tell me that I'm being politically incorrect and that I'm full of shit. She sees it as a trust thing. I betrayed her. She expects my loyalty. And with AIDs and herpes and whatever other diseases are out there, it's also a health issue."

"With Ash, it's a fear thing."

"Fear of what?"

"The fear of growing old and being alone, I guess. She'll tolerate my playing around at times because she doesn't want me to leave her."

A short silence came between them. Elliot found it odd that Dave was so open and conversational over the phone and quiet and reserved when they spoke in person. He swiveled around in his chair and stared out the window. The sun was bright and the day was unusually warm. He thought of leaving the office for the golf course.

"Elliot, what do you fear the most?"

"What do you mean?"

"What's your biggest fear?"

"I suppose I fear a number of things."

"Such as?"

"Well, if something bad happened to my son, or to my wife. Um…"

"Go on."

"At this moment I fear Karen leaving me and taking my son. I fear losing my reputation if my name is associated with this trick book. What will my employees think of me? Hell, I'm fifty-one and I still worry about what my parents will think when they find out about these prostitutes. I could go to jail. I could be charged with murder. There are a lot of things that scare the hell out of me at this very moment. And…"

"Keep going."

"Bankruptcy would be way up the list. Losing my business. My home. I thought I was going to have my throat slit that night in my hotel room."

"Ah, so you fear a violent death?"

"I don't think anyone would look forward to dying in a fire or a - "

"I don't mean some gruesome accident. I mean a violent death as in being murdered."

"Who wouldn't fear getting murdered?"

"When I was in college, I was a business major and had to pick an elective in the humanities. So I took a philosophy class, of all things. The only thing I got out of the course was this one lecture by the professor." Dave's voice was reflective, sounding far off. "He was lecturing on an English philosopher by the name of Thomas Hobbes - or was it John? – who wrote a lot about violence and how governments were supposed to deal with it. According to Hobbes, man's greatest fear is violent death: to be killed by your fellow man. What made him so paranoid of getting killed was that he lived during a very violent time in English history. There were the usual religious wars. And I think his king was even beheaded. Also, the Spanish Armada was setting sail for England. In fact, if I recall correctly, he was born prematurely during the Spanish Armada. He once said that his mother gave birth to both fear and himself."

Elliot was growing weary of Dave's conversation. He thought of leaving the office for an hour or so and going to the driving range.

"Anyway," Dave continued, "this philosophy professor asked the class to write down the one thing we feared the most. The majority of the class admitted - as Ash did when I asked her years later - that they feared growing old and living alone. A few mentioned things like murder and rape, but aging and loneliness topped the list."

"What was your answer?"

"To be murdered was my biggest fear."

Another long silence ensued.

After a while Elliot said, "I'm sorry, I think I missed your point. You lost me. I just haven't been able to concentrate since all this happened with the call girls."

"I understand. Here I am talking about a boring philosophy class that I had to take years ago. My point is, I think your wife plans to punish you some. Then she'll lighten up on you. Deep down, I think she fears growing old by herself like most of us. At her age, I think she doesn't want to start over. She doesn't like dealing with your faults, but she'll tolerate them as long as they're not too serious. A one-night stand isn't the same as having an affair or abusing her. So maybe this Hobbes didn't rate the fear of aging and loneliness as high as he should have. Of course, the century he lived in was a lot different than ours." Dave chuckled. "Elliot, I promise you I do better at business than philosophy. Also, I apologize for my behavior earlier; I cussed more in those few minutes than I've done in the last twenty years. I'm e-mailing you some info that I need you to look over. Give me a day's notice before you come down and I'll make reservations at a nearby hotel. And I promise, this will be a first-rate resort but free of any temptations. I'm looking forward to our doing business together."

## 36

"You've been pretty good about calling my office," Detective Hawkins said.

"I told you I would," Polita said. "I've left you five or six messages but didn't hear back."

"I guess I've had tunnel vision while working on Carmen's murder. Not to mention two other homicides. Sometimes my wife tells me that I get more wrapped up with the dead than with the livin'. Imagine your wife telling you that. But I guess she's right. I've been checking Carmen's e-mails, cell calls, blogs, Facebook - all of her social networkin' websites. So I guess I've been communicating more with her than with my own wife. Maybe it's time to retire."

They were seated in the interrogation room. The same female police officer sat next to Polita. The detective, with a folder spread out before him on the table, watched Polita with a grave expression as she sipped from a soft drink. She wore flat-heeled shoes, slacks, and a conservatively-cut blouse, but her hair remained brightly colored with its electric blue streaks, which from time to time the detective stared at disapprovingly.

"One of your messages said you moved to a new apartment," Detective Hawkins said.

"I wanted to let you know my new address. You told me to tell you everything."

"Why did you move?"

"I'm trying to start over. I thought changing apartments and jobs would help."

"You didn't change jobs – you were fired."

"I was going to quit anyway."

"Have you found a job?"

"Not yet."

"Are you looking?"

"Every day."

"You didn't answer my first question."

"What was the question?"

"Why did you move?"

"I thought I answered it. I'm trying to start over."

"Any other reason?"

"I needed a cheaper place."

"I think you're trying to hide from someone."

"What makes you think that?"

"Why don't you answer your own question?"

"I'm not afraid of anyone."

"Hmm. I'm not convinced. A friend of yours was just murdered. I think you have a lot to be afraid of."

"I don't want Dante to know where I live. But I'm not afraid of him."

"Why don't you have an answering machine at your new apartment? You had one at your other place."

"All I need is my cell. I don't need two phones. I'm trying to cut back. You and my mom have my number. I don't care to hear from anyone else."

"Who don't you want calling you?"

"Kim warned me about reporters harassing me. She said they've been calling her all the time. They've already found out where I moved to. This morning, a reporter showed up at my apartment. I closed the door in his face. I swear, I think they're following me."

"I talked to Kim about an hour ago. She's planning on making some money off this while the news is hot. Looks like she'll be cashin' in on her notoriety."

"I don't feel like talking to any reporters right now."

The scene around the table played out as it had before. The detective kept pushing his glasses up on his nose. Officer Rojas was quiet and gazed from Polita to the detective. Polita sipped from her soft drink.

"I've talked to a number of people who were at the marina the night Carmen was murdered," Detective Hawkins said. "Several witnesses told me you and Carmen got into a fight."

"There was no fight. We had a disagreement."

"Witnesses remembered hearing some shouting between you and Carmen. They said it sounded like a heated argument."

"I wanted to leave, she wanted to stay. It was no big deal. She was high or methed-out and wouldn't listen. So I left."

"It must've been a big deal because you knew that Carmen had a very expensive Rolex and a lot of cash on her."

Detective Hawkins glanced at the police officer.

Polita took a sip of her drink.

Detective Hawkins continued, "You said Carmen was on drugs. In her condition, why didn't you tell her to give you the Rolex and the money?"

"I tried to, but she wouldn't listen. And it was her operation. She was the boss."

"And when she didn't listen, you had an argument with her."

"You're putting words in my mouth." Her lips were dry and cracked, despite taking repeated sips from her drink.

"Did you ever see Mr. Anderson, the CEO from Boston, at the marina?"

"The last time I saw him was when he was lying on his hotel bed."

"He was seen wandering around the marina that night."

"Then I guess the knockout drops didn't work too good." Polita remembered that the bellhop had told her about his seeing Elliot at the marina. "He really fought it."

"What do you mean?"

"There for a while I thought he'd never pass out. He kept opening his eyes and struggling to get up. But then he didn't drink much to begin with. And I'm not sure how many knockout drops Carmen put in his wine."

"It was your practice then to get the hell out of the hotel rooms once you drugged and robbed your johns?"

"I tried to play it safe."

"Was Carmen being careless?"

"She was the few times I was with her."

She finished her soft drink. Nervously, she unwrapped a piece of gum and started chewing on it. While Officer Rojas watched her, Detective Hawkins looked through his folder.

"Go on," Detective Hawkins said, glancing up at Polita. "Keep talkin' to me."

"It was nerve-racking because she went about it so slow. It was like she was trying to make it more dangerous than it already was. Maybe it gave her a different kind of high. Maybe another cheap thrill. I don't know. She once told me that what she wanted to do was to make these men feel like they were being raped by her. She drugged them to make them defenseless. Then she'd embarrass them, especially the last one."

"Mr. Anderson?"

"The CEO from Boston, yeah. It wasn't just a sex thing, because she almost never had sex with them. She just wanted to -" Polita tried to think of another word, then shrugged - "humiliate them."

"Do you think this anger of hers was because she'd been raped?"

"She used to talk about some abusive men in her past."

"Did she ever talk about her father?"

"You asked about her father the last time I was here."

Detective Hawkins nodded but didn't say anything.

"Carmen never mentioned any names." Polita thought for a moment. "Like I've told you, I know very little about her private life. But watching how careless she was becoming, it seemed like she was trying to get arrested. Maybe it was her cry for help. She knew she was going over the edge. I mean, think about it, she robs this man and then she goes to a party that was practically under his hotel window. She was beginning a slide into erratic and even violent behavior."

"Boy, you are sounding like Dr. Phil again. You must've thought of majoring in psychology."

"You asked for my opinion."

"Maybe it was the other way around. Rippin' off johns had become too easy for her. Probably fifteen, twenty victims in six months. That was about one victim every five or six days. She was on a roll. She was becoming too cocky."

"Maybe," Polita said sullenly. She popped her gum once.

"Don't start gettin' an attitude with me."

Her forehead crinkled for a few seconds. "I can't say anything unless you talk down to me."

For what seemed like a full minute Detective Hawkins tapped on Carmen's trick book. He spoke briefly and quietly to Officer Rojas, who nodded. Once again Polita popped her gum. Detective Hawkins' eyes flinched each time she made that popping sound.

"Besides the johns in here, who would have a grudge against Carmen?" Detective Hawkins said.

"We talked about that last time too, and I told you I don't know."

"And I'll keep asking you. You've had some time to think about it. Name some names."

"I can't think of any one man who stands out, except for Dante and Ramón."

"Besides them."

"I don't know."

"You said Carmen used to date Allen, the bouncer. Then she dumped him, right?"

"I don't remember saying it like that."

"Let me put it this way. You said she quit dating him. Sound better?"

"Yeah, they went out some. Then they became friends."

"How'd Allen handle it when Carmen called off their romance?"

"Like most men, he didn't take rejection too good. He got pissed off and ranted and raved some. Carmen told me that one minute he'd call her a bad name, then he'd tell her how much he cared for her. That kind of thing."

"You ever see Allen get upset when he was around Carmen?"

"Maybe once. But like I said, I never knew much about her private life. Eventually, Allen gave up on her. The two of them got along fine when they went with some of us to Seth's brother's place in Everglades City. Everyone had a good time. All of us were just friends. It wasn't like Carmen and Allen were engaged or anything. They only went out a couple of times. You just don't get attached to people in our business."

"Was Carmen ever afraid of Allen?"

"She never said. They seemed to've gotten along OK. Like I said, in our line of work it doesn't pay to get attached."

"Did Carmen ever talk to you about a customer named Wink Ferrell?" Detective Hawkins flipped to another page in the folder and stopped.

"I heard that he used to be a regular at the café. Kim knows more about him than I do. She told me he was the friend of that businessman from Boston. That right there shows you how careless Carmen was becoming."

"Did you know that Mr. Ferrell was at the Luxuria the night of Carmen's murder?"

"I wasn't aware of that," Polita lied.

"Mr. Ferrell was there for the same business convention that Mr. Anderson was attending." Detective Hawkins read from his notes. "Mr. Ferrell's roommate at the hotel was a Mr. Dave Kornick. Mr. Kornick lives in Naples but has businesses in Miami and in Naples. When he's in town, Mr. Kornick has been known to visit the café with Mr. Ferrell."

"I don't know him. Kim would know more about those two men than I would. Why don't you ask her?"

"I have. And I've tried to talk to Mr. Ferrell and Mr. Kornick."

"Are they talking?"

"They didn't say much." Detective Hawkins turned a page in the folder. He was quiet for a moment. "This Dante Rivas fascinates me the more I talk to him. Tell me a little more about him."

"You want to know if I think he killed Carmen?"

"You can answer your own question if you want." Detective Hawkins chuckled as he glanced at Officer Rojas.

"I think Dante knew that Carmen was getting too reckless to suit him. I wouldn't put it past Dante to have someone kill Carmen for him."

"Someone like Ramón?"

"Maybe. Ramón would be the obvious choice. But I think Dante enjoys the attention you cops are giving him. His friends see him as a possible murder suspect. In their eyes they look up to someone who flaunts himself before the law. They'll start to think this Dante is dangerous. Someone not to mess with. A real badass."

"I've worked the streets long enough to know his type."

She continued to chew her gum, but without popping it. A minute or two of silence. Detective Hawkins glanced through the folder. He yawned. Officer Rojas was totally attentive and always kept her perfect posture. From time to time she stared with seeming distaste at Polita's hair.

"I think the man you want," Polita said, looking from Detective Hawkins to Officer Rojas, "is hiding in his big house in one of those gated neighborhoods with security guards. He's probably middle-aged, makes a lot of money, drives a fancy car, has spoiled kids, and his pretty stay-at-home wife is bored as hell and goes to charity events."

"That fits the description of just about every john in here." Detective Hawkins held up Carmen's trick book and waved it in the air several times.

"Those men in that book aren't a whole lot different than Dante and Ramón."

"Sounds like you're defending Dante."

"I could care less about him. I'm just saying that those johns are better educated and have more money and wear tailored suits and know how to hide their sleaze better than some punk like Dante."

"With your experience in these matters, I guess you know what you're talking about."

"Again, I'm just giving you my opinion. You asked me to think of someone who might've had a grudge against Carmen."

She looked away from the detective's probing stare. Moments passed. He returned to the folder. Deep in thought, he studied it while tapping his fingers on the table. Officer Rojas continued to stare at Polita.

"A stripper takes a big risk because of the possibility that an obsessed customer might want to stalk her," Detective Hawkins said, without looking up from his folder; he seemed to have read this statement from his notes.

"Is that a question?"

Detective Hawkins took off his glasses and gazed at her.

"A woman could walk through a shopping mall and take the same risk," she said.

"But your risk was obviously much greater. And you and Kim and Carmen took an even greater risk by going into this so-called escort service. And if that wasn't enough, you robbed your johns."

"It got one of us killed. What more can I say?"

"That makes you careless, too."

She cleared her throat slightly.

Detective Hawkins closed one of the folders and pushed it aside, almost to the end of the table, as if it troubled him to look at it. He glanced once at Officer Rojas. Then he stared for a long time at Polita. His silence troubled her. She met his gaze, wondering what he was thinking.

"You've been lying to me," Detective Hawkins said. He assumed his pouncing position by hunching up his shoulders and leaning over the table. His voice sounded deeper, almost a growl. "I've told you that if you cooperate with me I'll do what I can for you. You've deceived me about something that I consider very important."

"Like what?" Polita stopped chewing her gum.

"Why didn't you mention anything about the DVD?"

"You never asked."

"Think of a better answer."

"I never thought it was important."

"You didn't?"

"Is this a trick question or something?"

"I don't play tricks." Detective Hawkins looked at Officer Rojas, smiling broadly. Then he returned his gaze, slowly, to Polita. "You're the one who turns the tricks."

"Not anymore."

Detective Hawkins snorted something under his breath. His smile vanished.

Polita went to take a sip from her drink but realized it was empty.

"From what you've told me," Detective Hawkins said, "the Rolexes had become almost nickel and dime stuff after Dante got his cut. Dealin' with jewelry can be a hassle. But if you were to videotape your johns, then you could blackmail them for a lot more money. Like you said, these johns have families and reputations to protect. Y'all were gonna become extortion artists. Makes perfect sense."

"That was Dante's and Carmen's plan."

"He said it was yours."

"He's a liar. That's one of the reasons why Carmen wanted me to be with her that night. She asked me to videotape that businessman from Boston. To my knowledge, it was the first time she had tried it."

"Where is this DVD?"

"Carmen took everything with her. She made sure she kept the valuable stuff."

Detective Hawkins, his forearms resting on the table, continued staring at Polita. He made no attempt to press his finger against his glasses when they started to make the quarter-of-an- inch slide down his nose. The wooden Officer Rojas actually shifted in her chair. Her holster squeaked when she moved.

The detective finally took his eyes off Polita and silently read from another folder. Several minutes passed before his eyes lifted back up, slowly, and settled on Polita. For some reason, he and Officer Rojas were staring at her hair more than the last time they had been together. It was as though they noticed that her hair had been cut – chopped off – unevenly, in the back, by the bellhop.

"I want to go over one last thing with you," Detective Hawkins said. "There was a call girl who used to meet some of her johns at the Luxuria. She was murdered about a year and a half ago. Unlike Carmen, she was murdered in her apartment. Her throat was slit. Her apartment, we think, wasn't broken into, so she might've known this person and let him in. Her killer was never found. Now, I can't help but to ask some similar questions as I've done with Carmen's case. Was it one of her johns who killed her? Or was it maybe a hotel employee? Just out of curiosity, we reviewed all the johns in Carmen's trick book to see if any of them had ever checked into the Luxuria anytime over a year and a half ago, but we didn't come up with anything. By the way, we don't know if this other call girl had ever kept a trick book. Then, we did a background check of all the employees at the hotel. Naturally, there's a high turn-over rate among hotel employees. We managed to come up with seventy-three employees who've worked there for at least two years or more, from chambermaids to waiters to groundskeepers to managers. I want you to look at each employee's photo, which I have here, and tell me if you recognize any of them."

Detective Hawkins handed a folder to Polita. Inside, dozens of photos were arranged in plastic protector sheets; under each photo were the name and the job description of each employee.

Before she looked through the photos, Polita said, "I've only been to the Luxuria three times. I don't remember Carmen talking to any of the employees. Have you shown these to Kim? She's been to the hotel more than I have."

"I showed them to her earlier, but like I said, she hasn't been cooperatin' much. Now it's your turn."

Polita flipped through the photos while the detective and the police officer looked on. She showed no emotion when she came to the bellhop's photo. When she finished looking through the rest of the folder, she handed it back to the detective.

"I've never seen any of them approach Carmen when I was at the hotel," Polita said.

She took the empty soft drink can off the table and held it in her lap. Detective Hawkins placed the folder on top of his other paperwork.

"I want you and Kim to see me together sometime soon," Detective Hawkins said. "I'll call you both to give you the day and the time. You can go now."

"OK. So, I guess I'll be seeing you."

With both Detective Hawkins and Officer Rojas watching her, Polita walked out of the room. Before she reached the exit doors, she began to feel light-headed. She stopped at a water cooler for a drink. No matter how hard she tried, she couldn't get the bellhop out of her mind. The photo showed him in his khaki uniform, his white smile a leering curl, his slicked-back hair neatly barbered. Should she turn around, walk down all those hallways to the interrogation room, and tell Detective Hawkins about him?

A concerned police officer stopped next to the water cooler and asked if she needed help. Polita told him she was on her way out and opened the exit doors.

# 37

After soccer practice, Elliot and Jeremy returned home. Karen was in the kitchen preparing dinner. She greeted Jeremy with a hug and a kiss. Predictably, she had nothing to do with Elliot. Elliot and Jeremy went upstairs, cleaned up, and returned to the kitchen. On the table were two place settings of vegetable lasagna. Karen and Jeremy sat down and began eating while Elliot stood at the counter and made himself a sandwich.

"Jeremy, I want you to eat all of your salad," Karen told him. Without looking at Elliot she said, "Wink called about an hour ago."

That was the first time she had spoken to him in three days. He was getting used to those withering stares and punitive silences of hers.

"What did he want?" Elliot said.

"He called to give you an update on what's going on in hot and humid Miami."

"That's good to hear." He poured himself a diet drink.

"You look a little perplexed. I know what you're thinking: why would Wink call our home number? He didn't. You left your cell on the table and I answered it. Of course, Wink was surprised when he heard my voice."

"Hmm. I was looking for my cell at soccer practice."

"I hope you don't mind that I checked your messages."

"I'm not hiding anything."

A smirk appeared on her lips. "Oh, I'm sure you don't have anything to hide. I got Wink to tell me quite a bit about your dilemma. However, I hung up on him when he started to BS me with his flatter routine."

She turned her attention to Jeremy and asked him about school.

Jeremy, his mouth full of food, said, "Hey, Dad, why aren't you eatin' with us?"

"I haven't been invited," he said. "Someone's excluding me from all family functions."

He took the plate he had prepared and went to the living room. He turned on the evening news and called Wink but got no answer. After the news was over, and he had finished eating, Jeremy came into the living room and asked his father for help on his homework, so they went upstairs to Jeremy's room. Jeremy got out his crayons and told his father that he had to draw a map of Massachusetts.

"Dad, when are you and mom gonna quit fighting?" He stopped drawing and looked up at his father.

"Seems like we grownups argue more than you kids do."

"How long you gonna be staying in the guest room?"

"Until your mother and I make up."

"Then you'll be in the big bedroom with mom?"

"I hope."

After Elliot helped Jeremy with his homework, he went back downstairs and watched TV. He tried calling Wink again but didn't get an answer. Karen passed through the living room.

From his recliner he said, "What's the exercise program tonight, treadmill or stationary bike?"

She stopped and glared at him. "I can't hear you when you have the TV turned up."

He pressed the mute button on the remote and repeated his question. "Are you going to work out?"

"What's it to you?"

"I'm just trying to carry on a conversation with my wife."

"I've worked all day, cooked dinner, and cleaned up the kitchen. I'm too tired to work out. Trying to keep myself in shape was never good enough for you anyway, was it?"

"Forget I even asked." He pressed the volume button and resumed watching TV.

She started up the stairs but changed her mind and returned to the living room.

"What did Wink, your partner in crime, have to say?" she said.

"I couldn't reach him."

"I'm sure all this waiting is tearing you up inside."

"I'm not one to dwell on a very stupid mistake I made. I'm getting on with my life. With or without you."

"If you're so calm about everything, then why have you had such a hard time sleeping the past couple of nights?"

"How would you know if I'm sleeping or not? I've been down the hallway."

"I can hear you. The entire house shakes when you're tossing and turning and walking around."

"I miss sleeping in my bed."

"I heard you pacing the hallway and going up and down the stairs last night. Your conscience must be bothering you."

"I don't have a problem with my conscience. And I don't remember pacing."

"Then you must be walking in your sleep again."

"I'll try not to disturb you from now on."

"Did you ever hire an attorney?"

"I sure did."

"Who?"

"Jack Hartigan."

"Good choice. You must be very worried if you had to hire one of the best criminal attorneys in Boston."

"I don't settle for mediocrity at anything."

"Including the women you hire to fuck?"

He cut her a black glare.

"Why don't you try calling Wink again?" she said. "Are you worried I'll overhear how the two of you plan to get out of the mess you're in?"

He watched TV.

"I know one of the reasons why Wink wants to talk to you." She leaned back against the wall, arms crossed. "There have been a number of stories in *The Miami Herald* and on TV about the Rolex Bandits."

Elliot raised an eyebrow but said nothing.

"Oh, in case you wanted to know," Karen said, "The Rolex Bandits are lighting up the Internet. I haven't had any problems finding information on them. I'm surprised Wink hasn't been keeping you informed."

"He has been. But I'm not the least bit interested in what goes on down there unless it concerns my business deal."

"One article showed a picture of the three women together. They should be dubbed 'The Three Gorgons.' They're sexy and attractive in a sort of witchy way. Their wild hairstyles, tattoos, far-off, fuck-you gazes made them look possessed. They looked as though they had just crawled out of the underworld. I guess women like that turn on middle-aged men."

"Personally, I prefer the frustrated, full-of-anger middle-aged woman."

"Although I have to admit, there was one article about Carmen that turned out to be quite touching."

"That's interesting. Now you're calling her by her first name. A second ago she was Satan's girlfriend."

"I thought you would at least be curious to hear about the kind of life Carmen lived."

"I could care less about a dead call girl who scared the fuck out of me."

"That sounds cold-hearted."

"Then I must be a cold-hearted person."

"So it was a passionless murder committed by a passionless man, is that what you're saying?"

"Keep it up, Karen. You really enjoy verbally abusing me, don't you?"

"I've been doing some research into what happened after Carmen left your hotel room. I have a theory as to how it was physically possible for you to have killed her."

He turned up the volume of the TV. She stepped closer, within arm's length of his recliner.

"Your weak defense," she said, raising her voice, "is that you were too drugged to have been physically capable of hunting Carmen down and killing her. But wasn't it strange how quickly you recovered to go look for Wink? And while you were trying to find him, lo and behold, there was Carmen at the marina. She was probably high or drunk and vulnerable. You waited until she was alone, then you picked up a golf club and smashed her skull in. Then you pushed her off the pier and into the water, probably thinking that the tide would take her out to sea. But she got snagged under the marina. Am I right so far?"

"Why don't you talk a little louder so Jeremy can hear every fucking word you say?"

"Why don't you turn the volume down so I can speak to you in a normal tone?"

"I'm not interested in hearing your sick remarks."

She shouted, "I'll tell you anyway!"

Elliot, exasperated, turned red in the face and mumbled something. He turned off the TV.

"That's better." She lowered her voice. "My theory is based on the time we both got sick eating oysters."

"What in the fuck are you talking about?" A fierce crease appeared on his forehead.

"It was about eight, nine years ago. We were in the Keys visiting the Warrens and some of their relatives. Come to think of it, that was the last time you had asked me to go to Florida with you. The Warrens were having a fish fry and oysters on the half shell. Later that evening, two of their children got sick. Then, one by one, the adults started throwing up. The oysters turned out to be bad."

"What does any of that have to do with me?" The crease cut deeper into his forehead.

"It has plenty to do with you. You and another heavy-set man were the last to get sick, and when you did, it didn't affect you that much. You threw up some, took a short nap, and were back to normal within an hour or so. Everyone else stayed sick into the next day. Because of your size, your body was better able to absorb the toxin. That explains why you were capable of recovering so quickly after you were drugged by Carmen."

Karen's eyes glittered with delight. At first Elliot stared at her in disbelief. Then, slowly, he shook his head with a trace of a smile appearing. A short time later, his smile edged into laughter.

"That was the most asinine thing I've ever heard you say," he said. "Your anger has completely distorted your sense of reality."

"In case you're wondering, I pieced a lot of this together through my conversations with you and Wink. And the Internet has also been a big help."

"I'm not impressed with your research."

"Each newspaper story gets more and more intriguing. One of the big stories in *The Miami Herald* is if the police are going to start leaking information to the press about the johns. I can see the headlines about you in the *Globe*: 'Local businessman's name appears in trick book of a murdered Miami call girl.' Imagine what our parents and friends and employees - not to mention our own son - will think when your name is linked to a murder. And you can bet that our local TV news stations will be tripping over each other to get the inside scoop. Don't expect to be shown any mercy. I already have in mind a well-respected child psychologist for Jeremy. His friends at school and the players on his soccer team will ridicule him once they hear that his father – and their coach - is a pervert and murder suspect."

"If my name hasn't appeared on TV or in the papers by now, I doubt that it ever will."

A moment of silence passed between them. Karen sat on the sofa. A faint smile curved her lips.

"I was hoping you'd leave," Elliot said. "But I guess you want to hang around and rub more salt into the wound. You get your kicks making me miserable."

"That smartass comment of yours at my fortieth birthday is coming back to haunt you."

"What in God's name are you talking about now? First, it was oysters. Now it was one of your birthday parties."

"At my party, you told everyone that you might have to trade me in for two twenty-year-olds. Those were your exact words. You certainly did that, for at least one night."

"It was just a goddamn joke."

"A stupid one at that." She was no longer smiling. "Wink was at that party. Only you and he laughed at the joke. I bet he remembers it."

"Why don't you call and ask him?"

"I wouldn't ask that liar anything. I never did like him."

"When he lived in Boston, we spent quite a bit of time with him and his ex-wife. You got along OK with her."

"He ran around on her."

"She did the same to him."

"He used to bully her around when he had an audience."

"I wouldn't go that far. Wink just has a very forceful personality."

"His two kids have nothing to do with him."

"Most teenagers I know try to have as little as possible to do with their parents."

"I never had any respect for him. He's a loser."

"You called him that the other night. Think of a new name to call him."

"I'll call him a loser as long as I feel like it. He befriends people like you so he can use you for something. He tried to start at least three or four businesses on his own and failed every time. He keeps moving south with each failure. From Boston to Washington to Atlanta to Miami."

"At least he keeps trying. What makes you so special? Your parents gave you everything you wanted."

"So did yours."

"We were both very lucky. But I don't pass judgment on Wink. He never seems to get a break. I've seen some men almost destroyed because they have such shitty jobs and so much of a man's sense of self-worth is tied up in what he does for a living. Life's petty humiliations have tried to beat Wink down, but he somehow keeps getting back up. I admire him for that."

"All right, I'll give him some credit. At least he's a charismatic loser."

"Maybe that's one of the reasons why I like him. Ever since his ex-wife left him, I think he's been an intensely lonely man. He has had his share of problems, but he's a fun-loving person to be around."

"Behind those many smiles of his, he's full of anger."

"I don't deny his shortcomings, but I can count on him to be my friend."

"If you like him so much, why didn't you ever promote him to senior account executive? That would've made his career. It would've given him the stability his sorry ass needed. You kept him as a salesman."

"I probably would've promoted him, but that's about the time he was planning to go into business for himself. I needed someone committed to my company."

"I think one of the main reasons he left you was because he didn't think you were going to give him the promotion."

"I told him I wasn't sure if he would've worked out as the senior account executive. Wink's good at working with people, but not necessarily managing them. He would've made more money staying where he was."

"But he wanted the title. Deep down he still resents - maybe even hates - you for passing him over."

"All I know is he's getting a nice commission with the business I'm opening up in Miami."

"I wouldn't count him out as the one who set you up to get robbed. Did you ever wonder why he roomed with this other businessman and not you?"

"Wink knows how much I snore. And he knows I always prefer my own room."

"If he didn't set you up in some way, then I'm sure he's having a good time watching you squirm."

"Like you are?"

"You're a bully who deserves a comeuppance!"

Karen stormed out of the living room and headed up the stairs. Elliot turned on the TV but turned off the volume. For a long while he stared at the images on the screen. He was back at Café Sinsations with Wink and Dave. They sat among a crowd of businessmen, watching Carmen perform on the dance floor. She was dressed in her Indian outfit with a feather in her headband. She wore a feathered neon G-string. Her white moccasins were a blur as she danced. War paint was smeared across her face.

Elliot swallowed hard and rubbed his wrists.

# 38

Her arms around her updrawn knees, Polita was sitting in bed and staring out the window. The morning light that came through the blinds was diffused, a pale haze that drained the color from her complexion. She had endured another disturbing dream, and her fever-tossed sleep had left her with a headache. Her brain felt burned, hollowed out.

In the dream she was walking along the tideline of a deserted beach and noticed a salt-soaked, bloated body completely covered with seaweed. The body was desperately sucking in its last breaths. She began to disentangle the seaweed, but it was like an endless ball of yarn. The breathing grew faint and then stopped all together. By the time she removed all the seaweed, the body had disappeared; in its place was an open grave. Carmen lay at the bottom, her worm-eaten face half gone but her bulging eyes untouched and staring up at Polita.

An hour passed before she got out of bed and took a shower. Those gasping, wheezing breaths of the corpse in the dream still sounded in her ears.

After she got dressed, she watered the plants and flowers and vacuumed the apartment. She then sat down at her laptop and e-mailed a letter:

> *Dear Mama,*
> *I got your letter yesterday. Thanks for your support and love during these hard times. Your love means more to me now than ever. Also, thanks for asking me to come back home and live with you. As much as I'd like to, I can't leave Miami right now because of legal reasons. The cops want me to stay here while they continue*

*their investigation. Mama, I'll be going to jail soon. I know it's hard for you to accept that your only daughter broke some serious laws. I'm tying my best to cooperate, and I think the cops will help me out some. In your e-mail you tried to put some of the blame on yourself for what I've done, but you've been a great mother. I'm the one who has made all the mistakes. You warned me time and again. I was just too stubborn to listen. Remember our water taxi ride in Ft. Lauderdale when you last gave me some advice? Mothers who have daughters my age are going to their college graduations or are watching them get married. I'm sorry I've been such a disappointment and an embarrassment to you. I've hit rock bottom. I don't think I can go any lower. But one day, I promise, I'll bounce back and do something with my life. And then I hope you'll be proud of me.*

She stopped typing when she heard a knock on the door. She remained at the table, not making a sound. Several more taps sounded. Then silence. She waited a few more minutes. When she finally got up from the table, she saw Michelle's broad frame standing at the sliding glass door and staring at her with a wide grin. Polita invited her inside.

"I was taking my morning walk and decided to drop by and check out your new apartment," Michelle said.

"I hide every time I hear a knock because I think it might be a reporter." Polita knew from Michelle's expression that she didn't believe her.

"Seems you and Kim are in the news almost every day."

"None of it's flattering, is it? I try not to watch TV or read the newspaper."

Michelle shrugged. They sat across from each other at the table. Michelle wore gym shorts, a loose-fitting T-shirt, and cross-trainer sneakers. Her mannish hands were folded in her lap. Her nails were painted pink. Silently, her eyes took in everything around her.

"Do I make you nervous?" Michelle said, her eyes settling on Polita, who was tapping her fingernails on the laptop.

"No. Why do you ask?"

"You always seem to get fidgety when I'm around you."

"I'm just uptight right now, not because of you, but because I've got to see a detective in a little while." She glanced at the oven clock. Once again she noticed doubt in Michelle's eyes. She had lied about the detective; he had canceled today's appointment and rescheduled it for tomorrow.

"I won't keep you," Michelle said.

"I've got a few minutes."

Momentarily distracted, Michelle became quiet and gazed out the sliding glass door. Her presence did make Polita uneasy. Polita was relieved that she had an excuse to leave early. She kept her eyes on Michelle's hands, which were folding and unfolding in this big woman's lap.

"I quit at the café yesterday," Michelle said. Her shoulders slumped and she suddenly sounded dejected. "I feel bad for Miss Wanda because so many of us have quit in the past week or so. Allen quit. Then three dancers walked out the other day. They said they had a bad feeling about the café. One of them, Jo Ann, said she left because she thinks there's some crazy man preying on the dancers. Ever since Carmen was killed..."

"Is that why you quit?"

"I quit because of the manager." Michelle rubbed her hands together.

"Mark cut back your hours?"

"No, he kept me on my same schedule."

"You look troubled about something."

"You might be interested to hear about this. I was in the dressing room, in one of the bathroom stalls." Michelle's hands were moving in her lap. "I had my iPod on, so I didn't hear

Mark come into the dressing room, and he didn't see me in the bathroom stall. It was yesterday morning, and it was just me and Mark and one other employee getting things ready for lunch. When I flushed the toilet and opened the stall door, I surprised Mark, who was going through one of the dancer's lockers. At first he had a scared look. He was like a little boy who got caught with his hands in a cookie jar."

"Did he say anything?"

"He flipped out. He accused me of spying on him. He even yelled at me. I got upset, so I went out to my car. He followed me. We were arguing when Miss Wanda drove up. I was in tears and told her what had happened. She explained that she and Mark have the combinations to all the lockers, but I told her that he was going through the lockers without any of the dancers' permission. Miss Wanda and Mark got into an argument right in front of me. Then she went inside. Before Mark followed her in, he gave me the meanest look anyone's ever given me. I tried working past lunch, but I finally quit when I couldn't take the way Mark was staring at me."

"Did you catch him stealing anything?"

"That's what was strange. Miss Wanda called in all the dancers who worked lunch and asked them if anyone had anything stolen from their lockers. None of the dancers said they were missing anything."

"What do you think Mark was doing?"

"I think he had some kinky reason to go through our things."

"That means he could've gone through Carmen's locker. And mine."

"I don't trust him at all. He's real sneaky."

Polita, not knowing what to think of Michelle's story, stood up and said she had to leave. In silence Michelle approached Polita and put her hands on her shoulders. Polita turned away from her.

"I still make you nervous," Michelle said.

"Like Carmen, I'm just not the touchy-feely type, I guess. Nothing against you." Polita continued to keep her eyes on Michelle's hands.

"One of these days you'll like me."

Quiet and subdued, Michelle walked around the kitchen, stopping once, her eyes hardening into a brief stare at Polita. A moment later she glanced at the kitchen appliances, avoiding any eye contact at all. Polita found Michelle's different expressions hard to read.

Polita took her purse and walked outside with Michelle.

"Mind if I drop by from time to time?" Michelle said.

"You know where I live."

"Is that a yes?"

"Sure."

"I'll wait till things calm down. I know you've got a lot on you right now. But you've got me to talk to."

"Thanks. I appreciate that."

Michelle took out her cell phone and started texting. They went their separate ways, with Michelle walking down the sidewalk while talking on her cell phone and Polita getting into her car. While driving, she took out her cell phone and called Detective Hawkins and left a message on his voice mail: "This is Polita Flores. Just checking in. I'm going to some job interviews. See you tomorrow." She stopped at a traffic light, wondering why Mark would go through the dancers' lockers. She never remembered having anything stolen. Could he have found Carmen's trick book in her locker? If he had, he would have known all along about Carmen's illegal business.

# 39

Elliot opened his eyes to the darkness of the bedroom. His snoring had turned into a brief coughing fit, and he struggled momentarily to catch his breath. The blankets were wrapped around him so tightly that he could barely move. Drowsily confused, he thought for a moment that he was back in the hotel room. He sensed there was someone standing near him, and a scent of perfume hung in the room. He kicked the blankets free, sat up in bed, and switched on the lamp. In a cold sweat, he glanced around the room. Two separate portraits – one of his parents, the other of his mother and father in-law - stared down at him from the dresser. His parents, both in their early eighties, would be devastated, but embarrassingly supportive, when they found out that their only son was involved with two call girls. As for his in-laws, they would probably be hostile. His parents lived in Amherst, Massachusetts, and his in-laws lived in Stamford, Connecticut.

The scent of perfume meant that Karen had been snooping around the room when he was at work.

He got out of bed and gulped down two aspirins and a cup of water. He had been grinding his teeth, and his jaw hurt. The heat blew out of the vents and the house was warm. He checked on Jeremy, who was sound asleep. The hamster was nibbling on something in its cage.

He stopped at Karen's closed door and tried the doorknob. Locked. Back in his room, he got out *The Wall Street Journal* and read for half an hour.

The clock in the hallway chimed three times.

He set the newspaper down, took out a credit card from his wallet, and tiptoed down the hallway. Carefully, timidly, he inserted the credit card between Karen's door and the inside lock. The door opened easily. He sneaked inside the bedroom and sat in one of the chairs. It was too dark to see her.

He sat motionless and listened to her breathing.

The clock chimed four times before he returned to his room.

# 40

Polita stopped at the security office at the Luxuria Resort and Spa. She told the gray-haired female guard that she had an appointment to see Detective Hawkins. The guard checked for her name on a clipboard, marked it, and issued her a visitor's pass.

"Detective Hawkins wants you to meet him at the marina," the woman said. "Need any directions?"

"I know how to get there."

She drove down the winding, flower-bordered road until she reached the marina's parking lot. With her handbag strapped over her shoulder, she walked past a group of hotel guests who were filing into a tour bus. A security officer in a golf cart passed Polita, slowed down, then turned around and drove by her one more time. He stared at her but didn't say anything.

She met Detective Hawkins at the marina. The detective looked past her as if she was of absolutely no interest. He watched as a yacht was leaving the marina. The teal water below the planks of the marina was flat and clear and showed the sandy bottom and a carpet of seagrass. A gull's shadow appeared across the planks. The sun-sparkle on the water shone off the detective's glasses. Several pelicans, looking for handouts, were perched on pilings.

Feeling awkward and unimportant, Polita watched the gull circling the marina. A woman came from around the seawall and approached Detective Hawkins. She wore a navy blue pants suit, had short, wide hips, and was mid-forties. The two talked for a while, leaving Polita out of the conversation. She wished to escape the glowering sun and find some shade.

Detective Hawkins introduced the woman to Polita by simply saying, "Detective Avilia." He held that same steady gaze on the horizon. "She's been workin' on this investigation with me."

Detective Avilia nodded at Polita but said nothing. Her tiny black eyes had a cold glint in them. Polita shaded her face from the sun. She was wondering where Kim was, since she was supposed to be here.

"This is where Carmen's body was found," Detective Avilia said. She was looking at one of the barnacled pilings under the marina. "She was hit over the head, collapsed where we're standing, then fell – or was pushed - into the water. We believe this because there was blood only on these three planks. There was no evidence that she was killed somewhere else and dragged to this spot. At night this is the darkest area of the marina. The trees and hanging moss over here block off most of the landscape lights. And there are no surveillance cameras over here." She pointed to the end of the marina. "The yacht where the party was held was docked over there. That's where all the people were, and that's where it was lit up the brightest. Someone must've lured her over here. No one heard her scream, if she did indeed scream. I think she knew her murderer. She was facing him."

"Or her," Detective Hawkins said, taking his glasses off and wiping the bridge of his nose with his fingers. His watery eyes glanced at Polita.

Polita looked away from Detective Hawkins and gazed at nothing in particular.

"Why do you think Carmen was over here?" Detective Hawkins said. "She was away from everyone, and in the darkest corner of the marina, where there were no surveillance cameras."

"I don't have any idea," Polita said. She stared at the smooth water and the sun-drenched surroundings. "I thought Kim was supposed to meet us here."

"I don't think Kim wants to cooperate anymore. I can't force either one of you to come out here. Do you want to go?"

"Once I quit cooperating you'll arrest me."

Detective Hawkins put his glasses back on.

"I don't like being here," Polita said. "I'd like to forget about this hotel."

"I can understand that. It'll take just a few minutes. You want a soft drink or some water?"

Polita shook her head.

"Show me where you saw Carmen last," Detective Hawkins said.

"At the end of the marina, where the yacht was."

"We know she was on the yacht for at least fifteen minutes. But no one remembers seeing her leave the yacht." Detective Hawkins studied the area around the marina, his glasses glinting as he slowly turned his head. "An outside bar was set up by the pool, so she could've been walking this way to get a drink or to visit someone she knew. But why would she go to a bar over by the pool when there was a bar on the yacht? Why would she walk an extra three-hundred feet just for a drink?"

"I don't know why she'd walk toward the pool unless she was leaving."

"Let's take a walk. I want you to get a good look at some of the employees. If you remember Carmen talking to any of them, I want you to point them out to me."

They walked past the pro shop at the pitch-n-putt course. The golf pro was instructing a young woman on her putting technique. He glanced at Polita and the two detectives when they passed by. The security officer whom Polita had seen earlier drove by in his golf cart and nodded at the detectives. They passed flower-filled gardens that were bathed in a soft light. Groundskeepers worked nearby.

Detective Hawkins stopped and waited for a response from Polita. She shrugged and said nothing. Then they approached the pool around which hotel guests were lazing away in the sun or under colorful umbrellas. Hotel attendants delivered towels and carried trays of drinks and food to the guests. The scent of pool chlorine and suntan lotion filled the air.

"Anyone look familiar to you?" Detective Hawkins said.

"The only employees I saw Carmen talk to were the bartenders."

Polita, not knowing if the bellhop was working at this time, tensed up when the detectives approached the entrance to the hotel. They passed through the lounge. Detective Hawkins looked at the bartender, then to Polita. She shook her head. Both detectives and Polita sat on a bench in the atrium-lobby. Within minutes, four khaki-clad bellhops passed them pushing suitcases on carts; Phil wasn't among them. Polita remembered when Phil had told her about having to take a guest's makeup kit - "almost the size of a suitcase" - to the top floor the night Carmen had been murdered.

"Take your time and look around," Detective Hawkins said.

Polita glanced at the surveillance cameras and motion scanners above the entrances of each door and remembered that Carmen had warned her about them: *Be careful, the hotel's eyes will see you.* She was certain that both Carmen and Phil were too smart to have been seen together at the hotel.

"They could tell you more than I could," Polita said, staring at one of the surveillance cameras nearest to her. "They're here 24/7."

"We've checked them," Detective Hawkins said. "This resort has umpteen surveillance cameras and not one picked up Carmen with any clarity. She was like the fog that came off the sea; she was everywhere, but nowhere. She may as well have been a ghost."

Detective Avilia and Polita watched as three guests were getting off the elevator. Polita's eyes scanned each floor above her until they reached the top one. She saw no sign that Phil might be watching her from any balcony.

Ten minutes later both detectives and Polita stood up.

"I might have to ask you to come back tomorrow night," Detective Hawkins said. "I want to make sure we cover as many employees as possible."

"I've got to work tomorrow night."

"You found a job?"

"I'm working at a party."

"Oh, right, Kim told me about that. You're dancin' at a bachelor's party. I can see Kim doing that, but I thought you decided to go straight."

"I need the money because I'm hiring a lawyer."

"Oh?"

"Next time you see me I'll have a lawyer who can answer your questions."

"Everyone's gettin' themselves a lawyer." Detective Hawkins glanced at Polita, then up at the surveillance camera. "Suit yourself."

"I don't mean to be rude or anything, but I need a lawyer's help with your questions. I get all confused."

"You think I've been confusin' you on purpose?"

"No, I didn't mean it the way it sounded. I appreciate what you've done for me. I really have. I mean, I know you can arrest me right here and now. Honestly, I've been trying my best to help you. And even though I'm dancing at a party, I promise I plan to go straight."

"Dancin' at a bachelor's party doesn't seem to be the best choice. But, hell, do what you want. I tried to help."

"Like I said, I appreciate it. I'll have a bouncer with me. Everything will be OK. I just need some quick cash."

"Wantin' quick cash is what got you in this big mess to begin with."

"In a few days I plan to start working as a waitress or in a florist shop. I promised my mom that's where I'll start till I can find something better."

Detective Hawkins turned away from Polita and spoke to Detective Avilia. He had nothing to do with her. Slowly, haltingly, Polita shied away from them and went out the door by the pool. She walked straight ahead, avoiding eye contact with any of the employees.

# 41

Elliot was stacking the dishwasher when he heard Karen's Land Rover pull into the garage. It was past seven o'clock. Karen, looking haggard, entered the kitchen and set her briefcase next to the table. Without speaking to him, she took a bottle of water and a tuna sandwich out of the refrigerator. Then she sat at the table and began to eat. Elliot meanwhile was wiping off the kitchen counter and the top of the stove with a washcloth. When she finished her sandwich, she spoke first by asking about Jeremy.

"I tucked him in bed a few minutes ago," he said.

"This early?"

"He had a stomachache." He looked at her slumped shoulders. "Long day?"

"I had to fire an employee who worked for me for eight years. It's the one thing I hate the most."

"Feel like talking about it?"

"Not now."

"Let me know when you do."

Karen, yawning, opened her briefcase.

The past two minutes were the most civil she had acted toward him since their blowup over the call girls. He felt he had an opening and moved a little closer to her.

"You look really troubled," he said. "I can be a good listener if you want to talk about it."

"I've searched the Internet for some more interesting stories from Miami."

"I thought we were talking about one of your employees."

"That's what you would *like* for me to talk about. You always want to change the subject. I won't fall for your tactics."

Her voice was flat with no inflection. With a resigned expression, he wrung out the washcloth and placed it on the counter.

"Thanks for leading me on," he said. "I thought you would be too tired to ridicule me tonight. Your endurance at this is remarkable. I was hoping we could start trying to have civilized conversations around here. I guess I was wrong."

"The cops and the media are playing games about releasing the names of the johns in the trick book."

"I thought we had this conversation before."

"Wink hasn't called to tell you about any of this?"

"We seem to be playing phone tag."

"He'll end up deserting you before it's all over."

"You keep repeating that as if you want it to happen. No, despite all his faults, I think I can count on him. He left a message that he'll be picking me up in Naples this weekend. I've decided to fly down and finish my business deal with Dave by Monday."

She put her reading glasses on and read from a sheet of paper. He turned away from her and dried off some dishes.

"You might be interested to know this," she said, placing the paper on the table. "The police issued a statement yesterday saying that they're not going to release the names in the trick book – at least for now - because none of the johns had been arrested for anything."

"That's old news. My attorney called my office today to tell me that. Like you, he stays on top of everything that has to do with me. Except he's on my side."

"They will, however, continue to question the johns about Carmen's murder."

"My attorney said I won't be hearing from the police after he spoke with them."

"It doesn't mean that a detective won't leak the names to some enterprising reporter. You and the other johns are about to get caught in the vortex of a media storm."

"I'm expecting you to leak my name to *The Miami Herald*."

"Hmm. Now that's a thought." Karen's voice was showing signs of enthusiasm. She no longer yawned. "There are some complications, though. Did your attorney tell you that NOW is getting involved in this?"

"He doesn't care what any feminist organization has to say."

"He should, because NOW is stirring up some trouble."

"Which I'm sure you can't wait to tell me."

"NOW claims that if the two women - Polita and Kim - are arrested for prostitution, then the johns in the trick book should also be arrested for solicitation. NOW also claims that the two women have received a lot of bad publicity, and the johns have gotten away without one name being published."

"They're criminals. They should be getting bad publicity for what they did. And they should be in jail."

"Seems the talk of Miami is on two things: the Rolex Bandits and their trick book."

"People must be pretty bored in Miami."

"It's not a good time to be a john down there. Some neighboring cities are trying to out-compete each other on which one can come up with the most severe punishment for those who deal in the skin trade. You're not out of the woods yet. Do you want me to tell you about some of the ordinances?"

"I'm your punching bag, so please do. Get all your hostilities out of your system." Elliot sat across from Karen at the table and crossed his arms.

"The city of West Palm Beach is using an age-old deterrent for men who try to pick up hookers: public humiliation. Used to be that cops simply issued johns' citations, similar to parking tickets, and let them go home with a slap on the wrists. Starting next week johns will be arrested, fingerprinted, and will spend a night or two in jail. This should help detectives solve prostitution-related crimes, such as the one you still might be charged with. The humiliation factor comes in when the city will publish mug shots of them in the newspapers and on the Internet. Just think, we might find your mug shot next to the winning lottery numbers. Not to be outdone, Miami wants to come back with a stiffer ordinance. If the ordinance passes, anyone convicted of soliciting prostitutes will have his name, address, and arrest date broadcast on the city's public cable access channel. And the City Council in Ft. Lauderdale says it will start using both newspaper and the Internet to inform the public about its johns."

"I bet that makes NOW happy."

"That's what the ACLU said."

"Sounds like the big liberal guns are about to fight it out in Florida."

"All because of that little trick book that has your name in it. The ACLU claims that if the media publish the names of the johns, it would be a violation of their Constitutional rights, amounting to cruel and unusual punishment."

"Interesting. Finally the ACLU and I can agree on at least one issue."

"They've got your back, coach."

"Maybe I should send them a donation."

"It's kind of fun playing the devil's advocate in this controversy."

"You do have that devil's look in your eyes."

"West Palm claims that the names in arrest reports are public records and can be published. On the other hand, the ACLU argues that what West Palm is doing is equivalent to punishment used in Colonial America, that there is no attempt at rehabilitation, only public humiliation. And that it's a violation of one's civil rights to single someone out in contempt. But West Palm claims that historically, humiliation has always been used as a deterrent. I must admit, both sides present good arguments."

"You could teach them a thing or two about how to humiliate someone."

"A lawyer from the ACLU said that the reference to colonial times reminded her of *The Scarlet Letter*. Except this time, it's the johns who are going to feel like Hyster Prynne."

Slouched and sullen, Elliot stared at the table.

"You do remember Hester Prynne, don't you?" she said.

"What high-school student hasn't had to read about her?"

"In case you've forgotten some of the plot, allow me to give you a brief summary."

"Spare me."

"She was the woman in Puritan times who got caught cheating on her husband and was forced to wear an embroidered 'A' on her chest. But the important…"

"Do you ever listen to me?"

314

"I think you need to hear it."

He raised his eyes from the table to Karen. "I know the story. Like most high-school students, I read the CliffNotes. I'm just trying to wade through all your historical and literary bullshit to see what your fucking point is."

Instead of showing anger at Elliot's comment, Karen was smiling and having fun with her discussion.

"By the time all these cities pass their ordinances," she said, "each john might as well be walking around with the scarlet 'S' for solicitation printed on his shirt."

"The Nazis signaled out the Jews by making them wear the Star of David."

"That's a poor analogy. The Jews didn't commit a crime. You did."

"Give me some time; I'll try to think of an analogy that you'll approve of."

"Despite some good arguments by the ACLU, I think our society benefits when it inflicts a sense of shame on its criminals. Perhaps that's one of our cultural problems today: we've become shameless. Johns like you should face some public humiliation."

"*Johns* like me? I'm neither an alleged john nor a convicted one."

"You're a john in a trick book."

"I was a victim who could've been seriously hurt or even murdered. How many times must I remind you of that until it sinks in?"

"Oh, I forgot to mention one other story I read. There's a judge in a small town in Florida who gives his offenders a choice in punishment: go to jail, or in place of serving time, you have to stand on the busiest street corner holding a large sign that advertises what crime you committed. If you stole something, for example, your sign would read that you're a thief and you'll have to stand there eight hours a day, maybe longer, depending on your crime, so all your friends and neighbors get to see you. That's a throwback to when the Pilgrims were yoked in wooden stocks in the town square. A good example of shame punishment. In your case, your sign would read I SOLICITED A PROSTITUTE."

"Maybe if I could be yoked in a wooden stock there'd be a hole in it where my dick will hang out because of the mistake I made. Then you or someone from NOW could come by and take a whack at it. That's my version of being pilloried in the public square."

Karen and Elliot quietly stared at each other for a full two or three minutes. She smirked and squinted at him, her eyes full of scorn.

"Is that it for tonight?" Elliot said. "Any more hostile comments? How much more time do you think you'll need to get all this anger out? Another week? Maybe a month?"

"Maybe a lifetime."

He shot up from the table and kicked his chair back against the wall. He approached her, balling up his fists. His face was swollen and red. She watched him calmly, a provoking smile playing across her lips.

"Wipe that shit-eating grin off your face," he said.

"Make me. Go ahead and hit me." She continued to smile. "I dare you. That would look good in court, wouldn't it? That would prove to the prosecution that they have their man, if you can call that type of wife-beater a man."

Elliot, shaking, stepped back to the refrigerator.

"By the way," she said, "my parents wanted to meet us for dinner tomorrow. I told them it wasn't a good time. There may never be a good time. What do you think?"

He turned and stared at the refrigerator, breathing heavily and trying to calm down. He felt like slapping all of Karen's colorful Post-it notes off the refrigerator door.

"I guess you haven't told your parents about your involvement with the murdered call girl," she said.

"I'll give you the pleasure to fill them in on every detail."

316

"If you insist."

Another tense moment passed. She stared at him with icy silence. In frustration he pounded his fist on the table, knocking off her bottle of water, and walked out of the kitchen.

# 42

Polita was getting ready to leave for the bachelor party when she heard a knock. She opened the door, thinking it was Seth and Kim coming to pick her up; instead, Allen loomed in the doorway, wearing the same ridiculously small suit he had on at Carmen's funeral. He was holding a large gift-wrapped box with both hands and was smiling broadly.

"Can I come in?" Allen said.

"I've got to leave pretty soon."

"I won't be long. I've got a little surprise for you."

"That's an awfully big box to be carrying such a little surprise."

"Wait till you see it."

He entered the apartment and put the box on the kitchen floor. He motioned for Polita to open the gift. It was a microwave.

"I hope you like it," he said. Then he set the appliance on the kitchen counter. "I remembered you said you needed one when I was helping you move."

"You didn't have to do this."

"You're my friend, Polita, and I wanted to do something for you. I know you've been going through all kinds of hell."

"It hasn't been easy on you, either."

"Things couldn't be better for me. I got a job at Rico's as a short-order cook, and the owner said in a couple of months I can be assistant manager. While restaurants are going out of business left and right, Rico's has stayed busy. I know it's not much to write home about, but I had to get away from the café."

"It's the first time I've seen you happy."

"Let's see if this thing works."

Allen plugged the microwave in and started pressing various buttons while she took out a plate of leftover Chinese food from the refrigerator. She set it in the microwave and offered him a chair at the table while the food was warming up.

"Leftovers will be served in two minutes," she said, smiling.

After he declined a beer, she poured him a glass of water. She noticed the tattoos on each of his hands – the one from scripture, the other of the creature from *Alien*. They waited until the microwave made its buzzing sound.

"The first meal from the microwave is now being served," she said, placing the steaming plate of food before him.

After taking several bites, he said, "Mmm. Tastes great."

"You gave me a very nice gift, and how do I show you my appreciation? I cook you leftovers."

"Hey, that's what microwaves are for."

While he ate, she quietly flipped through a pamphlet that came with the microwave. Out of the corner of her eye, she saw his jaws working slowly as he chewed his food. Every once in a while he would smack his lips or take a loud sip from his glass. Hunched over his plate, he looked like an overdressed ogre.

"Finished," he said after washing his food down with one last gulp of water. He gazed at her and wiped his lips with a paper napkin.

She took the plate and the glass to the sink and turned on the tap. He came up behind her and gently grabbed her hand that was holding the washcloth.

"You did the cookin', I do the washin'," he said.

"All these dirty dishes are mine."

"I insist; I do the washin'."

He hadn't let go of her hand.

"I don't want you to get your suit dirty. Why are you all dressed up, anyway? Got a hot date?"

"I've got choir practice at church. I know you don't believe me, but I can sing. The choir director told me to just hum real low. Now come on, hand it over."

Polita gave him the washcloth. She was cornered between Allen and the counter, and he didn't show any indication that he was going to let her by. His densely built frame made the cramped kitchen seem even smaller. She took a nervous swipe at her hair.

"You wash and I'll dry," she said.

She maneuvered around him and grabbed the dish towel. He washed the dishes, wiped off the counter, and cleaned inside the microwave. When he finished, he wrung out the washcloth so many times that Polita thought that it had shriveled up in his huge hands.

"Seth and Kim should be here any minute," she said.

"I know. I'm getting ready to leave."

"That wasn't a hint." But she had meant it to be. "Why don't you stay till they get here?"

"Kim told me y'all are dancing at one of those bachelor parties." Allen looked away from Polita, as if embarrassed. "Carmen and Kim asked me a couple of times to work at a party like that as a bouncer, and I did it for some of the other dancers. Sometimes the guys at those parties can get mean after they've had a few drinks. I hope you're careful."

"I'll be all right. I'm used to dancing in front of men, remember? This will be a one-shot deal."

"I didn't mean to start giving you a lecture. What I mean is..." Allen had trouble completing his sentence.

"Go ahead, Allen, tell me what's on your mind."

"I know you got mad at me that night at the café when I told you that I thought Carmen and you and Kim did some evil things. I didn't mean it that way."

"It doesn't bother me what you think." She was annoyed and glanced at the oven clock.

"Polita, I want to tell you something, and, God-as-my-witness, I promise I won't bring it up again." He was thinking hard. "When Jesus met..."

"Allen." She put her hands on her hips and looked sternly at him. "I'm not in the mood to hear a lecture or a sermon. Not a day goes by that I don't hear or read something that says what a terrible person I am."

"I just want to tell you how I feel."

She took a deep breath and stared at the ceiling.

"When Jesus met the wayward woman at the well," he said humbly, "he wanted to help change her life, not throw rocks at her. I didn't mean to hurt your feelings that night by being so critical. Me, of all people, had no right to condemn you."

Her lips tightly compressed, Polita continued to stare at the ceiling.

"I was wrong when I judged you and Carmen and Kim for what y'all did," he said.

"I'd appreciate it if you'd just drop it."

"Then I'll change the subject. My church is having a social next Tuesday, and if you're not doing anything, I'd like to ask you to come as my guest."

"Seth asked me to go to his brother's this Saturday, and I may stay an extra day. He told me that you and Kim were also going."

"I'll be there with you on Saturday, but I'm driving back that night for a contemporary service. I promised the minister that I'd sing."

"Seth said his brother bought one of those boats that skim across the swamp," she said, changing the subject.

"An airboat. He also has three Jet Skis."

"I've lived my whole life in Florida and I've never been on an airboat or a Jet Ski."

"I've been to the lodge at least three or four times and have had a blast every time."

There was a knock on the door; it was Seth and Kim. While they spoke to Allen, Polita put what she needed in her handbag and went outside with them. The evening sun reddened the horizon.

"Y'all behave," Allen said.

"Thanks again for the gift," Polita said. "That's one microwave that'll get a lot of use."

Allen got into his car and backed out. When he drove by, he didn't return Polita's wave.

Seth drove Polita and Kim to the bachelor party. They entered an oceanfront high-rise condominium, spoke to an overweight security guard at the front desk, and were asked to wait in the lobby. Polita and Kim sat on a wicker couch, and Seth stepped outside and strolled around a small courtyard.

A few minutes later, the elevator doors opened and two men approached Polita and Kim. One of the men was Wink Ferrell. Polita sat motionless while Kim introduced the two men to her. Wink shook hands with Polita. Todd Levebrock, a balding man with silver-framed glasses, told the women that the party was in his apartment on the ninth floor.

Once Seth returned, the three men and two women entered the elevator. As they ascended, Todd presented each woman with an envelope. While Kim folded hers up and told Seth to keep it for her, Polita opened her envelope, counted out the agreed upon amount of $1,000, and stuffed it into her handbag. Wink watched Polita while he was talking to Kim.

They reached the ninth floor and walked down a carpeted hallway. Todd opened a door to an apartment and told the women they could dress inside; the party, he said, was across the hallway. Seth left with the two men, leaving Polita and Kim alone.

As soon as the door was closed, Polita said, "I can't believe you did this to me. Have you lost your mind? That man's too weird for me."

"Which one?"

"Which one? You know who I'm fucking talking about."

"The one named Wink? He's harmless."

"He's the one who was obsessed with Carmen. Also, he's the friend of that Boston businessman I helped Carmen rob. I told you that when I saw you talking to him at the café." Polita was visibly upset. "If I had known this was his party, I never would've come here."

"It's Todd's party, not Wink's." Kim was changing clothes.

"Did you know he was going to be here?"

"Todd said that Wink recommended me."

"There are at least thirty dancers at the café - probably hundreds, maybe thousands, in Miami - but this Wink recommended you? He's up to something."

"I didn't know it was gonna be such a sensitive subject with you."

"Shit, Kim, how many times do I have to tell you that I *robbed* his friend? Now he wants to do us a favor? No way. I don't like this one bit."

"I wouldn't worry about it. He won't say anything to you, not with Seth here. We'll dance for a couple of hours and then go home."

Reluctantly, Polita changed into her G-string and slipped on a bathrobe. She and Kim walked across the hallway and into another apartment where they met up with Seth. Twenty or so men were inside drinking and socializing. Wink tended bar at the kitchen counter and controlled the stereo equipment by keeping the music lively but not too loud. Seth stood in the corner of the room and ate pretzels and sipped a Diet Pepsi. He looked on as the women disrobed and danced for the men.

The party went smoothly for about thirty minutes until two men, drunk and vocal, tried to grab at the women. At first Polita tolerated their behavior, but when one of the men got too aggressive, she motioned for Seth to intervene. Seth calmly reminded the two men that touching the dancers was prohibited. One of the men apologized and sat on a sofa, but the other man drunkenly shouted for the women to have sex with each other. Seth asked him to take a seat.

"Who invited you?" the man said, staring down at the shorter Seth. He was in his late forties, tall, gangly, and wearing a blue sports jacket. "Does anyone here know this jerk? Who are you to tell me what to do?"

"Sir, I work for the dancers," Seth said. "Please respect our no-touching policy."

The man ignored Seth, took some money out of his wallet, and said, "I won't touch them, but I'll give each of the dancers $100 if they'll touch each other."

Both women ignored him. He laughed with some of the other men, then tried to stuff fifty-dollar bills down Polita's G-string. Polita recoiled as Seth once again reminded the man of the rules. Wink meanwhile had turned off the music, and everyone became quiet. The man in the sports jacket stepped up to Seth. Though Seth was obviously much younger and stronger, the man became verbally aggressive.

"I don't think I like you," the man said. "Who are you trying to impress? You come here wearing your tight shirt to show off your muscles." He looked to his friends. "Look at the guns on this guy. I guess we're supposed to be intimidated. This isn't a party for rednecks. That means it's time for you to leave."

"I'm just here for the ladies," Seth said, trying to be conciliatory.

"Did I hear you call *them* ladies?"

"Yes, sir. And they're to be treated like ladies."

Several men laughed. Seth was restrained, though the muscles of his jaw tensed.

"The only reason we wanted them to dance for us is because they're celebrities," the man said. "They're the infamous Rolex Bandits. Guys, you'd better hold on to your valuables with these two dancers around."

Seth continued to listen clench-jawed to the man's abuse, his biceps ready to burst out of their sleeves. His antagonizer held his drink unsteadily up to the ceiling light and tried to study it.

"They tricked me," the man said, sitting unsteadily on the sofa. "These call girls slipped drugs into my drink. Better check your drinks, gentlemen. They'll trick you too. Oh, I'm getting sleepy...I think I'm going to pass out...Oh..."

Sprawled on the sofa, legs spread, the man feigned sleep by snoring loudly. Some of his friends laughed, but others looked uneasy. Polita was embarrassed. Kim seemed to actually enjoy the humor of it all.

The man then sat up, yawned, and said, "I'm not getting my money's worth out of these bandits." With difficulty, and trying to balance his drink, he got up from the sofa. He slurred his words. "I want to see some X-rated action. These two babes are the hottest dancers in all of Miami. They do more than just dance."

Seth finally took control by handing the women their bathrobes and escorting them into the hallway. Wink and Todd followed them, apologizing as they went. Once in the other apartment, Wink approached Seth, shook his hand, and gave him a pat on the back. He then handed him two fifty-dollar bills as a tip.

"You handled that real well, young man," Wink said. "Unfortunately, some of our friends get silly when they drink. They don't mean any harm, but their behavior embarrassed both Todd and me."

"I'm only concerned about the ladies," Seth said. He was grinding his jaws.

"Would you believe that the man who gave you all the lip is the president of one of the biggest software businesses in Miami?" Wink said. He gazed at Polita, who had been staring at him. "Amazing what a few drinks can do to a man when he's got an eye on a sexy woman."

Pale with anger, Polita looked away from Wink.

Kim, not the least bit upset, said to Todd, "You want us to refund some of your money, since we didn't dance the whole two hours?"

"Not at all," Todd said. "You women didn't have to put up with that nonsense."

Seth shook both men's hands to show there was no animosity. Polita and Kim then went into another room and changed. A short while later, they came out carrying their handbags and followed Seth down the hallway. Wink met up with them at the elevator and rode down with them to the lobby. He continued to apologize for the man in the sports coat's abusive behavior.

"Except for one drunk," Wink said, "I thought the party went real well. I'm really sorry the Rolex thing was brought up. That was a real cheap shot."

As they were leaving the elevator, Wink asked Polita if he could talk to her in private.

"Why should I talk to you?" Polita said.

"It's just something I wanted to talk to you about," Wink said vaguely.

Polita told Seth and Kim that she would meet them in the car.

Alone with Polita, Wink said, "I've been trying to get in touch with you for a while."

"Talk. I'm listening."

"I'm not trying to come on to you or anything."

"You think I believe that?"

"I'll prove it to you."

"You've tracked me down so you could get back at me for what I did to your friend from Boston."

"Look, what happened to Elliot wasn't all your fault."

"Whose fault was it then?"

"He said it was Carmen who drugged him and who robbed him. She was the one who cut him up."

"What do you mean *cut him up*?"

"He said she cut at his wrists with a broken wine bottle."

"She never cut him. She was just playing."

"That's not how he described it."

"I was there. I saw it."

"If you say so." Wink looked confused. "All I know is Elliot isn't mad at you. He knows you tried to help him."

"Help him? I robbed him."

"But you stopped Carmen from hurting him."

"I told you, she was just playing around. Having a little fun."

"He said you tried to give him first aid."

"Look, I helped him some only because I thought he was going to croak on us. Last I heard, if a victim happens to die even accidently during a robbery, the criminal can get charged with murder. And that's what I am, a criminal, not a nurse or some goody two-shoes. You can be sure I didn't help him out of any kindness."

"Funny you said that. I told him the same thing."

"And I almost shot myself in the foot, because what little I did for him, it was enough to get him back on his feet a short time later to come looking for us."

"To be honest with you, I'm really not interested in the robbery anymore. Knowing Elliot, he'll find a way to get his insurance to cover the Rolex, or he'll simply go out and buy a new one. With his income, it's no big deal. There are only two things I'm still interested in. One is the DVD."

"I can't help you there." Polita had decided that she was going to hand over the DVD to Detective Hawkins. "What's the second thing?"

"I'd like to talk to you some about Carmen."

"That's still hard for me to do right now." Polita gazed sadly at the floor. A few seconds later she took her compact out of her handbag and checked her lipstick. "You know what I think you really want? You and your friend want some kind of revenge."

"Revenge for what?"

"Carmen did you and your friend wrong, and I was involved in it."

"Carmen didn't do anything to me."

"You trusted her to give your friend a good time and she let you down. She made you look bad in front of one of your rich friends. Look, Seth and Kim are waiting for me. For legal reasons, I'm really not even supposed to be talking about any of this."

"An hour or two is all I'm asking for."

"Why should I trust you?"

"We could meet at a restaurant. If it'll make you feel comfortable, tell Kim to join us. Hell, invite your bouncer friend. Here's my number." He handed his business card to her. "Let's try for dinner sometime soon."

"I can't promise anything."

"If you don't call, I promise I won't bother you again."

Wink slipped Polita six fifty-dollar bills.

"We've already been paid," she said.

"Just a little extra for putting up with that man's rudeness. The media has been savaging you for the past week, and you didn't come here to have to listen to his abuse. You can split it with Kim if you want. I hope to hear from you."

Wink entered the elevator, pressed the button, and smiled at Polita. After the elevator doors closed, Polita pocketed the crisp bills and went to the parking lot where Seth and Kim were waiting for her.

# 43

Elliot was sitting in an oversized leather wingback recliner, eating a bowl of frozen yogurt, and reading over some financial reports when Karen came down the stairs. She had ignored him since he had gotten home from work. It was 9 p.m., and she had spent all her time in her fitness room or with Jeremy. In each hand she was holding a number of DVDs. He continued to eat while he watched her. When she reached the middle of the living room, she tossed seven DVDs, one at a time, on the floor in front of his recliner. Elliot, about to take another bite of yogurt, withdrew the spoon from his mouth and placed it in his bowl.

"I cleaned out all of the disgusting porno stuff that you kept in the dresser," she said.

"I knew I couldn't enjoy one normal night around here. Looks like another night of living hell." He took his reading glasses off and set them on the end table.

"I want all these DVDs thrown away," she demanded. "Or burned. They've been in your dresser for years, and I don't want to see another one in this house. I'm sorry I ever let you talk me into watching some of them."

"I didn't exactly have to twist your arm."

"I can't believe I fell for your line that watching these could actually help our sex life."

"It didn't hurt it."

She stared at the DVDs and said harshly, "This X-rated stuff is a big reason why you're in so much trouble."

"What in the hell are you talking about now? Several nights ago you tried to draw a correlation between the toxicity in raw oysters and knockout drops. Then last night I had to hear an unsolicited lecture on *The Scarlet Letter* and why johns should be publicly humiliated. Little did I know that my least-favorite required novel in high school would come back to bite me in the ass thirty-five years later."

"Another thing that came back to bite you in the ass was watching those DVDs and fantasizing about different women."

"Here comes another riveting lecture."

"It's true and you know it."

"I don't need X-rated DVDs for that."

"But they serve as a sexual stimulus. You see a ménage a trios on one of your DVDs, then you go to Miami and hire two women to have sex with you."

He inhaled as if he were going to hold his breath for a long time. "Having to listen to another night about this Rolex stuff has become the equivalent of nails on a chalkboard. Will it ever end?"

"I find it ironic that you enjoyed watching all these DVDs," she said, "and then end up as a star in a homemade version of one."

"Me? A star? I was a real stud all right. Now I get to hear a lecture on irony. By the way, if you saw the DVD I'm in, I don't think you would find me too interesting and energetic."

"Who knows, one day I might get to see it."

"I hope you do. Then you'll see just how helpless I was." He was quiet for a moment. "Come to think of it, one of the few things I remember that call girl telling me while she was torturing me was that I was a big blob of helplessness. Looks like I got the last laugh."

"You sure did. With one swing of your golf club."

"Nothing like trying to have a conversation with an irrational and angry person."

Karen sat on the sofa. Elliot, his yogurt having melted, placed the bowl on the end table.

"I don't think anyone should laugh over another's misfortune," she said.

"You're having a good time with all the shit that's happened to me."

"I've had a change of heart after having read the articles on those three women."

"I've noticed. You sympathize with them and hate me."

"We hear about murder victims all the time, but they're faceless statistics until we get to know a little more about them. Having read about Carmen, I now see the human side of her."

"She was a thief. She lived a life of crime. She had a whole book-full of victims."

"I don't see johns as victims."

"They are when they're poisoned and then robbed."

"She was a victim, too. Johns like you exploited her."

"You need to hear my attorney's lecture on victims."

"The shoe is on the other foot, so to speak."

"What are you talking about now?"

"You said the johns in that trick book were victims. Well, maybe all of you johns now know what a woman feels like when she has been raped."

"Here we go again. You *johns.* You love rubbing that word in."

"I admit, Carmen did have her problems."

"I'd say she did. You wouldn't be calling her by her first name if she had held a broken bottle to your throat."

"I didn't say she was an angel. You probably scared her, and that was the only way she could defend herself. A man your size would scare anyone."

"All I can say is that you found out about my other life; that I lied to you and went to bed with another woman."

"With *two* women at the same time."

"OK. Fine. With two women. The bottom line is that it's pretty fucking pathetic and humiliating that I had to pay to have sex."

"Since when did I charge you?"

"The only reason I'm sitting through day after day of your abuse is because it shows a side of you that I didn't know even existed. It took me fourteen years to find out that you're a mean person, Karen."

"Carmen was young. She ran with the wrong crowd."

"Did you even *hear* a word I said? I was talking about you, not the call girl."

"I want to talk about Carmen."

"OK, if maybe one more night of this will put an end to it. Do you know what disturbs me about all these stories that you've read off the Internet? The media, I'm sure, have distorted everything by calling Carmen and her friends the Rolex Bandits. That gives them a cute, romantic sounding name that captures the public's imagination. You'd think they're the female version of Butch Cassidy and the Sundance Kid. Or maybe even Robin Hood, because they robbed from the rich. Maybe these bandits will all come to a violent end, like Bonnie and Clyde, guns a 'blazing. The media would like that."

"You're forgetting they never harmed anyone."

"Oh, they're just sweet, fun-loving outlaws. Diabolically charming little psychopaths."

"They came from tough backgrounds."

"That's become a cliché. I bet their families were dysfunctional, which means they were probably abused and suffered from low self-esteem, which therefore forced them into lives of crime."

"Actually, only the one named Kim fits that description. Polita's parents came from Cuba on the Mariel boatlift. They were called the Marielitos."

"Yet another reason to hate Castro. He should've kept them on his prison-island instead of dumping thousands of criminals onto our shores."

"Polita's parents are law-abiding citizens with jobs, not criminals."

"Can't say the same for their daughter."

"They're divorced now, but at least they were able to provide for her when she was younger. As for Carmen, her mother is mixed Seminole and Miccosukee and her father's Cuban."

"And I'm a WASP. So what?"

"There was a real touching story on Carmen's father. He told *The Miami Herald* that since Carmen's death he sees her every night in his dreams."

"So do I, except they're called nightmares."

Karen flashed an angry look. "Why is it that every time I make a comment, you have to counter with a smartass remark?"

"I'm only trying to soften your blows."

"I think you should know that of the three women, Carmen actually came from the more normal family. Her parents have been married for twenty-seven years. The mother was laid off recently, but the father works. They said Carmen was your average teenager. Her father said he disciplined her if she made bad grades or if she skipped school. She never gave them serious problems when she was growing up. The only time her father got truly upset with her was when he found out that she was an exotic dancer, but she was an adult by then and had already moved out of the house."

"Why are you telling me all this? I'm not the least bit interested in hearing about these vixens."

"I'm trying to put a human face on them."

"Vampire masks would be more appropriate."

"Carmen's mother said her daughter was very proud of her Indian heritage. Carmen used to make frequent visits to the Indian reservations in the Everglades."

"I'm sure the Indians there wouldn't be too happy to know that Carmen's strip act featured a feathered G-string and war paint."

"Polita and Kim haven't said much to the media about this Rolex Bandit story. The *Herald* quoted Kim a few days ago, but Polita has been quiet."

"You wait and see, they'll both cash in on their notoriety like other famous criminals. That's become a trend in the last decade or so. Before you know it, they'll be making an appearance on *Inside Edition* and posing in *Playboy*. Pretty soon they'll be able to afford their own Rolexes."

Karen went into the kitchen and poured herself a glass of wine. Elliot collected the DVDs off the floor and stacked them on the end table, next to his melted bowl of yogurt. He then resumed reading his financial papers. After a while Karen returned to the living room and sat down on the sofa.

"Make sure you don't leave those DVDs around for Jeremy to find," she said.

"Why did you bring them out to begin with and drop them in the middle of the floor?"

"To make a point."

"You made it all right."

Karen, sipping her wine, was quiet for several minutes. Elliot watched her without saying anything.

While staring at her wineglass, she said thoughtfully, without a trace of anger in her voice, "When you think about the last twenty years or so on Wall Street, those CEOs from Enron and WorldCom – they ripped off thousands of investors. And remember Milken and Boesky? They were also big-time corporate thieves. Prudential-Bache Securities was probably one of the biggest and sleaziest scams for any investment house in the history of Wall Street. But they're old news compared to what the investment firms and their sleazy casino-game derivatives did with the housing bubble, which almost brought down the entire economy. The Great Wall Street heist. I don't think one CEO from Bear Sterns or Lehman Brothers went to prison. The cofounder of Countrywide Financial, who was one of the main villains of the subprime-mortgage crisis, paid millions to settle a civil fraud case brought by the SEC, but that was a tiny fraction of his fortune."

Elliot looked at her, puzzled. "I must be tuning you out, because you've lost me. One minute we're discussing X-rated DVDs and how I ended up in one myself; then you bring up the Mariel boatlift; now you're talking about chicanery on Wall Street. Where the fuck are you going with this?"

Still staring at her wineglass, Karen continued as though he hadn't spoken. "So maybe a few white-collar criminals paid some fines, performed a few hours of community service, or spent a couple of months in some country-club detention center for wayward CEOs. Take our neighbor from across the street, Ian Wright. He invested in credit default swaps and made millions by betting on middle-class families losing their homes when the mortgage market started to collapse. Now he writes best-selling books on how he made his fortune and goes on speaking tours throughout the country. Your golfing partner and hospital-chain tycoon, Rob Swanson, was involved in one of Massachusetts worst health care fraud cases on record. His company cooked the books with fraudulent accounting and blatant overbilling. He defrauds Medicare, Medicaid and the military's Tricare, and what's he doing? Instead of going to prison, his company gave him a golden parachute worth hundreds of millions of dollars and now he's financing his own campaign for governor – of the same state he defrauded. And he's favored to win big. Only in America. Little Bernie Madloff, the Ponzi king himself, got prison time, but that was the exception. Yet Carmen and her two friends stole some watches and credit cards and look what happened to them. One got murdered and the other two will go to prison."

"Where they belong."

"Maybe. But maybe they should just pay some finds and do community service, like those CEOs. Derivatives, credit default swaps, subprime mortgages, defrauding the government, and Ponzi schemes hurt society more than some stolen watches and credit cards."

"Now I've connected your dots. Are you condemning all CEOs? As the saying goes, there are always a few bad apples. You're even a CEO. And since it will piss you off, I'm going to start donating to Swanson's campaign first thing tomorrow. And I'd pay to listen to one of Ian's lectures anytime. They didn't do anything illegal."

"They weren't caught. Carmen and her friends were."

"Good thing they were or there would've been more men without their watches and their dignity."

"Those kinds of men have dignity?"

"Can't you talk about something else? After I told you about what happened in Miami, you had nothing to do with me for the first few days. Can we return to those quiet but tense times? Now you just go on and on about the same thing. You've become obsessed with these call girls."

"Talking about them helps me deal with this."

"It doesn't do me any good to hear about them."

"In a way, don't we steal from our employees by paying them the lowest possible wages? Then we help influence the laws to lock them up if they steal back from us."

"I know you can't be serious. You're no longer that rich brat philosophy major at Mount Holyoke who used to quote Chairman Mao and Che Guevara. You went through that Marxist stage while your parents were paying your exorbitantly high tuition. Now you've grown up to become a successful owner of a marketing firm who has been a devoted Republican for fifteen years. You belong to a political party that represents about 13% of the registered voters in this state. So spare me all this phony liberal shit."

"All of us should feel some guilt."

"I don't, but maybe you should. I pay my people quite well, thank you. Through hard work I've built a company that has created hundreds – thousands - of jobs. And in several days, when I fly back to Florida, I'll be merging with another company that will create even more jobs. Good paying jobs. So go ahead and feel guilty when your advertisements try to convince people to buy more junk they don't need and can't afford so they can stay in debt."

"You've also made a fortune off government healthcare."

"I provide needed services."

"You've milked programs such as Medicare, Medicaid and Tricare. Yet you rant like these Tea-Party ideologues about being anti-government – unless it enriches you."

Elliot snorted, "I don't *milk* any program. I only rant against the state and federal bureaucracies when they act incompetent. When you have to fight through all kinds of job-killing red tape and regulations, it's a business like mine that corrects a lot of their mistakes and in turn protects the consumer."

Several minutes passed. Karen never took her eyes off her wineglass. Elliot tried to finish reading his financial papers but couldn't concentrate. Sunk in his recliner, he peered over the papers and noticed how sullen she looked.

In a more conciliatory tone, he said, "Karen, with all due respect, you haven't been making much sense lately. You've been talking a lot of nonsense in your anger to get back at me. This…this Rolex thing has disturbed you greatly, and I'm to blame for all of it. Once you get over your anger, if you ever do, I want you to realize that I paid to have sex with a woman and -"

"Two women." Her eyes left her wineglass to bore into Elliot. "You keep leaving out the other woman."

"As I was saying, what I did was wrong, and boy have you let me know about it. But I didn't have any feelings for her."

"For *them*."

He could only shrug.

"That says a lot about you," she said. "That you can fuck two women you just met. You didn't even know them."

"And that makes me a monster?"

"If you killed Carmen, it does."

"I was an adulterer for one night, not a murderer. All I'm trying to tell you is that at least I wasn't involved in some ongoing affair."

"That's supposed to flatter me?"

"What can I say?" He threw his hands up. "I have no excuses, no therapeutic explanations to answer for my actions in Miami. I wish I could think of some, but it was nothing but a primal urge. You were right about my fantasies and maybe those DVDs. It's like I have a sexually split personality. I desire and love you, yet I sometimes fantasize about other women when I make love to you. It's probably a normal thing to do, because sexual fantasies are all a part of eroticism, aren't they? Sexually, I don't think we're wired to be monogamous. So possibly to fulfill our caveman instinct, we fantasize about having other lovers. It's nothing more than harmless daydreaming. An escape. In some perverse way, my fantasies have enhanced my sexual drive when it comes to our love-making."

"And you said I was talking nonsense!" She laughed. "I wish I'd recorded that knuckle-dragging bullshit. You crossed the line from fantasy to reality when you fucked Carmen and Polita. Was Polita your Lolita? Was she your little nymphet? You and your erotic underground of X-rated DVDs, porn shops, strip joints, and prostitutes!"

"Once again, what can I say? You've caught me red-handed."

Elliot and Karen relapsed into another brooding silence. She finished her wine and stared blankly in front of her.

"We've been in this house for almost our entire marriage," he said, his eyes glancing around the room until they stopped when he noticed a spot one of his painters had missed between the crown molding and the ceiling. "There're many memories here. Great memories, and some that were sad. After you had those two miscarriages, I was beginning to think we'd have a childless marriage. Then we were blessed with Jeremy. Before Jeremy, I had almost everything I ever wanted. Great parents who gave me every opportunity to be successful. I was fortunate to play college football. I inherited and then helped build a thriving business. I have a beautiful and intelligent wife. But I had to wait until I was in my mid-forties to have a son. We've had our differences, but mostly it has been a wonderful ride. If you end up leaving me, I'll miss everything about you. And it'll tear me up to see Jeremy suffer through a divorce and especially any public humiliation that I bring on him and my family. That consumes me – eats me up – every waking moment."

Karen was silent.

Elliot said, "I missed you so much the other night that I snuck into your room and listened to you sleep for an entire hour."

"How?" Her eyes became focused. "I keep my door locked."

"A bedroom door isn't hard to unlock."

"Then I'll get a chain lock. I don't want you in my bedroom. I don't want you in this house."

"Karen, I hope that one day you'll realize that I'm a good and decent, if terribly flawed, husband and father."

Yet another few minutes of silence passed between them.

Finally he said, "I hope one day you can find it in your heart to take me back."

She remained quiet, but sometimes, when her eyes met his, her expression softened.

# 44

Detective Hawkins was sitting across from Polita and her attorney Mira Delgado in the interrogation room. Delgado was in her sixties, wore thick-lensed reading glasses, and spoke in a calm, measured tone. She had been asking why the detective had questioned Polita on three or four different occasions without her having had prior legal advice, and he had answered all of her questions. Their brief conversation had been tense, and after she was through asking questions, Delgado consulted with Polita for a while. Detective Hawkins folded his hands on the table and gravely regarded the attorney; she was a blade of a woman, with a thin face and sagging eyelids. She wore no makeup, and her thin gray hair was wispy, like cobweb. She was dressed in a masculine gray suit with a white shirt opened at the collar.

"Miss Delgado," Detective Hawkins said, "I've been workin' on a brutal murder of one of Polita's friends. She has agreed to cooperate, because she felt her life was in danger and..."

The attorney nodded dismissively. "Sir, whether a victim was bludgeoned, shot, stabbed, choked – are not most murders brutal? Miss Flores cooperated with you because you threatened to charge her with a few crimes if she didn't."

"A few?" Detective Hawkins smiled broadly. "I think it's more'n a few." He looked at Polita. "I ever threaten you?"

"We'll save that question for maybe later," Delgado said. She turned to Polita and consulted with her again for a few minutes.

The detective pursed his lips as he looked at the two women.

"I've allowed Miss Flores to make several important statements that should help with your investigation," the attorney said. "Go ahead, Miss Flores."

Polita met Detective Hawkins' stare and then looked away. She took a deep breath.

"An ex-dancer at the café came over to my apartment the other day," Polita said. "Her name's Michelle. She said she saw Mark Cerone, the manager of the café, going through some of the dancers' lockers." She paused for a moment to look at her attorney, who nodded for her to continue. "I guess what I'm trying to ask you, do you know where Mr. Cerone was the night Carmen was murdered?"

Detective Hawkins looked through his folder and stopped at a certain page and read silently. A minute later he looked at Polita.

"He checked in at the café at ten that morning," he said. "Then he left from five till six for dinner; then worked till closin'. The owner and several dancers confirmed this. However, he said he left several times to take breaks. He said it was a slow night."

"I was just wondering," Polita said. "You asked me to think of people who might've had something against Carmen."

"You think he did?"

"I don't know this for sure, but he might've been going through our lockers way before Carmen was killed. It's just a wild guess, but he might've seen Carmen's trick book and knew her schedule. Maybe he felt Carmen was going to be bad publicity for the café if she got caught. He lives and breathes the café, and I think it'd destroy him if he lost it because of some scandal."

"Last I heard," the detective said, "business has been boomin' there *because* of the scandal. That's how our system seems to work, huh? But I'm not sure I follow you on this Mr. Cerone. I thought he managed the place, and Miss Wanda owned it?"

"I think he's a part owner. He always kind of bragged about owning the whole thing one day, because Ms. Wanda has talked about wanting out. Maybe he has nothing to do with Carmen's murder. He's just so weird, but then I guess most of us who worked there are a little off." She paused again. The attorney asked Polita if she wanted a drink of water before continuing. She took a sip from a bottle of water and then continued hesitantly, "Someone broke into my last apartment the night after Carmen was killed." Her voice dropped off on the last word. She took several more long sips of water. "What I mean is, someone got into my apartment without breaking into it; that someone used a key or was clever to find another way in. I've let Carmen and Kim use my key before. I don't know if they gave the key to someone to make copies; I asked Kim, and she said she didn't."

"Who do you think was in your apartment?"

Polita looked to her attorney, who nodded and patted her hand. She gripped the sides of the chair.

"I think I know but I can't be sure about anything anymore it seems," Polita said, staring at the table. "But first I've got to tell you something else that's been on my mind. When I first saw you, I was confused and afraid. What I'm trying to say is" - her voice diminished to a whisper - "I've had the Rolex and the DVD all along."

"Speak up, Miss Flores, I can barely hear you." Detective Hawkins leaned forward on the table.

"Carmen gave Polita the Rolex and DVD while they were at the party," the attorney said.

The detective ignored the attorney. "Carmen just *gave* them to you?"

"Sir, your tone of voice intimidates my client," the attorney said.

"I was afraid to tell you because you would've thought I had stolen them," Polita said. "And when Carmen showed up dead the next day, that would've made me look real suspicious."

"You don't need to say anything more," the attorney told Polita.

"By the time I decided that I'd better turn them over to you," Polita said, "someone who knew Carmen blackmailed me."

"Who?" Detective Hawkins never took his eyes off Polita.

"He works at the Luxuria. His name's Phil Wiggins. He's a bellhop."

"Wait a second. You're switching gears here. I thought we were zeroing in on Mr. Cerone, the manager of the café."

"I was. Don't get me wrong, I'm still confused about him. But this bellhop was actually involved with Carmen."

"OK then. Let's talk about this bellhop. Did you give him the Rolex and the DVD?"

"I gave him the Rolex."

Polita expected the detective to show some emotion - surprise, maybe even anger - for not having told him about this earlier. Instead, his face was impassive. He eyed Polita while he flipped through one of the folders, acting as though he had expected Polita's information.

"As I'm sure you are aware," the attorney said to Detective Hawkins, "Miss Flores has been under tremendous duress."

Detective Hawkins again ignored the attorney and said to Polita, "Why did he blackmail you?"

"He told me Carmen owed him some money."

"A great deal of money," the attorney added.

"Was this a drug debt or something?" Detective Hawkins said.

"I don't know how much it had to do with drugs," Polita said. "He told Carmen about upcoming conventions at the hotel and he offered her protection. He claimed Carmen owed him money for it and never paid him. I didn't have the kind of money he wanted, so I gave him the Rolex."

Detective Hawkins found what he was looking for in the folder. He took the bellhop's photo out of its plastic sheet protector and showed it to Polita. "Is that him?"

"Yeah. That's the bellhop."

"I've got some phone calls to make. I'll be back shortly."

Detective Hawkins got up stiffly from his chair. With him gone, the attorney moved her chair closer to Polita.

"You handled yourself quite well," she said, patting Polita's hand and giving it a firm squeeze. "I'll stop him if his questions make you uncomfortable."

"Yes, ma'am."

While the attorney spoke to her, Polita was thinking about the bellhop's eyes filling with tears after he had touched her in her apartment.

Ten minutes later, Detective Hawkins entered the room, sat down, and placed a sheet of paper on the table. His nostrils flared with each breath as he read the paper.

"I've got a couple of detectives on their way to pay our bellhop a visit," Detective Hawkins said.

"Miss Flores is very concerned about her safety," the attorney said. "The information she has given you places her in extreme danger. This bellhop sounds like a very dangerous man."

"What do you know about him?" Detective Hawkins asked Polita, again ignoring her attorney.

"Just what I told you. I didn't know anything about him till he followed me to Kim's one night."

"This was after Carmen's murder?"

"It was after I left the marina, so if that was when Carmen was murdered, yeah."

"Carmen never mentioned him to you?"

"Never. I always thought there were only four of us involved in this Rolex thing - me, Carmen, Kim and Dante. Five, if you include Ramón."

"Did you see the bellhop at the hotel the night Carmen was killed?"

"I saw other bellhops and hotel attendants, but like I said, I didn't know anything about him then."

"Tell me something." Detective Hawkins looked closely at Polita. "Did you see him when I was with you at the Luxuria?"

"No, but I was looking for him. Had I seen him when I was with you, I probably would've told you about him right then and there."

"Has he ever threatened you?"

"He'll deny he ever did. It's his word against mine."

"Did he *threaten* you?" the detective repeated forcefully.

"Once, when he was in my apartment, he held a knife against my throat. He warned me if I ever told on him, he'd find a way to get back at me." She turned and showed Detective Hawkins the back of her hair. "He cut some of my hair and said he was going to keep it as a souvenir. You can hardly tell now that he did it because I've tried to even it out."

"Have you seen him since you gave him the Rolex?"

"No. And I hope I never see him again."

Detective Hawkins stared at Polita for a long time. A hard, aggressive stare.

"This has all been very traumatic for Miss Flores," the attorney said, ending the silence. "I'm very worried about her safety."

"You think the bellhop broke into your old apartment?"

"At first I thought it was Dante and Ramón. And like I said earlier, I wondered if the manager of the café got ahold of my key. But now, yeah, I think it was the bellhop."

He glanced again at the paper on the table. "Hmm. Says here that Phil Wiggins was named the Luxuria's associate of the year in 2009. There are no complaints against him. Always on time. Very courteous and respectful."

"None of which is relevant to my client's safety," Delgado said.

"Just doing some readin' for my own information," he said without taking his eyes off the paper. "Single. Clean cut. Also says that frequent guests have written recommendations for him. The Luxuria has asked him to consider training for various managerial positions. What else? Was a student at Florida International University. An engineering major."

"The Luxuria's associate of the year sounds like our murderer," the attorney said, mildly annoyed at the detective.

"Could be." Detective Hawkins took his eyes off the paper. "Could be."

"Your investigation would be going nowhere if it weren't for Polita's cooperation," the attorney said. "She is risking her life to help you find Carmen's murderer."

"I'll be getting back with both of you once I see this bellhop."

"Miss Flores will be spending a day, maybe two, in Everglades City with some friends. Then I've suggested that she move in with her mother, who lives in Tampa. It's for her safety, of course."

"I'll determine where she can and can't go." The detective pushed his glasses up.

"But you haven't charged her with anything because she has been cooperating with your investigation."

"The charges are forthcoming."

"Yes, you've explained that to me. But please let us know when you're going to get around to it. When you do so, her mother will be posting bail, and at that time all cooperation will cease. As of today, you can direct all of your calls to my office."

Detective Hawkins looked squarely at Polita. "Don't you have something you want to give me?"

"I have the DVD in my possession," the attorney said.

Polita finished her water as Detective Hawkins glared at her in disgust. She leaned back in her chair and looked on as her attorney presented the DVD to the detective.

# 45

A loud, smashing sound startled Elliot out of his sleep. In the darkness he raised himself on his elbows and listened to the wind through the trees. A limb must have fallen, he thought. After a moment of silence, he then thought he heard a distant weeping, a deep desolation, as if the wind had swept the sounds inside.

He got out of bed and checked on Jeremy, who was asleep and hugging one of his pillows. The weeping filled the hallway. He put his ear to Karen's door, but he couldn't tell where the sound came from. He turned the doorknob, expecting it to be locked; the door opened. The dresser, which he had heard Karen push against the door before she had gone to bed, was moved to the side. Her bed was empty.

He went downstairs and approached the kitchen. The kitchen light was visible under the closed door. He tapped on it.

"Are you all right?" Elliot said through the door.

"Don't come in here!" Karen shouted, trying to hold back her sobs.

He turned the doorknob but didn't enter.

"I said don't come in here! I'll call the police!"

"What's wrong? I thought I heard you crying."

He cracked open the door and looked in. Karen was standing next to the kitchen counter, gripping a golf club with both hands. She stared darkly at the counter, on which lay a cantaloupe. A deep gash had torn open the top of the melon, and loose chunks of it were scattered on the counter and floor, with one pulpy piece clinging to the head of the golf club. He entered the kitchen and stared at the mess, and then looked into her unblinking eyes.

"Have you lost your fucking mind?" he said. "Jesus Christ." He shook his head, mumbling, "What in the hell…? After our last conversation, I actually thought you were showing some progress and were beginning to reason with me. Now I know you definitely need professional help. Possibly even should be committed."

"You come near me and I'll hit you! I mean it!"

"Don't worry, I wouldn't think of coming anywhere near you. And you were the one who said that *I* scared *you?"*

Pointing the golf club at his chest, she continued to shout at him. "Leave me alone! Don't you come anywhere near me!" She was red-faced. Even her eyes were red from their broken capillaries.

"You're going to wake Jeremy if you keep shouting." He was ready to deflect the club if she decided to swing at him. "I don't think you want our son to see you in this condition. He'll have nightmares for the rest of his life."

The only audible sound was her panting. Never taking his eyes off the club, Elliot pulled a chair out from the table and sat down. He looked more weary than tired. An empty wine bottle and wineglass were on the table. Her crazed stare fixed on him one moment, then her eyes seemed to wander. She was unsteady on her feet. She lowered the golf club but continued to grip it tightly.

"This is like a scene out of *Psycho*," he said, stealing a glance at the damaged cantaloupe. "The only thing missing are the screeching violins sawing away."

"I had a dream tonight that we were playing golf together. We used to, remember?" She slurred her words. "When we were first married you used to take me with you, but I became a nuisance so you quit asking me to go." Her eyes took another flight around the kitchen. "In my dream it was a beautiful day. Sunshine and fresh air. We must've been in Florida, because I remember seeing palm trees. You went to swing at the ball but missed. Then you picked up the…um…what do you call it when you hack up a chunk of grass? I know there's a name for it but I can't..."

"It's called a divot."

"That's the word I'm looking for. A divot." To support herself, she used the golf club as a cane and leaned shakily on it. "I forgot what I was saying..."

"You were talking about a dream."

"Oh, right. You picked the divot up and waved it at me. You were laughing. The grass you were holding turned into a scalp, and your golf club was dripping with blood. Then you tossed the scalp into a pond and put the ball back on the tee and hit it like nothing had happened."

"A divot was a bloodied scalp? You've been reading too much about that Indian dancer." He examined the empty wine bottle. "I can't believe you drank all that. You of all people can't handle booze."

"Did you hear what I told you about my dream?"

"I heard every sick word of it. You're a very disturbed woman."

"You made a very revealing remark about Indians when I picked you up at the airport after your stay at the Luxur... whatever the name of that hotel was."

"It was the Luxuria. What revealing remark did I make concerning Indians?"

"Remember years ago when that mother horrified the country by drowning her two little boys? She let her car run off a pier and into a lake, with her boys buckled inside."

"I thought you were going to tell me a fascinating story about Indians."

"I am, but I'm trying to make a point first." She continued to slur her words.

"Then make it." He yawned.

"The mother of those boys claimed that someone kidnapped them. She even made her appeal to the kidnapper on national TV - lying to the entire country - to return her boys to her."

"I want to go back to bed. I was sleeping peacefully until I heard my wife destroying one of my golf clubs."

"Do you know how the cops started to suspect that she killed her sons?"

"No, but please tell me before I lose interest."

"She kept referring to her sons in the past tense. She would say things like, 'They were good boys. I loved them. They meant everything to me.' And so on. The more she talked about them in the past tense, the more the cops knew the mother was the killer."

"Somewhere, I missed the point of your story."

"You did a similar thing with Carmen. When we returned home after Jeremy and I had picked you up at the airport, I got onto Jeremy for pretending to shoot at something in our yard. You commented that when you were his age you were killing Indians. Ever since you told me about Carmen's murder, and the more I learned about her, the more I kept thinking about your comment. You gave yourself away."

"I hate to tell you this, but I really did fight imaginary Indians as a child. And since puberty, I tend to fuck imaginary women. Seems my imagination is getting me into trouble."

"But…um…subconsciously you…" She struggled with her narrative while staring at the golf club. "Oh, now I remember. For the past week I wouldn't dare go anywhere near your golf clubs, until tonight. Is this the kind of club you used to smash Carmen's skull?"

"The one you're holding is an expensive sand wedge that is now ruined. Smash as many cantaloupes as your heart desires, but not with my golf clubs."

"I was testing a theory."

"Looks like I'll have to start hiding my clubs if you're going to test any more theories."

"Why do you *really* want to hide them? Afraid someone might find out which one was the real weapon?"

"Now that you've demonstrated whatever theory you were trying to prove, hand over the club and let's go back to bed." He stood up from the table and extended his hand.

Raising the club over her shoulder, she said viciously, "I swear I'll hit you if you come close to me!"

"I just want my golf club back."

"So you can use it on me like you did Carmen?"

"Cut out the fucking hysterics."

She went into another rage. Eyes bulging, she turned and swung the golf club at the cantaloupe but missed badly, hitting the counter. She tried again and this time hit the cantaloupe, which fell apart with a cracking, sloshing sound. A chunk of the melon went flying across the kitchen and splattered against the wall.

Elliot sat back down at the table and rubbed his eyes hard.

"Jeremy, I hope you didn't hear that one," he said, glancing at the ceiling. "Your mother's going to wake everyone in the fucking neighborhood before she's through."

"Don't worry about Jeremy. He's a sound sleeper."

"Not if you keep slamming that club against the counter." He watched as she gazed at the crushed cantaloupe. "I've got this feeling that I'm sitting alone in a very small theater watching some avant-garde play. What a wonderful performance. Are you finished? Is there a second act? Is this supposed to be a comedy or a horror show? I don't know whether to laugh or have you committed."

"Carmen's dead and you're a free man."

"Whoever said life's fair?"

Her eyes focused on him in a stare of pure fury.

He sighed while shaking his head. "All right, I admit that comment went too far. Yes, unfortunately a woman has been killed, and her death is tearing apart the Anderson family."

Karen, crying, flung the golf club on the floor and rushed out of the kitchen. Elliot listened to her unsteady footsteps going up the stairs. When she reached her bedroom, he heard her push the dresser against the door. He picked up his golf club and washed it off at the sink. He examined the bent shaft and decided that the club would have to be thrown away. With a washcloth and some paper towels, he cleaned up the loose pieces of cantaloupe on the counter, floor, and wall. Then he wrapped the mess in a plastic bag, took it and the broken golf club into the garage, and threw them both into the trash can.

# 46

Polita locked her apartment door and walked to her car. It was a murky twilight, dark enough for some cars to pass by with their lights on. She had called Wink and told him she would meet him for dinner at a restaurant in Coconut Grove, and he had promised to talk only about Carmen, not Elliot. She had her doubts about his motives, but she was curious about the kind of relationship he had had with Carmen.

She got into her car and started to back out, but another car pulled up and blocked her in; it was Dante and Ramón. She stepped out and stood next to her door. Dante, sitting behind the wheel, rolled his window down. He was wearing a tank top and a backward MARLINS cap.

"Got the a/c workin' like a freezer," Dante said. He slapped the side of the door. "Feels like Alaska in here. What do you think, Ramón, it cold enough for you?"

"Cold as a witch's titties," Ramón said. He leaned toward the dashboard and stared at Polita with a scatterbrained smile. "I'm starin' at some right now."

"Move your car," Polita said. "I'm running late."

"I don't want to keep you from going somewhere important." Dante pulled up a few feet but still blocked her in. "Wonder where you'd be going all dolled up like that? Let me guess, I bet you're dancin' at another bachelor party. Or better yet, maybe you've gone into business for yourself turnin' tricks. Still hustlin' to make a couple bucks, huh?"

"I'm not going to tell you again to move your car."

"And if I don't?" Dante made a side-mouthed comment to Ramón that she couldn't hear.

Polita stood her ground.

"Maybe I'd better move," Dante said. "Shit, man, I forgot you're still packin' heat with that purse pistol of yours."

"I'll use it if you threaten me."

"Then we'd better protect ourselves," Dante told Ramón.

Ramón coyly slipped something out of the glove compartment and held it in his lap.

"That'd be fuckin' embarrassin' if my friends found out that I got shot by a pink pistol," Dante said. "A cute little Barbie Doll of a pistol."

"If you don't move I'll call the cops," Polita warned. She took out her cell phone. "All I've got to do is tell Detective Hawkins that you're threatening me and he'll lock your ass up."

"My, my. Why you so angry? Funny, you've always been on the run from the cops, now you're running to them for help. Fuck, man, they don't give a rat's ass about some whore like you. That detective is just waiting for the right time to lock your ass up. He knows you're the dangerous one. Me? He knows I'll negotiate with him." He leaned back in his seat and then stuck his leg out the window. "See this here ankle bracelet? You'll be wearing one real soon." He stared at her crotch. "I don't think these bracelets come in purple, to match your tight-ass purple jeans. Ramón's also wearing an ankle bracelet. Want to see?" Dante, laughing, put his leg back inside the car. "That detective got me and Ramón for dealin' in stolen goods. We spent a day or two in jail until bond was posted. Helps to have friends who look after you. The detective's getting really pissed at Kim 'cause she hasn't been cooperatin', so we'll be postin' bond for her before long. When it comes time to helping you out – sorry about your luck. You ain't got many friends left. Guess you'll have to run to your mama. You'll learn the hard way that when you're in a small business you don't fuck over your partners."

"Why are you even here?"

"To keep in touch. We haven't seen each other in a while. I thought I'd tell you that me and Mr. Detective had a long talk about that bellhop at the Luxuria." Dante paused to light a cigarette. "Yeah, that bellhop, he's in a shit-load of trouble, ain't he? Thanks to you."

Polita didn't say anything. She gazed at Dante's scrawny, tattooed arm hanging out the side of the door.

"Like I've always said, I knew you had the Rolex and the DVD the whole time," Dante said. "You never fooled me once. But I can't believe you gave a Presidential Rolex to a bellhop just to try to get your ass off the hook. Un*fucking*believable."

"Since I don't have it, then that means we don't have anything to talk about. So move your car."

"We've got plenty to talk about. You've embezzled money from our business by taking the Rolex and the DVD. Carmen didn't trust you or Kim. That's one of the reasons why she kept that bellhop around." He pointed his cigarette at Polita. "But what pisses me off more'n anything - except of course Carmen's murder - is that Dante never got the Rolex that was owed him. You had it the whole time. A bellhop - a little pussy that carries tourists' luggage - gets the Rolex and Dante ends up with zilch. Shit, man, it just ain't right. Know what I mean?"

"Wouldn't you want the bellhop to have the Rolex?"

"How you figure? Mr. Detective told me the bellhop has already got his money from the Rolex. The Rolex is long gone."

"My lawyer told me the detective is now all over the bellhop's ass. The pressure's off you and me. Sounds to me like the detective is getting ready to charge him with murder. Maybe two counts of murder. Carmen's and that other woman who used to work the Luxuria. What he got for the Rolex isn't going to help him once he goes to prison."

"No shit, Sherlock. Your lawyer is only tellin' you this just to make you and your mom feel like y'all are gettin' your money's worth. Mr. Detective ain't got much on that bellhop. That's why he can't cuff him yet, at least not for murder. All you done was get the bellhop fired from his job. You think you're so smart for turning the detective's attention on him. That's some good strategy, man, but I don't think it's gonna work. But it shows how slick you are. Fact is, it might backfire, 'cause that bellhop's gonna do his best to put the pressure back on you."

Polita imagined the bellhop circling her in her apartment. She remembered the bulgy-eyed hysteria in his expression as he cut her hair and ran his tongue along her neck and into her mouth.

"From what Mr. Detective told me," Dante said, taking a long drag from his cigarette, "that bellhop was running a nice little racket that goes back a couple of years. He had his female friend – a concierge - entertaining those rich executives at the Luxuria, while at the same time he was milkin' Carmen."

"You're not telling me anything I don't already know."

"I'm sure I'm not. You and that bellhop should get together more. Maybe go into business together, since you two think alike."

"That'd be hard to do, since he'll be in prison."

"Don't forget, all of us will be doing some time. Know what I told Mr. Detective?"

"I don't care what you told him."

"I told him not to put too much hope in the bellhop being the main man. You see, Mr. Detective is – to quote you - hot on the bellhop's ass 'cause he wants to wrap up his investigation. But I know what he's up to. He's got the bellhop's call girl all confused and she's confessin' to everything to cover her own ass. He planted a seed in her little brain to think he's murdered two call girls and that she might be next. And like so she's telling him everything he wants to hear. She's scared of the bellhop and the cops. Can't say I blame her. But I told Mr. Detective it's maybe more complicated than that. I told him we can't rule out that concierge. Like you, she's acting all scared and everything when she may've found out that the bellhop had this secret setup with Carmen. She may've gotten jealous or thought Carmen was sneakin' over on her turf. Maybe she decided to bury the golf club into Carmen's skull. Know what I mean? How's the saying go? Don't fuck with a woman scorned. Or something like that."

Polita didn't respond; she could only think of the ghoulish bellhop in her apartment.

"Know what else I told Mr. Detective?" Dante said. "I told him he still might be in for a few surprises regarding you. He told me that he knew Carmen didn't just hand over the Rolex and the DVD to you that night. He ain't telling too many people this, but he still thinks you had a big part in Carmen's murder."

"You know that's not true, so save your bullshit."

It was now dark, and Dante turned on his headlights. Polita tried to see what Ramón was holding in his lap, but he kept it hidden and every now and then would lean over and glare at her.

"You know, I've been doing a lot of thinking about you," Dante said. "I think you made a serious miscalculation about not taking advantage of all this free publicity. You would've been rollin' in the dough by now. Shit, man, you never would've even needed the Rolex and all the problems that came with it. You senoritas have become regulars on the TV news. Pretty soon you two could be starring in your own reality show.

Even ditzy Kim has finally started to cash in on her fame. Why don't you before it's too late?"

"For the last time, move your car."

"It hurts to say this, but I don't think you'll live to see your next birthday. But if you do survive this shit you're in, you're guaranteed at least a couple of years in prison. And when you get out, I see you dancin' at titty bars till you're in your forties – saggy tits and all – you douche-bag."

Disgusted that Dante wouldn't move, Polita finally returned to her car. She backed up until her rear bumper was inches from Dante's arm, which was still hanging out the door, then took the pistol from her handbag, placed it next to her lap, and rolled down the window.

"If you don't move," Polita called out, "I'll ram you."

"It was nice doing business with you," Dante said as he pulled his arm inside. "Oh, I forgot. Have a good time partyin' with your bouncer friends. Kim told me y'all are going to the lodge for a day or two. Better check with Mr. Detective and tell him where you're going. He wants to know where you are at all times."

As Dante pulled away, a scowling Ramón turned around and glared.

It took Polita fifteen minutes to reach the restaurant where Wink was waiting. She walked up to the entrance and then hesitated before opening the door. She became uneasy about the meeting and thought of forgetting about the whole thing, but halfway back to her car, she stopped and reconsidered. She was still curious about how involved Wink had been with Carmen.

The lights from the restaurant guided her around the outside of the building until she reached the bar section where Wink had told her he would meet her. From the sidewalk she looked in the window and saw him standing at the crowded bar, facing her. He was holding a drink while talking to a bald man seated at the bar who laughed at something Wink had told him. She observed the scene for a couple of minutes, still debating whether to follow through.

A short while later, the bald man finished his drink and got up from the barstool. Wink shook hands with him, patted him on the shoulder, and watched him leave for the restaurant section. He sipped his drink, called someone on his cell phone, and glanced at his watch. Remaining at the bar, he continued to gaze around him, apparently looking for Polita. He put away his cell phone and then used the window through which she was staring as a mirror to check his appearance. She stepped back into the shadows; he was looking directly at her. With his palms he smoothed his hair. He was snappily dressed in a Tommy Bahama brushed silk shirt, blue blazer, sockless white Docksiders, and pleatless white slacks. He appeared anxious while stirring his drink with a straw.

Another man sat down at the bar and immediately struck up a conversation with Wink, who continued to glance at the window from time to time to preen himself.

Polita finally entered the bar and approached Wink. He was surprised when he happened to turn and noticed her standing next to him. At the same time a hostess told him that his table was ready.

"Perfect timing," Wink said, flashing a pearly smile.

They followed the hostess to a table where a server pulled out Polita's chair for her and unfolded a cloth napkin and placed it on her lap. Two more servers approached their table with glasses of water and a basket of bread. Shortly afterwards, a waitress arrived and took their drink orders.

"Fancy place," Polita said after the waitress left. "I've never had so many people wait on me. Is this where you take all your dates?"

Wink smiled again, and he and Polita exchanged small talk for several minutes. When the waitress returned with the drinks, they ordered their food.

An awkward silence came between them, during which Wink seemed nervous and even a bit shy, he fidgeting with his napkin and glancing around the restaurant. Polita found it odd that he had been comfortable while talking to perfect strangers before she arrived but was noticeably uneasy around her.

"Thanks for calling me today," he said, ending the silence.

"I feel like you somehow talked me into coming here."

"Why do you say that?"

She sipped her frozen margarita while noticing that he was staring at her painted fingernails.

"You're a good salesman," she said. "I mean, I'm sitting in a fancy restaurant with a man whose friend I robbed. Now tell me, how crazy is that? You're a smooth talker, and I don't really mean that in a bad way."

"I promised you I wouldn't talk about my friend or the robbery."

"What the hell? I brought it up. You're still keeping to your promise. Tell me, did his Rolex have any sentimental value?"

"Do you really want to talk about this?"

"I'll tell you when I don't want to."

"His wife bought it for him for his birthday, or maybe it was for an anniversary. Who knows?" Wink shrugged. "He told me, but I forgot. I think they bought customized matching Rolexes. Now, how many couples do you know can afford to do that? They're always buying each other expensive gifts for whatever reason."

A server arrived with their appetizer.

"Are you good friends with him?" she said.

"I've been friends with Elliot for…let me think…maybe thirteen, fourteen years, something like that. When I worked for him, we didn't get along at all, but then, who does with the boss? We didn't become friends until I went into business for myself. There was no longer this boss-employee relationship. We've stayed in touch since I moved from Boston."

"So you wouldn't say you're best friends?"

"We're friends. We get together a couple of times a year to talk business and to play some golf."

"Carmen was killed by a golf club."

"That's…um…what I've heard." Wink's left eyelid twitched. "Ah, speaking of Elliot, I'm picking him up tomorrow so we can finish a business deal."

"Your friend will be back in Miami tomorrow? No wonder you wanted to meet me tonight. Can I expect a surprise visit from him? Seems every time I turn around I've got a visitor at my door."

"He'll be staying in Naples, but the business will be located in Miami. I don't think he wants anything to do with Miami for a while."

"Can't say that I blame him. Nothing good ever happened to me in this hellhole."

He sipped his drink and didn't respond.

"What do you have to do with his business?" she said.

"I introduced him to a friend of mine down here who also is in the health care field. They'll be one of my accounts."

"Your other friend, is he the one who used to go to the café with you?"

"He's been a few times."

"Was he in Carmen's book?"

The waitress arrived with the entrees. They began to eat. Polita absently divided her salad with her fork while Wink cut his food into tiny pieces. He ordered two more drinks for them.

"I guess you don't feel like talking about your other friend," she said.

"I was hoping we wouldn't talk about either one of them." He chewed his food. "Let me know when you want to change the subject."

"You and both your friends were at the Luxuria the night that Carmen was killed."

"We were. And?"

She raised her eyebrows. His ice cubes clinked in his glass.

"You know, we didn't hurt your friend that night we robbed him," she said. Unexpectedly, she smiled.

"That's true, you didn't."

"It's not like we pulled a gun or a knife on him. Now that would've been traumatic."

"It did seem a little harmless the way you and Carmen pulled it off."

"Carmen pointed that broken bottle at your friend only as a joke. She wasn't really serious about hurting him. I think I told you that after the bachelor's party."

"I always thought he was exaggerating."

"Using knockout drops to rob someone sounds to me like a pretty humane thing to do."

"If all crime victims could be so lucky."

She peered at him over her drink. "Are you trying to flatter me by always agreeing with what I say?"

"What makes you think I'd want to do that?" His wide smile deepened his crow's feet. "That Elliot, he ended up doing more harm to himself *after* you women left his room."

"Like what?" She found it curious that he was smiling at his friend's misfortune, and his teeth seemed too white.

"He stepped on a piece of glass from the broken bottle and had to limp around the resort. Then he nicked himself shaving. Plus, like most snowbirds, he got a pretty bad sunburn on his face while playing golf. I'm an ex-snowbird myself, so I shouldn't be talking."

"What has his wife said about all this?"

"You do want to talk about Elliot, don't you? Don't blame me for bringing his name up."

"I said it's OK to talk about him."

"What has his wife said? Karen's threatening to divorce him."

"So I did cause him a lot of pain after all."

"Don't worry about it. I seriously doubt she'll leave him. Her ego was bruised, but she'll get over it. That Karen, she can be real persnickety."

"I sense you don't like her."

"I wouldn't go that far. But the first time I met her she pretty much let me know that I was beneath her. Money has been in her family since the pilgrims landed. She can be a little too hoity-toity for me."

"Sounds like she's a fake and a snob."

"Not so much a fake as condescending. Now, Elliot acts snobby from time to time, but at least he can be one of the boys when he wants to."

They finished dinner. He offered to buy her another drink, but she declined and sipped her water. While a busboy cleaned off the crumbs in front of her with a crumb-scoop, the waitress gave Wink the check.

"Does your friend want to know what happened to his Rolex and to the DVD?" Polita said.

"You don't have to tell me if you don't want to." The drinks had relaxed Wink. "I don't think he cares anymore. Why should he? Have you ever known anyone who has heated towel racks in his house? Elliot has them. After you shower, you pull the towel off the rack and it's nice and warm. He has a heated driveway, too. No hassles with shoveling snow, unless it's a blizzard. Both he and my other friend who met Carmen live in fairy-tale neighborhoods. You know, those gated communities with private clubs and golf courses and yachts."

"I've never heard of a heated driveway. You're joking, right?"

"I'm serious. He's loaded. Trust me, he doesn't have to worry about a stolen Rolex. He owns one of the largest – if not *the* largest - medical supply companies east of the Mississippi. Hell, his bonus one year was more than you or I will probably see in a lifetime. As I told you at the bachelor party, he can afford to buy another Rolex. One for each wrist if he wants."

"I'll tell you about the Rolex and the DVD so you can tell your friend what happened to them."

"I'm not pressuring you to tell me anything."

"The cops have the DVD. And a bellhop at the Luxuria has the Rolex, which I think he sold. No telling who has the Rolex now."

"Hmm."

"I told you because I thought your friend might want to know."

"I'll tell him if you want me to."

"It's up to you."

"Come to think of it, Elliot did say that one of the bellhops was acting a little strange around him. Was this bellhop friends with you and Carmen?"

"He knew Carmen. Another call girl who used to work at the Luxuria was murdered a while back when the same bellhop was working there. And now there's a concierge at the Luxuria, who doubles as a call girl, who also got involved with him. The cops have already talked to them about Carmen's murder."

"Them?"

"Yeah. I guess they can't rule her out."

"Elliot said he had bad vibes from a bellhop and a woman who was hanging out on his floor. I thought he was being paranoid."

"That's probably all I should tell you."

"That's fine with me. Like I told you, you're not going to get any pressure from me. I appreciate the information though."

"My lawyer would probably be upset with me if she found out I was even talking to you."

"Mine too. So you've hired a lawyer?"

"Had to. The detective was being an asshole. Believe me, all this will wipe out my mom's little saving's account. It'll take years for me to pay her back."

"The detective was pushy with me too. But I guess that's his job."

"Yeah."

"The media have been really brutal on you."

"Someone tells me that every day. I've gotten to where I really don't care. I guess that's why no one calls me when I fill out job applications. Only old people with nothing to do read newspapers, and I don't watch much TV. I think Kim's getting ready to cash in on her publicity, though."

"Why not?"

"My lawyer hinted that I should too."

"Maybe you should."

"Nah."

"It'll help pay your legal bills."

"Why are you giving me advice?"

"I guess" – a shrug of his shoulders – "I was trying… It was just a suggestion, that's all."

"I appreciate it." She winked at him. "Maybe you're right. I should turn the bad publicity to my advantage. You know, you're the second person in the last hour to tell me that. Seems everyone wants to give me advice."

They both sipped from their glasses of water. Polita reached in her purse and handed Elliot's business card to Wink.

"Now I don't have anything that belongs to your friend," she said. "That's the only thing I can give back to him."

Wink looked at the business card, slipped it into his wallet, and took out his credit card.

"Did you have any feelings for Carmen?" Polita said. She covertly studied his reaction while he glanced at the check.

"She was a dancer at the café and I was a customer. I never saw it as anything more than that." He tapped his credit card once on the table.

"You were one of her regulars."

"The detective asked me the same thing. Carmen was the most popular dancer at the café. She had a number of regular customers who requested her."

"I wasn't popular like Carmen. You never knew I was a dancer till Kim told you. I guess I was just one of those average, forgettable dancers." She gave him a twisted smile.

"I remember seeing you dance." He looked like a smiling mannequin.

"You're just saying that. You don't have to bullshit me. That's the salesman in you."

"Everyone knows about the dancer with blue-streaked hair."

"That's all you remember me for?"

"Of course not." He handed the waitress the check and his credit card.

"You know what I think?"

"What's that?"

"I think you were obsessed with Carmen."

"Only a fool would've fallen in love with her."

"I didn't say *love*. There's a difference between love and obsession."

"Maybe there is, I don't know."

"Well, what was it?"

"You're sounding like that detective again."

"And you're talking like a politician. You're not giving me a straight answer."

"I thought Carmen was a very attractive woman. Sexy and fun to be around."

"I want to ask you another question, even if it'll make you mad."

"Go right ahead. I don't have anything to hide."

"Did you and Carmen set it up to rob your friend?"

Wink shook his head. He smiled but didn't show his teeth.

"No, I promise you, there was no setup," Wink said.

"I think it's possible."

"You do?" He tugged at his earlobe. "Funny you asked me that. Kim thinks you set it all up."

"Kim would tell you or anyone anything. But you and Carmen knew that your friend could collect on his insurance. I don't think the money motivated you. I think in some weird way you were helping Carmen out because you had a thing for her.

Maybe you were trying to help her out with drugs. I can't quite put my finger on it. But something got fucked up that night."

The waitress returned with Wink's credit card. He signed the check, and the waitress thanked him. He tapped the credit card once again on the table and then slipped it into his wallet, from which he took two twenties and a five and left them on the table for a tip.

"Well, are you ready?" he said.

They got up. While he wasn't looking, Polita took the bills off the table and pocketed them.

Outside, while escorting Polita to her car, Wink put his hand gently on her arm when a car approached in the parking lot. Caught in the glare of the headlights, his eyes froze for a second, wide and unblinking. As she unlocked her car door, he was standing close to her but wasn't making any physical contact. His face was in the shadows.

"You mad at me?" she said.

"Not at all. You had some questions for me, and I hope I answered them. However, I'd like to ask you one last question."

"Is it about your rich friend or Carmen?"

"Neither. We've talked about them enough, don't you think?"

"You're probably right."

"I'd like for you to join me for dinner again so we could talk about you."

"I think you have a thing for topless dancers."

"Does that mean you'll meet me again for dinner?"

"You're not some serial killer, are you?"

Clouds covered the moon and made it hard to see in the parking lot.

"You don't have anything to worry about," he said. "I'm not that type."

"What type are you?"

"I'm just a regular guy asking a very attractive woman out for another dinner date."

"You're lonely, aren't you?"

"I'm not seeing any one woman on a regular basis, if that's what you mean."

"I've seen a lot of lonely men at the café. Some of them are scary lonely."

"I'm comfortable with being by myself."

"I guess that's a fancy way of saying you're lonely. You ever been married?"

"My ex lives in Boston."

"You have children?"

"Pam is eighteen and Ryan is sixteen."

"I'm just a few months older than your daughter."

"No way." Wink sounded surprised.

"That was mean of me to say. I'm just kidding. Oh, well. I guess you don't fit the profile of a serial killer."

"Does that mean we'll be having dinner sometime soon?"

"I'm spending a day or so at a lodge in Everglades City. I need some time away from this dump. Like one of my friends said, where we're going is only an hour from Miami but it feels like a thousand miles. Maybe when I get back, I'll call you."

"If I don't hear from you?"

"Then maybe it's because I'll be in jail, so don't take it personal."

"Has your attorney given you any idea what you're facing?"

"She's been doing some negotiating. Worst case scenario, I'm looking at one to two years, maybe three. Best case is house arrest. I can't say any more than that."

"I understand."

Polita paused as she unlocked her car door. "Can you do me a favor?"

"Sure."

"Tell Mr. Anderson I'm sorry for all the grief I've caused him."

"OK. I can do that."

Polita got into her car. She knew that Wink was smiling because in her peripheral vision she could see his teeth but not his eyes.

"You've got my number," he said. "Call me any time you feel like getting together."

Polita told him good night and drove out of the parking lot. In her rearview mirror she noticed that another car had pulled out of the lot and was following her, keeping about a two-car length distance. Another car pulled in between them. She stopped at a red light, and when she continued on, the car behind her turned off, leaving the car that had been following her hanging back, so she sped up and weaved in and out of traffic. Several miles later, the only car behind her was a sports car, which eventually passed her.

# 47

As the corporate Learjet began its descent over South Florida, Elliot gazed out his window and at the vast expanse of the Everglades. He recalled watching television scenes years ago of searchers working in the Everglades after an airliner had crashed, imagining the passengers and their several minutes of terror as the plane nosedived at four-hundred miles an hour into the River of Grass and virtually disintegrated on impact. The only way searchers could reach the accident was by airboat and helicopters; alligators and snakes infested the area, so snipers, swatting mosquitoes and yellow flies, stood guard over the dive teams. The searchers also had to contend with razor-sharp sawgrass, with hydraulic fuel mixed with swampwater, and with pieces of flesh rotting in the stifling heat. After weeks of shifting through tons of mud, the searchers could only find a few human remains and some plane parts; the swamp had swallowed up everything else.

Strange piece of real estate, Elliot thought. Florida. Land of flowers. From the air, it was all swamp or concrete covered in a thick, smoke-like haze.

Elliot turned his thoughts to Karen. He had spent all yesterday and a sleepless night thinking about his wife's rage-twisted face and the crushed cantaloupe. She had become irrational and openly hostile, and he decided he would have to make plans to move out of the house. His presence there was making her fly into vicious rages, and it was only a matter of time before their violent arguments would start affecting Jeremy.

After the jet landed at the Naples Airport, Elliot and five other executives descended the gangway. The first person he spotted when he entered the tunnel was Wink, smiling his dazzling smile. Dave stood next to him and waved. Wink came up first and gave Elliot a firm, two-handed handshake, while Dave slipped his hand softly in and out of Elliot's grip almost upon contact. Dave's hand felt damp. Was he sweating? Possibly nervous?

"Elliot, it's great to see you again," Dave said.

Wink took Elliot's suitcase from him. "Here, big fella, let me have that."

With a tight smile Dave said, "No golf bag?"

"This trip is all business," Elliot said.

"Of course," Dave said. "We'll be like boy scouts this time."

They walked to the main exit.

"You're not limping," Wink said.

"Foot feels fine," Elliot said. He noticed that Wink was wearing new leather shoes, which creaked with each step he took.

"Your wrists and neck are all right?" Wink squinted for a better look at Elliot's neck. "Those were some godawful marks, that's for sure."

"I've recovered from all my wounds." Elliot wanted to change the subject. "What's the schedule for today?"

"Ash and the kids insist that we have a cookout at the house," Dave said. "After we eat, Wink will drop you off at your hotel and you can look over some papers I've prepared for you. Later, if you feel like it, either Wink or I will show you around Naples, maybe drive over to Marco Island; last time you said something about wanting to own a condo on the gulf since you'll have a business down here. We'll save the financial and legal matters for tomorrow."

They got into Wink's white Infinite and left the airport. Wink and Dave sat up front and talked business. Tired from a sleepless night, Elliot rested his head against the back seat and listened as Dave discussed investment possibilities with a health maintenance organization. Neither man mentioned anything about the call girls.

Wink crossed residential bridges and drove through different neighborhoods, past golf courses, an orange grove with symmetrically planted trees, canalside homes, marinas, and pastel-colored strip malls. Eventually, he turned onto a road lined with palm trees and sun-soaked flowers that led to a security office. An officer waved Wink through once Dave identified himself, and they entered a gated community named Hidden Cove. A golf course with tightly-mown Bermuda grass spread throughout the community. Lushly treed streets and tall-trimmed hedges practically hid the homes, most of which either bordered the golf course or overlooked the aqueous Gulf of Mexico. They passed cypress ponds and salt marshes where wading birds fished the banks. Spanish moss hung from the heavy-limbed oak trees.

Wink turned into Dave's curving, brick-paved driveway and passed an opened wrought-iron gate. Close-clipped Japanese Yew served as an eight-foot tall natural fence for about two-hundred feet between Dave's house and his neighbor's. Wink parked in front of a three-bay garage. Two groundskeepers were working in front of the house, a Country-club Colonial with the neighbor's home on one side and the gulf on the other.

Dave, Wink, and Elliot climbed out of the car and headed toward the front door. Elliot could smell the sea. Sailboats passed within view. Gulls screeched and flew low to the house.

They entered the house and met Dave's wife who was standing at the kitchen counter preparing the food for the cookout. She was short and plumpish and wore a bright-colored muumuu. Straight blond hair touched her round shoulders.

"This is my lovely wife Ash," Dave said. He kissed her on one of her chubby cheeks and put his arm around her waist.

"Nice to meet you," Elliot said. He shook her hand. Her handshake was firmer than her husband's.

"I've heard so much about you," Ashley said.

She smiled, but there was no glitter in her green eyes.

"Where are Tara and Hannah?" Dave said.

"They're with little David, and the three of them are waiting for us at the grill," Ashley said. Her arm flab shook as she was seasoning some steaks. "I hope Elliot and Wink don't mind that our girls want to be the chefs today."

"Tell them I like my steak medium-rare," Elliot said, smiling.

Ashley took the plate full of steaks to the deck in the backyard, and the men followed her. The tree-shaded deck overlooked their swimming pool, fruit trees, a private putting green, a one-hundred-fifty-foot dock, and, their yacht. Dave's next door neighbor had a small castle of a house with turret-like rooms.

"There are daddy's little chefs," Dave said. He hugged his girls, ages six and eight, who wore braces and had blond hair. The infant was in his crib. Dave leaned over the crib and oohed and aahed at his son.

Ashley watched as the girls put the steaks on the grill; her smile was warm when she looked at her children, but she rarely looked at Elliot. On the picnic table were plates and glasses and a pitcher of iced tea. Elliot was the first to sit down while Dave used a video camera to film his daughters as they served the steaks. On the deck, a soft drink in hand, Wink seemed distant and watched with indifference as the girls hammed it up before the camera.

"Aren't you going to eat?" Dave asked Wink.

Wink sat next to Elliot, and the girls served him, but he didn't seem to be listening to the conversations around him.

The air smelled of fresh-cut grass and a salt breeze.

Elliot gazed at the gulf and at a sleek powerboat - the shape and color of a silver bullet - that skimmed the water as if airborne. Wink was looking past Elliot, at Dave's yacht. About a dozen pelicans flew in a tight formation above the water.

After the picnic, everyone cleaned off their plates and went inside. The girls watched TV. While Wink helped Ashley with the dishes, Dave took Elliot on a tour of the house. He led him into a room with hand painted tiles and a carved and painted wood ceiling where a redwood sauna and a bubbling whirlpool bath with underwater lights sat in the corner. Tropical plants surrounded the whirlpool, and built-in aquariums were along the wall.

"This is my new pride and joy," Dave said excitedly. "I had it installed several months ago. The whirlpool is completely computerized. While sitting in it, I can regulate a number of household appliances, such as the microwave and the air-conditioner. It also has a surveillance system." He demonstrated by pressing a button on a hand-held remote unit and pointing to a TV monitor screen. "I can also see who's at the door. If I want to let anyone in, I press the remote and it unlocks the front door. And get this, if I'm leaving the office and Ash isn't home, I can call from my cell and reprogram the bath to fill so it's already hot and bubbly by the time I get home."

Dave looked at Elliot with a smugly self-satisfied expression. He was very relaxed and easy-going, with none of the rigid smiles Elliot had remembered from his stay at the Luxuria. They went into the dining room where Ashley and the girls were serving dessert and coffee. Tara, the younger girl, was getting tired and moody. Dave put her on his lap and asked her for a kiss. She said no and rubbed her eyes. Elliot watched as Dave babied his daughter.

"Please," Dave said. "Just a teensy-weensie kiss." Tara shook her head. "You just worked too hard as mama's little helper, doing all that cooking and helping her with the picnic. I'm so proud of you."

Elliot and Wink were ready to leave. Dave, carrying Tara on his back, went outside with them. Shortly afterward Ashley and Hannah joined them. Ashley was holding the baby.

Elliot told the girls, "That was the best steak I've ever eaten."

Both girls beamed. Dave and his smiling family waved as Wink and Elliot got into the car and pulled out of the driveway. Wink drove past the security office and told Elliot he was taking him to the hotel.

"Do you have a room?" Elliot said.

"No, I've got some errands to run. Also, I'm afraid I won't be able to meet with you and Dave tomorrow morning." Wink spoke in a flat, neutral voice.

"That's no problem. It'll be just some attorneys and financial advisors with us. Nothing too exciting there."

"You and Dave were gone for a while when I was helping his wife with the dishes. Were you talking about Carmen?"

Elliot turned and looked at Wink. "Are you kidding? In his house? With his wife around? Neither one of us said a word about her. He was showing me around."

"I'm sure he showed you his new whirlpool."

"He did. He was like a kid with a new toy."

"I get tired of hearing about it. All he ever does is talk about himself. Kind of wears you down after a while." He paused for a moment. "So you two didn't talk about Carmen?"

"No, we didn't. We're not the least bit interested in her."

They drove the next two miles in silence.

"Dave's a different man around his family," Elliot said.

"Yeah," was Wink's only response.

"Dave and Ashley seem to get along really well, especially after what just happened."

"It's a good front. She puts up with his bullshit and verbal abuse. I thought she would leave him after he told her about the trick book. Since none of your names have been published yet, Dave acts as though a ton of bricks have been taken off his shoulders."

"I feel the same way."

"The local TV news stations are competing with the national ones. I'm afraid it's only a matter of time before some of the names of the johns – maybe all of them – will be leaked."

Elliot felt a slight headache at the base of his neck. "Until it happens, I guess there's nothing I can do. Has Dave said anything more to you about the detective or the investigation?"

"All he told me was that his attorney has everything covered."

Wink stopped at a security office at the Blue Dolphin, a six-story hotel. After the security officer cleared him, he pulled up to the front entrance where a bellhop took Elliot's suitcase and a valet parked Wink's car. Deeply tanned, with wavy blond hair, the bellhop looked like a surfer.

"This is one of the nicer hotels in Naples," Wink said.

"Looks good to me. And safe."

A doorman in a red jacket and white gloves greeted Elliot and Wink and opened the main doors. The hotel was clean and spacious. A three-tiered fountain with two sculptured dolphins splashed in the middle of the lobby. A slit-skirted, long-legged, flame-haired concierge walked across the marble lobby floor and smiled at Elliot as he was checking in at one of the front desks.

With the bellhop following behind them, Elliot and Wink took the elevator to the fourth floor and went to Elliot's suite. Elliot tipped the bellhop, then opened the curtains and looked out the balcony at the courtyard with flowers and topiary, the hotel's swimming pool, and the Gulf of Mexico.

"This is at least one notch below the Luxuria," Wink said, looking around the room. "I know you stay at only the best."

"Don't even try to apologize. It's very nice. Looks like a resort. This suite is big enough for a family of four." Elliot opened his suitcase, took out a dress shirt, and hung it up in the closet. "I'll never set foot in the Luxuria ever again."

"There's not much to do here. Looks more like a retirement community." He revealed a small cold smile. "Wonder what time bingo starts."

"Had I played bingo last time I was in Florida instead of going to a topless lounge, my life would've been a whole lot less stressful. I plan to stay put and read over the documents that Dave gave me. Then it's lights out."

Wink, still standing, stared out the sliding glass door. Something seemed to be bothering him.

"I've seldom seen you so quiet," Elliot said. "You hardly said anything at Dave's. By now I would've heard at least some obscene joke. And you're not even trying to imitate some country hick. What's up with you? You should be happy. By tomorrow morning you'll have a new account."

"My boss told me the other day that I'll be losing three accounts by the end of the month. Things aren't going too well right now. Fucking economy just seems stuck. Two wars, Katrina, and the worst recession since the Great Depression – did Bush do anything right?"

"I wouldn't blame him; it was just some bad timing. By the time Obama is through, we'll be overtaxed and the country will be facing bankruptcy. We'll end up like Greece and Italy."

"I've been through recessions before, but nothing this hellacious."

"You know you can have your old job back with me if you want it."

"Thanks, I appreciate that. But to move back to Boston would give me a whole new set of problems. The ex still lives there, and she's after me for some back payments."

"Maybe Dave has something for you. You two seem to get along real well."

"I'm sure you've noticed that Dave's all about himself. He treats me like I'm his errand boy. Do this, do that; take me here, take me there – that's all I ever hear. Seldom does he deliver on his promises." Wink's frown turned to a smile as he went into his country accent. "Gosh darn it, I'll be just fine. Things always turn out for the best. And I've got you as my best friend for-evah, ain't that so, big fella?"

"Karen and I were talking the other day about some of the bad breaks you've had."

"I'm happy to hear that you two are communicating. So things are starting to get better on the home front?"

Elliot had to sit down to answer that one. "Afraid I don't have Dave's luck there. The hostility in Karen's eyes says it all. She'd like to kill me. I've watched my wife - a very poised, intelligent and self-assured woman – become unraveled."

"She needs to get over it."

"She seems to get meaner with each passing day."

"Can't she accept the fact that we all make mistakes?"

"I found her in the kitchen early this morning screaming like a raving lunatic. I wouldn't dare tell you what she was doing."

Lost in thought, Wink walked around the room with his hands in his pockets. Elliot could only think of the cantaloupe splattered all over his kitchen and Karen's ever-increasing paranoia.

Wink ended his silence by saying, "You probably don't want me to talk about it, but I thought I'd at least mention that I saw Polita last night."

"Oh?"

"She gave me this." He opened his wallet and handed Elliot's business card to him. "She said that now she doesn't have anything that belongs to you."

Elliot put his business card in his wallet. He then spread out some documents on the bed.

A moment later, while glancing over the documents, Elliot said, "Did she say anything about the Rolex or the DVD?"

"The Rolex is history. And I think she said the cops have the DVD."

"Great. It's nice to know there's a video of me buck naked with a whore sitting on my face. And that it'll be in some detective's filing cabinet for the rest of my life. I'm sure when the cops get bored, they can just watch the DVD for a good laugh. Hell, it almost became one of those grainy snuff films."

"You might want to know one other thing. You were right, there was a bellhop at the Luxuria who was involved with the Rolex Bandits. He also had another woman, a concierge, working for him. She must've been the one who you kept seeing hanging around your floor."

"I told you I thought there was something funny going on."

Elliot acted indifferent while arranging the documents.

Wink let a full minute pass. "Polita told me one other thing about the bellhop. She said the cops are trying to get the evidence to arrest him for Carmen's murder."

"Hmm."

"I guess they're trying to piece it all together."

"Have you said anything about this to Dave?"

"I mentioned it to him, and he just shrugged. The only thing he cares about is the trick book with his name in it."

"He and I are on the same page there." He paused. "So I'll never see the Rolex?"

"Afraid not. It's long gone. It could be on someone's wrist in Miami, Rio de Janeiro, Berlin, or Moscow. Theft has gone global with everything else."

While reading over one of the documents, Elliot said, "Not that I really care, but what do you think will happen to the other woman?"

"Polita? You know, the whole time I was talking to her I kept wondering the same thing. I've said it all along, I don't trust her. I still think she's dangerous. Or doomed."

"Doomed?"

"Yeah. One minute when I was talking to her she seemed real cocky and full of herself. Then the next I couldn't help but see a hint of fear in her eyes. I guess she'd better be looking over her shoulder. She could be a damsel-in-distress - or she's a killer."

"Hmm." Elliot turned another page.

"You're not going to believe this, but she told me to tell you that she was sorry for all the pain she had caused you."

Elliot cleared his throat, took out his iPhone, and scrolled through to see how his stocks did for the week.

Wink watched him close his cell phone. "What do you think of her apology?"

"If someone doesn't slam a golf club into her skull," Elliot said after a long pause, "she'll probably one day look back and say that what she did to me was an example of youthful indiscretion. I bet she doesn't spend one day in jail." He looked at Wink. "Well, when do I see you next?"

"I need to see my kids sometime this summer. Maybe we can catch a game at Fenway."

"I'd like that."

Wink glanced at his watch. "Well, pardner, this here salesman had better start poundin' the pavement before I done lost another account. Hard to believe I'm pushin' fifty and I still have to make cold calls." Then, in a more serious tone, he said,

"I know that you and Dave made a sound investment with this merger. And I hope you and Karen work things out. Maybe you should ask Dave for advice on how to save a marriage. He's getting to be an expert on that."

"He has already given me some advice over the phone. I don't think anything will work with Karen." Elliot took the ice bucket off the dresser. "I'll walk with you to the elevator."

They went down the hallway. Wink pressed the elevator button and waited.

"Speaking of Polita," Wink said, "she's not that far from here."

"She's in Naples?"

"No. She's spending a little time near Everglades City. She said something about going scuba diving or something."

"Since when do criminals get to go scuba diving? I thought she'd be in prison by now."

"I think she cut a deal with the detective. She'll end up doing some time, but not much. Plus she and Kim are celebrities now. You don't have to feel sorry for her."

"What makes you think I feel sorry for her?"

"I don't think you or I want to see her end up like Carmen. Call me naïve, but I think she's really trying to turn her life around."

"I could care less. For a while Karen was giving me nightly reports on those criminals. I don't want to ever hear about them again."

"You behave and get a good night's sleep, hear?"

"I'll be on my best behavior."

Wink smiled, barely, said goodbye, fist-bumped Elliot, and rode the elevator to the lobby. Elliot filled his bucket up with ice and headed back to his room.

A half hour later, his cell phone rang. It was Dave. He wanted to know if Elliot was pleased with the hotel. Elliot heard Dave's girls playing in the background. After Dave made sure everything was all right, he said goodbye and hung up.

Elliot then called his home number. After the answering machine came on, he said, "Karen, it's me. I just wanted to let you and Jeremy know that I'm in Naples and will be staying at the Blue Dolphin. Please call my cell if there's an emergency. My flight leaves tomorrow afternoon, and I'll be in Boston around six. Someone from the office will pick me up."

He paused. "I love you both very much."

# 48

Seth piloted an airboat, its giant fan blades spinning, through hydrilla beds of a swampy lake. Polita was sitting next to him, with Kim, Allen and Seth's brother Paul seated in the back. Seth, hiding a can of beer, slowed down when he approached a populated area. A marine patrol boat motored by in the distance. Men in jonboats drift-fished in the lake. Seth waved to an elderly man and woman with straw hats and cane poles who were fishing from a pier. The sky was hazy with heat.

Seth guided the airboat through a narrow creek bordered with cypress knees and cattails. A hawk, perched on one of the cypress knees, watched them as they passed. When Seth reached a shallow-flooded prairie, Allen started to whoop and holler.

"I want to see how fast this thing can go!" Allen yelled. He turned his baseball cap backwards. "Let's have some action!"

Seeing no boats or marine patrol officers, Seth finished his beer and revved the engine while Allen and Paul cheered him on. He put the engine on full throttle, and the bow lifted. Polita gripped the handrail to brace herself, and the boat skimmed over the water as the endless scenery of spartina grass flew by. The blast of air rushed against Polita's face.

A wall of tall cypress trees stood at the end of the prairie. Without slowing down, Seth headed straight for the trees. His passengers screamed with laughter. Polita closed her eyes and covered her head while Allen and Kim embraced each other. Just before reaching the trees, Seth turned sharply and sent a spray of water high into the air. Allen and Paul yelled some more. Polita and Kim were laughing.

"Let's do it again!" Allen shouted.

"Maybe later this evening, when it cools off some," Seth said.

Seth maneuvered the boat through the trees until he reached another lake fed by numerous creeks and cypress bogs. They passed a fish camp, trailers, and homes with docks and screened porches. He turned down one of the creeks, which moved muddily along the banks. Sharp slices of sunlight penetrated a thick-limbed, twisting canopy of trees. He idled the boat and pointed at a pond in which an alligator disguised as a log lay perfectly still. A few yards away, on the bank, a malnourished dog sniffed at something.

"Gator bait," Seth whispered. He opened another can of beer. "When the locals want to get rid of one of their dogs, they just let them wander down here knowing there'll be a gator waiting on them. A gator won't leave a trace of bone or hair."

"That's cruel," Polita said.

"Unfortunately, I've seen this one nab a few," Paul said. "He's a bull gator who owns this pond."

"How can you tell 'em apart?" Allen said. "They all look the same to me."

Paul shielded his eyes from the sun for a better look. "He's over thirteen feet and he's blind."

"No way," Kim said.

"I'm serious," Paul said. "A couple of years ago some teenagers shot him in the face with buckshot. He has to hunt by smell. The locals named him Ray Charles."

The gator moved closer to the dog.

"There used to be another bull gator that lived in a pond not far from here," Paul said. "We named him Boss because he was the biggest and baddest gator around. But Boss got careless and lazy and ended up getting shot. Turned out that some local hunters kept losing their prized hunting dogs that just happened to disappear when they were sent out in this area. Then one day a couple of determined hunters went looking for their missing dogs by following the beeping sounds that were coming from the tracking collars. The sounds brought them to Boss, who was sunning himself on the bank, just as fat and happy as he could be. After the hunters shot Boss and opened him up, they found over a half dozen tracking collars in his stomach. Old Boss had been dining off the best hunting dogs money could buy, not to mention any stray mutt that wandered into his territory."

With the gator closing in on the dog, Polita stood up in the boat and shouted, "Go! Get out of here!"

The dog raised its head, looked at Polita, and scratched itself. Except for Polita, everyone else was laughing. The gator moved a few feet closer.

"Get out of here you dumb mutt!" Polita shouted, clapping her hands. "You'd better run!"

She pretended to throw something at the dog, which finally scared it away. The gator sank, and then scooted under a dense mat of water lettuce. A few seconds later, the gator's snout broke the surface and looked at them with unseeing eyes.

"You just cost Ray Charles his dinner," Seth said.

"He looks pissed," Kim said.

Polita sat back down and didn't say anything.

"Don't act so serious," Kim said. "We were just having some fun. None of us wanted to see that dog get eaten. Did we, guys?"

"Of course not," Seth said. Everyone but Polita was laughing.

Seth poled the boat through a hyacinth-clogged section of the creek until he reached a pier. A large gator, coated with algae, lay camouflaged on the opposite bank of the creek. He tied up the boat, and everyone followed him to his brother's weathered, wood-shingled hunting lodge on cedar pilings. Paul and Allen carried the ice chest and life preservers and piled them on the pier. Inside the lodge, Paul, dressed in moccasins, black jeans and black T-shirt, and smoking a cigar, served his guests sandwiches and soft drinks at a table. The lodge had cypress walls and pine flooring, with modest furnishings, including a billiard table, a sofa, one wicker chair, and two bar stools. Mounted animal heads - two deer, one boar - hung above the mantel.

"Some friends are coming by in a little while," Paul said. "We're going hog-hunting. Anyone care to come along?"

"Sounds like fun," Seth said.

"I thought we were going scuba diving in the gulf," Kim said.

"We can go diving anytime," Seth said. "But when do you get a chance to hunt wild hogs?"

"Count me out," Kim said. "I might be from the country, but huntin' was never big on my list of things to do."

"You'll have to count me out, too," Allen said. "It's fun riding an airboat through the swamp, but I don't like walking through all that stuff. I'll be leaving soon anyway."

"Looks like Allen and Kim aren't going," Seth said, looking at Polita while sipping his beer. "How about you? Are you game?"

"Sure, why not?" Polita said. "I've never been hunting before."

"I knew I could count on you," Seth said.

"We'll wait for you back here," Kim said.

"Where it's safe," Allen added, and laughed.

"I didn't think *Alien* was afraid of anything," Seth said.

"I'd rather deal with sharks in the gulf than with what's out there in this swamp," Allen said.

Polita noticed that Paul was staring at her. When she returned his stare, he extinguished his cigar and got up from the table. He stepped up to the window and gazed outside.

"My brother may not look like much," Seth said after they had finished eating lunch, "but he owns more land around here than almost anyone except the government."

"It's more swamp than real estate," Paul said.

Paul gave Seth a cigar and took him aside to talk to him, glancing once at Polita. Then, while Seth used his knife to cut off the tip of his cigar, he asked Polita to follow him out back. Hunters in their mud-splattered pickups and sports utilities were arriving. The vehicles pulled trailers with four-wheelers and airboats. Several hunters showed up on horseback. Seth drove one of his brother's four-wheelers out of the garage and parked between two pickups loaded with dog boxes.

"You and I will hunt by riding in this," Seth told her. "There's no need to go on foot in these woods and step on something that doesn't like being stepped on."

One hunter was opening up the dog boxes while another hunter was tying the dogs to a long rope. They both wore snakebite-proof chaps.

"This is Randy," Seth said, introducing Polita to an overalled hunter with discolored teeth. "Randy's been hunting with my brother for a long time. He's the owner of most of these dogs. They may not be pretty, like their owner, but they sure are good hunters. They're hog dogs. Mixed breeds and a couple of pit bulls. Those two over there are Dixie - the light-colored one - and Magnum." He flicked his cigar at the two lean, muscle-tight pit bulls. "Dixie and Magnum are Randy's prized dogs. A boar can weigh over five-hundred pounds and have razor-sharp tusks four-inches long, so you're going to need some mean dogs that'll fight it, not just chase after it. Look at the battle scars on Dixie and Magnum. They have no fear. A T. Rex could be out there and these two would take it on. None of the other dogs mess with the pit bulls."

Seth's brother pulled up in his bright orange four-wheeler and handed Seth a rifle and a .357 revolver.

"We're waiting for another couple of hunters to show up," Paul said. "We'll go back to the lodge for an hour or so, let it cool off some, then we should be ready to go."

"You know how to handle one of these things?" Allen said as he admired Seth's rifle.

"I've hunted a few times with my brother," Seth said.

"My daddy owns all kinds of guns," Kim said.

"But Seth's a city boy," Allen said.

"I can hold my own," Seth said. "More than half of these hunters live in the city - Miami, Homestead, Naples. Only Randy and a few others are truly from the swamps. Isn't that right, swamp man?"

Smiling shyly to hide his bad teeth, Randy was setting out his supplies on top of one of the dog boxes: ammunition, knives, a snakebite kit, two first-aid kits with sutures for sewing up the dogs' wounds, and several radio collars for the dogs.

"Speaking of the city," Allen said, "Miami's a whole lot safer than out here."

Kim laughed. "Miami? Safe? What do you think, Polita?"

"I'm more nervous in Miami than out here," Polita said.

"Randy, can you make sure all the four-wheelers are gassed up and ready to go?" Paul said.

"Will do, boss" Randy said.

"One more hour and the hunt is on," Paul announced.

Randy spat out a stream of chewing tobacco. "The dogs are already chompin' at the bit."

On their way back to the lodge, Paul said to Polita, "You don't have to go if you don't want to."

"I've never been on a four-wheeler," Polita said. "I'll be OK."

"You'll ride with Seth. He's pretty good at handling one through these woods. The trails are marked and pretty easy to see. I think you'll have fun."

# 49

One of Elliot's associates had picked him up at the airport and was dropping him off in front of his home when Elliot's cell phone rang. It was Dave.

"How was the flight?" Dave said.

"Everything went smoothly. We're just now pulling into the driveway."

"Good…Good. Is your wife with you?"

"No. Why?"

"You said 'we.'"

"One of my sales reps drove me from the airport. Hold on for a second."

Elliot got out of the car and opened the backseat door to retrieve his one suitcase and briefcase. His associate offered to take the suitcase inside, but he waved him off.

"Thanks for the ride," Elliot said. "I'll see you at the office tomorrow." Holding his cell phone to his ear while getting out his keys to open the front door, he said to Dave, "What's up?"

"Are you alone now?"

Elliot opened the door and called out, "Anyone here?" No one answered. "As expected, I've arrived at a deserted home."

"I thought the merger went really well."

"I was impressed. You have a great business model." He left his suitcase near the front entrance and sat down. "Did we forget anything? I wasn't expecting you to call so soon. Everything OK down there? Your voice sounds a little flat."

"Wink hasn't called you?"

"I haven't heard from him since he dropped me off at the hotel."

"Well, there's a little bit of bad news out there, I'm afraid."

"What now?"

"The good news is that everything went so well with the merger. Didn't it? That's what we'll focus on, right?"

Elliot changed hands with the cell phone. "Dave, quit beating around the bush and tell me what's going on."

"About an hour ago, all the TV news stations released the names from Carmen's trick book."

Dave's answer seemed to take a full minute to reach Elliot's ear. Elliot lowered the cell phone to his lap, let his head rest against the back of the chair, and stared at the ceiling. Dave's muffled voice could be heard talking into Elliot's lap, but it took some effort for him to raise the cell phone back to his ear.

"Are you still there, Elliot?" Dave's voice sounded almost frantic.

"Yeah. I'm here. I heard most of your conversation."

"We must have a bad connection."

"No, I just went a little numb. Every time I turn a corner in this ordeal something new pops up in front of me. But nothing should surprise me. It was just a matter of time."

"I know what you mean. I was trying to will it away. My phone has been ringing constantly. Every reporter in the area wants to talk to me. Have you had any calls?"

Elliot's voice was resigned. "I haven't checked the answering machine. So far, I don't have any voice messages on my cell. What did your wife say?"

"She's been in the bedroom with the door closed, crying. She's had calls from her relatives and friends telling her about my name being in the news."

"Just more pain and humiliation we keep handing out to our families." He continued to stare at the ceiling. "I waited over forty fucking years to have a son and look what I'm about to do to him. His friends are going to eat him alive."

"It's all about damage control from here on out. I'm going to admit to my family and friends - and my employees – that I made a mistake and that I can only try to do better. To be a better person, and that will come with time and some counseling. Those are words right out of my attorney's mouth. He's going to draft me a statement. He has been worth every penny."

Elliot's heavy sighs sounded like an asthma attack. "I'm just curious. Were most of the names from the Miami area?"

"Less than half is my guess. There's one major celebrity – the football player, Matt Owens, of the Dolphins - and a minor one, a city council member. The rest are business executives from all over. I remember hearing Madrid, Seoul, Sidney, to name a few. Our Rolex Bandits had gone international with their little crime spree."

"I'm the only one from Boston?"

"I think so. There's a CEO from New York, a lobbyist from D.C."

"Being the only one from Boston makes me stand out. I guess I'll be on the evening news. Maybe Karen has already found out and is in hiding with Jeremy." He motioned his arm back and forth as though he wanted to throw the cell phone against the wall. "Amazing what we put our families through for trying to get a piece of ass."

"I'm getting out of Dodge for a week or so. That should cool off the paparazzi for a while. Call it therapy time with the family. And I'll probably do a video conference with my employees, to let them know that I made a mistake but that I'm still in charge."

"Sounds like some good advice. Because of my wife's hostility toward me, I can cross out the family vacation. But I'll make a statement to my employees, then I guess I'll go into hiding. Probably right here in my own home, unless Karen kicks me out." He glanced around the living room. "I should give my attorney a call. I always feel better after I listen to him."

"Same here. Good luck. And keep me posted. We'll get through this, Elliot. Together."

They hung up. Elliot called his attorney. "Jack. Elliot Anderson. I have some bad news for you."

"Don't keep me in suspense."

"They've released the names from the trick book."

"Who are they?"

"I don't know who leaked them but the names are all over South Florida. It's only a matter of hours – minutes - before the names go national."

"Your voice sounds shaky. Try to relax."

"How the fuck can I relax?"

"Just take it easy. Sounds like we have a few PR issues, not legal ones. Has anyone from the media tried to contact you?"

"I just returned from Florida and haven't checked my phone messages here at the house."

"There's nothing to worry about."

"How can you say that?" Elliot ran his free hand through his hair.

"It's going to be all right. Look, Mr. Anderson, I'm not the cheerleader type. My job is not to give you a pep talk and tell you what you want to hear."

"Maybe I need a fucking pep talk." A slight edge of hysteria crept into Elliot's voice.

"Remember what I told you to say to the detective?"

"Ah…I'm not sure what you told me. How can I keep anything straight when my world is collapsing around me?"

"Of course you're not in the right frame of mind to think clearly. I'll think for you. I told you to keep quiet around him."

"Why are we talking about the detective anyway?"

"Because I want you to treat any reporters the same way I told you to handle the detective: keep quiet. These reporters are going to snoop around your home, your workplace. They'll try calling you at all hours. They smell blood in the water. Expect nothing from the tabloid press but sensationalism and trash. Ignore them. It's the gotcha type of journalism – if you can call it journalism. If you open your mouth and mumble any response – that reporter has gotcha saying something. If you want to really get verbose tell a reporter, 'No comment.' You've got to let me handle everything."

"If you say so." Elliot was shaking so badly that he almost dropped the cell phone. He switched hands. "All of this has already traumatized my wife. And now my name on TV and in the papers will only make her worse. And of course there's my son…And my parents…Not to mention all of my employees. All of my friends. My clients. The whole fucking city of Boston…"

"And I'm ready for it, Elliot. It comes as no great surprise. We talked about how an ambitious district attorney or detective might pull this stunt. Clearly, they must be getting desperate. Look, you are in no condition right now to be rational, Elliot; you too are traumatized. I know this is tough. Let me handle everything. And I mean everything."

Holding the cell phone against his chest, Elliot wept silently in shame.

The attorney waited a moment. When he next spoke, his steely voice sounded surprisingly gentle, "Would it make you feel better if I came over and we talked? I can be there in fifteen minutes."

Elliot tried to compose himself. He wiped the tears from his eyes.

"I'm sorry," Elliot said between half-sobs.

"You have nothing to be sorry for."

"I'll be all right. I've got to deal with both my wife and my employees. I'll have to make a statement to the *Globe*. I don't know what to say. I was thinking of at least meeting with my top assistants to at least give them an update."

"Elliot, because of the trauma you're going through, I don't think you heard me. One, you don't have to tell anyone anything. Two, an update of what? Third, frankly, it's a private matter and no one's damn business."

"I just can't ignore my employees. Besides, it'd give me an excuse to get out of the house to meet with at least a few of my assistants. I'm walking on eggshells around here. I feel like the walls are closing in on me, and I haven't been home for more than ten minutes."

"If you want to get out of the house for a while, why don't you go play golf- by yourself? It's supposed to be a nice day. I don't want you to associate with anyone for the next couple of days."

"I want to make at least some statement."

"I wouldn't."

"I have to. It's the honorable thing to do, which coming from me sounds like a contradiction."

"I won't accept that kind of talk."

"Will you help me or not?"

"If that's what you want, of course I will. For starters, we should keep the statement simple."

"Like what?"

"Personally, I'm in favor of our 'No comment' statement."

"Come up with something better."

"Off the top of my head…um…'What happened reflected a serious error of judgment,' or 'I very much regret the incident and I accept full responsibility for my actions.' Something like that. Give me a little time and I'll come up with something short and sweet."

"Add to that, 'Criticize me, but leave my wife and child out of it.'"

"The less said the better. We want to keep it ambiguous. No specifics."

"Right now my biggest concern is how all the negative publicity will affect my son."

"I'm here to help you on all fronts, whether it's family, business, or having to deal with the media." The attorney's voice was resolute. "I'm going to get you through this. Put everything on my shoulders."

"My friend in Naples who's also in the trick book suggested that I…"

"Elliot, I will repeat this until I'm red in the face – you have no friends when it comes to what happened to you in Miami. I am your only friend. Now listen to me carefully. Are you listening?"

"Go ahead."

"Screen all your calls – from cell to home to office. Don't answer your door. Make sure your secretaries and assistants protect you from any intruders at work. These reporters will swarm you when you least expect it. When you're not at work, you stay at home. Your home is your fortress. Don't even go out to eat. If you have to leave the house, wear a disguise. All this will blow over. Usually the media's attention span lasts a week or two on something like this. Then they seek out the next headline or tragedy. All of this will blow over, and you'll be able to return to a normal life."

# 50

Paul led Seth and Polita out of the lodge and they met up with the hunters and their barking dogs. The four-wheelers were being started up, so the air was full of gas fumes.

"Out there are thousands of acres of pine forest and swamp," Seth told Polita. He holstered his .357 and placed the rifle next to him. "There are lots of trails and some dirt roads. We'll stay out of the real swampy areas. You look a little tense. You had fun on the airboat, right?"

"Yeah," Polita said.

"Well, the four-wheeler is just as much fun."

"Aren't there any seatbelts?"

"Nope. Just hold on."

The hunters unleashed the dogs. The men on horseback got a head start and galloped into the flat piney woods. A moment later a half-dozen four-wheelers sped off and followed the horses. The dogs' howls and barks shrieked above the sound of engines. Paul took the initial lead.

"I just love the sound of dogs on the hunt!" he yelled.

Polita put her arms around Seth's waist and braced herself by pressing her feet against the floorboard as Seth and his brother exchanged leads on a heavily-rooted path. The racing four-wheelers produced a thick cloud of dirt and bluish exhaust fumes.

Farther up the path a huge boar was ripping apart a snake when it saw the dogs and immediately ran for the thick underbrush. The howling and baying of the dogs reached a fever pitch. Seth listened to the ear-shattering cries and followed the pack while Polita huddled up behind him to protect herself from low branches that slapped against the four-wheeler. The hog, with a piece of the snake hanging from one of its tusks, crashed through the palmettos, the dogs in full cry behind it.

Paul raced past Seth, yelling, "These four-wheelers aren't built for two if you want speed! You can't hang with me!"

Minutes later, Seth came to a stop. Ahead of him, Paul had pulled over and climbed off his four-wheeler. With a .357 in hand, Paul walked quickly toward a field of scrub oak and palmettos. He motioned for Seth to follow him, but after he'd walked a short distance, the palmettos shook violently. The hog and the pack of trail dogs chasing it suddenly burst forth. Paul wore a look of both terror and exhilaration as the squealing hog charged him. He fired once, missing, then ran. He jumped back in his four-wheeler just in time to escape the hog's tusks.

Seth grabbed his rifle and stood up in his four-wheeler, waiting for a good shot. One of the quicker dogs ran the hog down and leaped at it. The hog turned and started slashing. The dog emitted a high whine and retreated with a deep gash across its throat. Soon another injured dog limped away. The enraged hog, popping its jaws, spun in circles in an effort to gore any dog that came near it. The hair on its back bristled.

The two pit bulls finally caught up with the rest of the pack of dogs and, without hesitation, swarmed the hog. Their gnashing teeth filled the air. The hog slashed at them repeatedly. Dixie jumped the hog from behind and clamped its jaws onto one of the hog's ears. Magnum attacked the hog's throat. The hog was squealing, frantically whipping its head about to disengage the tenacious dogs by slamming them to the ground or against a tree. None of the other dogs joined in the fight; they circled the hog and gnashed their teeth and barked but didn't attack.

Too weak to fight anymore, the hog just stood there, both pit bulls locked onto it with their bloodied fang teeth. Blood poured from its throat. Its flanks sucked in and out. Dark drool, mixed with blood, dripped from its snout. The hog's ear that Dixie was hanging onto looked like a piece of tattered leather.

With the hog under control, Seth discarded his rifle and jumped out of the four-wheeler. He ran up to the hog and shot it twice at close range with his .357. The hog collapsed. Both dogs fell with the hog and remained clinging to it. The mixture of blood and saliva on the dogs' mouths made them look rabid.

"That was one mean hog," Paul said, appearing next to Seth. He was almost out of breath but laughing. "Damn. I've had them come after me before, but that one wanted to gore me up against the four-wheeler. He's one of the biggest hogs I've seen out here, and I've been hunting these woods for a long time." He looked at Polita, who remained seated. "Are you all right?"

Polita, gazing at the dead hog, said nothing.

"Too much excitement for one day?" Seth asked her.

Polita stared at Seth. The squealing of the hog was still ringing in her ears.

"Oh, I thought it was *fun*," Polita said. "Let's go watch the dogs maul another hog."

"Hey, I'm sorry. You said you wanted to come with us. Hunting sure is exciting, but no one claimed it was going to be pretty."

Eventually, the remaining hunters arrived and marveled at the size of the hog. Nearby a dog lay dead from its neck wound, while another that had been gutted by the hog lay staring blankly at the ground. It took the owner of the pit bulls a while to pry them loose from their prey. Another hunter loaded up the rest of the dogs into their boxes. Polita looked away as yet another hunter picked up the shivering and whining dog that had been wounded, took it behind a thicket of scrub oak, and shot it.

It took four hunters to load the hog onto the back of a four-wheeler. Except for Seth, who was drinking another beer, Paul and the rest of the men left for the lodge.

Alone with Seth, Polita remained in the four-wheeler and watched him stare at the ground where the hog had lain. Blood pooled on the ground and stained several palmettos. In full frontal view of her, he pulled out his penis and, regarding her with an ineffable smirk, began urinating. She looked at him in mute astonishment. The arc of his urine went over a trampled palmetto bush. Then he urinated into the puddle of blood. After he finished, he shook his penis a number of times and zipped up his jeans. He returned to the four-wheeler and sipped his beer. He smelled of urine.

"Carmen liked coming out here," Seth said, staring at nothing in particular. "There were at least four or five times after she'd gotten off work that she'd ask me to take her to my brother's. It was the peace and quiet that she enjoyed." He gazed at Polita and smiled. "Maybe it was the Indian in her."

"I want to go back to the lodge." She slid farther behind him, to the edge of the seat.

"Yeah, Carmen really enjoyed it out here." He started up the four-wheeler. "Let's take a ride. I'll show you some of the places where she liked to go."

"I don't care where you used to take her. I'm ready to go back to the lodge."

"I'll take you back. In a little while."

Seth drove down a dirt path.

"Is this the right way?" she said.

"I think so." He looked around. "But on second thought, all the paths look the same to me. We might be lost. I hope we get back before dark. If you get lost at night, you want to cover yourself with palmettos and stay put. Don't move around. Everything out here hunts at night. By the way, you know who also hunted at night?"

"What are you talking about?"

"Call girls like you and Carmen and Kim – the Rolex Bandits – stalked their prey at night."

"I've never seen you act like this. You're drunk."

"If you think I'm drunk, then you'll have to tell me how to get back to the lodge."

"It's the other way. Turn around."

"If you say so. You're the navigator."

He turned around and drove for about a half mile until a fallen log blocked their way.

"I didn't think this was the right direction," he said. "I bet you're trying to get me lost. Are you trying to take advantage of me."

"Seth, why...?"

"Why what?"

"Why are you acting like this?"

"What way am I acting?" He turned the four-wheeler around and took another path.

"You knew this wasn't the right way."

"Hey, I don't live out here. I just visit my brother once or twice a month. It'd take a swamp Indian to know his way around this place. I bet if Carmen were here she'd be able to help us."

"Please don't bring her name up again."

"Why can't we talk about Carmen? You were always jealous of the attention she got. Don't deny it."

"Watch where you're going!"

Seth almost drove into a pine tree. He increased his speed.

"Do you know how Carmen got that Indian name that she used at the café?" Seth said. "My brother gave it to her. He knows about some of the Indian folklore because he lives out here and is into that kind of stuff. If you haven't noticed, he's a mix between a hippie and a yuppie. I enjoy getting away from the city to visit him, and he leaves his business concerns around here to visit me in the city. And he'd always drop by the café, which is where he met Carmen." As Seth talked about Carmen, Polita gripped her hands on the metal handles of the seat and listened with mounting uneasiness. "And wouldn't you know, those two hit it off when he found out about her Indian heritage. After the first time he met her, he started calling her Chechoter. That's what got her started into that Indian act of hers." He shook his head and grinned. "That war dance she performed had almost all the men at the café ready to jump on the stage with her."

Seth drove erratically, one hand on the steering wheel and the other groping at Polita. She squeezed herself against the back of the seat. He then came to a sudden stop in the middle of the path. They were in the open, in a palmetto-and-wiregrass field, with the nearest pine, cypress or scrub oak at least three-hundred feet away.

"The four-wheeler makes too much noise," he said. "I can hardly hear myself think." He turned off the ignition and climbed out. "This would probably be a good time for us to talk about Carmen's murder. It's real peaceful and quiet, the way Carmen would like it."

"I told you I don't want to talk about her."

"Well, I do. So there."

Polita tried to get out of the four-wheeler, but Seth grabbed her by the arm. Afraid to look at him, she stared down the snaky, dirt path. Her throat was dry from the heat and from having breathed in the exhaust fumes and dirt.

"We talked some about her murder on our way to the lodge," she said. "I told you about the bellhop and the concierge and how the cops are trying to piece together the evidence."

He was quiet. She turned and looked at him, expecting him to be angry. Instead, he was calm and smiling.

With his left hand he took his beer can from a cup holder, finished drinking it, and tossed it on the floorboard. He thought for a moment while his right hand remained gripping Polita's arm.

"You're hurting me," she said. "Let go of me."

"I didn't mean to hurt you." He applied less pressure to her arm but continued to hold onto her. "You had something to do with that bellhop, didn't you?"

"I tried not to have anything to do with him. Seth, let go of my arm."

"The reason you asked me to park in front of your apartment that night was because he was there, wasn't he?"

"Yeah. It was the bellhop."

"You two were up to something."

"I asked you to be nearby, in case he was going to hurt me. He may've been the one who broke into my old apartment and destroyed everything. That was my warning. I was afraid of him."

The whine of mosquitoes sounded around Polita's head.

He slurred some of his words. "I've got a confession to make. I knew about your call-girl operation several weeks before Carmen was even murdered."

The shadeless palmetto field made Polita perspire and feel light-headed.

"My brother told me that every time Carmen was around him, he'd end up missing money or something valuable," he said. "And she even had the nerve to borrow money from him while at the same time she was ripping him off. Which she never paid back. Paul was just being dumb. Both of them were acting stupid. Drugs fucked up Carmen. And a drop-dead gorgeous woman was turning my brother into a moron."

The sun continued to send hazy waves of heat beating upon Polita. She wanted to leave while she still had the strength, but Seth kept a vice-like grip on her arm.

"One day I decided to investigate for my brother," he continued. "I waited for Paul and Carmen to go out on the airboat, then I looked through her purse and handbag. Sure enough, she was hiding one of his rings and a wad of cash. She even stole some of my things. As you know, she was one desperate woman with a very expensive habit. You name it, she was doing it. Crack. Heroin. Meth. She was a 'tweaker.' Then I found her trick book. I saw yours and Kim's initials in it. I figured out most of the codes. It didn't take a rocket scientist to figure out that LR&S stood for the Luxuria Resort and Spa."

Sweat stung Polita's eyes. She thought she was going to pass out.

"Yeah, Paul and I were a little hurt about the trick book," he said. "I told him about it before I drove Carmen back to Miami. He didn't say anything to her. He just let her go. We thought that you and Carmen were like the typical dancers at any topless joint: You liked the money but hated the way you had to go about getting it. Like most dancers, you and Carmen would work three or four years, save some money, then get the hell out of the sleaze and turn to something more respectable. We knew you two weren't the 8-to-5 office-types. But we never thought that both of you would turn out to be con artists and call girls. Kim - maybe - but not you. You and Carmen had us fooled."

Seth's voice came slowly out of the heavy, humid air. His words seemed to smother Polita, making it hard for her to breathe.

"You told me while you were helping me move out of my old apartment that you still wanted to be my friend," she said wearily. She was surprised to hear her own voice. "And that was after you found out about my involvement with the Rolexes."

"I guess it bothered me more than I thought."

"You called me a lady when that man was making fun of me at the bachelor party. No one's ever called me a lady before." Her voice was so weak as to be almost inaudible.

"I called *you* a lady? Well, I can change my mind, can't I? You're a whore. And a con-artist. And probably a murderer."

An animal-like breath of a breeze wafted across the palmetto field.

"I think my brother handled it pretty well when I told him about Carmen and her trick book," Seth droned on. "He wasn't in love with her, but he cared for her more than he wanted to admit. He exploded only once - the day I told him about the trick book. He told me that he was going to follow her to the café or to the Luxuria, but I talked him out of it." His eyes followed the path that led into the darkness of the trees. "Of course, he couldn't do anything to her out here because it'd look too suspicious. But I think he got over her. One good thing about the trick book was it didn't have his name in it. At least on paper, he wasn't one of her johns. But I mean, goddamn, she was using him as much if not more than some of the johns in her book. It pissed me off how she used him. And he was afraid she might blackmail him because they were both into drugs. I wasn't going to let her ruin him. He has a good business. And he's going to let me go into business with him."

While Polita slapped at the steamy swarm of mosquitoes, Seth didn't seem to notice the insects. He continued to stare off in the direction of the trees. For some minutes he was silent. The four-wheeler smelled of urine and beer.

In his dreamy monotone he said, "I learned a lot about Carmen just by reading through her so-called appointment book. I knew how much she charged, what she stole, what kind of sex she was supposed to have. Needless to say, details like that got under my brother's skin, though he knew she almost never had sex because her johns were drugged. I also got to know more about her personal life. I knew when she got her hair done, what her work schedule was, what tattoo artist she went to, the birthdays of her brother and parents, things like that. I knew her ATM number and her locker combination at the café. Anything to do with numbers, she kept in her book."

Seth took a ring of keys out of his pocket, undid two keys, and examined them. "I even have the key to Carmen's apartment. And this one" - he held it out for Polita to see - "is the key to your old apartment."

Polita's shoulders slumped, and she stared at the hand gripping her arm. Fear crawled into her bones.

"That's one of the fringe benefits of helping both of you move four or five times in one year," he said. "I got to know quite a bit more about her by going through her apartment when she was at work."

With no warning, Seth threw both keys into a slimy pond about thirty feet away. He then fingered the .357 in his belt holster, eyeing Polita.

"I don't believe you," Polita said shakily. "That wasn't my key. Stop playing this cruel game."

"Believe what you want. My brother was afraid that either you or Carmen knew too much about him. I had to make sure. He didn't want any violence, of course. But, well, what can I say? Don't forget, I did help you clean up your apartment. I don't know why, but I did."

"You worked that night Carmen was killed."

Seth stared at Polita for a long time with fixed, dead eyes. He no longer gripped her by the arm but instead held her by her hand. Their fingers intertwined, like lovers'. She tried to free herself, but his urine-scented hand tightened its grip.

The lunatic chirping of cicadas now drowned out the whine of mosquitoes.

"You're right, I worked that night Carmen was murdered," Seth said. "So what? You know how it is at the café on slow nights. I take long breaks or run errands for Miss Wanda. Maybe that detective got a little sloppy in doing his homework. I did an early liquor run, then checked out. The Luxuria is only a few minutes from the café. None of the security people at the hotel could ever identify me if they had to."

"But surveillance cameras are everywhere. Detectives check out things like that; they'll see you on them."

"I moved like an Indian. Silent and deadly. Like Chechoter. Don't ask me why I decided on that night. I wasn't going to confront her out here, or at the café. It had to be at her apartment or on one of her dates at the hotel. I figured if I nailed her at the hotel, the cops would think it was one of her johns. I had to get to her before my brother decided to do something foolish. I had to protect my big brother."

"Why are you telling me all this?"

"Does there have to be a reason for anything? I guess I had to tell someone. I didn't want to tell my brother. He's the real nervous type." He smiled. "And wouldn't you know it, just as I spotted her by the marina, there you were. I just wanted to see her at the Luxuria, to catch her red-handed. To tell her off for what she had done to my brother. But then I saw what you did to her. I ran back to my car and got the hell away from the hotel."

"No, that's not true."

"Oh, yes it is."

Polita was wide-eyed in shock. Her temples tightened at the deafening rattle of the cicadas. Several minutes passed without anything being said. She glanced at Seth's rifle strapped to the side of the four-wheeler.

"I'm sure your brother must be looking for us," she said, trying to regain her composure. She glanced at the surrounding palmettos. "I know Allen and Kim are probably worried."

"Allen and Kim would be the last two people I'd count on. Besides, Allen has probably left for Miami by now. Remember, he had to go to church or something."

The cicadas were making so much noise that she could barely hear him.

"I'd like to go back to the lodge now," she said.

"Then let's go. Don't tell my brother what I just told you."

"I promise, I won't tell anyone."

"I was really pulling your leg."

"I don't understand..."

"You don't have to understand. I really don't understand much, either. In fact, my brother and I are kind of lost about all the stuff that has happened."

Seth climbed back onto the four-wheeler and drove toward the pine trees. The path was bumpy and narrow. He increased his speed.

"You're going to flip us if you go any faster," Polita warned.

"You said you wanted to go back to the lodge. You seem to be in a hurry."

He floored it, and she held onto the seat lest she be thrown out. Each bump in the path jolted her. Around one corner the four-wheeler struck a deep hole, went over an embankment, and spun out of control. They went airborne and landed in a scum-coated pond, the force of the impact driving their lower torsos under the front steering column. For a moment she lay stunned, unable to move. Her neck hurt from the whiplash, and her knees were bruised from having struck metal. The steering column pinned Seth against Polita and the seat. His lip and forehead were swollen; he spat out mud and blood.

The four-wheeler momentarily floated, and then slowly sank until it settled in about two feet of water, which covered the floorboard and engulfed half of the vehicle. Polita maneuvered herself so that she could sit upright and on top of the seat, but her movement rocked the four-wheeler and made it slide and sink into another half-foot of water. The four-wheeler tottered on several underwater logs. Chest-deep in water, Seth stared at the floating flora around him with a look of amusement. Blood dripped from his forehead and ran down his nose and chin.

"That was fucking wild," he said. "I felt like I was on a roller-coaster." He gazed at the steering wheel. "I'm stuck, and I can't move my arm. I think it might be broken."

She tried to get out, but once again her movement made the four-wheeler slip deeper into the water.

He said casually, "If I can't get out of here, I guess I'll be gator bait. Or I'll drown. What a way to go, huh? Drown in this shit or be eaten alive. This place is full of the fuckers."

"I don't know what to do. Every time I move I'm afraid it'll sink."

"When you move, all this thing wants to do is rock-n-roll." He sounded calm and unhurried. "Go ahead and get out. But take it easy."

"I'll try to find your brother."

"Just get out. Your extra weight is sinking this thing."

Polita worked fast but carefully. She climbed out of the four-wheeler and stood on several sunken logs. The pond was too muddy to see to the bottom, so she felt her way by taking one small step at a time. She balanced herself by holding onto the mossy limbs hanging closest to her. She slipped once, scraping her already bloody knees. Unable to leap the four or five feet to dry ground, she got off the log and waded through the muck and pondweed.

Seth meanwhile tried to free himself from the steering column, but he moved with infuriating slowness; something always seemed to distract him from the task at hand. One time he stopped to whistle at a bird that landed on a nearby branch. Another time he watched with fascination when a dragonfly buzzed around his head.

"If I had a bullfrog's tongue I'd get that fucker," he said. He stuck his tongue out at the dragonfly.

Polita, exhausted and covered with mud, reached dry ground and bent over with her hands resting on her knees. It took her a moment to catch her breath. Aquatic plants formed a carpet across the pond interrupted only by the murky hole where the four-wheeler lay half-submerged. She watched as Seth played around. With his back against the seat and his head turned to her, he grinned and blew her a kiss.

"Go ahead and drown," she said. "Why should I care?"

"Gee thanks. Some friend you are."

"You're drunk."

"Me? Drunk? Nah." A look of childlike bewilderment entered his eyes.

She approached the pond, sloshing through the mud, but stopped before she entered the water. He had scared her, and for her own safety, she should leave him and try to find his brother. But she was lost and knew that if she left him he could drown within minutes. Without advancing any farther, she stood in the mud and stared at him. The four-wheeler took in more water, which crept up to his neck.

Seth's voice was starting to sound shaky. "Hey, look, as I've already told you, I was just kidding about all that stuff I said about Carmen. And I was never in your apartment. Like I said, I helped you clean it up. OK, I admit. I guess I am a little drunk. Like you said, I was playing a cruel game. Just to get a rise out of you. Come on, I need your help. And I promise, I won't tell anyone about seeing what you did to Carmen. It's our secret. My brother has a lot of money and will get you the best legal help."

"You're so drunk you don't know what you're saying." She didn't move.

"Are you just going to stand there?" he shouted, his voice suddenly a high shrill. He no longer looked amused but frightened. "Help me!"

"I don't know what to do. Every time I get near that four-wheeler it moves and sinks a little more. You said so yourself."

"Damn you! You're going to let me drown!" He sounded hysterical. "I can't believe you. You fucking helped a scrawny dog escape a gator but you won't help me! And you almost cried when you saw that bloody hog and what it did to those two hunting dogs!"

The four-wheeler took in yet more water and was up to his chin. He struggled to keep his head above water. He shouted profanities at the pond. At the four-wheeler. At Polita.

"I told you I was only kidding!" he screamed.

She waded back into the pond. With each step she took the mud deepened around her legs. He continued to rant and rave until his head disappeared underwater. She climbed onto the submerged logs as he frantically waved one hand above the water. By the time she reached the four-wheeler, his head reappeared and he jumped up on the submerged seat. He raised his strongly muscled arms in triumph, one hand holding the broken steering wheel. Weeds and mud dripped from his face. He was laughing.

"Fooled you!" he shouted. "I was never trapped. I could've moved the steering wheel any time I wanted to. I had everything under control."

He dropped the steering wheel into the water and climbed out of the four-wheeler.

"I thought you said you hurt your arm," she said.

"I guess I exaggerated a little. But I did hurt my leg some. Why are you so pissed? You should be happy that I didn't drown."

He sloshed toward her. Furious, she waded back to dry ground and walked down the path. Seth, dripping wet, limped behind her.

"Hey, I want to talk to you," he said.

"Leave me alone!"

"I was just having some fun, that's all."

The path widened. Horse dung, fresh and steaming, buzzed with flies. Four-wheeler tracks marked the area. The hunters had been there, so she knew the path must lead back to the lodge. She passed several vacant and roofless tarpaper shacks. Vines crawled into the broken windows.

He called out, "Slow down! I can't keep up with you. My leg hurts. I just want to talk to you. Don't go back to the lodge mad at me."

"You scare me!" Without stopping, she turned to look at him. She then walked faster.

"Don't be afraid. I can help you. I hate to tell you this, but you're going the wrong way. This path goes nowhere."

"You're lying! Stop playing these fucking mind games with me! Why are you acting this way?"

"The hunters were here, but this area is used as a kind of rest stop."

Every couple of hundred feet or so, she stopped to rest her sore knees. He was gaining on her. He moved with a flat-footed, stiff-kneed gait, his head cocked to the side, his eyes wide, zombie-like. Was this another act of his to scare her? Up ahead the path narrowed. Despite the pain in her knees, she quickened her pace. The path twisted and turned at sharp angles. A while later, without slowing, she checked behind her and didn't see him. Where did he go? She was gulping air. She stopped to catch her breath and to look and listen.

Through the trees she spotted him making his way toward her with those same uncoordinated, stiff movements. She left the path and pushed through the tangled underbrush, blindly running with her hands outstretched before her against branches and spider webs. The hardwoods gave way to pines, pines to marshes. She was running now through palmettos and fetter bush, occasionally turning to locate him. Sharp reeds slashed her legs. The ground was soft and spongy. The area bubbled around her with the swamp odor of wet earth. Smelly black muck sucked at her feet, nearly pulling off her sneakers. There was very little air. The world was steaming, suffocating, thick with mud and heat.

She approached a tannin-colored creek, too wide to wade across. Clusters of floating vegetation drifted by. Ankle-deep in slime, she stopped at the creek and looked around; Seth was nowhere to be seen. This swampy area was unnaturally quiet. A moment of eerie calm settled around her. A quivering vapor hung over the creek.

She remained still for a long time until she started to sob. She pressed her hand against her mouth, trying to muffle the sounds that seemed to awaken the area around her. She heard first the creek murmuring, as if whispering. Then the screeching cries of an osprey sounded as it flew over the trees. Soon the air was buzzing with insects. She heard - or imagined – slithering sounds in the grass and in the bushes.

She wanted a drink, or to at least wet her parched lips. She knelt down, eyeing the creek. The swamp-water stench made her gag. She pushed away a layer of rotting leaves and wet her lips. Something moved in the green slime. The crawling slime turned into a watersnake that wound its way across the creek.

She tried to find her way back to the path. Her face and neck were swollen with insect bites. A cloud of gnats followed her, and gnats were crawling into her nose and ears. Worse than the sting of mosquitoes and yellow flies, the gnat bites covered her body like needle pricks. Her scalp was on fire with them. She could slap the fat mosquitoes and yellow flies that gorged on her blood, but trying to keep the gnats away was impossible.

She heard the sound and movement of hogs. On a grassy flat, a sow and her brood were rooting until they spotted her. The sow advanced toward Polita and then turned and ran to the protection of some underbrush with her brood close behind. Beyond the grassy flat she found a dirt path, much wider than the one she had been on, which she proceeded to take without bothering to look for Seth. She was too exhausted to care.

The sky had turned blue-black, and it looked as if it might rain. A warm, blustery wind whipped through the trees. She welcomed the sudden wind; it kept the insects off her.

She heard something move. The wind in the pines, perhaps? No. The sound came from behind the trees. More hogs? She walked faster until she tired. She stopped. Silence, except for the wind. The pines quivered.

From behind the trees Seth suddenly appeared in front of Polita. He had taken off his shirt. His muddied .357 was in his holster. For an instant she stared at him, fixed in place. Shadow and light crisscrossed his face, his gaze resting about a foot over her head. His eyes appeared lightless, empty of any emotion. Slowly, she backed away from him, her mouth open in terror. She took short, desperate breaths.

"Why did you run away from me?" he said, as if in a daze. "You would've left me back there."

"Why do you keep doing this to me? I don't know when to believe you!"

"Now I'll have to make you pay for what you did," he said in a flat, dead tone.

"What are you talking about? You keep confusing me! You're not making any sense!"

In one fluid movement Seth struck Polita in the face. She let out a low wail and fell on a soft bed of pine needles.

On hands and knees, Polita, dazed, spat out blood and broken teeth.

The pine needles in the trees sounded like windchimes.

When she looked up, he was standing above her. He didn't reach for his .357 or for his hunting knife. She tried to crawl away, but he grabbed her by the hair. He continued to show no emotion. His face wasn't angry or raging; even his eyes were blank. He said nothing. He pulled her up by her hair and swung again, but he missed her face and struck her shoulder. She swung back and hit – and clawed – at his face. Her resistance made him pause briefly. She kicked and swung again, hitting him repeatedly. She pulled out pieces of his hair. Each blow made him look more amused. For a moment he seemed impressed with the fight she was putting up.

The next blow she received came so quick and hard that she didn't see it. She screamed once into the wind. Into nothing.

Once again she passed out briefly but came to when Seth started dragging her by one of her arms. He stomped and kicked at her a couple of times. She moaned. Her eyes rolled. Her arm was being pulled out of its socket. With her free hand she tried to hold onto anything – roots, stumps, underbrush, sharp palmettos – to keep him from dragging her off the path and into the woods. Her fingernails broke off. Her bloodied fist flexed around dirt, leaves, and pine needles. Her mouth was full of more dirt and blood. Sweaty strands of wet hair stuck to her face and covered her eyes. She was too dazed to try to scream.

Seth tripped over something and momentarily lost his grip of Polita's arm. Too exhausted to crawl away, she lay face down in the soft pine needles. Her entire body was numb, except for her ears. She heard Seth screaming at her, his beery breath hot against the side of her face. The screaming intensified. More kicks and blows struck her. She wanted to go to sleep. The pine needles felt like a soft mattress. She heard more screams and expected more blows, but if they came, she didn't feel them.

Polita felt herself being turned over. To protect herself from Seth's fists, she tried to cover her face with her good arm; the other one dangled helplessly at her side. The screaming continued. Through her blurry vision she watched him kneel next to her. His face came up to hers, just inches away, as if he were going to kiss her. But the face looming before her wasn't Seth's.

The overalled hunter with discolored teeth and a cheek bulging with chewing tobacco cradled her head in his lap while another hunter came into her view and used his T-shirt to stop her mouth and nose from bleeding. The screaming she had heard came from both Paul and Seth as  Paul was trying everything he could to restrain his brother. It took three other hunters to aid Paul as they wrestled Seth to the ground. Once subdued, Seth's screams turned to sobs.

Polita closed her eyes and found herself falling into a deep, quiet sleep.

# 51

Jeremy, in his pajamas, entered the guest room where Elliot sat on the edge of the bed while putting on his sneakers. Jeremy gave his father a hug and sat next to him.

"You going for a walk or something?" Jeremy said.

"I'm getting ready to meet some workers outside."

"Are they workers from your business?"

"No. A maintenance man is coming to repair the garage door. And our landscapers, Kevin and Carlos, have some work to do."

"But the grass doesn't need to be cut."

"Not yet. They're here to check the sprinkler system and do some lawn maintenance. That last ice storm took down some pretty big branches."

"I have a soccer game today. You gonna help coach?"

"Not today, son." Elliot put his arm around Jeremy. "I'm not feeling very well, so I'll probably stay home and check on the workers. Maybe next time."

"Mom's sick also. She's been crying a lot."

"Yes, I know. I heard her. She probably has an upset stomach."

Elliot had been kept up for most of the night because of Karen's sobs. After she had listened to the news yesterday evening, she had cried intermittently for the next six hours. They had both watched the evening news in their separate bedrooms, but she had turned up the volume on her TV so far that Elliot muted his and heard everything: the news station had devoted over two minutes on how Elliot's name was associated with a murdered call girl's trick book. Through the walls he had heard all of her hysterics: the crying, the throwing of things, the phone conversations to a couple of her closest friends, and the shoving of her furniture against the bedroom door. Except for their having checked on Jeremy from time to time, both Elliot and Karen had barricaded themselves in their own rooms. She had finally cried herself to sleep around two-thirty in the morning, after which time he had been able to doze off for an hour or two.

"Since mom isn't feeling well," Elliot said, "why don't you crawl in bed with her? You always bring a smile to her face."

"Her door's locked."

"She'll let you in. Just tap on the door and tell her it's you."

"I hope she'll be OK when Pa-Pa and Gramma come over."

"Oh, they're dropping by?"

"Uh-huh. But mommy's been throwin' up, so you and Pa-Pa will probably have to take her to see a doctor."

"Your mom isn't that sick." His cell phone rang. "Let daddy take this call while you go check on your mother."

Jeremy hopped off the bed, said, "OK," and went down the hallway.

Elliot swallowed hard as he watched Jeremy knock on Karen's door. His eyes moistened.

"Hey, Jeremy, I sure do love you."

"I love you, Daddy."

The call was from Elliot's attorney. "Did I get you at a bad time?"

"Has there been a good time lately?" Elliot heard Karen open her door for Jeremy, who entered her bedroom, and the door was locked behind him.

"I tried calling and texting you after the news last night but you didn't respond."

"I wasn't in the mood to talk to anyone."

"That's what I thought. I'm ready to take control of the situation."

"Do you have a statement prepared for me?"

"I have one, in case we need it."

"Could you read it to me?"

The attorney paused for a moment, then said, "'I deeply regret the pain and embarrassment that I caused my family. What I did was a morally reprehensible act of which I am ashamed. While current press accounts are erroneous, I take full responsibility for my actions and lapse in judgment. I pray that one day my family and friends will forgive me.'"

"Hmm." Elliot thought as he stroked an imaginary beard. "That's all?"

"In my opinion, that's four sentences too many."

"Could you repeat the second sentence?"

The attorney reread the entire statement.

"Not bad," Elliot said. "Not bad, except it sounds too lawyerly. Could you make it more sincere? Needs to come from the heart."

"I'll keep revising it until you're satisfied."

"I like that you used the words 'pray' and 'forgive' in the last sentence. Could you add 'I have sinned' somewhere in there?"

"Let's not overdo it."

"Yeah, you're right. Maybe we could get some ideas by researching Clinton's press releases during Zippergate." Elliot's attempt to laugh sounded like a muffled cough.

"He was the master of obfuscation, that's for sure."

Elliot changed hands with the cell phone. "Have you read today's newspaper?"

"I have."

"I haven't. I saw it on the doorstep early this morning and imagined it was an I.E.D. I expected it to blow up in my face."

"You didn't miss much. Your story was practically the same one that ran on the TV news. It was front page, with a picture of you and the three bandits."

"I hid the paper from Karen, as if it matters. I'm sure her parents will be happy to give her their copy when they come over."

"Elliot, as expected, the media came out swinging hard at you with ignominies and demeaning comments. Don't you help them by beating yourself up over the same thing. Take it easy on yourself, because they won't. You've got to keep repeating it over and over: You made a mistake. People need to forgive and forget. And that means you. You need to forgive and forget what you did."

While the attorney was discussing his strategy, Elliot heard Karen unlock her door. She and Jeremy went into his bedroom, where she helped him dress. A moment later they descended the stairs and entered the kitchen.

Elliot told his attorney, "Let me call you back. My wife and son are getting ready to leave for a soccer game."

"Call me anytime, Elliot. As I've told you, put all of your concerns and worries on my shoulders. I'll take good care of you."

"I needed to hear that."

After Elliot hung up he left the bedroom, but he stopped halfway down the stairs when he heard Karen laughing with Jeremy in the kitchen. Hearing her laugh surprised him, especially after all the miserable sobbing he had listened to throughout the night. It was a loud, boisterous, house-filling laugh. He went down the remaining stairs and entered the kitchen. Upon seeing him, Karen, dressed in jeans and a sweater, stopped laughing and prepared Jeremy a bowl of cereal. Jeremy, giggling, told his father to eat breakfast with him.

Pouring himself a cup of coffee, Elliot said, "What's got you so tickled, son? I could hear you laughing when I was upstairs."

"Mommy was telling me a soccer joke. Huh, mommy?"

Karen answered by nodding. She sat down on a kitchen chair and laced her running shoes. Never once did she glance at Elliot.

Also avoiding eye contact with her, Elliot was looking at his son when he said, "Jeremy told me he has a game."

She was slow to reply, and when she did, her voice was just above a whisper, "The parents are doing a fundraiser."

"So it's not a real game?" He sat across the kitchen table from her, the wooden chair making a squeaking sound as it absorbed his weight.

"The players are going to scrimmage and then have their pictures taken with their parents."

Her voice was so soft and abstracted that he had to lean forward to hear her. They both avoided eye contact.

"I want you to get your picture with us," Jeremy said.

"Probably not today, son. Maybe next time." Elliot now looked directly at Karen. "Why wasn't I told about the fundraiser?"

"You were in Miami," she said distantly, staring at her cup of untouched yogurt and a glass of orange juice. Her eyes were flat and opaque.

"I was in Naples this time, not Miami. I didn't step foot in Miami. I was careful to leave you an explicit message stating that I was in Naples."

"I'm surprised Jeremy didn't say anything about the fundraiser before you left." She looked downward, as if talking to the floor.

"Since when does anyone around here communicate with me?"

She blinked but made no comment. He felt a sudden urge to reach across the table to touch her hand. Seeming to sense this, she slid her cup of yogurt and glass of orange juice away from him and closer to Jeremy.

"We need to be leaving soon," she told Jeremy.

"I'm hurryin'."

"I don't want you to hurry. I just want us to try to be on time."

"Then I'll get my ball."

Before she could stop him, Jeremy sprang out of his chair and headed for the garage.

Elliot used Jeremy's absence to say to Karen, "Look, you know this really isn't about my attending the fundraiser. Those parents would eat me alive if I showed up. My concern is with Jeremy – and you - taking the abuse that's meant for me. Why are you two going at a time like this? I want to protect him from the ridicule... from all this...this...media shit, at least for as long as I can."

She nodded but said nothing. Deep sighs sounded between them. Absorbed in their own thoughts, they quietly moved their utensils and cups back and forth like chess pieces. They both cleared their throats.

After a moment of silence, he tried to illicit some response from her. "You're being awfully quiet. You don't have any comment to make?" Her silence was beginning to unnerve him. "You have nothing rude or insulting to say about the release of the names from the trick book?"

With some effort, Karen lifted her eyes from the table. In silence they stared at each other. Her gaze at him was distant, but there were no expressions of contempt, of hostility.

"So now you're going to give me the silent treatment?" he said. "That's just as poisonous as your verbal abuse."

In her mild-mannered voice, she said, "I've decided not to concern myself with what happened in that hotel room. All of that is beyond my control. As far as your being on the news and in the newspaper, I'll just have to deal with it the best I can."

"I find that hard to believe. What about all those Rolex Bandit stories you keep telling me about? You know what's going on in Miami more than I do."

"I'm not going to let it control me anymore." Her only emotion was a shrug. "I'm burned out. And I've lost interest in it. I'm numb to it all."

Jeremy entered with his soccer ball only to be told by his mother to wait for her outside the kitchen.

"The yard people are here," Jeremy said.

"They know what to do," Elliot said. "Tell them I'll be out to talk to them in a little while. Your mom and I need a few more minutes together." After Jeremy left, Elliot said to her, "You were saying?"

She seemed to have lost interest and relapsed into silence. More quiet, distant stares. More throat-clearings between them.

He let a minute pass and said, "I'd like you to complete what you were saying. For the first time in over a week I was able to have a brief conversation with you without anything ugly being said."

"I would feel more comfortable if I took Jeremy to the fundraiser."

"I just want to know why you're not humiliating me because of the bad publicity. Last night you had the TV news turned up to where half the neighborhood could hear every sordid detail. Then I heard you cry and cuss and fume for half the night."

After a long pause, during which she repositioned her cup and utensils, she said, "You were right, I was letting what happened to you change me. I was full of anger." She raised an eyebrow but not her voice. "As I said, I'm letting go of it. All of it. I have a small business where people depend on me. I owe it to them and to myself to be at my best. And most important, I have a son whom I love with my whole heart. I want to protect him. Those are my priorities. Everything else is irrelevant."

"Including me?"

Her attention drifted. "I…What did you say?"

"Nothing. You just answered my question."

"I thought I was talking about Jeremy."

"You were. I was hoping we could protect him *together*; that we could raise our son *together*. He's going to need both of us to get through this hell that I created for all of us."

In that far-off, retrospective voice, she said, "I spoke to my parents last night and to several of my friends about the bad news. Now I guess I'll find out who my true friends are. I've decided not to go into hiding. I'm not going to run from it. That's one of the reasons why I decided to go to the fundraiser. Some of my so-called friends will laugh at our misfortune." Her voice momentarily lost its delicate tone and became firm. "But what I won't tolerate is snide or vicious remarks aimed at Jeremy."

"Neither will I."

"Jeremy and I will have to get on with our lives."

"With or without me?"

Without replying, Karen finally took her first sip of orange juice.

"I guess that means without me," he said.

"I need more time to think things through."

"How much time?"

"I don't know."

"You don't know. So there's maybe a slight chance we can save this crumbling marriage?"

"Please don't pressure me."

"I'm not pressuring you." Elliot raised both eyebrows. "Did I hear you say 'please'? I thought I'd never live to hear you say that word to me again."

Throughout their conversation Karen's voice remained passionless; there was no recriminatory tone, no facial expressions contorted with rage. Where was the bitterness? Where were the tears? There was no spark, not even a hint of fire in her eyes. She was composed, relaxed, even serene. Too relaxed, he thought. She was at peace with herself. Her transformation from near hysteria a few hours ago to complete calm troubled him.

"So what you're saying between the lines is that we have to separate?" he said.

She nodded. Her eyes lacked intensity; they wandered some.

"How long is this separation supposed to last?"

"Only time will tell."

"Only time will tell," Elliot said, mimicking Karen's quiet tone.

"I'll leave now if you're going to lose your temper."

"*Me* lose my temper? Who was standing right here the other night swinging a golf club at a cantaloupe?"

Strangely calm, she took her purse off the table and started to leave. He blocked the kitchen door and held out both hands.

"All right," he said. "I'll try not to be an asshole."

With purse in hand, Karen gazed beyond Elliot, into some empty space. She continued to exhibit that inner, unshakable composure.

"So for now," he said, "I assume I'm to stay in the guest room?"

"I don't think that would be a good idea."

"We've been separated for – what? – almost two weeks now. Seems we can co-exist if we make the effort."

"Separation means living apart."

"This is a big house. Over five-thousand square feet worth." He raised both arms and gestured toward the ceiling. "I'll stay out of your way."

"For Jeremy's sake, one of us should move out. If you want to stay, I can look for another place."

Karen's voice was matter-of-fact, detached, coolly clinical. She gazed affectlessly at that spot somewhere beyond where Elliot was standing. He stepped aside to indicate that she was free to pass him. She saw her opening to the hallway and to the garage but remained where she was.

"Don't let me keep you and Jeremy from your fundraiser." He paused, then added, "You know, I might not be here when you get back. I'm fucking tired of groveling."

She crossed her arms and looked at the floor. Looking anywhere except into his eyes.

"That's exactly what I've been doing since I told you about what happened in that hotel room. Groveling. Begging. Kissing your ass. And now with my name all over the news you want me to grovel some more. And you've enjoyed every minute of it. Well, fuck it! If you can't find it in your heart to forgive one *stupid* decision of mine – then the hell with you! When I needed you the most – when my whole fucking world is collapsing around me – you turn to stone. Fuck whatever love you claimed to have had for me."

With eyes cast downward, with an expression of patient attention, Karen listened to his rant in silence. Never once did she try to interrupt him.

While still looking at the floor she said in her same soft voice, "Are you finished?"

"Maybe."

"This has been hard on everyone."

"Then make it a little easier on us by getting over this anger of yours."

"I'm trying."

"You don't think it's gut-wrenching to know what I'm about to put you and Jeremy through? Since the six o'clock news last night the Anderson name has become shit. And it's not only you and Jeremy. Look at what I'm about to do to my father. Because we share the same name, people will have him confused with me. I can hear them now ridiculing an eighty year old man with a weak heart: Hey, Elliot, I didn't know you were involved with call girls. And I know what you're thinking: Why didn't I think of all that when I had those call girls in my hotel room? I didn't think of the consequences. What else can I say?"

Jeremy re-entered the kitchen. "Mom, I thought you said we were ready to go. I've been waitin' forever."

"Son, give us two more minutes," Elliot said. "Your mother will get you there on time. It's warm outside. Go kick your ball some."

"I'll be there shortly," Karen told Jeremy.

When she looked at her son, Karen's eyes brightened, but when her eyes settled back on Elliot, her gaze had no depth or ⁓th.

⁓liot said, "I've been doing all the talking. Your ⁓ been about as cold as this past fucking winter. For once, can't you just get mildly annoyed?" With no response from her, he said dismissively, "Go ahead and take Jeremy to the fundraiser. While you're gone, my attorney and I will be preparing for the firestorm."

Karen walked past Elliot, but before she opened the door to the garage, she turned and took several steps forward. She stared at him with that same strange dreaminess.

"Forget something?" he said.

"I want you to know that you said something to me the other night that wasn't true."

"I wondered how long it was going to take before you'd call me a liar."

"I'm not calling you a liar." She had no animosity in her voice. "You called me a mean person. That's not true."

"I called you mean?" He took a deep breath. "Hell, you're not mean. You're fucking *cruel*."

Karen received the insult by merely blinking once, pressed her lips together, turned and entered the garage. Elliot felt a constriction in his throat. Acid reflux? No, he hadn't eaten anything. Perhaps he didn't want to admit that he was choked up with emotion. He stepped into the garage as she was backing out her Land Rover. He knew it was too late to apologize. As Jeremy waved at him Karen set out down the driveway, never once glancing back in his direction.

Elliot wandered over to where the landscapers were working. One was checking the pump to the irrigation system, while the other was stacking broken branches on a cart hitched to his four-wheeler. Despite his dour mood, it pleased Elliot to see activity once again on his property after the long winter. The sun shone brightly. The sky was clear and cloudless. The maples and elms showed new buds. He breathed in deeply. The warmth made him feel like doing yard work or hitting golf balls at the driving range.

After he spoke to the landscapers, Elliot entered the garage, gathered up his golf bag, and loaded it into the trunk of his car.

As he was pulling out, a truck was turning into his driveway. He stopped and motioned the driver to roll down his window. It was the maintenance man, whom he knew well.

"Tim, I left the garage door open," Elliot said, wondering from his expression – and those of his landscapers – if they had heard the news about him. "I've got cabin fever, so I'm going to hit some golf balls for thirty minutes or so. You have my cell number in case you need me."

Elliot turned onto the road and headed to the driving range.

# 52

An incredible darkness enveloped Polita, a weightless emptiness numbed her. Any sense of time, or place, had disappeared. All she heard, barely, was a soft, seashell-like hum in her ears as she dreamily floated in a void.

Then sometime later – minutes? hours? - far off flashes of light and high-decibel sounds pierced her consciousness. She wanted to cry out, but her voice was muffled. Currents of pain shot through her body. She became cold. Everything pulsed around her.

Barely able to open her blackened and swollen eyes, she noticed flashing monitors and heard electronic beeping. She blinked back tears. In her blurred vision everything appeared murky, unfocused. She thought she recognized someone's vague shape standing above her, but on second glance, as her vision began to improve, the shape next to her became a clear plastic drip bag attached to an IV-stand. Blinking back more tears revealed a hospital room. A meal cart was parked next to the door. Because she couldn't move her head to the left, she could only see the window side of the space. The blinds were partially closed, and the beeping sounds became muted, so the room was menacingly quiet and dark.

She lay in bed at an incline; her head, slightly tilted to the right, rested on a pillow. A sharp pain prevented her from looking to the other side of the room, and a neck brace restricted her movement. The left side of her face was swathed in white gauze; the right side was covered in cuts, scratches, and bruises. Her skin's waxy yellow complexion made her look terminally ill. No matter how hard she tried, she could only half-open her swollen eyelids, but as she settled into consciousness, she no longer teared up, and her vision sharpened. She noticed three fingers on her right hand were in a splint. Her left arm was in a sling. There were I.V. tubes going into the back of both hands, in her nostrils, and in the crook of her elbow. Tubing seemed to be everywhere.

She stared dully out the window at the retention lake and a chain-linked fence below. Bottlebrushes and palm trees surrounded the lake. Pond birds, flashes of white in the stark sunlight, foraged in the shallow water. Turtles sunned on logs.

Her eyes slowly closed, and she began to fall back into that same void as before, but this time she found herself following Carmen down a long hallway of closed doors in a deserted building, presumably a hotel, which was in such disrepair that its damp, mossy walls exuded an odor of decay. Carmen checked various doors until one finally opened into a room that shimmered in waves of heat, and before Polita followed her inside, both Carmen and the room disappeared.

Nearby voices, sounding like crackling, high-pitched interference on a radio reawakened Polita, who managed to turn her head slightly, painfully, to the left, away from the window.

How long had she dozed off? Two people were sitting next to her. It took her eyes a few more seconds to refocus, and appearing before her were her mother and her attorney. How long had they been sitting there? They looked like sisters, stooped, thin, with gray hair, wearing dark clothes and rimless glasses. Grief-stricken, her mother appeared lost in a grim haze. She held a rosary in one hand, a cup of ice in the other. Her purse and a Bible containing yellow Post-it notes were on the table next to her. She nodded at everything the attorney was telling her.

Polita stared at a thin wooden crucifix around her mother's neck, fascinated by the detailed beauty of its craftsmanship. Intricately carved, each feature of the tiny Jesus showed the blood streaming down from the crown of thorns, the eyes turned upward, the agonized expression, the protruding ribs, the gashed side, the ragged loincloth, and the nails through the wrists and feet.

Mira Delgado, the attorney, stopped talking when she noticed Polita looking at her mother. In addition to moving her eyes, Polita also shifted her weight. A faint gurgle sounded at the bottom of her throat. Her breath tasted of blood, and her tongue was as thick and dry as leather; she was thirsty. Her mother gently extracted a piece of bloodied cotton from her daughter's mouth and held the cup to her lips. Polita noisily sucked on the ice for some time. Her mother was so distraught, so nervous, that the cup was shaking and several pieces of ice fell on Polita's gown. The attorney reached over and helped the woman hold the cup.

Polita dozed off again. When she came to, the two women and the items in the room seemed to reappear hazily. She noticed her mother's lips moving expressively as she was saying the rosary, and Polita thought she looked fragile, almost childlike. She tried to say something but was unable to. Her mother stopped reciting her prayers when she noticed her daughter's eyes had reopened. For some reason, Polita was staring at her broken, dirty fingernails. She gestured with her splint hand for more ice. A dry-mouthed fear swept over her when she realized that her dream of the building's damp walls converged with the more powerful smell of the swamp. The mud and heat and thick underbrush of the swamp and its sound of insects – the beeping of hospital machines? - suffocated her. She panicked by trying to kick and throw off all the wires and tubes attached to her. Her mother, seeing the terror in her daughter's eyes, restrained her by holding her hands.

"It's going to be OK, baby," her mother said, comforting her. "You're safe. I'll never leave you. Don't you ever forget that." Her voice started to break. "I…"

Polita closed her eyes and collapsed into herself. A nurse intervened. Once she knew that her patient had calmed down, the nurse studied a chart, checked the drip bag, changed the catheter-receptacle under the bed, and began speaking to the two women at Polita's bedside. Polita opened her eyes and tried to exercise her jaws. Her mother and the attorney held her by the hand. After the nurse left, Polita tried again to speak but found it hard to pronounce a word.

"Shh, you don't have to say anything," the attorney said. "I know it hurts. Just rest."

Polita's lips made a sound, and with her voice hoarse and barely audible, she managed to whisper, "How long have I been here?"

"Baby, you're going to make it," her mother assured her.

"How long?" Polita repeated.

"Not too long."

Her mother, kissing her crucifix once, looked away, her tearstained face and glasses reflecting off the monitor's lights. Her hair was pulled up in a tight bun.

"About two days," the attorney answered.

"Have I been in a coma?"

Ms. Delgado hesitated before answering. "You had a severe concussion."

Polita stared at her sling, her broken fingers, and at what remained of her dirt and blood-encrusted nails. "What did he do to me?"

Her mother tried to answer, became choked up, and twisted the rosary in her hands.

"Tell me, what did he do to me?"

In a gentle voice the attorney said, "You had a concussion and…"

"What else?" Saliva mixed with blood drooled down Polita's chin. "I want to know."

The attorney looked warmly into Polita's eyes. "You have two broken ribs. A broken nose. Three broken fingers. A broken collarbone. Bruised kidneys. Some busted teeth. A strained neck. A dislocated shoulder." The attorney took a tissue and wiped the tears from the mother's cheeks. "And your mother has a broken heart. Let's talk about something else."

Polita found it hard to put more than five or six words together. Her voice was still hoarse, low, and cracked.

"Where is he?" Polita said.

"He was arrested," the attorney said.

"For what?"

"Assault with intent to commit grievous bodily harm."

"He tried to more than harm me. He wanted to kill me."

"We would need to prove intent."

"Look what he did to me."

"I know. I'm going after him."

"What about Carmen's murder?" She glanced out her window. "The things he told me out there."

"There's not enough evidence to connect him yet. Our main concern right now is with you."

"He told me…"

"Whatever he said out there would be his word against yours. We'll go over all of that later, when you're feeling better. Now's not the time."

Polita swallowed hard. The taste of blood was now in her throat.

"I want a mirror," Polita said to her mother.

Without responding, her mother gripped Polita's uninjured hand firmly.

"I want to see what he did to me," Polita said. "Mama, I know you keep a compact in your purse." She glanced at the attorney. "If my mama won't give me hers, then I know you've got one."

Neither the attorney nor the mother retrieved a mirror. Polita squeezed her eyes shut. Another sharp pain shot through her side.

Polita's voice remained hoarse, drained, still a whisper. "Has Detective Hawkins seen him?"

The attorney said, "Seth's brother has hired an attorney and, to my knowledge, there has been little contact between him and the detective. But it won't do us any good to talk about this now. Our goal is to get you feeling better."

"Just be up front with me about him. That's all I ask. Be honest. I promise, I won't go nodding off on you again."

"I'll understand if you do." The attorney glanced at Polita's mother, then back at Polita. "Seth admitted that he was drinking when he lost control of the ATV and struck his head. He claims everything after that became a blur. He doesn't remember attacking you. When the cops showed up, he complained of severe headaches and started vomiting. He kept passing out. He was taken to the hospital where a doctor drained fluid from his skull. He had some stitches on his forehead and on top of his head. His doctor said he suffered from subdued hematoma, a swelling of the brain. It can make a person very emotional and unpredictable, capable of anything from a temper tantrum to homicidal behavior. His attorney will use the head injury as his defense: it was the impact of the collision that made him go off the deep end. He had everything going for him. He was two months from graduating. He was going to work for his brother's

427

business. Why would he have done something so irrational as to attack you when at least ten hunters had just left you two together? And, you wanted me to be up front, so expect his attorney to drag your name through the mud by claiming that you helped provoke him. May I stop now? Have you heard enough?"

"He already dragged me through the mud. He was going to beat me to death."

"I know, I know." The attorney patted Polita's hand. "I didn't mean to sound so matter-of-fact. We'll find all kinds of holes in their defense. We also have several hunters as witnesses."

"His brother is good friends with all of them. He'll pay them off. He'll…"

"We'll worry about that later."

The attorney waited a full minute for Polita to respond. Because her swollen eyes were mere slits, it was hard to tell if they were closed. Had she fallen asleep again?

"I spoke too fast and said too much," Ms. Delgado said. "Is there anything you want me to repeat? In your condition, I know it was a lot to comprehend."

"He's got all of you fooled." Polita's voice was without expression.

"I don't think he has any of us fooled. It's just the defense he'll use."

Polita glanced to the left, in the direction of the door. "You said he was arrested."

"Yes."

"He's not in jail, is he?"

"Not yet. He's being transferred later today."

"That's because he's being transferred from here, isn't he? He's in this hospital."

The attorney looked at Polita's mother. "Yes, he's here. But he's under 24/7 security."

Barely able to shake her head in disbelief, Polita said, more to herself than to the attorney, "The man who tried to kill me is in the same hospital." It hurt her to try to smile. She spit up some blood. "Maybe he's in the room next door. Maybe we share the same nurse."

"You don't have anything to worry about. In a few hours he'll be transferred to Miami."

"Isn't that where we are?"

"You're in a hospital in Naples."

"I'll spend more time in prison than he ever will, you can count on that." She looked at the attorney. "I don't understand it. He just went ballistic..."

"As I said, he'll pay a price for what he did to you."

"Sure he will. Look who his brother is. And look at me. Just look at me. That is, if I don't scare you."

"His brother has been trying to visit you. He feels terrible and has offered to help with the medical expenses."

"He's trying to get us to take it easy on his brother."

"That'll never happen."

"I don't want his brother in this room."

"I promise you, he'll never set foot in here. I'm preparing a solid case to..."

The attorney's voice floated away.

Polita's mother continued to pray by touching each rosary bead in her trembling hands.

Exhausted, Polita smiled at her mother as she closed her eyes.

"I'm tired, Mama."

"Go back to sleep. I'll stay right here. I'll never leave you."

It comforted Polita to feel her mother's rosary-wrapped hand holding hers. Her entire body hurt. She wanted to reenter that quiet, in-between station that didn't have a name or a location, where there would be no pain, no time, and no memories, that cool, airy, impenetrable place.

Alan Mowbray is the author
of two novels, *The Diary of a
Dissident* and *Beautiful
Woman.*

Made in the USA
Charleston, SC
13 June 2013